# PRAISE FOR FIRST STRIKE

"The universe's safety is at risk in the gripping science fiction novel *First Strike*, which features an exciting array of extraterrestrial entities. About sacrifices made for others… *First Strike* jets among planets, galactic intrigues, and varying lifeforms across the stars."

—*Foreword Clarion Review*

"Haas' neat storytelling style is reminiscent of that of genre master Alan Dean Foster; the tale never takes itself too seriously, and it's fast-moving enough to distract readers from asking too many questions. Readers may also be reminded of the Marvel film *Guardians of the Galaxy* and other seriocomic cosmic capers…. Sequels are planned, but this one can be read as a stand-alone. A deft, slightly tongue-in-cheek escapade among the stars."

—*Kirkus Reviews*

"Angela Haas delivers an energetic science fiction tale…. The story is fast-moving, with plenty of action, and the author's light touch adds a playful sensibility."

—*Blue Ink Review*

Brenda!

Thank you for supporting my dream!

Angela Haas

**1**
**KEEPERS**
OF THE
**UNIVERSE**

# FIRST STRIKE

A N G E L A   H A A S

**First Strike: Keepers of the Universe Book 1**
Published by Spotted Owl Publishing
Colorado Springs, CO

Publisher's Cataloging-in-Publication data

Names: Haas, Angela, author.
Title: First strike : keepers of the universe , book 1 / Angela Haas.
Series: Keepers of the Universe
Description: Colorado Springs, CO: Spotted Owl Publishing, 2022.
Identifiers: ISBN 978-1-7361962-0-5 (paperback) Subjects: LCSH
Surgeons--Fiction. | Space warfare--Fiction. | Women--Fiction. | Science
fiction. | BISAC FICTION / Science Fiction / Space Opera Classification:
LCC PS3608 .A2345 F57 2022 | DDC 813.6--dc23

Cover by Jeff Brown and interior design by Victoria Wolf, copyright owned by Angela Haas.

Spotted Owl
PUBLISHING

This book is dedicated to everyone who thinks they are too old to start their dream, to change their life, to take that big leap. You are not old. It's not too late. Get up and go do that thing.

# 1

# STELLA

## EARTH, PRESENT DAY

**DR. STELLA JAYNE WALSH FROZE,** the hair on the back of her neck rigid as her body reacted to the sense that someone was behind her. *Relax,* she thought. *You know what to do.* A creak in the floor gave the person away and Stella whipped around, snatched the man's fingers, and bent them back on his hand. He cried out and fell back. She thrust her palm into his chest and, as he coughed, she sent him to the ground by kicking his legs out from under him. He grunted as he hit the floor, cringing from the pain.

She pounced on top of him and punched him in the chest again. "Okay! Okay! Stop!" he shouted.

"Stella, that's great, no, I think you, yes—" said another man behind her.

Her self-defense coach called to her, and his hands touched her arms. "Wow! Great job, Stella," Brian said, "but what's one thing we could have done differently here?" He turned to address the rest of the class as they stood in a circle around Stella and Dan. Brian pulled Dan up from the floor, and Dan shook his head as he massaged his sore fingers. Stella was about to apologize when her phone rang, calling to her from her bag on the bench next to the sparring area. It was the special ringtone for the hospital, Mercy General.

"Hello," Stella said. "Yeah, oh … okay. I'll be right there."

When she hung up, she felt a touch on her arm.

"It's 2019, Stella. I can't believe you still have a flip phone," said her friend Sarah.

"I know, but I only need it for actual phone calls, and I hate texting," Stella said. She zipped up her winter jacket and brushed her hair out of her face.

"You okay?" Sarah asked.

"Yes, I've got to get into surgery, but other than that—"

"No, I mean, you kind of pissed off Dan, I think."

They both glanced over their shoulders to see Dan scowling at them from the other side of the room.

"He'll be fine," Stella said.

"Are you sure you're all right? It's not been that long since the shooting."

Stella's gaze hit the floor. It was as if someone hit a rewind button and it took her back to the day a disgruntled man burst into the main entrance of the hospital with an AR15. Stella walked up to the front desk just as the man, upset over the passing of his cancer-stricken wife, stormed through the hospital entrance. She stepped in front of the nurse closest to the armed man. She hoped her words of sympathy would calm the man down, but as she inched closer to him, the color drained from his eyes. With black, wild eyes and a finger on the trigger, the man opened fire. Stella threw herself over a nurse, shielding her. An off-duty officer returned fire, but not before the shooter got off several rounds.

In the commotion, Stella didn't realize a bullet hit her until she saw the bright stream of blood oozing down her right sleeve, staining her lab coat. Six people died that day in the lobby, including a newly married intern. The searing pain in her shoulder was nothing compared to the pain of losing her colleagues in an act of violence. She had never felt that helpless or out of control. She never wanted to feel that way again.

"Stella?"

Stella shook her head. "Yes?"

"Look, I know we only took this class together because we found that Groupon, but I think I'm going to buy another package. Will you keep coming with me?"

"Uh, I don't think so."

Sarah frowned.

"Hey, I've had fun and I love that I get to do this with you, but I'm good. Really. I've learned some self-defense basics. Hopefully, I will never have to use them." Stella's phone started ringing again, buzzing her palm.

"You better go, huh?"

"Yeah, sorry," Stella said. "We're on for dinner tomorrow though, right?"

Sarah smiled and said yes, but Stella was already halfway into a cab by the time the word left Sarah's mouth.

# 2

# FIRST LOSS

**"THAT'S IT. THAT'S ALL WE CAN DO."** A nurse covered the broken twelve-year-old boy with a sheet.

"Time of death 23:17," said another nurse.

Gasps and whispers filled the room. Stella had been a trauma surgeon for New York City's Mercy General hospital for the past five years, and in all that time she had never lost a patient. Tonight, a boy died on her table.

She peeled off her mask as she stared at the lifeless form; the boy's small hand stuck out from under the sheet.

*This boy. Someone's child. Someone's friend.* These words rattled Stella's mind.

The sounds of cleanup replaced the gut-wrenching silence that had hung in the room. Stella kept staring at that small hand, her mind racing, trying to think of what else she could have done. As the staff waited for her next command, one nurse shook her head while another stood with her mouth open. Stella quivered under the weight of their stares because she, for once, did not have an answer.

"Dr. Walsh?"

Silence.

"Doctor?"

"Yes." Stella wiped the sweat off her face. "Thank you all for your efforts. I will, uh, notify the parents."

Stella stopped in the hallway and paced. Once she gathered her thoughts and silently practiced what she was going to say in a hallway, she found the boy's parents in the waiting room. Stella fumbled over her words but delivered the message. The father's angry screams echoed in her ears.

"How could this happen? We brought him here because you were supposed to be the best! 'She's never lost a patient,'" the father screamed. "How did you lose him?" Moments later, Stella closed the door to the physician's lounge and poured herself some stale coffee. Her hand shook so much that she almost spilled it. She sat down at a table and rubbed her temples, trying to bring some relief to her throbbing head.

"I can't believe it," she mumbled out loud.

"Can't believe what?" asked a voice.

Stella jumped in her seat and clenched her chest. "Mark, you scared me."

"Sorry, Walsh."

Dr. Mark Stanton took a seat across from her. He had been her mentor when she first arrived at Mercy General. "I'm not going to ask if you are all right because I think I know the answer."

"I shouldn't have lost him. It doesn't make sense."

"I saw the reports. Was a nasty car accident. He wasn't belted in. He was thrown from the car. Massive head and chest trauma. Tough to come back from that."

"I know, but I've seen and saved worse. Why this boy? Why now?" Stella asked.

"You did everything you could. We know that. At least now we know you're human. I was beginning to think you were from another planet. Every doctor loses patients. It just took you five years to get to your first one."

"Mark—"

"Go home. I will stay on."

"I'm fine. I just need to eat something," Stella said.

"You've been on for too long. Get some rest. Go home. That's an order," Mark said. "I'll call you in the morning."

Stella didn't want to leave. She wanted to get back in the OR and save someone to prove she was still the woman people turned to, to save those who were impossible to save. As she stood up, a wave of nausea shook her. She grabbed the table to steady herself.

"Let someone drive you home," Mark suggested.

Stella waved him away.

"Walsh, this is nonnegotiable. If I need to take you home myself, I will, but you're done for the day."

Stella gave Mark a nod of agreement, and he patted her on the back before heading out of the lounge. She collected her things and hailed a cab.

The door of her brownstone creaked open. She tossed her keys toward the entryway table, and while they had always landed in a dish before, this time they missed the table and clattered on the floor. Instead of placing her coat on the hook by the door as she always did, she took it off and let it fall on the floor. She kicked off her shoes instead of stepping out of them and placing them in their spot in the hall closet. The clock on the wall ticked in time with her heart pounding in her ears as she trudged up the stairs to her bedroom.

It was just as she left it, bed perfectly made, with just enough pillows to rest her head on comfortably. There were no real signs that someone was living there other than a table lamp on either side of the bed and a painting of azure watercolor strokes resembling the ocean.

She took the painting off the wall next to her bed and placed it on the floor, revealing the cabinet behind it. She reached toward the back of it, pulling out a wooden box with an ornate carving of a figure 8 on top. She sat down on the bed and began to sift through the contents of the box.

She set aside a heart-shaped locket and a sprig of dried lavender. Under those was a photo that sat on her mother's desk for years. It was a picture of her mother, Kate, and two of Kate's closest friends, Willow and Maren. Stella remembered how happy her mother was and how she almost glowed when she was around them.

The only other item in the box was a book her mother used to read to her every night before bed. "The Keepers of the Universe," she said aloud as she ran her fingers over the tattered leather cover. Stella thumbed through the book, hearing her mother's soothing voice as she scanned the words. Stella stopped when she got to the chapter titled, "Keepers of Health, The Healers."

A familiar paragraph stood out to her. "The health of the Healers is vital to the survival of the others. They heal all around them; however, the Healer's powers are strongest when all the Keepers are joined together. The Keepers can be separated for a time, but if that time stretches, their powers will dwindle. Their light will dim, and they will age and contract illnesses. As Healers, they will lose their vision, their ability to see ills in the body, and ultimately their ability to heal others, as well as themselves."

Stella stopped reading and closed the book. Her heart fluttered in her chest.

*This is crazy. I'm losing my mind. Just had a bad day. Just had a bad day.*

She shook it off, left the book on her bed, and put everything else back in the box and slammed the lid shut.

The doorbell rang, almost knocking her off her feet. She frowned after a quick glance at her watch. It was well after 1:00 a.m. She tiptoed down the stairs and looked out her door's peephole to see a short man with a gray suit and the ugliest orange tie she had ever seen.

"Yes?" Stella asked.

"Dr. Stella Jayne Walsh?" The man with the ugly orange tie asked.

"Yes, what is this about?"

"My name is Detective Scott Zimmer. May I come in and speak with you a moment? It's about the accident victim you had tonight." He flashed a badge and put it away before Stella got a good look at it.

Stella remembered that a drunk driver hitting the car head-on caused the accident. It was possible authorities needed more information, but why would they just show up like this in the middle of the night?

"No. Why are you here at this hour?"

Zimmer paused. "There have been some recent developments, and this can't wait. May I come in?"

Stella peered through the hole again. He did not appear dangerous, but there was something odd and out of place about him.

"No," she said, reaching for a baseball bat she kept by the door. "Leave a card in the door, and I will call you tomorrow."

He shoved his hands in his pockets, turned, and walked down the street out of view. She breathed a sigh of relief and double-checked her locks. She stretched her neck and climbed the stairs. A warm bath and then bed were all she wanted.

Stella opened her bedroom door and screamed when she saw Zimmer standing in her bedroom. The door slammed behind her and two bulky arms grabbed her. A prick from something sharp stung the back of her neck and a rush of stiffness flooded her body. It must have been a paralytic drug because she was still alert, but unable to move. A giant, burly man lowered her to the floor and crossed her arms over her chest. "Told you she wouldn't let you in," the burly man said.

Zimmer rolled his eyes. "Prepare to teleport."

He pressed down on his ear as if he were speaking to someone else. "Yes, we have her. Just need to get the man. Transport for three from this spot. Yeah, I'll clean up here and shut down the house as usual."

Zimmer knelt beside Stella. Her eyes were bulging and her jaw tightened so she couldn't close her mouth, but her breathing was slow and steady. "Don't worry, Dr. Walsh, you're going to be fine." He nodded, and the burly man scooped her up in his arms.

Zimmer stood up, and his mouth fell open as he noticed what was lying on her bed. He picked up her book, *The Keepers of the Universe,* and thumbed through it.

He held it up to her and in an acidic voice asked, "Where the hell did you get this?"

# 3

# THE INSPIRION

**PEOPLE SHOUTING AND RUSHING IN THE OR** flashed through Stella's mind as she lay dreaming—the boy being wheeled into surgery, the dread overtaking her as she knew she had to tell the parents, running out of the hospital, the man with the ugly orange tie appearing in her room. Stella kicked at him as hands grabbed her from behind. She couldn't get away. They held her down. She tried to scream, but no sound came. She felt as though she was being sucked through a vacuum, and she blasted out of her coma as if a light within her suddenly switched on. Her eyes opened, but they strained from the brightness that engulfed her. She decided not to move and sent her fingers out to investigate her surroundings. They let her know she was lying face down on a cushiony bed. The sounds of stillness enveloped her, but something else told her she was moving.

She blinked to lift the fog from her eyes. She was in a room bathed in white and pastels. White walls, blush carpet, a white sofa next to a gold table, and a soft lavender lamp sat next to the white bed she had been sleeping on. Everything looked new and in perfect order, and it looked as though one was meant to enjoy the splendor of the room but not touch anything. She sat up like a creaky door struggling to open, and cringed. Her body spiked with pain.

Her throbbing head became an afterthought as she noticed something else in the room. Behind her was a large circular window. The scene on the other side called to her as she rose from the bed in a trance. She tried to process what she saw, but the moment was difficult to capture. Gone were the buildings, streets, and streams of people of New York City. In its place a fantastic, inky blackness littered with millions of tiny sparkling stars. Stella touched the frosty glass of the window and immediately recoiled. She wasn't looking at the stars; she was moving through them. She backed away from the window and tried to remain calm, though her heart pounded in her throat.

*No, I'm still dreaming. It must be a dream, a nightmare.*

The trauma from losing her first patient must have prompted her brain to create this escape, an alternate reality. She held her head as another sensation swept over her. She touched her sides and gasped. Someone had changed her clothes. She moved closer to an ornate mirror on a wall. A long, white gown with a plunging neckline, a high slit up her right leg, and a bodice decorated with embroidery and sequins had replaced her OR scrubs. She looked down at her feet to see glittering, golden high heels. Her long, red hair was curled and pinned in a decorative design at the nape of her neck. She leaned closer into the mirror to see fake eyelashes, rosy cheeks, and red lips.

"Oh my God," she said out loud.

From behind a door, a toilet flushed, followed by the sound of running water.

She glanced around for something to protect herself with, but the room contained only beautiful, comfortable things.

The door opened, revealing a tall man dressed in tuxedo pants and shirt. He was tucking his shirt into his pants when he looked up. "Oh, whoops! Hi, you're awake." He zipped up his pants and tried to straighten his disheveled hair.

"Stop!"

"Um, I was just, I needed to use the restroom."

"Where am I?" Stella demanded.

"I, uh, I don't—"

"Who are you? What do you want?" Stella shouted.

"Relax, okay?" The man put one hand on his chest and one hand out in front of him. "My name is Elliot, Elliot Driver. I'm not the one who brought you here."

"You were there, there in my house," Stella said, trying to remember.

"No, listen," Elliot stammered.

"Tell me where we are!"

"I don't know! I don't know where we are!" Elliot winced and held his head. "I was not in your house, because I was in my apartment … getting attacked by this … God, my head is killing me. Does your head hurt?" Elliot tried to move back to the bed.

"Stay right there!" Stella grabbed a lamp off the nightstand by the bed. "I want to know what you did to me!"

"I didn't do anything to you!"

Stella took a swipe at Elliot, but he jumped back just in time. The motion caused her to wobble; she was still unsteady on her feet.

"Okay, okay." Elliot backed away from her. "Calm down, okay? I'm not going to hurt you, and I didn't bring you here."

"Shut up!" Stella lunged at him again.

"Hey! Just, stop! Okay? Whatever is happening to you is happening to me too, all right?" Elliot put his hand on the back of his neck. "Wait. I remember. I was sitting in my living room, and this little guy shows up at the door—this dude wearing this crazy orange tie. Man, it was awful."

Stella lowered the lamp. "That's the man I saw."

"Right? The other guy was big, and he had muscles I didn't know people could have."

Stella nodded.

"Is there a mark from where they stuck something in your neck?" Elliot asked.

Stella touched the side of her neck where she found a bump that stung when she touched it. "What did they do?" The pace of her heart increased.

Elliot put his hands on his hips and stared at the floor. "I don't know. Whatever it was, it was weird. I was awake, but I couldn't feel my body."

She stared at Elliot as he rubbed his neck. She set the lamp back down on the table. Elliot sat down on a nearby chair and buried his face in his hands. "All I remember was coming home. This man was at the door. Next thing, I woke up here with you lying beside me. I got up to use the bathroom. Then you're trying to bash me with a lamp, and then … I have no idea beyond that what is happening. Oh, God, I feel terrible."

Elliot patted his pockets. "They took my wallet, keys, and cell-phone—everything I had. And somehow dressed me in this tuxedo, which fits perfectly by the way. How did they do that?"

"Then, I guess you have no idea how I ended up in this?" Stella spread her arms out.

Elliot cleared his throat. "Uh, not sure, but may I say something? You look stunning." He scratched his left ear. "I mean, we just met, but—"

Stella crossed her arms across her chest. "So, to sum it up, we both were drugged, kidnapped, and then dressed in formal wear."

"Yep, there's that, and then … there's that." He pointed to a table across the room.

Stella got up and walked to the table, where she found the most frightening thing yet: two sets of champagne glasses, a chilled bottle of Dom Perignon, and a note. Stella read it out loud. "To the happy couple, we heartily welcome you to your new and grand life together."

Stella whipped her head toward Elliot, her mouth falling open. He just shrugged and pursed his lips. They both jumped when a light shot out of the coffee table. It projected a crystal-clear image of a woman dressed in a flowing yellow gown.

"Welcome, new citizens of Balance," the woman said in a grand, booming voice. "Today marks the first day of the rest of your life on a wonderful new sphere."

"What the hell?" Elliot said.

Pictures of a lush green landscape faded into a scene with blue ocean, which then faded into a garden of enormous blooming flowers.

"Please enjoy your gifts of celebration; the ship's captain will be with you shortly." The woman smiled as the last image dissolved.

"The ship's what?" Stella asked.

"What ship?" Elliot asked.

"What is this?"

Elliot looked around the room. "A dream, a reality TV show. We've clearly been robbed, so maybe we've been abducted by some serial killer who likes to dress up his victims."

Stella furrowed her brow.

"Um, but let's say this is a reality TV show. That sounds like the best option," Elliot suggested.

"I don't think that sounds like our best option."

Elliot frowned. "Well, do you have a better idea for what all this means?" He gestured to the window where the stars were passing by.

"No. I'm hoping I'll wake up any moment." She got up and moved to the window again and then turned back to Elliot. "Although, if this is a dream, why are you in it?"

He smiled. "Well, I'm not the worst man to show up in a woman's dream."

Stella scowled.

"Right. I need some water. You want some water?" Elliot got up and went back into the bathroom. "No cups," he said when he returned.

"Of course not."

Elliot grabbed the champagne glasses. "It is odd that we are both having the exact same dream though, right?"

"Nightmare," Stella said. "This is a nightmare."

"Right. I guess I wouldn't really call it a nightmare," Elliot said after some reflection. "I mean, I'm here in this beautiful room. There are thousands of twinkling stars floating outside the window, and I wake up to a beautiful woman. That's not bad."

Stella closed her eyes, but that only caused the room to spin.

"If only we could open this door," Elliot said. He stared at a control panel and tried pressing buttons. Stella joined Elliot at the door. It was solid steel with no handles. He stepped aside. Stella reached out to tap a button, and the door slid open before her finger made contact.

Zimmer and a man wearing a military-looking uniform with a long cape walked through. The man in the cape had shiny blond hair, and when he smiled it was like he had too many teeth.

"Hello! Oh, I'm so pleased you both are awake," he said. "Welcome to The Inspirion! We hope you two will enjoy your stay with us!"

Stella recognized Zimmer instantly, not just from the tie, but also from his sharp eyes, small button nose, and the salt and pepper crescent of hair that hugged his scalp.

"Our stay with you?" Stella shouted. "Where are we staying? Who are you?"

"Yes," Elliot said. "What's going on here?"

The man with the cape continued with a jovial voice. "I am Captain Shamus Stallworth, and this is my ship, The Inspirion. Congratulations! You both have been abducted by aliens."

# 4

# RYDER

ONE YEAR EARLIER

**JOHN "RYDER" ALEXANDER** dove for protection behind one of the last boulders still standing. Rocket fire grazed the edge of the charcoal-colored rock, spraying his head with dust and filling his mouth with dirt. Ryder was bleeding from a shot to the arm, had only one functioning energy revolver, and heard a series of Hovertanks moving in, but those were exactly the conditions under which he thrived. He spit out the dirt as he tried to reload. He craned his neck around the edge of the rock. It was only twenty feet to the protective bunker where the rest of Ryder's army and the B'aik were waiting. He had stayed back to cover the others in his unit so they could get the last citizens on the surface to safety underground.

It was the seventh day of the Miner's War on the planet Juntö. Ryder's infantry had flown in to support the B'aik, the native people of Juntö who worked as miners extracting the planet's valuable resources. The defenseless B'aik sent out a distress call when a band of Rovers invaded and attempted to take over the planet and claim its valuable ore and minerals for their own. Rovers scour the universe looking for anything they can plunder, and if they must take innocent lives in the process, so be it. Ryder and his army had pushed the Rovers back, but his unit took a hit and they now needed to call for backup from their home world.

He peeked out, firing off six more blasts that brought down a lone fighter perched on a nearby boulder. Once it was clear, he took off. For his average height, he was muscular and agile. When he ran at a dead sprint, he could outrun almost anything, even if it had four wheels. The last torrent of adrenaline fired in his veins as the bunker came into his sights. His eyes stung from the toxic mix of burnt flesh, gunpowder, and dust kicked up off the battlefield.

Mortar fire exploded behind him, and he knew they had spotted him. More shots passed over his head as he shouted to his team on his wrist radio. "Open the damn doors! I'm coming in." A group of Rovers barreled down the bloodstained path behind him. He shot his blaster over his shoulder to give him a few more seconds. Shots from the Hovertank sparked off the edges of the bunker door as it slid open.

Ryder launched himself at the door, enemy fire narrowly missing his legs. He somersaulted in, grunted as the door closed, and realized he was staring down the end of a jumbo blaster. A blond woman smiled as she aimed it at his head.

"Who taught you how to shoot?" Kara Alexander asked her brother.

"You did, Pip," Ryder said with a grin. Pip slung her blaster over her shoulder and helped him up. He dusted himself off as she peeked through a scope by the door that gave her a bird's-eye view of the battlefield.

"How long have we got?" she asked.

"Long enough," Ryder said. "Their numbers are down, but they still have some firepower. If we can get those reinforcements, we can finish off the Rovers."

"We keep sending out distress calls, but so far, no response."

"They'll answer," Ryder said. "Where's everyone else?"

"In the primary command center, trying to regroup. We took a hit, lost a lot of people. Thought we lost you."

Ryder smiled. "You will never lose me."

Pip wrinkled her brow. "You've been shot."

"Just grazed."

"How are you not shaken right now?" Pip asked as they hustled through a tunnel toward the unit command center the Miners had set up for Ryder's army. Pip leaned in, and the security system scanned her retina. Once they were through, a steel door twelve inches thick lowered back to the floor.

"I'm never shaken. You know that. And neither are you," Ryder said. "What's wrong?"

They walked through the entrance, but Pip stopped once they were on the other side. "Something doesn't feel right this time."

"Of course it doesn't feel right. We're losing a battle. We're usually winning."

"No, it's something else. I don't know why, but my gut tells me no one is coming to help us."

Ryder tilted his head and focused on Pip for a moment. He noticed her expression tighten. In all the battles he had fought alongside his sister, she faced everyone without fear. Now she stood in front of him, shifting on her feet—something he had never seen before.

He reached out for her hand. "We're going to be fine. We've got each other and the others. Let's go check again on that callout. I bet there's an explanation for the delay. Besides, we're safe in here. The bombs from the Rover Hovertanks can't penetrate this bunker."

"I know. I just hope our supplies hold."

"They will. C'mon."

They both laid their palms on the next security entrance and the doors parted, revealing a large open area with two levels and a frenzy of people trying to send out distress calls. Some studied digital maps of the battlefield while others received medical attention in a small, makeshift infirmary for the severely wounded.

"There he is!" a voice behind them said.

A man with a thick, dark beard ran over to them. He wore a blast repulsion vest that barely covered his barrel chest. It was their brother, Hunter. He reached out for Ryder and pulled him in for a half hug, slapping him on the back before releasing him.

"Thought I was going to have to come out and rescue you, princess," Hunter said.

"I was only out so long because I had to save your weak ass, brother," Ryder replied.

Hunter let out a booming laugh. "Well, glad you made it, and with only a scratch. Nice work."

Ryder looked down at the wound in his arm he had almost forgotten. The bleeding had stopped; the wound healed. Ryder and his people were Kaygun, a race of people who possess regenerative abilities, which make them difficult to kill since most superficial wounds they receive repair themselves almost instantly.

"So, what's the update? Where's our backup?" Ryder asked. He walked around a wide, flat table that was the bunker's main computer terminal.

"We aren't sure," Hunter said. "Butani and his unit should have been here by now. We've sent out four calls, and we have yet to hear a response. Reports from home show they left at the agreed time, but they missed their landing window. Not sure what the holdup is unless they crashed somewhere or were shot down."

"They are bringing in five heavy air units. There's no way the enemy forces have enough juice to bring those down," Ryder said.

Ryder studied the screen in front of him. The Miners lived underground, only going to the surface to work, but he still wondered how long they would last. It also unsettled him that Pip was so rattled. She was always the fiercest one of all his siblings, especially in battle. The more he mulled things over, the more he knew Pip was right. Something was off.

Ryder cracked his knuckles, causing his siblings to cringe.

"I hate it when you do that," Pip said. "Isn't there some other way you can release your anxiety?"

"You know that sound gives us the creeps," Hunter added.

"Sorry, can't help it."

"Fine, what are you thinking?" Pip asked.

"We should call the Sentinels for help," Ryder said.

"The Sentinels? They'd never reach us in time."

"They might," said Pip, perking up. "I can get out a call to them right now."

Pip reached out to start a signal to the Sentinels, who were intergalactic allies and sources of protection for all in the universe. Just then, a call came into the terminal.

Ryder, Hunter, and Pip all exchanged glances. The signal code was Butani's.

Ryder answered. "Butani?"

There was only silence on the other end, though they heard noise as if someone had answered but was only listening.

"Butani? Are you there?"

"Uh, yeah, man. Butani here. Coming up on your bunker now."

"What happened to you? You should have landed a day ago?"

Static cut through as Butani tried to answer.

"We lost him," Ryder said.

Hunter grabbed his two blasters off an adjacent table. "Let's go meet him at the door. They're probably just trying to give us the all clear."

Pip shook her head. "Something's not right."

"What are you talking about? They made it. He ran into a little trouble, that's all," Hunter suggested.

"That guy *causes* trouble wherever he goes. I've never liked him," Pip said.

While Ryder agreed with his sister, he wanted to give Butani the benefit of the doubt. Butani was a bit of a rogue, but he was still Kaygun and a damned good soldier. At the same time, Ryder did not want to disregard his sister's feelings. "Pip, go ahead and send the call to the Sentinels. Doesn't hurt."

Pip punched in distress calls, and Ryder prayed the Sentinels would answer them in time. While there was no one else he would rather have beside him in battle than his sisters and brothers, he still worried about their safety.

"What do we do with Butani?" Hunter asked.

"Let's round up some people and go check it out," Ryder said, picking up a large canon rifle. Pip hesitated and then grabbed another rifle and powered it on.

They made their way back through the tunnels. When they got to the main entrance, Pip checked the scope again. The dust had settled on the surface. Butani and several others were waiting outside.

"Why are they just standing there?" Hunter asked.

"Don't know," Ryder said.

Butani pushed his face toward the scope, tapped on his ear, on his wrist, and then shook his head.

"Their comm is out. That's all it is," Hunter said.

"They shouldn't be out in the open like that," Pip added.

"Everyone in position. I'm opening the door," Ryder said as he entered a code in the pad next to the door. The battered bunker door blew dust up around them as it lurched open.

Butani, a bulky man with a shaved head, threw away a cigarette and stepped inside, throwing his hands up.

"Whoa, it's me!"

"Stay right there," Ryder said. He kept his rifle focused on Butani.

"What is your problem, man? We're here to help you. You called us."

Pip chimed in. "You should have been here days ago. What happened?"

Butani's gaze hit the floor. "We, uh ... we ran into ... we got delayed."

*He's lying, something's wrong.*

"You always were a terrible liar," Ryder said.

"We came to help you!"

Ryder took two steps toward Butani. "And why don't I think that's what you intend to do?"

Butani lowered his hands. The corner of his mouth twitched. Before Ryder got a shot off, an intense boom sounded behind Butani, who dove back out of the bunker. Pip screamed as they fell to the ground, and Ryder shielded his sister. A white light surrounded them all as their world faded to black and the bunker fell silent.

# 5

# TRINKET

**KANDICE MARIE SHOOK UNLOCKED** the double doors of her suite in an Aldemaran high rise. She had converted the once lackluster office by taking out a wall and creating a space where she could work and take a nap if she was so inclined. She threw her purse on her desk and stopped to straighten an empty pink frame hanging behind her chair. It was a frame that would have held her master's degree if she had finished school. She made her way from the south to Silicon Valley. The subjects of science and engineering had always come easy to her, but as she furthered her education and began to outpace her colleagues, she was constantly dismissed by the faculty in the field based on how she looked and dressed. She looked like a million bucks and dressed however the hell she wanted—typically more like a woman from the cover of a fashion magazine than a bio-mechanical engineer. Tired of being bullied by women and harassed by men, she dropped out.

One night, she returned home from a dinner and a man wearing a cape was standing in her living room. He offered her a better life out in the universe, and she took it. She charmed her way through different spaceports and made deals where she could. She ended up in Aldemara, the capital city of the planet of Ozex where she had her own laboratory, her own private security, and a personal assistant.

That assistant, Taylor, had just walked into her office. He was a lanky man with curly blond hair. He wore the same thing every day: a pressed white shirt with a collar, a black vest, and black pants. Everything irritated him, especially when Kandi asked him to do his job.

"The old lady has been calling forevs," Taylor said. "Now she's on her way up here."

"I told you I didn't want to talk to her," Kandi said.

"She would not listen to me."

"Did you even try to stop her?"

"Not very hard, no."

Kandi rolled her eyes. "Just go get me something hot to drink."

Taylor scoffed as Kandi's current employer, General Lovella Law, pushed her way through the heavy golden doors.

"I've been calling you for the better part of an hour," Lovella said.

Kandi picked up a ceramic trinket of a pig in a bikini. "Do you know what makes pigs so special?"

"Excuse me?"

"Pigs are smart. Smarter than dogs or chimps. They can solve problems, you can train them to do specific tasks, and yet, because of how they look, the only thing we do with them is eat them."

"I don't have time for your mind games, Ms. Shook. While you've been here skulking about, the lab staff notified me that your acquisition has come out of his last surgery and you've ordered them to bring him here to your suite."

Kandi grinned, stood up from her desk and straightened the red dress that clung to her every curve. "I can't wait to see what they did."

Lovella followed her around the desk. "They also informed me that you intend to revive him here without using restraints on him?"

"Yes. That poor man has been through so much. The med team thought he should wake up somewhere more soothing than that sterile old med bay. They told me you okayed it." Kandi shuffled to the large, round mirror hanging over a credenza and applied the most shocking shade of pink lipstick she had in her cosmetic arsenal.

With a strained voice, Lovella continued, "I did not authorize any such thing, and you know this."

"Well, that's what they told me. They really were just trying to follow your orders."

Lovella's face flushed, and her jaw tightened. "He will be waking up in the lab with restraints on, not in your suffocatingly pink boudoir."

"Oh, goodness! Well, I guess the lines of communication got crossed. Isn't it frustrating when your staff doesn't listen to you? It's probably too late to change the order, though."

"This man is not some new pet. He is one of the most decorated soldiers in the history of this galaxy. He is going to wake confused, enraged, and dangerous. Do not underestimate him and his desire to return to his home planet. If we do not contain him from the beginning, our plan will fail."

"Relax, honey. He's just a man. They're all the same. Besides, he won't have a choice once he finds out what's at stake for him if refuses to be my little pet."

"This operation is bigger than that. We need him to help solidify our alignment with the Zuldari. We did not acquire this man to be your toy. His purpose is to fulfill a very specific mission. Your purpose is to follow my directives. I'm not funding your operations in the lab just for the hell of it. If he fails—if you fail—you will spend the rest of your days in the Thenaria Nickel Mines."

"Hey, I work for you, sweetie," Kandi said. "I was just trying to think of his well-being."

Lovella sighed. "Kandi, what I'm offering you is a place beside me at the table. Once we solidify our alliance with the Zuldari, you will be my right hand in all we accomplish with them. We need to work together from here on out."

Kandi flashed a crooked smile, folded her arms, and leaned back onto the credenza. "Of course. I'll make sure he wakes up in the med bay. Just as we want him to."

Lovella looked Kandi up and down and then narrowed her eyes. "We need to get this right."

"Absolutely," Kandi said, turning away to apply one more layer of lipstick. She smiled at Lovella in the mirror. *We'll see who ends up in the Nickel Mines when this is all over.*

# 6

## PINK

**RYDER FELT LIKE HE WAS FLOATING**, as if he were not in his body, but hovering above it. The heaviness of his tactical gear and armor fell away as he drifted, surrounded by soft, white light. He saw Pip. She smiled and laughed, and then her face twisted with pain. She screamed and reached out for Ryder. He called out to her, but there was no sound. His arms stretched out for her again, but her face disappeared in a fireball. He screamed as all the weight of his body fell back on him. When he woke, he was panting and sitting in a place that was not the battlefield he last saw.

It took a moment for his vision to return, and to his horror, he could see out of only one eye. His hands shook uncontrollably, and another sight caught him as he tried to make sense of where he was. He recoiled as he realized he was not in the dark bunker or on the scorched battle-field, but covered in a soft, satin, pink sheet on a large king bed with more pillows than he had ever seen. Above him, a pink canopy covered the bed. His chest tightened, and he flung the covers off and launched out of the bed. He lost his footing because his sight couldn't adjust with one working eye. He pulled himself up and tried to catch his breath.

Ryder had been a prisoner of war before. He had woken up submerged in ice baths, chained to walls, beaten, and bound. Those were scenes he had learned to cope with, but nothing in his life had prepared him for the atrocities he was seeing in his new surroundings. Pink everywhere. Pink wallpaper, hot pink velvet sofa, pink shag rug. The smell of perfume was so strong it was as if several bottles had broken on the floor, releasing an overwhelming pink cloud of scent.

He was in a bedroom that opened into an expansive living area. A chill ran over him as he realized the only thing he was wearing was a pair of pink boxer briefs.

Something else caught his eye as he explored the room. It was horrifyingly decorated with small pig figurines. They all seemed to grunt and grin at him.

Straight ahead, on the wall in front of him, was another shocking sight. A painting of a curvaceous woman with large, perky breasts and round hips filled the entire wall. She had glistening sun tanned skin, full lips, and long, hot pink fingernails. Her streaked blond hair blew around her as if the wind had caught it when the photo was taken. Ryder shook his head, trying to shake off the nightmare unfolding around him. He stepped back and fell over a puffy hot pink ottoman, hitting his head on the floor. He was so preoccupied with the gold and sparkling white trim of the ceiling that he almost did not notice his arm.

Ryder scraped himself off the floor as he looked in terror at his left arm. Instead of a triceps muscle and a fleshy elbow, there was a piece of shiny steel. He flexed his arm and felt as though he were going to be sick. To his right was a bathroom with a mirror. Light filled the room when he stepped in. He held himself up on the bathroom counter and there, in the rhinestone-framed mirror, was the reason he could see out of only one eye. When he lifted the eye patch, the color drained from his face. Where a bright right eye had been, machine parts and a glowing red light filled his eye socket. His vision was then split: normal images appeared in the left eye, and he could simultaneously see heat signatures in the room from the right eye.

Nausea churned up from his stomach. The motion from his hand caused the faucet to turn on, and he shoveled as much water into his mouth as he could so he wouldn't get sick. That's when he heard a door open.

A short woman wearing a tight, red dress glided in. It was the woman from the painting. Ryder glared at her, but she ignored him. She sauntered in, eating a large cupcake with mounds of pink frosting.

"Hey baby! Welcome back!" she said after taking a seat behind her desk. She licked the frosting off one of her fingers. "Damn, you look fine."

"Who are you?"

"Kandice Shook, your newest best friend. But call me Kandi, sugar."

Ryder clenched his teeth. "What have you done to me?!"

"Baby, I saved you. You were dead, hon. A plasma bomb tore through your little hideout and wiped y'all out."

Ryder searched his memories for any shred of the last moments in the bunker, but he could not remember anything beyond opening the door to Butani.

"I know a body dealer who found you and two of your siblings. You were all dead and gone. Well, you were mostly dead. Y'all were steaming like slugs on hot blacktop when they found you. Turns out you still had a little life left in you."

Ryder glared at her. "I was dead?"

"Kind of," Kandi said. "My people said that y'all can regenerate to a certain extent. With our help, we brought you back to this gorgeous

29

life. There were some parts missing though so we had to … uh … fill in the blanks with our own pieces."

"Where is *here*?"

"Aldemara."

"Where is my family? Butani?" Ryder asked.

"Listen honey, we'll get to that. Why don't you sit and relax? You've had a long day, am I right?" Kandi batted her velvety eyelashes.

Ryder growled, and with all the force of a hurricane, he pushed all the trinkets off her desk, sending everything crashing to the floor. Kandi shot to her feet.

"Answer me!" Ryder shouted.

Kandi ran her hand through her hair and exhaled as she leaned over the desk, pushing her breasts up. "Your siblings are still in our lab." Kandi pressed a button on her desk.

Ryder took a step back as the wall with the painting opened to reveal a network of computer screens. He tried to focus through his eye, and his mouth fell open at the sight of Pip, beaten and bruised. She was submerged in a giant tank of glowing green liquid in what looked like a laboratory.

Ryder lunged over the desk at Kandi and leapt on her, throwing her to the ground. He wrapped his powerful hands around her slender neck and squeezed, shaking her. "Release them!"

She did not struggle and only laughed in between coughs and gasps for air. "Can't … only you can."

Ryder was so focused on extinguishing the life from Kandi's eyes that he did not hear someone charge through the doors behind him. A blast of light hit Ryder in the shoulder, but he didn't flinch. He kept squeezing, though his flesh was burning and intense pain rippled down his arm. He slammed Kandi's head into the ground. Her laughter then turned to a scream. A second blast hit Ryder in the chest, and he fell back. A man shot one more time before Kandi put up a hand to stop him. Two of Kandi's guards rushed in with blasters drawn, and Ryder stayed down, his body spiking with pain.

Kandi rubbed her neck. "Thank you, Taylor," she said to the man pointing his blaster at Ryder.

"Why are you doing this?" Ryder asked.

"Doesn't matter why," Kandi said. She straightened her dress and combed her hair with her fingernails. "What matters now is how y'all earn your freedom, and to do that, you will work for me and do everything I ask. Got it, honey?"

# 7

# STALLWORTH

### PRESENT DAY

**"WHERE WHO WHAT NOW?"** Elliot asked.

"You can call me Captain Stallworth, and this is my lovely assistant, Mr. Scott Zimmer."

Zimmer released an exasperated sigh as he stepped forward and handed Stella and Elliot each an electronic tablet. "These tablets will describe to you, in some detail, the alien abduction experience."

"Aliens?" Elliot asked. "Wait … oh my God …is this…?" Elliot looked around the room. "This must be the TV show."

Stallworth cocked his head to one side. "Show?"

"This is crazy," Stella said. She threw her tablet on the bed behind her.

"Is this a new show where you kidnap people and say they've been abducted by aliens? And you dress us up, and we will have to fight for survival on a desert island? You guys are running out of ideas, aren't you?" Elliot asked.

"Mr. Driver, I can assure you this is not a *show*."

"What happened to our clothes?" Stella asked.

Stallworth threw back his head and laughed as he held his chest. "My dear, those were not *clothes* we found you in. Those were hideous, tattered rags. You may now enjoy the finest wardrobe Balance offers."

"Balance?"

"Your new home, Dr. Walsh."

"Captain, I need to begin check-in so we can process them before we land," Zimmer insisted.

Stella opened her mouth to protest, but Zimmer held up his hand to silence her. "The sooner I can get you checked in, the sooner you will be on your way."

Stella massaged her eyes. *This is just a dream. Just a dream.*

Zimmer pulled a small mic out of his tablet and spoke into it. "All right, starting with the female. We have one Stella Jayne Walsh, Caucasian, five feet, nine inches tall, approximately 140 pounds, 37 Terran years of age, red hair, eyes green, unwed, no descendants, surgeon by trade," Zimmer paused. "What is this? You have here: no pets, does not cook, and has username Bubbles17 on Reddit. Captain—"

"How dare you!" fumed Stella. "How do you know all of that?"

Stallworth ignored her and smiled. "Yes, yes. Now do the man."

Zimmer scrolled down. "You have here: Elliot James Driver, male, Caucasian, six-foot-two, 225 pounds, 38 Terran years of age, hair: brown, eyes: blue, unwed, no descendants, warrior by trade—"

"Uh, that should be American Ninja Warrior," Elliot corrected. "I passed qualifying twice, just can't make it to finals, but that won't stop me from training. This is only my hobby, though. My day job is working at Spartan Ink Advertising. Want to make sure they get a good promo out of this." Elliot pointed to the notes.

Stallworth and Zimmer exchanged glances.

Stella gawked at Elliot, shaking her head at how calm he was. "I don't know how you know all of that about me," she said, turning her attention back to Zimmer and Stallworth, "but I'm calling the police, and I'm getting out of here."

"How do you expect to call the police, Dr. Walsh? You are far from everything familiar to you. Now, back up, please." Zimmer said with a pinched tone. He scrolled through the rest of the notes. "Captain, I'm sorry, but your team has once again compiled useless information. After six months of scouting, all we have here is that Mr. Driver collects beer steins and enjoys blues music. The officials of Balance will never sign off on this. We need health records and criminal backgrounds, not what their inane interests are."

"I think when they see how fine these specimens are, they will sign off. Look at this man. He possesses impressive musculature, handsome, perfect teeth, and Balance will need a warrior with skills. This woman is beautiful and spry and comes with a knowledge of medicine. They are a perfect match. They will produce fine offspring."

"Excuse me?" Stella and Elliot said in unison.

"We have selected you both to help populate our newly discovered planet. We need to reach a certain population number to be counted in the Intergalactic Alliance of Planets, which is how we will receive credits for new buildings, byways, and the like. Dr. Walsh, Mr. Driver, say hello to your new mate."

"Now this I like," Elliot smiled.

Stella moved to the door, but Zimmer whipped out a small weapon that looked like an oddly shaped gun. "I said, step back."

Stella looked down at the gun and scoffed. "Uh, I work at Mercy General, so I hate to disappoint you, but this is not the first time I've had a gun in my face."

"If you do not cooperate, I will stun you," Zimmer said.

Stallworth laughed nervously and stepped in front of Zimmer. "That won't be necessary. Our guests are a little confused by all of this, and rightly so. Let's just everyone return to a calmer state, shall we?"

Zimmer put his gun away. "I'm going to get their profiles processed before we land," he said before leaving the room in a huff.

"I do apologize for Zimmer. He has no patience. That will not happen again. Take a seat, Dr. Walsh. You look pale."

She took a seat next to Elliot on the cozy, beige sofa. If this was a reality TV show, she could play along, although she knew her lawyer would have a field day with this production after he learned they rendered her unconscious and threatened her with a weapon.

"So, you're an alien?" Elliot asked.

Stallworth raised his eyebrows. "In one sense, yes, but from what I'm sure you have been told about space aliens, no. I'm an alien to you because I don't reside on earth, but I'm human in every other sense. Not what you were expecting?"

"No," Elliot said.

"Well, I'm sorry to disappoint," Stallworth said. He sat down in a chair to the side of them.

"No, it's fine," Elliot continued. "I just thought, aliens had … you know … big, black eyes and skinny little bodies with, like, pointy heads or something."

"Ah, yes, those are elaborate costumes. We use them only when we want to frighten people," Stallworth said with a chuckle. "Although there are some life forms from the outer rims that do resemble what you speak of. The Greys, as your people call them."

"Sure," Elliot said, nodding. "The Greys."

"There's something else that may disappoint you, Mr. Driver."

"Oh?"

"Most all life-forms in this part of the galaxy speak English, as it was a language created on another distant planet and not on Earth."

"Oh, c'mon," Elliot said.

"I know this will take some getting used to, but it will be only a short time before you realize the rewards of living a life outside Earth. Your tablet will tell you more about your abduction. For now, if you are feeling better, we have a complimentary tour of the ship laid out for you."

"Ship?" Stella asked. "You want us to believe we are on ... a spaceship?"

"Yes. At this moment, you are flying on a spaceship through the universe."

"No, I'm sorry, no. I have to go." Stella stood up. "I do not want to be on your show. Please take me home as I have patients and a hospital to help manage and—"

"I am sorry, Dr. Walsh. We cannot do that. You are far from home, and those things you spoke of are things you must forget because you are never to return to Earth. You have a new life now—the life we are going to give you on a new, wondrous planet. Yes, your life will never be the same. You should embrace these facts. Resistance will only break you down after a while."

Stella shut her eyes again. *Wake up, Stella. Wake up.* When she opened her eyes, the scene was the same. She frowned.

"Give it time to sink in," Stallworth said. "Meanwhile, try to enjoy yourselves while you are here. I'm sure you will find our ship quite comfortable and fun."

Stallworth led Stella and Elliot out of their temporary chamber and through the ship. It looked like the inside of a luxury hotel, except that carpet covered everything, even the walls and ceilings.

*What if it's true? What if this is happening?* Stella thought. Elliot asked Stallworth questions as they passed through the ship's corridors. Stella wanted only to get back to the hospital and her patients and did not realize she mumbled that last statement out loud until it was too late.

"You need not worry, Dr. Walsh. A replacement surgeon has stepped in to assist with your work. He has trained his entire life for this moment."

Stella snickered. "Replacement surgeon? Right, I'm replaceable. I don't think so."

Stallworth squinted and forced a smile. He gestured through the next open doorway. "This is the lounge up here to the left. Now, we will land shortly, so sit down, order a drink. Zimmer will be back for you momentarily."

# 8

# PKIS

**THE LOUNGE WAS DIMLY LIT** with a ceiling covered in tiny, blue, twinkling lights that resembled a small galaxy. A pleasant bustle of people laughed, talked, and drank, while blues music wandered out of speakers in the ceiling. After much coaxing from Elliot, Stella agreed to take a seat in a booth.

"I will say, if this is a TV show, they have outdone themselves as far as creating the set. I'm surprised they made everyone look like your average human," Elliot said. "You would think they would have a few more alien creatures with, like, fifty eyes or tentacles. Kind of lazy on the director's part, if you ask me." He rested his cheek on his hand and started to read through the tablet.

Stella glanced around the room. No one looked like how Stella envisioned an alien. Some people were dressed in formal wear, some wore uniforms like Stallworth's, and some were dressed in other forms of casual attire. Occasionally, people would look over toward Stella and Elliot, whispering and smiling as they chatted, but other than a few curious glances, everyone seemed calm and normal, just as they would be if Stella and Elliot were having dinner in a Manhattan restaurant. "Maybe I have PTSD," Stella mumbled.

"Huh?" Elliot winked at the server who had just winked at him.

The server approached the table and set down two cocktail napkins. "Hi! My name is Rianne, and I will tend to you. Here are your TEDs." Rianne set down two glasses filled with a bright glowing liquid.

"Our what?" Stella asked.

"Your teleportation easement drinks. TEDs. They will help your head."

Elliot sniffed his drink. "Interesting color. I thought this was a lit candle."

"First time in space?" Rianne asked.

"Why yes, yes it is," Elliot said, beaming.

"Don't worry. You'll love it up here. I was ... let me see ... abducted in 1994. It was amazin'. It happened right in my own back yard in Fenton, Indiana. I was out there, stringing some sheets on the line, and bam! I was out like a light and then woke up here. And now I'm having the time of my life. You will too, once you get used to it. Now, what would you like?"

"That's an incredible story, Rianne," Elliot said. "I guess I will have something equivalent to a scotch on the rocks."

Stella remained silent. She was thirsty, but she struggled with how casual everyone around her was.

*Just play along. Maybe you'll wake up any second.*

"Do you have some sort of sparkling water with a lime?" Stella asked.

"Nothing from the bar, dearie?" Rianne asked.

"Sparkling water?" Elliot repeated.

"I don't drink alcohol."

"Oh, so not even—"

"Nope."

"That's a shame. You know, it may help you feel more at ease, sugar," Rianne said.

Stella folded her arms across her chest. "It won't."

"Sure thing," Rianne said, her bright smile fading as she walked away.

Elliot frowned and continued to scroll through the information in the tablet. "Wow, listen to this: The title of this manual is 'For PKIS or Persons Kidnapped In Space. Penned for the Intergalactic Council (IGC) by Doctor Wiffle, Doctor Spineti, and Doctor Kyan of Arcas 7, 406th space year,'" Elliot read. "This is so awesome. 'This manual contains lists and tips for easing oneself into abduction. The first sensation a new abductee will experience is that of a pounding headache. It is the body letting you know that it is adjusting to space teleportation, which will always offset one's equilibrium. Your captor is required to give you teleportation easement drinks to ease the symptoms. For information regarding what becomes of PKIS, skip to page 5.'" Elliot swiped on the screen. "It just says, 'It all depends.' That's not very reassuring."

"Why are you reading that?"

"I mean, why not?"

"Because it's insane."

Elliot swiped left on the screen several times. "Listen to this: 'Mercenaries to Avoid. Be warned that there are dangerous beings running about that want nothing more than to spy, maim, steal, and kill for themselves or the people they serve. They classify some as Rovers. Rovers are looters and marauders who patrol the galaxies for anything they can steal and then later barter. This includes people, flora, fauna, and anything else they deem of value. There are other mercenaries who are skilled assassins. They carry out tasks for the people who own them. These tasks can include, but are not limited to, murder, torture, kidnapping, revenge, and debt collection. The following pages will show the top ten most wanted assassins the IGC is hunting for capture.' Wow, look at this guy."

He turned his tablet so Stella could see the picture of a man's face. He had a fade haircut and a five o'clock shadow. He looked like a normal man except for the fact that the left side of his face had a blue eye, while the other side had a red, glowing eye.

"Yep, he looks like a scary guy," Stella said, rolling her eyes.

"'Ryder is known throughout the universe as one of the most evasive fugitives in intergalactic history,' Elliot continued. "'He wears a long, leather coat that can cloak his body, making him invisible. One of his eyes has built-in night vision, heat sensors, and a chip scanner. Skilled with a multitude of fighting techniques and the ability to regenerate from most wounds, Ryder is almost impossible to find and even more difficult to kill.' I hope I never meet that dude." He swiped further ahead in the manual and didn't look up until Stella made a scoffing sound. "What? What's wrong?"

"I'm sorry, I don't know why you seem so okay with all of this."

"I'm not okay, but what else should I be doing? This is the most exciting thing that has happened to me in months. Well, there was a blind guy I thought needed help on the A Train. Turns out, he wasn't blind at all and was just trying to steal my wallet."

"I'd much rather be dealing with that right now than this nonsense," Stella said.

"And what *would* you be doing right now?"

"I would get out of this stupid dress, take a shower, and go to sleep. In the morning, I'm hoping to wake up, having realized this was all a dream, exercise, have a piece of avocado toast, and go back to work."

"Sounds awful," Elliot said.

"Excuse me?"

"First, avocado toast is the worst. Second, I hope this is not a dream. I hope this is all real, and I can't wait to see what happens next. I'm going to have an open mind. You should try it."

"Is your life that bad that you would rather embrace this delusion than wake up and just go to work tomorrow?"

Elliot paused. "Not bad, but could be better. I've got a place to live, but the upstairs neighbor has like sixty cats. I've been meeting women, but my last date wanted a list of my ex-girlfriends so she could consult with them before she agreed to a second date. Work is fine, but they passed me over for a promotion because the boss's son needed a management position. I guess you could say I'm ready for some excitement."

Stella softened and let one part of her mouth give into a slight upward curl. Elliot intrigued her.

*Look at him. He's like a kid at Disneyland. How does he do that?*

She admired his openness, although she kept those thoughts to herself, not wanting to encourage him. Rianne returned with more cheerfulness and their drinks. Elliot took a swig, while Stella squeezed the lime into her water.

"What about you? You're a doctor, a scientist, right? I would think all this would fascinate you. Why can't you just let go and accept the fact that you are on a spaceship about to discover new lands, explore alien worlds, all with the most handsome man you have ever seen?"

Stella shifted her gaze away from Elliot's lively eyes. "I just can't."

"Why?"

"Because it doesn't make any sense. None of this makes any sense."

"So?"

"And besides, my life was just fine."

"Oh? Really? Okay, tell me, is there a man or ... hmm ... maybe a woman in your life?"

Stella's eyes shot back to Elliot's. "No, and no."

"When was the last time you went on a date?"

She couldn't remember. "I, I don't have time ..."

"When was your last vacation?"

"I went to Long Island last fall," Stella said.

"That's not a vacation. I'm talking exotic locales—the beach or maybe a rugged adventure in the mountains. When was the last time you went to a movie?"

"There aren't any movies I like."

"Do you have any kids or pets or plants even?" Elliot asked.

"I don't think this is any of your business."

"Look, I get it. You save lives for a living. There's probably not much energy left to take care of you or anything else. Not even a cactus, which is the plant I would say most matches your personality."

Stella wanted to laugh but brought her fingers to her mouth halting her smile. She cleared her throat. "Hey, there's nothing wrong with cacti. They need little water to thrive."

Elliot grinned. "That's true."

The sudden hush of the lounge caught Stella's attention. People who were once laughing and chatting at a loud hum were now whispering or quiet as they turned their gazes toward the window. Elliot turned in his seat to look behind him.

"What the ..."

"Maybe they are changing the set," Stella said.

"Then why does everyone look so scared?" Elliot asked.

Stella peered over her glass as she drank her water. Everyone in the lounge was staring out the window. What looked like a warehouse slowly replaced the stars on the other side of the window. An alarm sounded through the lounge, piercing the stillness. Stella jumped, spilling water all over her face, but she wiped herself off while the other guests screamed and ran out of the lounge in a panic. People overturned tables and shattered glasses as they pushed to get out of the lounge. Stella and Elliot remained frozen in their booth.

"So, I guess that's going to be a 'no' on getting a refill," Elliot said.

Stella massaged her temples. Elliot started for the bar when loud pops sounded on the other side of the lounge door.

"Whoa, that can't be good."

"Well, I've had it. I'm tired of waiting, tired of playing along. I'm going to go find Stall-whatever, and I'm getting out of here." Stella slid out of the booth toward the lounge doors.

Elliot caught up to her and blocked the door. "Wait. I swear those were gunshots. Shouldn't we get back to our room?"

"And do what?" Stella asked, trying to step by him.

Elliot put up his hands. "And get away from the gunshots. Hello?"

"I doubt that's what they were. I'm tired of sitting here. I want to go home."

"Haven't you ever seen a horror movie? You never open the door."

Stella had taken a step closer to the door, but she stopped before triggering the censor that would open it. "You really think those are gunshots?"

"Yes, and I think we should go out the opposite door back to the room."

"But the captain went out this door."

"So? He probably just got shot!"

"I'm ... uh ... sure it's fine. It's quiet now. I'm sure whatever caused the commotion is gone."

Stella hesitated but decided she was done waiting for Stallworth to come back for them. She stepped forward and the doors slid open, revealing an empty corridor.

"See? Nothing to be afraid of."

She took one step into the corridor when a laser blast flew past her right ear. She yelped and slammed herself against the wall. Elliot cried out and dodged another blast that missed his torso just as the doors closed again. Steam wafted up from his shoulder where a laser blast had torn through his flesh.

Elliot winced and grabbed his arm. "I've been shot. I've been shot. Okay … um … I think we should get out of here now."

Stella nodded with her mouth open. "Oh my God, I'm—"

"Let's go!"

They made it to a familiar door, and when Stella touched it, a woman's voice said, "Welcome to the happy couple. Your chamber awaits."

The door slid open, and Stella and Elliot hustled in, the sounds of blasts and gunshots echoing through the hallway behind them.

"Okay, that was intense," Elliot said, out of breath.

"Your arm …" Stella said.

Elliot looked down and cringed.

"Are they allowed to shoot at you on reality TV now?" Stella said as she examined Elliot's wound.

"This isn't reality TV. I'm pretty sure this is actually happening."

"Don't say that." Stella ripped Elliot's torn shirt away from the wound. "It's not too bad, but this will bleed more if we don't get you some first aid."

"Shhh," Elliot said.

Screams echoed in the hallway, followed by more pops.

"We need to barricade the door," Elliot said.

Stella helped Elliot pull a table and two chairs in front of the door. More screaming sounded and then faded away. Men shouted in the hallway and banged on the door. The woman's voice that had greeted Stella and Elliot said, "I apologize, but we do not permit you to enter this room."

A man on the other side shouted an obscenity at the voice and shot at the door. Stella and Elliot stepped back when smoke puffed through the furniture barricade as the forces on the other side broke through. Elliot flipped over the sofa, and they both hit the floor behind it as the men blew a hole through the door. Elliot shielded Stella by wrapping himself around her. Her screams were drowned under the sounds of bombs exploding as bits of the couch, tables, and ceiling pelted them. The sofa was disintegrating with each laser blast, and if the shooting didn't stop, there would be nothing left to shield Stella and Elliot from the enraged mob forcing their way into the room.

# 9

# INTERCEPTION

**THE SOFA HAD ALL BUT DISINTEGRATED.** They needed to get further away from the door. Stella motioned to Elliot and pointed to the other side of the room. He nodded, and just as they slid flat on their stomachs, the mob stopped shooting into the room and seemed to focus on something in the hallway.

Stella was about to push herself up to her feet when a larger blast blew the doors to the room wide open. She and Elliot crawled to the other side of the bed and Stella pulled her legs out from view.

Stella made a "shhh" gesture to Elliot, who wriggled onto his back as loud voices entered the room.

"They are in here. I know I hit one of them," said a voice.

There was more than one man in the room looking around, but not with much urgency. One of them guzzled the champagne, burped, and then threw the empty bottle against the wall. She tried to hold her breath, but her nose began the familiar tickle from all the falling debris. She buried her face in the floor, which helped the sneeze subside. Elliot could not stop himself in time, and he sneezed into his sleeve.

"Hello there," said a voice. "Found them."

A garish looking man grinned with an almost toothless smile as he pointed a rifle at Stella and Elliot. Another man with a shaved head and an eye patch stood over them with a smaller gun.

"What do we do wit' dem?" asked the man with the eye patch.

The man pointing the rifle at them answered. "Kill the man. The woman will bring some bounty."

Stella's pulse raced as the man focused his weapon on Elliot. The man's finger pulled back on the trigger. Elliot rolled to protect Stella, but she screamed and threw up her hands. The men's eyes widened as lime green sparks flew out of her hands. They burst out like mini fireworks, then fizzled like a motor that couldn't quite get started.

"What are you?" The man holding the rifle asked. Before anyone could answer, something tore through the back of him, blowing a hole in his chest. Blood sprayed out, and he fell on top of Elliot, who winced and pushed him off to the side. The man with the eye patch returned fire, but another shot blew him back. Another man in the room charged at something Stella couldn't see. He yelled, but a shot silenced him. Stella and Elliot pushed themselves up to see a giant silver robot grab a fourth man and slam him to the ground. A woman dressed in a black leather catsuit shot two more men who tried to enter the room.

"Are you hurt?" The woman asked, reaching to help Stella up.

"Who are you?"

"We're Sentinels, here to help. Rovers have seized the ship. We need to get you both to safety." She pulled Elliot up, whipped around, and fired at another Rover entering the room.

The woman shouted for Stella and Elliot to follow the robot who was waving them into the corridor. As they ran behind him in the hallway, the robot's body absorbed blasts from other Rovers that popped out from hidden spots along the way. The woman dashed behind them, blasting away at anyone who tried to follow. Stella ducked stray beams of light and pulled Elliot down as one just missed his head. They hustled down a small ramp and into an extensive airplane hangar. The ramp to another aircraft was down, and people, including Shamus Stallworth, ran up it while others in white military uniforms returned fire on the Rovers shooting from what was left of The Inspirion.

"Get on board!" shouted the woman. She fired into the crowd of Rovers, picking them off one by one. The robot turned and shielded Stella and Elliot as they scurried up the ramp.

Zimmer waved to them from the top. "We got them. Let's go," he yelled into a device on his wrist.

Zimmer shuffled them into the cargo hold of the new aircraft. Stella recognized some people from The Inspirion's lounge. Sobs and gasps from those on board echoed in the room while everyone attempted to collect themselves. The woman in the black catsuit and the robot were the last to make it up the ramp, as tremors shook the room. Through an octagon-shaped window that ran from the ceiling to the floor, Stella saw the ship pull out from the hangar and rocket out into the stars.

Stella still did not want to believe anything unfolding before her was real, but there was now actual blood on her dress, most likely from one of the men the woman shot. Stella's knees buckled, and it was as if everything were moving in slow motion. Zimmer broke through the crowd of people in the cargo bay and guided Stella and Elliot down more steel hallways to another room that resembled a medical facility. The woman in the catsuit followed and guided Stella and Elliot to two flat tables.

"Do you have any injuries?" she asked Stella.

"What the hell is going on here?" Stella asked.

The woman narrowed her eyes. "I'll take that as a no. Wait here, please. The captain will be down shortly."

Elliot sat himself on one of the tables, and the woman assessed his injuries.

*Great. I've just been kidnapped, shot at, dressed for a sham wedding, and now I'm going to have to help with all these injured people.*

"He's been shot at twice now, you know," Stella said.

The woman in black frowned as she helped Elliot out of his tux shirt. "I can see that."

Stella caught herself staring at Elliot as he peeled off the rest of his shirt. He was tan and sculpted, with muscles that rippled when he moved his arms. Stella tried to keep a straight face, though she wanted to smile. Elliot was a handsome man, and she could see how he could be mistaken for a warrior.

"What? What's wrong with my arm?" Elliot asked.

The woman cleared her throat and pressed a button. A small tray of instruments and devices Stella had never seen hovered over to the table.

Stella stepped in front of the woman and tried to examine the burned gash in Elliot's shoulder. "What type of weapon would do this kind of damage?"

"A 72-C Pulse Rifle. Sends out a blast of laser light that can penetrate almost anything. He's lucky it only grazed him."

"I'll need something to clean this out with, and I'll need something for the pain," Stella said.

"I'm fine. It doesn't hurt—aaaahhhh!—that bad."

Stella applied pressure on the wound. She smirked, and then continued. "I need a pair of gloves and—"

The woman glared at Stella. "What you need is to go sit on the bed over there." She pointed to the other flat exam table. "The captain will be down shortly to speak with you and Mr. Driver."

"How do you know his name?" Stella asked.

"Go sit down."

Stella glared back at the woman in the catsuit and sat on the nearest bed. She folded her arms across her chest and surveyed the room. It was unlike any medical facility she had ever seen. No one had personal protective equipment on. There were no IVs of fluids, no ventilators, or many other things Stella was used to seeing in an ER. The beds were flat and looked like they contained built-in computers around their edges. Stella watched as electronic devices treated minor injuries. One device healed a substantial gash on a woman's head in just seconds. Another man lay flat on his back on a table. A woman in a lab coat placed his arm in a steel tube, set a timer, and then walked away. She returned minutes later, removed the tube, and moved the man's arm back and forth as he nodded.

Stella took a deep breath. This room was the closest to anything familiar to her, but she couldn't help anyone as she had always done. Instead, she was sent to time-out like a child.

*What is happening to me? How did I get here? Where is here?*

The questions kept popping up in her mind, and there did not seem to be many answers. She hoped the captain would have some, and if he didn't, she would question everyone on the ship until she got to the bottom of what was happening.

Just then, Zimmer entered the room with a man who was about his same modest height, but with a stockier build. His chin almost disappeared in a mustache that sat at attention on his top lip. He had a wave of brown hair graying at the temples. From his uniform, Stella discerned he was an authority figure.

*Must be the new captain.*

Stella narrowed her eyes as Zimmer handed the captain something, though she couldn't quite make out what it was. The captain's eyes passed over hers. He looked both concerned and intrigued by whatever Zimmer was telling him. She missed bits of their conversation because of the surrounding noise, but she still could make out a few fragments.

"That's why I radioed you for help—that and, well, the fact that Stallworth doesn't take any travel precautions," Zimmer said. "We can't let anyone know she's here."

"That's easier said than done, my friend, but we need to get her back to Verbatim and figure out what to do."

"I'm fine, by the way. I know you were all concerned," the robot said, breaking Stella's concentration as he joined Zimmer and the captain. The captain shoved something in a chest pocket as he walked toward Elliot. Stella stood and approached them; she was over being in time-out.

"Are you the captain?" she asked. The woman in black, the robot, and Zimmer all exchanged glances.

The captain smiled in a way that unnerved Stella. She had never seen the man before, but the way he looked at her, it was as though she was familiar to him.

"Captain Finnieous Rex, but please call me Rex. And you are the good Dr. Stella Jayne Walsh," he said, extending his hand.

Stella crossed her arms over her chest. "How do you know my name?"

"We track abducted Terrans. Zimmer here provided us with the information we needed so we could locate you, and lucky he did. Nasty bunch of Rovers back there." Rex patted Zimmer on the back.

"But he's the one who abducted me," Stella said.

Rex's eyes darted around. "Uh ..."

"I've got to take this phone call," Zimmer said as he shuffled around for a phone that hadn't been ringing. He hustled through the crowd and out of sight.

"Seriously? The fake phone call?" Stella asked.

Rex put his arm around Stella and squeezed her as if she were the grown daughter he hadn't seen in months. "Dr. Walsh, I'm sure you must be exhausted. You can get some rest while you are here, and we can go over any questions you may have soon enough."

"And where is here?" Stella asked.

"You are safe and sound on our ship, The Pygmy Train," Rex said.

"Are you going to explain to us what's happening?"

"As I said, in due time, Dr. Walsh. We will get you and Driver checked out, make sure you are okay, and then we will have a nice, long chat in my chambers."

"Why can't we have that chat right now?" Stella insisted.

Rex turned to the robot. "For all that's holy, Gary, you can return to your normal state now."

The giant silver robot looked down at himself. "Hmmm? Oh, yes."

Stella gasped and stepped back as the robot morphed before her eyes. Slabs of silver metal folded inward and changed position like puzzle pieces that were taking themselves apart and putting themselves back together again. He shrank and transformed into a man with curly hair, wearing a Hawaiian shirt, Bermuda shorts, white socks pulled up to his calves, and sandals. He also wore a fanny pack from which he pulled a cloth, dabbing his forehead as if he had just come off a ride at an amusement park.

"That was the coolest thing I have ever seen," Elliot said.

Gary grinned. "Isn't it?"

"What are you?" Stella asked.

"Right. Introductions are in order, I believe. Dr. Walsh, Driver, this is my bold, and may I say beautiful, number two in command, Iris," Rex said as the woman in black nodded. "And this fine gentleman is Gary."

Before Stella could react, she felt herself being scooped up in Gary's firm grasp. Her arms went limp and she was thankful Rex pulled them apart.

"Gary, what have we told you about hugging people you first meet?" Iris said.

"I know, I know, I know, but—oh my—this is a moment. My heart just burst into a thousand rainbows. I couldn't help myself." Gary released Stella. She stood frozen with her arms outstretched. Gary then turned to Elliot, who hugged him tight. Elliot laughed the entire time, like he and Gary were old friends.

"Gary, let us do it like we practiced," Rex said. "The Terran custom is to exchange more formal pleasantries when you meet. Then, if the human is open to your use of the embrace, you may proceed."

Gary gasped and straightened his fanny pack.

"Let's try that again," Iris said.

Rex cleared his throat. "Dr. Walsh, Mr. Driver, I would like you to meet ..." Gary started hopping in place. "... Gary. He is a P32 Operational Assistant Morphing Droid."

Elliot reached out to shake Gary's hand. "This feels a little funny. I mean, we just hugged, but, hello. Great to meet you."

"Excuse me, but you're a ... a robot?" Stella asked. His human appearance baffled her. He even had fuzzy hair on his forearms and legs and little wrinkles around his small eyes.

Gary frowned. "The term robot is so pedestrian. I prefer droid, but I'm really a perfect Gary, and as of this morning, I'm proud to announce that my technicians downloaded a level three emotion pack. I now have authentic saltwater deposits that drip from my eyes."

"Something that may be the ruin of us all," Rex said. "Now, I must have a word with Stallworth and get back to the helm. Iris, bring them to my chambers when you finish here."

Iris nodded as Rex exited the room. She went back to work on Elliot's shoulder. She placed a device on his skin and pressed a button on its side. Moments later, it beeped. "All done, Mr. Driver."

"Wow, like it never even happened," Elliot said.

Stella ran her hand over where the wound used to be. Only dried bits of blood remained. She was in awe of the fact that a wound healed in seconds with the machine when it would have taken Stella time to close it with sutures. "How does that work?" she asked.

"It disinfects with UV light and then helps the cells repair themselves. Now, I need to run a contaminate scan on both of you before releasing you to the rest of the ship. One moment," Iris said. She left them and walked to the other side of the room.

"You good?" Elliot asked as he put his shirt back on.

"I honestly don't know."

"So to be clear, and I'm not trying to pry, but in the vein of attempting to prove I'm not totally losing my mind …" Elliot stopped mid-sentence, his eyes glancing down at her hands. "But … um, when I was almost shot to death back there … did … did green sparks of light shoot out of your hands?"

She looked down at her palms. "No. No, I think that was a hallucination brought on by an extreme fear response."

"Right. A hallucination. That sounds good. We'll go with that."

# 10

# THE PYGMY TRAIN

**"WHAT HAPPENED BACK THERE?"** Stella asked as Iris led them to Rex's office.

Iris sighed. "Captain Rex can explain things to you. Zimmer and I will be back, in a moment, to take you to the helm."

Iris pressed her palm on a panel by the door. A digital female voice announced her arrival, and the door opened. Rex stood up from behind his desk.

"Ah! Welcome, brave friends!"

"Hello!" Elliot said. "Wow, this place is amazing!"

Stella sighed, annoyed that Elliot could act like they were on vacation instead of in a never-ending nightmare.

Rex's chamber was a grand office suite. Big and bold leather furniture surrounded a desk with ornate carvings around the edges. Shelves with books and other odd collectibles stood behind the desk. A window showcasing the glittering galaxy took up half the room.

"Why thank you, Mr. Driver. Please sit," Rex said, extending his arm toward a seating area.

Elliot plopped down on a leather couch and spread out his arms while Stella sat in a solitary chair to the side of him and folded her arms across her chest.

"May I offer you a drink?" Rex asked, motioning toward a small selection of spirits in beautiful crystal jars. "I've got some libations a Terran would recognize. I am especially fond of gin, though I do prefer a bit of bubbling water to take the edge off it." Rex admired one bottle before popping the top.

"No, thank you. I don't drink," Stella said.

Rex looked up while he was pouring. "Oh. That's a damn shame."

"I would love something," Elliot said. He popped up out of his seat and took the drink Rex crafted.

"So where are we now?" Stella asked, unable to withstand any more of the pleasantries.

"You are on the glorious ship, The Pygmy Train." Rex took a sip of his drink and punched digital keys on a display on his desk. A 3D projection of a massive aircraft appeared in the center of the room. Stella couldn't tell the scale of the ship from the projection, but she could see it looked very long, with a ring of thrusters on the back. It did not look like a graceful ship; rather, something more clunky. "Don't let the size fool you. This ship is quick as a whip with lots of firepower. We take her out on diplomatic missions, but she is handy in battle as well. There are several cargo holds, and on this mission, we had to aid the refugees from Largo 219. Lucky for The Inspirion we were nearby."

"Please, stop," Stella interrupted. "I don't care about the … the ship. I want an explanation for what's happening. Why am I here? How did I get in this wedding gown? Who was Stall-what's-his-name, and when can I go home?"

Elliot nodded in agreement. "Yeah, I mean, this has been an interesting experience, but I've been shot twice, which seems like the opposite of how you should welcome people to outer space."

"You're right. I am sorry." Rex sat down behind his desk and took on a more professional tone. "Let me start at the beginning."

Stella closed her eyes. "I don't think we have time for that. How about a summary?"

"Okay, well, I'll do my best. Summaries are not my forte. You are here because of an alien abduction. Captain Stallworth is the president of a new planet called Balance, but they do not have a large enough human population to be counted as an official populated planet by the Intergalactic Council for the Intergalactic Alliance of Planets."

"The Intergalactic...what? What's all that?" Elliot asked.

Stella punched him in the chest. "That's not important right now."

"The IGC is just the governing forces of the IAP. As I was saying, Stallworth sends out operatives to scour your world and others for individuals they feel would be ideal mates. They wait for the right moment— for the moment they feel like they have enough information on their subjects—and then they abduct them and whisk them away to Balance. You would have loved the setting there: lush plant life, sprawling vistas, and a temperate climate."

"Sounds neat. Can we rewind to the part where you mentioned the fact that alien abductions are real?" Stella asked.

"Yes, very real. Although it surprises most that abductions are most often carried out by humans with similar DNA to Terrans. Some of these so-called *aliens* are from Terra themselves. They just find promising careers out in space."

"I knew it," Elliot said.

Stella glanced at Elliot.

He shrugged. "I saw a UFO once."

"Ah yes, unidentified flying objects, as you call them. Earth, or Terra as we refer to it, was more of an experiment in the beginning. One civilization brought large reptile beasts called dinosaurs to Terra, hoping to create an adventure park for galactic civilizations to enjoy, but an asteroid thwarted that, although they saved many of the animals. Now, Terra is a mix of all cultures and beings. The UFOs you see are just visitors and travelers conducting business as usual. This gin is hitting all the spots, isn't it?"

Stella and Elliot shifted nervously in their seats.

Elliot broke the silence first. "Wait, you're saying the dinosaurs came from outer space?"

"Of course, along with many other technologies, businesses, ideas, and beings."

"Sure ... I mean, of course," Elliot said.

Stella pinched the bridge of her nose with her fingers. She wondered if this was the moment she should start drinking. "This is all so ridiculous."

"I know this is difficult to believe. I must say you two are more resistant to accepting this information than other Terrans have been. I had quite a chuckle when Zimmer informed me you both thought you were on one of your television shows."

"Tell me about Zimmer. He works for you, but he also works for Stallworth abducting people?"

"In a way."

"That would mean you have to save the people your own employee kidnaps?" Stella asked.

"I'm not sure that's how I would describe it," Rex said.

"Okay, how *would* you describe what he does?" Stella asked.

Rex rubbed his mustache. "Scott Zimmer is a man of all things in the universe, taking work where he can get it. He is no one's employee, and yet he is everyone's employee at the same time."

"What the hell does that mean?"

"Interesting fact about Zimmer is that he resides on my home world of Verbatim, but he is originally from Cleveland, Ohio, USA, Terra."

"Really? My aunt lives in Cleveland," Elliot said.

Stella sat back in her chair. "Fine. You're clearly not going to answer my questions about Zimmer. Let's try some different ones. What now? How do we get home?" Stella asked.

"Now *that* we can help you with."

"Who's we?" Stella said.

"The Sentinels," Rex replied.

"Oh, yeah. I learned about the Sentinels in that manual we got. You all are something like our military, right? I think that's what I read."

"That's correct, Driver. Yes, galactic military is one way to describe us. We live in service to protect all beings. We are traveling back to Verbatim, which is the Sentinel capital of the universe. You will be safe there until we can return you to earth." Rex stood up, moving images with his fingers off the screen on his desktop so they were free-floating above the desk. "We have a state-of-the-art teleportal that takes you straight to Terra."

The images showed a cylinder the size of a typical New York skyscraper that was smooth and round. A demonstration showed a person walking inside with a protective suit on. The image showed a man dissolving and then emerging on his earthly destination back in one piece. The person in the video smiled and gave a thumbs up, but Stella did not think teleportation seemed safe or fun.

"Now, you have a choice, of course," Rex said.

"What choice?" Stella asked.

"If you would like to remain on Verbatim, we will give you full citizenship, lodging, digital credits, which are the universal currency out here, and work, if you want it. You will have a new and prosperous life or …"

Stella leaned forward in her seat. "Yes?"

"You can return to Terra. Take some time to mull it—"

"I would like to go home, thank you," Stella said. She wanted nothing more at that moment than to walk into her apartment, place her jacket on its familiar hook, crawl into her bed, get up the next morning, and go to work.

"Oh, uh, me too," Elliot said. "I would like to go home as well. Don't get me wrong, the other offer sounds nice, but I better get back before rent is due. You have no idea what I had to go through to get my apartment."

Rex sat down and leaned back in his chair. He tapped his fingers on the desk. "Very well. We shall return you to Terra in no time at all. In the meantime, I hope you will enjoy The Pygmy Train. We will land shortly on Verbatim, and Zimmer and Iris will bring you to the helm to see the spectacle."

Stella narrowed her eyes at Rex as he got up and shook Elliot's hand. She didn't know why, but she felt as though he was not being entirely forthcoming. The way he looked at her, some of his explanations of things; there was more that he wasn't revealing.

# 11

# HEALING WATERS

**KANDI KICKED OFF HER HEELS** and scurried back and forth on the slick tiles of the main floor of her laboratory in Aldemara. She wiped the sweat off her brow and placed a steel mask over her face. She fired up a blowtorch and sparks flew as she fused two steel pipes together at the base of a large, vertical tank filled with green liquid. Once she finished, she slid a cover back over the exposed pipes and then shouted at her lab tech, Mr. Owen.

"Try now," she said, pulling off her mask.

Mr. Owen sat behind a computer terminal and tapped on the keys, eventually nodding.

Kandi pushed a button sending a jet of liquid into the tank.

"Yes!" she said. "Now we're in business like an ice cream truck in the desert."

Kandi designed and helped build the laboratory as a place to work, create, and see her greatest ideas come to life—something she knew she couldn't do working in stifling Silicon Valley.

She had the lab built toward the outskirts of Aldemara, where the chaos of the nightlife and Lovella would not bother her. The lower level had a sprawling lobby with smaller rooms where Kandi and the other lab workers tested her creations. Exam rooms lined the second floor, and the top floor contained Kandi's creation room: Inventions and Experiments.

One of the first things Kandi designed for the building was a state-of-the-art security system. The only way into the building was with an authorized retinal scan and voice recognition, and that's only after four sets of guards allowed a person through the main entrance.

Kandi had been so immersed in calibrating a new function on a tank that she did not notice Taylor standing in the doorway with Kandi's nightly coffee in hand.

"Um, hello?" Taylor said.

"Just set it over there, baby." Kandi pointed to a clear resin desk in the corner holding her bright pink purse. Taylor did as he was told and then sat behind the desk to scroll through his tablet.

"Why are you working so late?" Taylor asked, sipping another coffee he brought for himself.

"Is it late?" Kandi asked.

"Yes, you have been here for hours."

"Lordy, I had no idea. I'm almost done."

"What are you even doing?" Taylor asked.

"Mr. Owen, let's show him what we've been working on."

Mr. Owen straightened his neat bow tie and pushed his glasses up his nose. He joined Kandi near an oblong table that held various objects in different states of construction.

"Well, uh, here we have a device, or … um … a patch, that, well, it sends a synthetic cover for your heart, lungs, and all your pulse points to make it appear you are deceased when, in fact, you are still very much alive." Mr. Owen held up a rather nondescript patch of fabric.

"Okay. Why would you ever need that?" Taylor asked with a pinched expression.

"Oh honey, nothing ever impresses you, does it?" Kandi said.

Taylor shrugged.

"Many animals play dead to escape danger. I've got an order of these going to the warriors of Delumi 6. They'll use these to play dead on the battlefield. Once their enemy thinks they have won the war, boom, baby! The second wave begins."

Taylor shrugged again and pointed to two small pieces of plastic. "I guess. What are those?"

Kandi held up a small plastic disc on her fingertip. "Contact lenses that let you see through walls. Kinda basic, and pretty easy to make."

"They, uh, also read heat signatures so you know what is on the other side of the wall," Mr. Owen added.

"Better. What else?" Taylor asked.

"Tell him about the big project, Mr. O. Let's see if we can get some reaction here."

"Oh, uh, sure. We've been working on these tanks for some time. We designed them to keep a subject alive and comfortable in a state of sleep while the tank extracts resources from them. We tested this on a subject who had antibodies for cancerous tumors in his blood. We extracted the antibodies and developed a cure for the tumors with the help of the medical team."

"And it happens pretty quickly, correct?"

"Uh, yes, it's a very rapid process compared to others. The tank nourishes the subjects while they experience a deep sleep. These hoses funnel whatever we need to remove from them, and then these machines behind the tanks convert what's extracted into liquids, or even solids."

Taylor pointed to the one empty tank in the room. "What's that tank for?"

"That is for a Healer," Kandi said.

"A who?"

"A Keeper of Health—a Healer," Mr. Owen said.

"I'm still not getting enough information to care about this," Taylor said. Kandi rolled her eyes, tapped on the digital display in front of her, and produced a visual for Taylor. Normally, Kandi wouldn't tolerate someone with his attitude, but he reminded her of a friend she had back home in the valley. He had an attitude, but Kandi enjoyed laughing and gossiping with him in their neighborhood coffee shop.

Taylor was one of the first people she met when she arrived in Aldemara, and it was Taylor who listened and offered to help. Now, they gossiped over their coffees, about how Kandi enjoyed finding alternative ways to torment Lovella and Ryder, and how it was the one thing that reminded her of the good times she had in California. Kandi knew that underneath all the sass, Taylor had her back.

"Who are these people?" Taylor asked, referring to the images of women in a virtual dossier that popped up from the desk in front of them.

"They are called the Keepers of the Universe," Kandi said.

"Oh yeah, I've heard of them. Thought they were a myth."

"They're no myth, honey. They're real," Kandi said. "And that's both a good thing and a bad."

"Okay, so what are they? What do they have to do with the tank? Tell me, because I'm getting bored." Taylor pulled up a chair and sat back in it, putting his feet up on the computer terminal. Kandi nodded at Mr. Owen.

"The Keepers were, long ago, protectors of the universe. Working with the Sentinels, the special forces of the military, the Keepers kept us safe," Mr. Owen said.

"But now, I'm the only one who's going to keep us safe, right baby?"

Mr. Owen straightened his glasses. "Uh, yes."

Taylor sat up in his chair. "What does this have to do with the Zuldari? They're so gross and slimy, and they smell."

"That's where we come in, babe. The Zuldari are sick. They need some healing waters from us." Kandi walked over to the tank and rubbed her hand along the glass. "If we can find a Healer, we can use her essence to create a healing serum. We heal the Zuldari, and they help us get rid of the Keepers."

"Get rid of them? Sounds like a lot of work. Seriously, who cares?"

Kandi glanced at the images in front of her. "I care! The Keepers are all women. Can't have a bunch of broads running the show." Her eyes flashed anger, and then contempt. "Women are all the same. Since I can't trust 'em, I gotta kill 'em all. The only woman who should have power in this universe is me."

Taylor threw his head back. "Do you hear yourself right now? I love you, but please."

"If you just came here to sass me, then you can show yourself out."

"Fine, so, where you going to get a Healer?"

Kandi folded her arms across her chest and rubbed her chin. "I think I already found one. Just waiting for confirmation."

# 12

# ACID RAIN

**THE SKYLINE OF ALDEMARA DIMMED** for a moment as the sun tucked itself into its nightly nap. Darkness wandered across the city. Though far from home, Ryder always found some comfort in the nightly ritual of the city lights blinking on and cuing the Aldemaran nightlife to stir. The lights flickered until the cityscape filled with light, but not from the source that made it so hot.

Ryder never thought Aldemara was an attractive city during the day. The plain, steel buildings were packed together like people riding in uncomfortable silence on an overcrowded train. During the day, the city was still as the hateful sun made the planet hot and the air prickly. But at night, the city glittered with lights of all colors. Bright magentas glowed from the main medical plaza; lime green lights shone off the shopping district. Yellows and golds burst off the arts district. The many small cafes and pool halls gleamed with reds and blues as their signs burned all night, luring patrons in from their holes so they could move around again without being punished by the heat.

While the city usually strummed alive as darkness fell, the citizens were shut in this night because the forecast called for acid in the rain. This was common on the industrial planet, which is why the buildings were built to withstand the harsh weather. With a crash of lightning, the rain fell and it stung anything living that did not heed the warning to stay inside.

Ryder waited with Lovella in her office on the twenty-fourth floor of the capital building. They were waiting, as they always did, for Kandi to grace them with her presence. As Lovella sat at her desk entering data into a 3D computer screen, Ryder stood in front of a large window that ran from the floor to the ceiling in Lovella's sprawling suite. He shook his head as he watched those foolish enough to be out in the rain scream and run for shelter. Once he grew tired of watching the mice scurry into their holes, he turned and took a seat in a chair across from Lovella's desk.

"And how do you find yourself this evening, Master Ryder?" Lovella asked.

"Well enough," Ryder said. "How long must we wait?"

Lovella looked over her thick octagon-shaped eyeglass frames. "As long as it takes."

Ryder studied her for a moment. She always dressed in a simple black dress and heels. Her long, silver hair was pulled back into a taut bun at the base of her neck. She was stern, ruthless, a total professional, and someone Ryder would rather serve than Kandice Shook. She had worked her way up through the ranks of the Intergalactic Military Forces to become a general. She settled in Aldemara after the Great War and became a leader Aldemarans loved, although most people who encountered her found her incredibly intimidating. Ryder respected her immensely and wished he knew her under different circumstances.

"Is there a reason for your smile, Master Ryder?" Lovella asked.

Ryder straightened in his chair and cracked his knuckles. "No, General."

"I appreciate your promptness, and I apologize for the wait, but Kandi also must hear what I am about to tell you. Soon Commander T'Adox will arrive, and I need you both to be ready."

"T'Adox, the Zuldari leader?" Ryder asked. He leaned forward in his chair.

"The same."

"I thought the Zuldari died out after the Great War."

Lovella stopped working and looked past Ryder as if she were remembering something. "Most did, but there are survivors."

"You were there, weren't you? In the Great War."

Lovella hesitated and then answered. "I was."

"Which side were you fighting for?"

"That is a conversation for another time." She focused back to the screens in front of her.

The click-clack of something sharp hitting the floor outside the door caught their attention. The sound of Kandi's voice followed. It filled the hallway as she neared. Ryder rose from the chair just as the hair stood up on the back of his neck. He stood away from the desk as Kandi strode in. She was dressed in a hot pink pantsuit, an oversized hot pink bag and beige, puffy fur coat slung over her arm. Kandi ignored Lovella and Ryder as she finished the phone call. Though they were staring at her, she continued laughing and slapping her hand on the table as her friend on the other end of her phone rambled on.

"Okay babe. Well, I will call you tonight. Yeah, yeah ... I'm here ... I know, right? So boring ... Love you too! Kisses!" Kandi ended her call and slipped her phone in the purse. She shuffled around in her bag, found her lip gloss, and it was only then, when her lips were shiny, that she finally acknowledged them.

"You're late," Lovella said.

Kandi cackled and raised her eyebrows. "Oh no, honey, I'm not late at all. This is exactly when I wanted to be here."

Ryder cracked his neck, his face tightening under the strain of having to be in Kandi's presence.

"Well, if you refuse to be on time to our meetings, can you please dress appropriately? As an employee of my organization, you should be wearing a uniform by now," Lovella said,

Kandi narrowed her eyes. "Excuse me?"

"That outfit you're wearing is incredibly inappropriate."

"Oh really?"

"Yes."

"I get it. You're just jealous that you're too old to pull this off, right baby?" Kandi blew a kiss to Ryder. He folded his arms across his chest and slowly shook his head. "I'm kidding. God, y'all are boring." She smiled condescendingly. "I kind of think of this *as* my uniform. But I'll be a good girl and wear a better set of threads if that makes you happy."

"Right," Lovella said, glaring at Kandi over the rim of her glasses. "If we may move on."

"Certainly. What's up?" Kandi asked.

Lovella got up from her desk and went to a large terminal, waving her hand until the screen came alive. "In the coming days, Commander T'Adox, a prominent Zuldari leader, will land here to inspect the tanks in the lab and see how they're progressing."

T'Adox had a pronounced furrow in his brow, and the skin of his face hung on him as if it couldn't decide to commit to the shape of his skull. This was typical of the Zuldari people. They looked like amphibians with some human characteristics. They stood upright but still had scales and eyes with slits. They wore uniforms to look more civilized, but to Ryder, the Zuldari looked as though they should swim around in a lake rather than work through treaty negotiations.

"Will you be able to provide a lab update once Commander T'Adox lands, Ms. Shook?"

"Of course," Kandi said as she flipped through images on her phone. "Shouldn't we have a Healer in the tank first?"

"Ideally, but locating a Healer is not that simple since they went into hiding. We have a few leads, but we need to use caution."

"Come on," Kandi threw down her phone beside her. "We've got leads; let's go get one of these bitches and throw them in. What are we waiting for?"

Lovella squeezed the bridge of her nose. "We need to do this right. This is a delicate operation. We will acquire a Healer, but it must be the right one. We need one no one will come looking for."

"You're the boss," Kandi said, flipping her hair.

"Ms. Shook, I assure you, you will have the glory you seek for your inventions. I need your patience right now and not your attitude. When the commander lands, I would like you both by my side to great him."

Ryder nodded.

"Thank you. That will be all," Lovella said, returning to her desk.

Ryder smirked as he turned to leave. He knew Kandi would not appreciate being called to Lovella's office for such a brief meeting. He also had a feeling that is exactly what Lovella was hoping for.

He closed the door behind him just as Kandi fired off some insults. He had almost made it to the elevator when he heard the familiar click-clack of her heels running after him.

Kandi blocked Ryder's path, her pungent jasmine perfume enveloping him as it snaked through his nostrils. He found a spot on the wall in front of him to fixate on while she spoke.

"Why're you running away so fast, handsome?" Kandi said. She grabbed the lapels of his trench coat and pulled him to her.

Ryder kept his eye on the wall as he waited for the elevator to arrive. "What do you need?"

"I need you to get someone for me." Kandi pulled her phone out of her purse. She projected an image on the wall. It was of a woman Ryder did not recognize.

"Who is this?"

"The Healer I need for my tank. Our operative has just informed me of her whereabouts. Here is her tracking chip number. Scan this with your eye so you can keep track of her movements once she lands on this location."

"General Law just told us to wait."

"Yes, yes she did, but the sooner we find the Healer, the sooner we can get in good with that slimy T'Adox dude. Trust me, you are so close to your reunion with sissy." Kandi projected the coordinates of the woman's location from her smartwatch.

Ryder narrowed his eyes. "Those are the coordinates of Verbatim—Prehma to be exact. There's security there even I can't breach."

"Which is why you will take my new G-50 stealth plane so you can transport in undetected. Our operative will radio this target's location to you. All you need to do is port her back to the ship with you. Once you make it back here, I need you to bring her to the lab. You're going to land on the outskirts of Aldemara when you bring her in and ride your little bike to the lab with our girl."

"My motorcycle is not a little bike."

"You're right, sugar." She winked at him. "You have the biggest motorcycle there is. Just bring her to the lab on it. We need to get that ship back to the shipyard before Lovella realizes it's gone."

"The Sentinels won't let her go willingly. You really want a Sentinel arsenal to land in Aldemara to retrieve her?"

Kandi furrowed her brow. "You better stand down, hero. You don't get to question my orders. Now, shut your hot mouth and listen."

Ryder swallowed and focused his gaze back on the wall.

"You will plant some plasma bombs. Choose buildings you think have a lot of people inside. That should keep them busy. They won't even notice this bitch is gone. I'll assemble your ship and crew, but don't you say a damn word to anyone about this, got it?"

Ryder clenched his jaw. "Got it."

The elevator door opened, and Ryder tried to step in.

Kandi blocked his path and nuzzled up to his neck. "Hey baby, I don't like it when we fight. When you bring the Healer to the lab, I'll let you see sissy, okay?"

Ryder finally made eye contact with Kandi. So many times she had said this, and so many times there was some reason it couldn't happen. She looked up at him and smiled, but his chest tightened, and he could feel the heat from blood flushing his face.

"I will complete this mission, but after this, I'm done until I see my sister in person," he said.

"You do not get to tell me—" Kandi started.

Before she could finish, Ryder grabbed her by the neck and slammed her into the wall. "I will see my sister after this, whether I'm let into the lab or I have to break in. Got it?"

Kandi flared her nostrils and pushed his hand away from her. "You just get the job done, hero, and if you ever touch me like that again, sissy is dead."

She pushed past him and delivered one final warning before going back into Lovella's office. "Don't get any ideas about causing my demise either," she said. "I'm the only one who has the code to get sissy out of the tank. Something happens to me and she rots in there forever."

# 13

## R & R

**A WOMAN'S DIGITAL VOICE ANNOUNCED** that Zimmer was at Rex's door. Rex admitted him as he stood up from his desk. "How goes it, friend?" Rex asked.

Zimmer sighed. "Finally calmed Stallworth down."

"Outstanding! And how is he now?"

"He's accepted the credits as compensation, but he didn't want to let these two go," Zimmer said, his eyes lingering on Stella.

*Why does he keep looking at me like that? I'm going to figure out who he really is if it's the last thing I do.*

"Poor bastard," Rex said. "But the Terran Rights Activists are moving closer to completely shutting down his operation. He needs to get used to being disappointed."

"Terran Rights Activists?" Stella asked.

"The TRA," Zimmer started. "They wish to stop the mass abductions and the interactions galactic visitors are having with Terra. If we don't get you home, they will knock on our door next."

The female voice announced that Iris was waiting outside.

"Will you join us as we land the ship?" Iris asked, forcing a smile as Stella, Elliot, and Zimmer joined her in the hallway.

Elliot winked at Iris. "Why, yes. Thank you."

"Is there something in your eye, Mr. Driver?" Iris asked.

"Uh, no, uh …"

Stella laughed as Rex waved them on. "I'll join you shortly," he said.

They piled into a sleek steel elevator and rode in silence until Elliot asked a question that he and Stella had both wondered about since their arrival in space. "Dude, what is with that tie? I can't stop looking at it, and not for good reasons."

Zimmer ran his tie through his fingers and shrugged. "It was a gift from my mother, the last Christmas we had together. I realize it's a shocking shade, but it reminds me of her."

Stella and Elliot exchanged glances.

"Oh, um, it's actually very lovely," Stella said.

"And I meant that I … I can't stop looking at it because it really goes with your suit."

The corner of Zimmer's mouth curved upward. "Thanks."

They rode up the rest of the way in an awkward silence. Stella mulled over everything Rex had said. She had always looked up at the stars when she would sometimes walk out to the street on a brief break from the OR, and now she was flying through them on a spaceship.

The elevator doors opened, revealing an area of the ship with more crew members scattered around sitting at various computer stations while others shuffled back and forth as The Pygmy Train approached a blue-green ball. Each crew member sat at a computer terminal in a chair shaped like the letter S. Gary waved excitedly from a terminal in the corner.

"Welcome to the helm," Iris said. "Rex wants you to take your seats here next to his captain's chair so you'll have the best view."

Stella stared at the massive window that enveloped the helm. The planet Verbatim filled the entire view as they neared. Crew members, prepping for landing, bombarded Rex with questions as he walked in.

"Beautiful, isn't she?" Rex said to Stella as she took her seat. Elliot sat down on the other side.

"It looks like earth," Stella said.

"Verbatim has an atmosphere similar to Terra's, but it's a smaller planet with a more uniform climate. You'll find no icecaps or weather below thirty degrees. There are dense forests and the most spectacular bodies of water you have ever seen," Rex said as he sat down and pulled a computer terminal toward him. He placed his hand on a screen and moved it to pilot the ship as it entered Verbatim's atmosphere.

The ship shook as it broke through the first layer of atmosphere. Stella's fingers ached, and she realized it was because she was squeezing them so hard with her other hand. She closed her eyes, taking a deep breath, trying to reassure herself that every rattle of the ship did not mean something catastrophic. She opened one eye to see what the others were doing, but everyone seemed calm, even as a startling wave of fuchsia light surrounded the ship.

The Pygmy Train steadied as it bounced into the fluffy, cheerful clouds of Verbatim's sky. Underneath the pale mist was a city surrounded by a shade of water Stella had never seen before. The sunlight glinted off the azure water, which was a stark contrast to the dreary gray of the Hudson River she was used to. Towering buildings dotted the city below as plush, prehistoric-looking trees filled the spaces in between the buildings. Ships plunged in and out of the water as others buzzed about like busy bees in the air.

"Crew, prep for landing. Welcome to Prehma, capital of Verbatim," said the ship's digital voice.

The scene in the Starport was a dizzying mix of ships large and small landing and taking off with people scurrying about.

The streets of Prehma were pristine. Not a speck of trash on the ground, and the sidewalks and other pathways appeared as though they never had been used. A piece of paper glided on the breeze and landed on the sidewalk in front of Stella. Before it fully settled on the ground, a robot claw hand came out from a tile that shifted on the sidewalk, grabbed the debris, and pulled it under as the tile closed behind it. Even the air felt soothing to her lungs. It smelled of sweet flowers, surprising for such a densely populated city.

Stella craned her neck upward, mesmerized by the sculpted design of the buildings in Prehma. She glanced back down, but not in time to avoid bumping into a woman with purple skin and dozens of tentacles jutting out from her head. The woman chirped at her in a language she didn't understand. Stella fumbled over her words as she tried to apologize, but the woman kept chirping and pecking at Stella's face. Thankfully, Rex stepped in and shooed the woman away.

"What just happened?" Stella asked, looking back over her shoulder.

"Nothing serious. That's simply a visiting foreign citizen who is cranky due to the temperature of the day. Her kind prefers colder climates."

"This is amazing!" Elliot said as they entered the inside of the Starport.

Rex chuckled. "Glad you think so, Driver. We are lucky souls to get to live in such a glorious place."

Rex stopped and gathered everyone in a huddle before they entered the food and shopping district of the Starport. "Driver, Dr. Walsh, again I am sorry for the ordeal you have been through. I will meet with my engineering team, and we will run some tests on the portal to Terra to make sure it's safe. We will get you on your way in the morning. For now, you both can rest and enjoy the sights of Prehma."

"Yay!" Gary exclaimed.

Iris smiled and grabbed Gary's arm, trying to get him to calm down.

"Now Gary, I want you to take our guests through the Starport. They will need nourishment and a change of clothes. I imagine that formal wear is not comfortable."

Gary jumped up and down again.

"Gary," Rex grabbed him by the shoulders. "Keep it together, man. You are to show them around and take them to the shops, not smother them with love. Yes?"

"Of course, of course," Gary said, biting his lip.

"Right! If you will excuse us, we must attend to the other passengers of The Inspirion." Rex opened his arms and led Iris and Zimmer off in another direction.

Gary clapped his hands together. "Oh my! There is so much to show you."

"Wait, is that what I think it is?" Elliot asked, running ahead through the brightly lit corridor of shops and restaurants. Stella and Gary followed.

"I can't believe there's a Starbucks here, in space!" Elliot said as he emerged moments later with the familiar paper cup. "Are you serious? They always spell my name wrong."

Stella looked at his cup that read "Elly Ott" and laughed.

"How is there a Starbucks here?" she asked Gary, who was waving at the woman with green skin working behind the counter.

"This is actually the first Starbucks. Most people are incorrectly informed that the first Starbucks is on Terra. The man who first brought Starbucks to Terra was passing through here and loved the coffee so much that he bought part of the franchise."

"Right, he was just passing through." Stella put up her hand, indicating she did not want to taste his coffee after Elliot offered it to her.

She settled on a bottle of Verbatim water instead.

"Don't tell me you don't drink coffee either?" Elliot asked.

"I do. I drink the coffee I make myself in my home coffeemaker."

"Sounds about right … Oh, this tastes so good." Elliot licked foam off his lip. Stella and Elliot followed Gary through the rest of the Starport, walking behind him as he stopped and chatted with people he knew. "Actually, did you know the best coffee is from this Turkish coffee cart right outside my office?"

Stella smiled. "I did not know that."

"There used to be another one at the end of the block," Elliot continued. "Not sure what happened to that guy."

"Where do you live in New York?" Stella asked.

"I used to live in Williamsburg but upgraded to a place in Brooklyn Heights when I started at Spartan Inc. It's a tiny studio, but it's mine and I love it. *Was* mine, I guess. If I don't get home soon, I'm sure the real estate vultures will be circling."

Stella touched Elliot's arm. "What's your address?"

"102 Remsen Street. Why?"

"124 Hicks Street."

"Seriously?"

Stella nodded.

"We literally live a few blocks from each other?"

"I guess so," Stella said.

"This gets better and better," Elliot said. "You don't have much of an accent, though. Have you always lived in New York?"

"As long as I can remember. You don't have one either."

"That's because I'm originally from Wyoming. Grew up on a ranch. That's when I started training for Ninja Warrior. Kept me busy, you know? But I couldn't wait to get out of that one-horse town I grew up in. Actually, the town had three horses, I think. Anyway, I headed east and never looked back. How did you get a place on Hicks? I've seen those. Did you win the lottery?"

Stella laughed. "It was my mother's. I lived there with her until she disappeared when I was in med school."

Elliot stopped walking and looked at Stella with wide eyes. "Disappeared?"

"Yes." Stella glanced at the floor. She remembered the moment she learned the news only because it had haunted her nightmares every day since. "My mother went to work at her hospital in Queens and never came home. Her car, purse, and a shoe were left behind. It looked like someone had kidnapped her, but they never found another trace of her."

"I'm so sorry," Elliot said. "That's terrible."

Stella was thankful she could see Gary coming back toward them because she had nothing more to say about her mother. It had been ten years, but it still pained her to talk about it.

"All right, I've transferred credits to some shop owners here," Gary started.

"Credits?" Stella asked.

"Galactic currency, all digital and universally accepted. Anyway, I'm sure you are ready to ease into more reasonable clothes until we can return you to Terra."

This was something Stella was in favor of, as her dress was clinging to her in unnatural ways. Stella picked out some items at a clothing store and then joined Elliot and Gary at a place called Galactic Annie's Gastro Café. Stella ordered something that resembled a salad. She wasn't sure if it was just because she was starving or if it truly was because she was on a different planet, but every bite tasted like a parade in her mouth.

*Can't believe even a simple salad literally tastes out of this world. I guess I'll let myself enjoy this tonight, but tomorrow heads are going to roll if I don't get in that portal and get home.*

Gary left Stella and Elliot as he again saw someone he knew.

"I still can't believe that dude is a robot. He looks just like a normal human, and he's so social for a robot."

"He even has veins in his arms. It's incredible," Stella said, finishing the last of her meal.

"So what do you think now?" Elliot asked between bites of his cheeseburger. "What do you think about all of this? Is it real, or are we still dreaming? This burger tastes pretty real."

"It's real, but I guess I don't understand why this would happen to me now. I feel like there's more going on that these people aren't telling us, but I honestly don't care anymore. I just want to go home."

Gary returned, and once Stella and Elliot finished their meal, he took them out of the Starport terminal to a street where a car shaped like a bubble waited for them. The air cooled as the sun tucked itself into the horizon. Gary closed the door behind him and programed coordinates of their destination into a panel.

Gary and Elliot chatted on while Stella took in the view. The driverless bubble was see-through from their waists up, giving them a 360-degree view of their surroundings. The shroud of night covered the landscape, and thousands of glittery lights reflected off the city as the bubble car glided along on its track. The city lights dimmed into the darkness as the car's track took it over a large body of water that connected the heart of the city to other buildings that stood tall on the outskirts.

Their destination was a disc-shaped building, hardly visible behind the dense bushes that appeared as though they were growing out from the top and bottom. Mist from two waterfalls above filled the air. The water cascaded off the roof and drained into two pools on either side of the structure.

"What is this place?" Stella asked.

"It's lodging for special guests of Rex and other Sentinel leaders. You will both be safe here," Gary said, handing them keycards to their rooms as they walked inside.

"Safe from what?" Elliot asked.

Gary cleared his throat. "Uh, safe from gawking Verbatain citizens, of course. Now, enjoy your lodging. Iris and I will come for you in the morning to take you to the portal. Goodnight, my dumplings."

Stella still stiffened when Gary hugged her, although she brought herself to pat him on the back this time. Elliot again squeezed Gary, and they both laughed as Gary waved goodbye.

"Love that guy," Elliot said. He turned to Stella and sighed. "Well, I'm not sure if this has been fun or terrifying, but I have to say that I'm glad I got abducted with you."

"Thanks," Stella said.

"Hey," Elliot said. "Since we live a few blocks from each other, we should hang out sometime when we get home."

Stella paused. *I already have three friends in New York. Can I really handle another one?* "Let's just see if we make it home tomorrow."

"Sure, yeah, of course. If you can't sleep, you know where to find me." Elliot nodded and slipped into his room.

# 15

# TRANSPORT
# FOR TWO

**RYDER SAT IN A CHAIR**, his arms spread wide on each armrest. He tapped his fingers on the cushions as he waited. He had teleported down to Verbatim, and with one touch of a button on his long, leather duster, he dissolved into his surroundings so no one could see him tiptoeing through the city as he set his plasma bombs. Then, the stealth technology of the G-50 plane teleported him into a room where he waited for his target. He wouldn't normally wait in such a comfortable position, but he decided the target was not a threat based on the photo Kandi had shown him.

His ears perked up to voices on the other side of the door: a man, a woman, and a casual conversation. Ryder heard a woman say "good-night" as the door to the room slid open. She strode in looking tall in her high heels. She was dressed in a frilly white gown and had a bag in her hand that she threw on the bed. He quieted his breath and observed, hidden in the corner. The woman rummaged intently and then pulled out a pair of pants from the bag. She held them up and said, "Finally!"

Ryder cocked his head to one side and watched for a moment. He had never before seen someone so excited about a pair of pants. She was beautiful, with flame-red hair and athletic build, but with some curves. By the looks of her and how she was dressed, he thought this was going to be one of the easiest assignments he'd ever had.

*It's a shame I have to drag this one back to Shook.*

He could have sat in the corner longer, but he knew he could not be idle. He purposely let the creaking leather from his jacket give him away, and the woman turned her head toward him as he stood up from the chair. He removed the cloak and stepped toward her.

*Piece of cake.*

The corner of his mouth curled slightly as he saw her staring at him with her mouth open. He pressed a button on his smartwatch. "Target acquired. Initiate transport for two in five minutes. "Wait ... make that two minutes."

"You. You're that guy," the woman said, pointing at him. "How did you get in here?"

"I'm what guy?"

"The, the ... you're in the manual, the tablet. You're the mercenary to avoid."

Ryder furrowed his brow. "Sounds about right."

"What do you want?"

"This isn't about what *I* want, but you need to come with me," Ryder replied.

"I'm not going anywhere with you."

He said nothing and stepped closer. The woman's eyes searched for something on the bed, and he ducked when she threw a large shoebox at him and raced toward the door. He fired a beam of light from a utility device on his wrist, causing sparks to fly out of the door's control panel. She tried to open the door, but the keyboard was dead. He lunged at her and grabbed her from behind, wrapping his arm around her neck. She squirmed and shouted for help.

A man's voice sounded on the other side of the door. "Hey, are you okay? What's going on?"

The woman screamed and the man pounded on the door.

Ryder shouted into his wrist. "Start transport!"

"Stella! Let me in!" the man demanded.

"Can't open the door!" Stella shouted.

"I'm getting help!" the man said after his failed attempts to break in.

Ryder covered Stella's mouth with his free hand and attempted to keep her still for teleportation, when a shooting pain burst through his right side. She jabbed her elbow into his ribs, knocking the wind out of him. He winced but did not let go. She hit him again with enough force for him to loosen the grasp on her neck. She grabbed his right arm with both her hands and yanked his arm closer to her so it created a small gap between him and her neck—enough for her to wriggle out her head.

Stella spun around and rocketed her open hand right into his throat. He coughed violently. He fell back, trying to gasp for air. Pain surged up from his groin from the swift kick he received. He fell to his knees, reeling from the pain. Ryder grunted through the pain and popped up, lunging for her as she pounded on the door calling for help. Ryder grabbed her, and with teeth clenched, tried to hold on even as she punched and kicked him. He wanted to get better control over her, but it was too late. The teleportation had overtaken their bodies and for a moment Stella stopped fighting and gasped as it lifted them out of the room.

# 16

# FIGHT AND FLIGHT

**STELLA'S BODY CAME TOGETHER**, and a scream that was silent through teleportation violently returned as her feet hit solid ground again. She gasped, desperate to calm down and fill her lungs with air. Her body felt as though she'd had twenty shots of espresso all at once. Every part of her trembled from the shock. She stopped pushing against the man once she saw where she was. The room was cold and dark, with only a few lights overhead. Wires and pipes hung down from the ceiling. They stood on a platform in front of two men in uniforms who watched them from behind a control panel.

Hands snatched her arms and pulled her away from the man who took her from Verbatim. She tried to wriggle out of the grip of the two men who were dragging her away until she felt something sharp jam into her side. A zap of energy exploded in her body, and she went limp. The men dragged her down a dark hallway that was lit only with dim green light.

"Where am I now?" Stella asked them when the feeling returned to her body. The men only grunted as they stomped with heavy feet through another tunnel. They stopped in front of a steel door; it opened when one of them placed his hand on a panel outside the door. They pushed Stella into the room and shut the door.

"You can't keep me in here! Why are you holding me?" she shouted.

This new environment would not offer as much comfort as the one she woke up in on The Inspirion. No windows, one door, and a bench that was attached with heavy chains to the far wall.

She tried calling again for someone to let her out, though she stopped when she heard no sounds on the other side of the door. She could not stand to be at the mercy of anyone else. She wanted to be home, saving lives, calling the shots, putting out fires, not stuck in a steel room waiting for whatever was going to happen to her. The more she thought about it, the more frustrated she got, and the only thing she could do with that energy was pace around the room.

Wherever she was now, it was quiet except for a few vibrations that swept through the room. She was not sure how much time had passed when the room rattled more consistently. It was the same rattling The Pygmy Train made when it breached Verbatim's atmosphere.

She put her ear to the door when she heard footsteps coming again. They differed from the ones before, and it was just one person walking. She pressed herself up against the wall to the left of the door so she would be out of sight. The door opened and she spun out from the shadows with a balled fist, but instead of making contact, a fist wrapped around her hand, stopping it cold.

It was the man with the creepy, red machine eye. He twisted her arm behind her back and slammed her up against the wall. She felt steel wrap around her wrists, and with a click, she was restrained. The man then whipped her around, and though she kicked at him, this time he seemed prepared for her to fight back.

"Stop," he said, pushing the muzzle of something that looked very much like a gun under her neck. "Stop! I'm going to take you out of here, and I need you to be calm. I don't want to hurt you, but I will."

Standing face to face, Stella looked deeper into the red eye to see small lights flashing, along with wires and circuits. He gritted his teeth and wrenched her away from the wall. The dim overhead lights flickered as they walked through the hallway.

"Where am I?" Stella asked.

Ryder did not answer.

Stella halted and pulled her arm out of his grasp. "Answer me. Where am I?"

Ryder looked down at the floor, his face flushing. "You're Terran, yeah?"

Stella neither nodded nor shook her head, but she was listening.

He continued stepping in closer to her. "Which means that it doesn't matter what I tell you because it won't make sense to you anyway."

"That's a bullshit answer. Just tell me what's going on and let me be the judge of what makes sense to me."

Ryder twisted his head from side to side until it made a popping sound. "Fine. You were teleported to this G-50 stealth plane that is taking us to the city of Aldemara. Once we land, I'm taking you to the city's laboratory where I will turn you over to a woman named Kandice Shook. She wants to run tests on you to confirm your identity. That is all I know."

"What tests? Who is Kandice Shook?"

"I don't know what the tests are, and Shook is another Terran like you."

He was right. It did not make sense to her, but that was something she was getting used to.

"And what are you, exactly?" she asked.

"I'm a man who doesn't like to answer questions."

Ryder hustled Stella down the ramp of the ship. The environment of Aldemara differed from Verbatim, although Aldemara looked more like home to Stella. Skyscrapers, thousands of blinking lights, signs inviting people in for assorted activities of pleasure, and air so thick a person could chew on it. No flora, no fauna; just steel and concrete and neon. There was not one person out in any of the walkways. For a city that looked so alive, it was completely empty.

To the left was a long walkway leading up to a building that looked like an observatory. It was not a very tall building, but it was wide, and it had a dome-shaped roof with a circular window that appeared to look up to the stars. Ryder pushed Stella toward a massive motorcycle parked across the path. The tires looked like they should be on a semitruck, and the exhaust pipes looked as though they would launch rockets.

Ryder stopped to debrief a crew member who disembarked. "We need to be quiet about this. I'm taking her to the lab. Take this ship back to the shipyard with the stealth on."

While the crew members distracted him, Stella looked behind her into the city.

*If only I could make it to one of those buildings.*

Her chest tightened and she swallowed, trying to keep still even though her adrenaline was spiking.

The crew members walked back up the ship's ramp, and it closed behind them. Dust and debris kicked up around them as the ship pushed off the ground.

Ryder pulled out his gun again. "Get on the bike," he ordered. Stella straddled the seat, and Ryder pressed the barrel of the gun in her back. The cuffs that bound her released, freeing her hands, though the shiny, black cuffs remained on her wrist. The bike shifted as Ryder slipped on behind her.

"Hold onto the front bar," he said.

Stella wrapped her hands around the front bar. As soon as Ryder leaned toward her, she brought her head up and, with a crack, the back of her head hit Ryder in the face. Pain shot through her skull and Ryder cried out. She jammed her elbow back into his ribs and hopped down to the pavement. Her head throbbed, but she punched him in the side again, causing him to fall to the ground. She kicked off her heels and sprinted into the city. Her heart pounded in her ears as she scanned the path in front of her.

*There must be somewhere to get help.*

A sudden gust of wind blew her back, but she kept running. She ran to the first door she saw and jiggled the handle, but it was locked. She pounded on the door, but no one came. She ran down side streets and into alleys only to find every door locked and not a soul answering her calls for help. She slipped to the side of a building to catch her breath and look behind her, but Ryder had not followed. A crash overhead made her jump, and when she looked up into the sky, a static arm of lightning stretched out of the clouds, its long tentacles lingering in the air. Prickly goosebumps appeared on her arm and her hair stood on end.

She ran back out onto the sidewalk, hoping to find an unlocked door, and that's when the first drop hit her. It seemed like normal rain, but when more warm droplets landed on Stella's upturned hand, it sizzled and burned. Stella shook her hand as more drops fell on her shoulders, burning holes right through her dress. More and more drops of acid rain fell on her, and she ran under an overhang to get cover. The wind picked up and she winced as the rain blew in, gnawing at her bare feet.

Gusts from the storm blew drops inward and she inched up against the building, but biting water splashed onto her, stinging her skin. She threw up her hands and gasped as green sparks flew out, this time forming a bubble around her, but it lasted only a mere second and then fizzled away. She wasn't sure what was more shocking—the fact that rain was eating away at her skin or that the green sparks appeared out of her hands once again.

The sound of screeching tires tore through the heavy rain. Ryder pulled up on the bike under a protective window that shielded the entire vehicle. Once it opened, he shot off the bike and flung his jacket over Stella.

"What the hell are you doing?" he yelled. His nose and lip were bleeding from Stella ramming her head into his face. "Get on the bike!"

This time Stella nodded. Ryder wrapped her completely in his jacket and he winced when the rain hit him. The bike's shield closed, and when the rain hit the protective dome it sounded like thousands of mini explosions.

Stella straddled the bike, glad to be out of the storm, though her stomach was still in knots. Ryder peeled the jacket off her and threw it on the seat behind him. He pulled out his gun again with one hand. With his other hand, he pressed a button on his smartwatch. Her cuffs snapped together from two powerful magnets.

This time, Stella held onto the front bar as the bike ripped out down the road.

"What exactly was the plan there?" Ryder asked.

"To get help; to get away from you," Stella said.

"And how did that work out for you?"

Stella didn't answer. Her entire body ached as if the same bee had attacked her repeatedly. She noticed another sensation coming over her as Ryder's muscular arms held her tight while he was driving. She felt his breath in her hair, and it sent a shiver down her spine. She was not sure what was in store for her in the building they pulled up next to; she only hoped the Sentinels were looking for her and would reach her in time.

# 17

## SHOOK

RYDER TRAINED HIS GUN BACK ON STELLA. "I'm going to take you inside. You can try to run again, but this time, I won't come for you when you get lost in the storm."

"Fine. Let's just get this over with," Stella said.

He almost wished he didn't have to take her inside, but he knew it was the only way he could see his sister. Ryder covered Stella with his jacket so he would take the brunt of the rain as they made their way through the lab's security checkpoints.

Once they made it to the lobby, Ryder shook out his jacket. He had welts all over his body and holes burned through his shirt, but one by one, each welt got smaller and smaller until they shrank away completely. He looked up to see Stella staring at him. She watched intently as the last welts on his hands dissolved, his skin good as new. His nose and lip had healed as well, though they still felt sore. He wiped the last bits of blood away and scowled at her, feeling uncomfortable under her gaze. With his gun focused on her, he took a small device out of his pocket.

"Stop staring," Ryder said. He tried to place the device on the side of Stella's mouth.

She jerked her head out of reach "What is that?"

Ryder stuck the device on Stella's face, and a sheet of metal covered her mouth by attaching to her other cheek. Ryder smiled. It was more for his sanity than her safety that he wanted to keep her mouth shut.

Kandi instructed Ryder to bring Stella up to a room next to the lab and wait. When they finally made it to the top floor, Ryder saw a room marked with a sign that read Inventions and Experiments. The room's door was ajar, and he could hear Kandi whispering to Taylor.

Ryder pushed through the door.

"What the hell is this?" Kandi asked. "What happened? She looks like hammered shit."

Ryder ignored Kandi and handed Stella off to a lab security guard. He wandered over to the tanks with his mouth open and his stomach churning with acid. There she was: Pip floating in suspended animation in a large tank of green liquid. Her blond hair surrounded her like waves of gold. Her arms were spread out as if she were gently descending to the ground from the heavens. She looked peaceful, even though it was a horrific sight.

"That's far enough," Taylor said, aiming a plasma blaster. "You've seen her. Now it's time to go."

Ryder pulled out his gun. "I'm not leaving without her."

Kandi put up her hands and stepped in between Ryder and Taylor. "Let's just everyone calm down, all right? Please, y'all are givin' me a headache."

"You said—" Ryder started.

"I said you could *see* sissy. I said nothing about y'all leavin'. Let's deal with this thing you dragged in first, then we talk about you and sissy."

"Is she alive? How is she alive in there?" Ryder asked.

"She's alive and she's doin' fine," Kandi said. "Chipper as a bullfrog. It's like she's asleep. Getting all the nutrients she needs and with the memory modifier in there, all she is doing is dreamin' beautiful dreams. When she wakes up, she won't remember ever being asleep. She's fine, baby. Now, put down the gun."

Ryder lowered his gun and put it back in its holster.

Kandi tugged on Ryder's arm. "Come on, let's take this thing you brought into an exam room."

Ryder brushed past Kandi and grabbed Stella again. Kandi slipped past them and opened the door to a smaller medical room across the hall from Inventions and Experiments. Ryder sat Stella down in a metal chair. There was a steel table with straps laid across it and a counter that had various instruments and devices set out.

"Honey, you didn't need to put that thing over her mouth. We need to have a little chat," Kandi said.

"I don't recommend removing it," Ryder said.

Kandi ignored him and removed the seal from Stella's mouth. Ryder leaned up against the wall and folded his arms across his chest. He hated being this close to his sister without being able to do anything to help her. If he played along, maybe he would be one step closer to gaining Pip's freedom.

"Hmmm. She doesn't look like much," Kandi said. She looked Stella up and down.

"I would say the same for you," Stella replied.

"I see what you mean, hero," Kandi said. "Better watch it, baby. Let's not get off on the wrong foot." Kandi stood with her hands on her curvy hips, staring at Stella. "So, you're the Healer?"

"Healer? I'm a surgeon. I work at Mercy General."

Kandi narrowed her eyes. "You don't know who you really are, do you?"

"I do. I just told you who I really am. Who are you? What do you want?"

"The name's Kandice Shook. I'm happy as a clam in high tide that you're here. Can't wait to get you in the tank and pump all those healing juices out of you."

"I don't have healing juices, and I'm not going in one of those tanks."

Kandi looked over at Ryder with her mouth open.

"Told you," Ryder said. He coughed into his shoulder to hide his smile. Stella impressed him with her fervor.

Without warning, Kandi hit Stella in the face with the back of her hand. Stella shook her head, stunned by the slap. Kandi tried to hit her again, but Stella put up her bound hands, pushed Kandi's away, and shot up from the chair.

"Pretty tough, is that it?" Kandi grabbed a device from the counter. "Sit down, you spoiled bitch." Kandi plunged a stun gun into Stella's chest. Blue lightning burst into Stella's body, and it forced her back into the chair. Kandi then hit her again. "You need to learn that acting tough around me is a bad idea."

Stella licked the blood from her now split lip and gasped to catch her breath.

"That's enough. You asked me to bring her here. I did. Now I'm done," Ryder said, making for the door.

"Not so fast, hero," Kandi said. She replaced the seal over Stella's mouth. "I need you to help Mr. Owen run some tests on her. Need to confirm her DNA. Make sure she doesn't have a tracking chip on her."

"You run the tests," Ryder said. "I've done my part."

Kandi nuzzled up to Ryder's neck and he stiffened. He clenched his fists so they would not reach out and strangle her.

"You're so close. Just a little longer. Get this nasty little bitch in the tank, and you get your sister out."

Ryder glanced at Stella and then back to Kandi and nodded reluctantly.

# 18

# CHIPPED

**STELLA'S BODY SHOOK** from the electricity coursing through her. She cried out when Kandi stunned her again before leaving the room. Kandi ordered Ryder to stand by until Mr. Owen could come to run the tests. Stella flinched when Ryder neared her, and it surprised her when he removed the mouth seal. She gasped for more air, trying to calm herself from the electricity that left her body trembling.

Moments later, there was a soft knock at the door. Ryder reached behind him and opened it while keeping his weapon pointed at Stella with the other hand. A short man wearing a lab coat walked in. He pushed his glasses up his nose and wiped a bead of sweat from his brow.

"Oh my! Um, hello. I am Mr. Owen. I'm a physician here in Aldemara and Ms. Shook's lab tech. I know this is not ideal for you, but I need to, um, run some tests and draw some blood. I do not want to do this, but I am ordered to do so. I hope you understand."

Seeing Mr. Owen's face flush, she knew he was under duress. She nodded, and Mr. Owen's shoulders relaxed.

"Okay, we'll just undo these," he said. He removed Stella's restraints and she massaged her aching wrists.

"Oh goodness, you have been out in the rain," Mr. Owen said, noticing the welts all over Stella's body. "I can help with the sting of those. If you wouldn't mind sitting up on the table here."

"No thank you," Stella said.

Mr. Owen glanced at Ryder, who shrugged.

"If she doesn't want to feel better, then don't bother," Ryder said.

"Yes, well," Mr. Owen said. "I know this must be frightening. Uh, but I promise, I want to help you. I'm a doctor, like you. What we use for these welts … oh dear … not sure how to describe this as something a Terran would recognize. It's a potion that soothes acid rain burns."

Mr. Owen reached in a cabinet and showed Stella a bottle of the spray he wanted to use. He sprayed it on his face to show her it was safe. His skin didn't have a reaction. While Stella wanted to protest, her welts itched, so she welcomed any relief. She got up and pushed herself up onto the table.

"Miss Stella, if you are comfortable, may I undo the back of your dress to spray this on your … um … shoulders and back? It will help with all the burns."

Ryder gulped.

"Fine," Stella said.

Before anyone could say anything more, Ryder holstered his gun and opened the door. "I'll be waiting outside."

*Good. At least the threat of seeing my bare shoulders got him out of the room.*

Mr. Owen carefully unzipped Stella's dress, and she pulled it down over her shoulders. The spray hit her skin, cooling and soothing her. The itch of the welts immediately subsided, and she closed her eyes, relishing the sensation.

"I apologize for Ms. Shook's treatment of you," Mr. Owen said. "She doesn't like women."

"Doesn't appear like she likes men that much either."

"This is true, but she detests women. All the employees in the lab are men. The only reason I'm still alive is because I am … um … a male, I think."

"If that's the case, then you shouldn't let her push you around like that."

Mr. Owen, speaking in a hushed tone, said, "I … um … don't have much of a choice. Mostly what I do is try to keep her calm. When she gets angry, her eyes go dark, almost like she leaves her body for a moment. And then, she does … she does horrible things."

"Why would this city put her in charge?" Stella asked.

Mr. Owen zipped Stella's dress back up and continued to spray her arms, face, chest, and legs. "She's not really supposed to be in charge. General Law is … um … the leader here, but Kandi has created many allies because she brings a lot of credits to Aldemara with her tech and med deals. We also have a new fleet of military vessels because of her. She's pretty good at fooling people who don't know her very well into thinking that she's normal. There now, how does that feel?"

"Better, thank you," Stella said. The welts were all but gone on her arms.

"Now, I need to check you for a tracking chip."

Mr. Owen waved a small device over Stella's body. There was a green light on the end that stayed green over her head, shoulders, and torso. It remained green over the lower half of her body and her left arm. It suddenly switched to red when Mr. Owen got to Stella's right wrist. A pill-shaped object shot a digital projection in the air.

"Oh no. You do have a tracking chip embedded in your wrist."

"A tracking chip?"

"Yes. It means that someone could track your location."

"I know what it means. How did it get there?"

"Where did Ryder pick you up from?"

Stella had to think. "A place called Verbatim."

The color drained from Mr. Owen's face. "Oh my, the Sentinels."

"They can find me with this, can't they?"

Mr. Owen nodded, and Stella hopped down from the table.

"Oh, please wait. I still need to draw some blood."

"I don't think so," Stella said.

"Please, you don't understand," Mr. Owen said. "This is nothing I ... um ... want to do, but something I *have* to do. If I don't get your blood, I will experience retaliation and punishment from Ms. Shook. I used to be a respectable physician here. I helped people, cured diseases, invented alternative medicines. Ms. Shook came, and now I'm forced to complete her requests. If I refuse, she will hurt my family. Please, I only need a little of your blood."

Stella knew the Sentinels would be looking for her, and she felt even better knowing there was a way they could find her. "I'm sorry, but you're not drawing my blood."

"Please, sit down. There is surveillance in these rooms. Maybe ... um ... maybe we can help each other."

Stella's expression softened. She sat back down on the table. "I'm listening."

"I ... um ... need to take your blood, but I can delay the test results. The Sentinels will most likely be retrieving you any moment, and I will make sure Ms. Shook doesn't find what she wants to with your blood."

"And what does she want to find?"

"She has gotten information that you're a Healer ... that you are one of the Keepers. If you are, she will draw out your healing powers and sell them in liquid form. I can cause a delay and say I didn't find a tracking chip."

Stella sighed. Seeing Mr. Owen standing in front of her, red-faced and sweating, she could tell he did not want to do this. "Well, I am not a Keeper. I am a surgeon from Earth, but ... if you need to do this to help your cause, then do it."

Stella stuck her arm out and Mr. Owen relaxed once again.

"Thank you," he said. He placed a clear cylinder on Stella's left wrist. He pressed a button on the top and it sucked the blood out before she could blink. When he took the cylinder away, Stella rubbed her wrist, noticing there wasn't even a mark on her skin.

"Amazing," she said, marveling at the technology. "Now what?" she asked after Mr. Owen placed the cylinder in his lab coat pocket.

"I'll get Ryder. Not sure what comes next for you, but I do hope the Sentinels are on their way."

Stella smiled. "Thank you for being kind."

"Thank you, Miss."

Mr. Owen slipped out and briefed Ryder. "She's clean, no ... um ... chips that I could locate."

"Good," Ryder said. He came back in the room with his gun pointed at Stella. "Get up."

"Where are we going now?"

"To a different room."

"And if I refuse?"

"Don't. Don't refuse."

Stella looked past Ryder into the empty hall behind him.

*How will I know if the Sentinels are coming?* Her eyes darted around the room looking for a place to run to.

"Think carefully about how your last plan turned out. This is a very secure building. You run in here and you won't make it ten feet. Now get up off the table and let's go," Ryder said. He frowned at Stella and motioned with his gun toward the door.

Reluctantly, Stella stepped down off the table and he took her arm again.

"I can bind you and seal your mouth, or shoot you, or you can walk with me peacefully. Your call."

"If you really wanted to shoot me, you would have done it already," Stella said, stopping.

"Believe me when I say, I *will* shoot you if I want to."

"But that woman has leverage over you too, doesn't she? That woman in the tank ... she's your sister? Is that why you have to do what you're told?"

"Shut up!" Ryder thrust Stella into the wall, knocking the wind out of her. "I'm done with your questions, and I'm done with you. Now let's go!"

Ryder attempted to re-cuff Stella, but as he grabbed her wrist they both froze when a blue light blinked under her skin.

"You're chipped!" Ryder roared. "No, no, no, no, no!"

Ryder dragged Stella back to the exam room. She pulled back, and he knocked her in the face, stunning her. He slammed her down on the table. He grabbed a sharp object and plunged it into Stella's wrist. She screamed and pushed on Ryder. Blood gushed out of her wound, but the blinking blue continued. Ryder was so focused on cutting out the chip that he didn't see Stella take a scalpel off the tray next to her. Just when he noticed the knife in her hand, she plunged it into Ryder's red eye. He recoiled instantly and fell to the floor howling in pain, sparks flying out of his face.

Stella popped up and ran out the door. She ducked behind a wall as she heard Ryder stumble out of the lab screaming for backup. An alarm sounded in the building, and she knew she had to get out whether the Sentinels were waiting for her or not. Guards shouted, and other lab workers emerged out of other rooms to see what all the commotion was about. She stopped and caught her breath. She tore a strip of fabric off her dress and wrapped it around her wrist to slow the bleeding.

Voices echoed down the hall. The guards were getting closer. She raced down the stairs, glancing over her shoulder to see who was following when she ran right into his arms. They were powerful arms that closed around her tightly. She thrashed and howled trying to push him away. Stella punched and screamed and tried to wriggle free, but he didn't release her.

"Hey! It's me! It's me! It's me!"

Stella stopped thrashing and looked at the man in front of her.

Elliot.

She was so relieved to see him, she flung her arms around his neck. Elliot squeezed her briefly and released her once a shot whizzed past them. Iris ran into the lobby and shot down a guard on the second floor.

"Let's go!" she shouted.

"Yes!" Elliot shouted.

"We've got them. Get back to the ship," Iris yelled into her watch. Ryder stumbled down the staircase. He fired on his way down, and he made it to the bottom a few feet away from them. Gary rushed through the door of the lobby in his silvery giant form to cover the others as Elliot and Iris hustled Stella out. Zimmer appeared from behind a corner and shot a guard, who fell from the top railing and crashed into the floor of the lobby. Gary absorbed multiple blasts while Iris shot through the security checkpoints, clearing their way out of the entrance. Ryder was closing in but was still wobbly from the damage Stella had caused. Stella and Elliot ran out, ducking from guards firing at them. Gary aimed a plasma cannon and fired, sending Ryder to the ground. Ryder skidded back on the floor until he hit the wall. He lay motionless on the floor, smoke coming off the wound in his chest.

The acid rain had subsided, allowing them all to run back to a small ship that had landed to the side of the lab.

"Are you okay?" Elliot asked once they were on board. "You're bleeding. Jesus, what did they do to you? Hey, she's bleeding. Hello?" Elliot yelled.

"I'm okay," Stella replied.

"Hang on, friends. Let's get out of here," Rex shouted from the captain's chair, flipping switches on the ship and sending it into the sky.

"Wait, wait! There are people in that building being held hostage. There's a woman in a tank!" Stella said. She held onto the back of Rex's seat as the ship throttled and shook. Iris hopped into the seat next to Rex to help him outmaneuver three Aldemaran fighter planes chasing them through the sky. Gary morphed back into his human form to help Zimmer attend to Stella with first aid.

"Stella, sit down and tell me what happened," Zimmer said. He guided her to a bench where Elliot had already buckled up. Zimmer knelt so he could attend to Stella's wrist. He placed a device on her wrist like the one she had seen them use on Elliot. A warming sensation followed, and the bleeding immediately stopped. The pain subsided, and the device beeped happily as it finished its work.

Gary handed her some water, which she gladly accepted as her mouth felt like she had been sucking on sawdust. "We need to help that woman I saw in the tank."

"What woman? What tank?" Zimmer asked. He tried to inspect her split lip, but Stella waved him away. "Someone called Shook is holding a woman hostage in a tank of green liquid. It's Ryder's sister. They were trying to put me in a tank because they think I'm a Healer ... a Keeper?"

Zimmer shot up to his feet.

"What?" Stella asked.

Zimmer opened his mouth to speak, but a rocket blew over the ship, just missing it as Rex maneuvered to avoid the missile. "Let's just get you back to Verbatim, and then you can tell us everything," Zimmer said.

"That woman's life is in danger," Stella said.

"We can't do much from up here. We will try to help if we can, but first we need to get out of here alive," Zimmer replied.

# 19

# THIN ICE

**KANDI FLEW DOWN THE STAIRCASE**, followed by Taylor and Mr. Owen. Lovella and several armed Aldemaran troops rushed through the front doors of the lab. Lovella's eyes were bulging. Kandi knew what was about to happen, and she didn't want to deal with it. Mr. Owen checked the bodies strewn about and announced they were all dead.

"Check him," Kandi said, pointing toward Ryder's body.

Lovella approached Kandi, stepping over the dead that littered the lobby.

"Do you have an explanation as to why there was a Sentinel ship here and why they breached your highly secure lab, a place you refuse to let me into?" Lovella asked through clenched teeth. Her normally fair skin looked hot and flushed.

"I'm just as horrified as you are. I don't know why they were here," Kandi lied.

"How did they find this place? How did they get in?"

"I told you I don't know, but I'm going to get to the bottom of it," Kandi said.

Mr. Owen helped Ryder sit up.

"What's his status?" Lovella asked.

"He is alive, but it looks like they hit him with a plasma cannon. I need to take him to the mechanic."

Ryder coughed and then collapsed when he saw the ash-colored burn on his chest.

"Get him out of here," Kandi said. She felt so much anger boiling up inside her, but there weren't enough people left alive to yell at. Now Lovella had seen the lab, which meant that she was going to be more invested in what, exactly, Kandi was doing.

"You've got a lot of cleanup to do around here, and after that, you will report to my office. Then you can tell me exactly why the Sentinels were here and what they wanted," Lovella said, holstering her gun. She signaled to her troops to haul away the dead.

For once, Kandi remained silent. She had a contingency plan in place for exactly this event; she didn't realize she would have to execute it so soon.

# 20

# REPAIRS

**RYDER'S EYE BLINKED OPEN.** From the look of the ceiling and the familiar smell of sandalwood, he knew where he was. It was the one place other than his small apartment that brought some comfort to him. His entire body rippled with pain, but the repairing light of the operating table was helping his cells turn over rapidly. The hole in his chest had healed and he sat up, but a force pushed him down again.

"Not so fast, bro. Not finished with you yet."

Ryder sank back down on the flat steel table.

"My head," he groaned.

"Yeah, no wonder. Whoever jammed that knife through your eye really made a mess. It's going to take me a bit to restore sight to this, and it's going to take even longer to get the rest of your damn head to stop ringing," said Tana, his mechanic and his only friend in Aldemara.

Ryder groaned again, and Tana grabbed a small, metal cylinder and injected pain medication into his arm. "That should help. I hope you killed him … the dude who did this to you." Tana sat in her chair and pulled an X-ray scanner from the ceiling so she could better see Ryder's circuits. She pulled magnifying glasses, that were attached to a headband, over her eyes.

"She," corrected Ryder.

"She? A *she* did this to you?"

Ryder nodded and focused his good eye elsewhere in the room.

"And is *she* dead?"

"No."

"Hmmm, that's different. Not normal for you to end up on the losing end of a tussle."

"I did not lose. I …" Ryder stopped, too tired to explain.

"Did she also hit you with a shot of plasma?"

"She didn't, but a droid did."

"Mercy! What happened over there?"

Ryder sighed. "Long story."

He clenched his teeth as Tana pulled out the tattered old hardware of his eye and threw it in a nearby tray. Though most of the nerves around his right eye had been dead for some time, it still pained him to have the metal and wires taken out of his skull.

"Apologies," Tana said. "But hey, I've been working on some new hardware for you, and this one …" she concentrated as she carefully placed the new mechanical eye in Ryder's socket, "… will be even better. Better clarity, better heat-seeking, and when you put on the new prosthetic I made to cover the machine parts of your face, this eye will let you see as well as the other one, like you used to."

"Good. When can I have the prosthetic?"

"Not finished yet, but soon."

Tana wiped Ryder's forehead with a cool cloth and finished securing the new eye. "There, all done." She brushed ringlets of her dark hair out of her face and pushed her glasses up. They rested in between the two thick, curled horns that grew out of her head. "Blink for me, then tell me what you see."

She helped him sit up and turn so he was facing her, his feet dangling off the table.

"The room … you," Ryder said.

"Now, how many fingers am I holding up?"

Ryder's mouth curved upward. "Three."

Tana put her tools away and cleaned up her workspace. The room she worked in was not pretty, but she kept it clean. She had two operating tables with wobbly lights overhead, a sink with a leaky faucet, and an old rug she used to keep her feet from touching the cold concrete floor. She had a large computer system that took up most of the space and the energy in the room. She had always worn her perfume when she came to work to cover up the odors of gasoline and oil since she specialized in repairing droids and other machinery. When Kandi first brought Ryder's lifeless body into Tana's workshop, Tana had never worked on a human before, but Kandi forced her to put Ryder back together again. Since then, Tana's expert hands always repaired him.

"Tana?"

"What's up?"

"I need you to do something for me," Ryder said.

"Name it."

Ryder punched three buttons on his smartwatch, which cued the projection of a number in red writing. "Can you to look up this chip number? Want some more information on this person."

Tana nodded and said the number three times out loud as she went to her computer terminal. She motioned her hands to pull screens out of the computer and stack them three dimensionally on top of one another to the right side. She read the number out loud so the computer could process it.

"Oh ... wow," she said as the computer filled the room with pictures of Stella.

Ryder slipped off the table, still holding his sore ribs to have a closer look at all the information loaded onto Stella's chip. 3D images, videos, and sounds of Stella and her life on Terra surrounded him.

"Is this ... *she*?" Tana asked.

Ryder nodded.

"I see. Hmmm ... Terran. Stella Jayne Walsh. Huh, not what I was expecting. Doesn't seem like she could do that much damage to you. But damn, she's scrappy isn't she?"

More photos popped up in the room. Pictures of Stella in grade school, pictures of her playing soccer in high school, family photos and vacation photos of her and a woman Ryder assumed was her mother.

"Pretty lady."

Ryder stiffened. Tana laughed and looked back to the photos. "Beauty and brains, yeah? Interesting...she's a doctor, a surgeon."

Tana cued a video. "That must be her in surgery on Terra. And this video looks like ... Whoa, that man is pointing a gun at her! Terran media headline says, 'Man opens fire in Mercy General after doctors couldn't save his wife.'"

Grainy video showed Stella in her doctor's coat standing in front of members of her staff with her arms outstretched, trying to talk to a man who held a revolver and waved it around shouting in the hospital lobby. The man fired, and Stella hit the floor with the rest of her staff as police breaking in from the outside shot the man. Stella writhed in pain on the floor of the ER entryway.

"Lots of information here about that incident."

"Wait, cue that one," Ryder said, pointing to a video of Stella on the program *60 Minutes*. Stella was talking to a journalist. Tana turned up the volume.

"So, when did you start taking self-defense classes?"

"Almost immediately," Stella replied. The footage cut away to Stella in a gym sparring with a man who was trying to choke her. The video cut back to Stella and the journalist. "I decided that I would not live in fear. I decided that I was not going to be a victim. I wanted to learn how to defend myself, so no man could ever terrorize me again."

The video cut out.

"I like her. I'm glad you didn't kill her."

"How much information is there?" Ryder asked, his eyes glued to the screens in front of him.

"Lots. Her abductors surveilled her for six Terran months. Wait, something else just popped up." Tana clicked on the keyboard panel. "It's this chip number … an old number. She's…she's not Terran at all."

Ryder raised his brows, reading the panel in front of him as Tana continued.

"Can I take all this to go?" Ryder asked.

"You want all her Terran surveillance?"

"Yes."

"Nah, if they catch you with that, it'll be my ass."

"Just do it. Tell them I stole it."

"There's a lot here. Why do you want all this?" Tana asked as she uploaded the files to a tiny computer chip and handed it to Ryder.

"I …uh … have to locate her. This will help me find her."

Ryder never liked the look Tana gave him when she knew he was not being truthful with her. He made a break for it before he had to answer any more of her questions.

Ryder picked up his leather coat, wincing as he stretched his arms through the sleeves.

"You better take it is easy now. Your body took quite a beating. "

He made it to the door and then turned. "Just a typical day. At least I've got you to put me back together again, yeah?"

Tana wiped her hands. "You bet."

# 21

# CONFLICTED

**RYDER UNSHEATHED HIS ENERGY REVOLVER** and checked behind him, as he always did when he entered his studio apartment. Kandi said she wanted him close to her in the city, so she gave him a place in the high-rise next door to her office suite. But he never felt settled until he tactically cleared the inside and outside every time he walked in.

It was silent, as usual.

It wasn't much of an apartment, and it was sterile since he never considered it really a home. It was just a place to get cleaned up and sleep. There was a bed, nightstand, computer terminal, and table. The only thing he enjoyed was that every room, office, and apartment in Aldemara had windows that ran from the floor to the ceiling so everyone could enjoy the nightly view.

He placed his revolver on his nightstand, peeled off his clothes, and took the hottest shower possible. He stretched his aching arms out on the shower wall and let the steaming water run down his back.

As images of Stella flashed in his head, he wished he could wash those away. He was still unnerved, because when she stared at him, it was not out of fear but out of curiosity. Her eyes stared at him in his mind, and he shook his head, trying to get her out. He knew that Kandi would not stop until she got what she wanted, and that meant that Kandi would order Ryder to pursue Stella again.

He got a bite to eat, settled in front of his computer terminal, and pulled up everything Tana gave him on Stella. This time, he lingered over every piece of information. He read every Terran news article published on her and rewatched the hospital shooting and the disappearance of her mother, Kate. He studied every photo, from her childhood to her adult years. He laughed at a grade school picture that popped up of her in pigtails.

*How did this girl grow up to punch me in the throat and smash me in the face with her head?*

He scrolled through her past until something popped up that intrigued him more than anything he had seen so far. It was Stella's chip number and how she acquired it that caused him to reread the information three times.

Ryder sat back in his chair and took a big gulp. If the information was correct, Stella was not the Terran she thought she was. She was part of something Ryder only knew to be myth and legend. The Kaygun soldier Ryder used to be would have sworn an oath to protect someone like Stella, not mistreat her as Kandi had ordered. Reflecting on the many crimes he committed for Kandi, he knew he was not that soldier anymore, but the duty he swore to uphold never really left him.

He shut off the computer and got up. His mind was buzzing with images of Stella and the horrifying image of Pip in the tank. Pip would not have wanted him to do all this for her, for the chance to earn her freedom. She had sworn her oath to protect those who needed it as well, and she would have been happy dying for that, not frozen in a dream state.

Ryder lay in his bed, but he would not sleep that night. In his mind, a plan formed to free Pip. Now that he had seen the lab, he knew what he was up against. He tossed and turned and eventually got up. His mind would not be quiet. He was going to rescue his sister, even if it meant he would die trying.

# 22
# HOME

**WHEN STELLA WAS A LITTLE GIRL,** her mother had sprigs of lavender in vases all around their brownstone. She also had a little perfume roller of lavender and mint oil that she would rub on Stella's wrists to help Stella sleep at night. As Stella turned on her side in the bed, she felt soft blankets engulf her, and she smelled that lavender again.

It must have been a dream. She knew it. Just a dream. She must have passed out after the shock of losing her patient. Maybe someone found her and sent her home. Stella's eyelids stretched open. There was someone in the room with her. Someone she had not seen since ...

"Mom?"

"Hi, Peanut."

Kate stepped out of the shadows and sat down on the edge of the bed. It surprised Stella how calm she was. She had not seen her in years, but it felt like not a day had passed.

"Where were you?" Stella asked, stretching.

"Here. I've always been here, Peanut."

"I couldn't find you," Stella said. She tried to turn her head, but she couldn't move.

Kate reached out her hands and gently ran them down Stella's arms. Kate smiled, but it quickly faded as her gaze became fixed and icy.

"Mom?"

Silence.

"Mom? I can't move. Mom?"

She tried to scream, to move, but she couldn't. The lavender smell dissipated. The image of her mother dissolved. Her eyes blinked open to a blur of dim lights in a room. She heard familiar voices, and she could make out three blurry figures standing over her as she blinked away the fog in her eyes.

"There she is," said a voice.

Elliot with Zimmer and Gary stood over her. She was in a room that had medical equipment, but it was not part of a hospital. She pushed herself up in the bed, wondering why she dreamed of her mother. The answer came when she saw sprigs of lavender in a vase on a table by the bed.

"What happened?" Stella asked.

"You passed out," Elliot said. "Right after we got you back to the ship."

"Dehydration, I'm sure of it," Gary said.

Stella rubbed her head. "I'm getting a little tired of asking this, but where am I now?"

"Rex's house," Zimmer replied. "You'll be safe here."

"I've heard that before," Stella said. "How the hell did I get a tracking chip in my wrist?" Stella asked.

"Oh, all Terrans get them the moment they arrive in space. Thank goodness it was undetectable until we were very close. We may not have found you," Gary said.

"I have one too," Elliot said, proudly showing his wrist.

"I am sorry if this offends you, Dr. Walsh," Zimmer added. "It's standard protocol; we wouldn't have located you if not for that chip, and we would have found you sooner but Ryder set out plasma bombs in the city, which detonated when his ship took off."

"Saints be praised, you're awake," Rex said as he entered the room. Iris followed behind Rex, but she remained in the doorway and did not greet Stella as the others had.

"Rex, what about the people back there? What can we do?" Stella asked.

"We will get to that, Stella. We want you to tell us everything you experienced," Rex replied. "But first we need to get you cleaned up and get you a fresh change of clothing."

Gary reached for Stella's hands and helped her to her feet. She didn't want to wait to tell Rex what she saw, but her dress, half burned with holes, splashed in blood, smudged with dirt, was about to disintegrate at any moment. "All right," she said.

"Follow me." Gary led her out of Rex's private medical chamber. They walked down a small hallway to a beautiful room bathed in tropical colors. Stella craned her neck, gawking at the twenty-foot-high ceiling. A sprawling canopy bed with multicolored pillows spread across it greeted her from the middle of the room. Beside it, a cobalt blue sectional sofa. They stopped in the bathroom with a massive bathtub that looked like a backyard swimming pool.

"I have drawn a bath for you, taking special care to fill it with healing oils that will cleanse your sinuses. There's clothing laid out for you on the bed. Take your time. We'll be down in the great room at the end of the hall when you're ready." Gary smiled and blinked his eyes rapidly.

Stella cocked her head to one side. "Are ... are you okay?"

"Oh yes, dear me, I'm trying to wink. It's an adorable Terran gesture and one I have yet to master."

"I see. Well, uh, you'll get there. Just watch how Elliot does it. He is a professional when it comes to winking."

"Good thinking. Yes, I will have him help me with this." Gary closed the door, gently blinking as he exited.

Standing at the edge of the steaming bath, Stella dipped in her toes to test the water and found it was the perfect temperature. She had so many questions, but the bath looked so inviting she couldn't help but slip in. The warm vapors of eucalyptus consoled her as she slipped under the bubbles, holding her breath for a moment. Images of what she saw in Aldemara popped into her mind. The acid rain, sparks flying out of her hands, the woman in the tank, Kandi hitting her in the face, and Ryder's red eye flashing as he slammed her against the wall. She exploded out from underneath the water, gasping for air and disturbing the quiet of the bathroom. She tried to shake the pictures of Ryder and the lab from her mind and hoped that Rex was about to tell her she could finally go home.

She toweled off and was happy to find a pair of pants waiting for her on the bed. The fitted tank top and cotton shirt hugged her perfectly. When she walked out of her bedroom, Elliot emerged at the same time. He smiled brightly, his cheeks revealing his dimples. He had combed his hair into a neat formation on his head, a refreshing change from the matted mop Stella had gotten used to seeing.

"My goodness, that bath! Did you have one?" he asked, buttoning the last button on his fresh shirt.

"Yes. It was amazing."

"I usually hate baths. Something about soaking in your own dirt … but that was incredible. How are you? I was worried about you," Elliot said.

"I'm much better now that I'm out of that dress. How are you? Surprised to see you with Rex's crew," Stella said.

"They let me tag along because they still think I'm a warrior. They gave me a gun, but I had no idea how to use it, so I just punched a guy in the face when we stormed that building."

"Really?"

"Yeah, my hand still hurts," Elliot said, flexing his right hand a few times.

"When are you going to tell them you are not the warrior they think you are?" Stella asked.

"I was thinking … never. I kind of like it. Like them thinking I'm a warrior, I mean."

"Don't you think they will come to the conclusion that you are not, in fact, a warrior?"

"Not if we don't say anything. Are you going to tell them green sparks flew out of your hands?"

Stella opened her palms, staring at them. These were the hands that had performed hundreds of surgeries. They had always been something she could count on—predictable and steady. How could she explain this new revelation when she didn't want to believe her hands were capable of something so bizarre?

"It happened again, didn't it?"

Stella nodded. "Only this time, this green bubble came out, like a shield, then it just went away."

"You need to tell them."

"No. It's a trick my mind plays on me when I am stressed, okay?"

Elliot narrowed his eyes. "I see. Well, I'm glad we found you. You'll have to tell me what happened."

"I will. Hopefully, when we are on our way home," Stella said.

Stella and Elliot were the last to arrive in the great room where Rex, Iris, Gary, and Zimmer were already gathered around a long table. Rex and crew were talking in hushed voices as Zimmer flipped through images that shot up from the center of the table. The voices stopped and all eyes turned to Stella as she entered the room.

"What's going on?" Stella asked.

"We are assessing the damage Ryder caused with the bombs he planted. The odd thing is that he didn't destroy anything that was occupied. All were vacant buildings save for one," Rex said. He pointed to an image on the screen.

It was the one building Stella recognized: the Terran portal and their way home.

"Oh no," Elliot said, sitting down at the table.

"What does this mean? We can't get home now, can we?" Stella asked.

Rex rubbed his mustache. "No, it means that Elliot can't get home. Stella, you can't go home to Terra because you already *are* home."

# 23

## GRAVITY

**"EXCUSE ME?"** A chill tickled the back of Stella's spine.

"Please sit down. This won't be easy for you to hear," Rex said.

"I'm not a child. I don't want to sit down. Let's see, so far, I've been abducted by people calling themselves aliens. I've been put into a wedding dress and told that I was to mate with a stranger on a new planet. I was kidnapped by a man with one red eye and was assaulted by a woman who wanted to put me in a tank so they could syphon healing juices out of my body to sell in liquid form. Whatever you have to tell me, it can't be any more difficult to hear than anything I've already heard!"

Silence passed through the room as Stella's words settled on them. Gary let out a quick gasp. "Rex, I'm not sure that *I* can listen to this." Stella furrowed her brow.

"Iris, dear, would you please take Gary through the gardens? It will allow us to speak with Stella without interruption," Rex said, motioning toward a door off the great room that led to the outside.

"But Stella may need my emotional support," Gary protested.

Rex smiled, clasping his hands together. "That's just it. You have become too emotional; therefore, you will be ineffective in terms of offering support."

Gary turned up his nose. Iris tried to hide her smile as she offered Gary her hand. Gary reached out his hand for Elliot, who took it.

Rex got up and patted Elliot on the back as he was leaving. "I'm sorry Driver. We will repair the portal straight away, and we will get you home to your world as soon as we can. That's a promise."

Elliot pursed his lips and nodded.

Rex continued. "Now then, Stella, there is a tracking chip in your wrist. Most Terrans receive them when they first arrive in space. The chip number carries data on it about said Terran, and these chips are also equipped with a device that lets others with the right technology locate that person as well."

"I know how tracking devices work," Stella said. "What does this have to do with you saying this is my home, which is crazy by the way."

"Iris researched your chip number, and there was an anomaly. You did not receive your chip when you arrived in space; it was given to you when you were sent to Terra, I assume so you could be located at a later time," Rex said.

"Sent to Terra?"

"What we are trying to say is that chip has data about you and your DNA," Zimmer added.

"My DNA?"

"DNA that suggests you are not Terran, Stella. That woman in Aldemara was right about you. You are a healer, and not just any healer. You are a Keeper of Health," Rex said.

"No, I'm not."

Zimmer took a book out of his chest pocket and threw it on the table in front of her.

"Where did you get that?" Stella asked, and as soon as the words left her lips a memory sparked in her brain of Zimmer holding up the book when she was first abducted.

"You know where *I* got it," Zimmer said. "What I was asking you that night is where *you* got that book—a book that was given only to the Keepers after the Great War as a record of their lives and who they were. You can't just find this at your local bookstore."

Stella reached for *The Keepers of the Universe.* "This was my mother's. She used to read from it to me every night. It's just a story."

"Incorrect. It's *your* story," Rex said. He tapped on the table's keypad. Images of Stella's mother, along with the two other women she once saw in the photograph on her mother's desk, projected out of the table.

Willow and Maren.

Stella's eyes bounced around over the images of them fighting in the war. Kate was flying over what looked like troops on the ground. Green beams of light shot out of her extended palms and the beams merged, forming a protective bubble around the other women fighting on the ground.

Rex pressed a button, freezing the video. Kate appeared younger and in a uniform like the Sentinels wore. She was levitating in the air, in a war that, until that moment, Stella thought was part of a fable that had been read to her at bedtime.

"This is impossible," she said.

"It only feels that way," Zimmer said.

"No, it's literally impossible. I was born in New York."

"You were actually born here," Zimmer said, pulling up another image. A blue-green planet appeared in front of her. "It's called Tulavarus. You and your family lived there until you moved here, to Verbatim, so your mother could help in our medical facility. After the Great War, she moved you to Terra to hide you and keep you safe."

The blood drained from Stella's face. Her stomach tightened. "This is insane."

Rex sat down and paused, pressing his mouth into his fingertips. "Stella, haven't you ever wondered why you had never lost a patient until now?"

She stared at him, hard. "I'm good at what I do, that's why."

"From what I gather about Terran medicine, it is fairly rare, in fact almost impossible, to have the record you had. Didn't you ever wonder how it came so easy for you?" Rex asked.

"It wasn't easy. None of it came easy. I busted my ass in med school. I worked my way up, sacrificing everything to get to where I was."

"That may be part of it, but part of your abilities come from your ancestors, the Keepers of Health," Zimmer added.

She shook her head, angered by their words and their insinuations that her abilities were superpowers and not the result of hard work. "I don't have to listen to this." She turned to walk back to the bedroom.

"Your mother is alive, Stella," Rex said.

Stella whipped around, her eyes wide. "What did you say?"

"Your mother is alive," Rex insisted.

"Stop! Just stop! Why are you doing this?"

"Because we need your help. Your mother needs your help," Zimmer added.

Stella suddenly felt chilled as if she had walked outside into a snowstorm. "My help? I haven't seen my mother in ten years."

"We realize that," Zimmer said.

"Okay, so where is she?"

"We don't know. We need your help to locate her," Rex said.

"How am I supposed to help?"

"Stella, please sit down. I realize this is all so shocking, but allow us to explain further." Rex came around the table and pulled out a chair for Stella.

She looked again at her mother soaring through the air and then back at her own hands, gripping the back of a chair so hard they were turning white. She couldn't dare tell them that the green light shooting out of her mother's hands was the same light she saw emerging from her own hand since she arrived.

"No, I will not sit down, and I will not listen to this nonsense. I don't care what it takes, but you fix that portal, and you get us home. I'm an emergency room surgeon who works at Mercy General, Manhattan, New York, USA, Earth. That's who I am, that is my home, and that's who I help. My mother is gone. It took me ten years to accept that. If I can do that, so can all of you."

# 24

# BEDTIME STORY

**STELLA MADE HER WAY BACK** to the bedroom and walked out on the attached balcony. It overlooked a far-reaching sea that tickled and splashed happily against the rocks on either side of it. The moonlight reflected off the ripples in the water, and Stella leaned over the marble railing, inhaling the salty air. At the hospital, even though every hour led to something unexpected coming through the door, she was prepared and in complete control of every situation. She knew what to do, even when everything fell apart around her. For the first time in her life, she did not have the answers. She did not know what to do.

"Hey."

Elliot's silhouette filled the doorway.

"You could have knocked."

"I did knock ... twice," Elliot said. "Rex wanted me to bring this book back to you. He showed me everything. Told me to talk to you."

Stella raised her eyebrows. "Did he? Not sure what good that is going to do."

"I agree," Elliot said, handing Stella the book and walking to the corner of the room to a gold-rimmed cart full of crystal glassware and various bottles of spirits. Elliot took off the top of one, sniffed it, then poured two glasses of it.

Stella took a seat on the sofa across from Elliot, who poured the drink down his throat and grunted as if it burned on the way down.

"He told me about your mother, your superpowers—which I think is completely awesome, by the way—and he told me you should read that book again." Elliot offered her a drink and when Stella waved him away, he drank it himself.

"It's a bedtime story," Stella said, throwing the book on the table. She leaned back and folded her arms across her chest. "I've read it. I don't need to read it again."

Elliot picked it up off the table. "What if it wasn't?" He opened the book to the first page.

"What do you mean?"

"What if it was real?"

"It's not."

"But what if, for tonight, since we are stuck in this, um, beautiful place … did you look at the ceiling tiles? So ornate."

"Elliot."

"Right." Elliot got up and approached Stella's side of the sofa. "May I?" he asked before sitting down.

Stella nodded, half smiling, and Elliot took a seat next to her. "What if tonight, we read this not as a story, but as a record of something totally amazing that actually happened?"

Stella exhaled and sank further into the sofa. "You can read it all you want. That doesn't mean I have to believe it."

She was used to the story being read to her, so she pulled a nearby blanket across her and listened as Elliot read.

"The Keepers of the Universe ..." Elliot said. He settled in comfortably. Quietly, he said, "Chapter One."

# 25

# THE KEEPERS

**BEFORE THE GREAT WAR**, the diverse beings of the universe lived in harmony. Beings were free to live, to work, to play, and to love. During this time, the protectors of this harmony ensured that everything remained in balance. The universe knew them as the Keepers. Keepers of Mind, Keepers of Body, and above all were the Keepers of Health. The Keepers of Mind have psychic energy manipulation, psychic navigation and other psychic abilities. Keepers of Body possess great strength. They can be shields in battle. Their bodies resist pain and illness, and they can use their strength to help others. The Keepers of Health not only can heal other beings, but they are also the ultimate guardians of the other Keepers. The Healers are the connectors to all. Without the Healers, the health and powers of the other Keepers will eventually dim. The Keepers are stronger together. Their powers are strongest when they all work as one.

"This is awesome. I can't believe you're one of these Keepers. Do you want me to keep reading?" Elliot asked.

Stella nodded. One chapter flowed into two and then four, each one exploring more about what made each Keeper special. Elliot stopped to sip some water as he said the scotch had made him drowsy. He started Chapter 6 titled "The Great War."

The Great War against the Zuldari people changed the universe forever. The Zuldari waged the war on many galactic beings to sterilize the universe of all diverse races and to create spaces where only the Zuldari existed. The Keepers and the Sentinels joined with the forces of good to help drive the Zuldari back to their native world. The Keepers and Sentinels finally gained the upper hand in battle, and ultimately the Zuldari retreated, but not before making this threat: they would return in great numbers and extinguish the fire from the Keepers once and for all. Many Keepers and Sentinels perished in the Great War. The remaining Keepers then went into hiding to preserve their lives and legacy.

Wow," Elliot said, "so you're basically a superhero."

Stella chuckled. "I don't think so."

"This book says you are, and since they gave this book only to … what did it say?" Elliot flipped through the pages. "'Keepers each have a copy of the sacred text to preserve their record and their place in galactic history.' Did you hear that? This is a sacred text. Yep, you are a superhero." Elliot shut the book and handed it to Stella.

"I don't care what it says."

"Why can't you accept it? Rex showed me that picture of your mother with the green light shooting out of her hands. What if that is what the green sparks are? What if that's your body trying to show you what you can do?"

Stella opened the book and searched the chapters, finding the one named "The Keepers of Health and Healing."

"How can I just accept all this? According to the *sacred* text, I can fly and, oh, 'surround warriors on a battlefield with a protective healing shield that prevents injury,' and I can also 'withdraw poisons from a wound with my bare hands,' and I love this one: I can 'heal wounds with psychic wave energy.'" Stella shot up from the sofa and threw the book on the cushion.

"What you just read makes you even more amazing."

"I can't do any of those things," she said. She went back out to the balcony and peered out over the edge. She didn't want to believe. It scared her that when she first saw the picture of her mother frozen in time on the battlefield, for a moment Stella thought she was looking at a picture of herself.

"How do you know?" Elliot said, joining her on the balcony. "How do you know that you can't do those things if you never have tried to do them?"

"Because they aren't possible. Psychic wave energy? There's no such thing. I'm sorry, I'm not like you. I can't openly embrace the unknown. I need proof."

"I think that's what this is—a big book of proof."

"I need more than a story to convince me."

Elliot was quiet for a moment. "Oh wait," he suddenly said. "You know what all this really means, don't you?"

Stella let out an exasperated sigh. "What?"

"You are the hero of this story."

"Elliot."

"And so, do you know what that makes me?"

"No, what does that make you?"

"The sidekick. I'm your sidekick!"

"Please."

"Seriously, I get to walk beside you and say things like, 'What do we do now, Boss?' And I get to help you out of a jam," Elliot said. "I can't wait."

Stella smiled at Elliot as he picked up the book once more. There was something about him that both irritated her and comforted her at the same time. He was the absolute opposite of her in that he seemed to roll with whatever was given him while Stella struggled to embrace her out-of-control state. Although she found him exhausting, he was a welcome distraction to her, especially when he finally put the book down and they began again to talk about their lives back in New York. She had always lived alone and swore she didn't have time for relationships, especially one with a man. But in talking to Elliot, she realized she had missed out on some things by dedicating her life solely to Mercy General.

She eventually excused herself to the bathroom and decided to tell Elliot it was time for him to go to his room. She returned to find him sprawled out on the canopy bed fast asleep. She pulled a blanket over him.

"Goodnight … sidekick," she said before wrapping herself in a blanket and slipping onto the sofa.

# 26

# NEW DAY

**THE SUN PEEKED INTO THE ROOM** and washed over Stella as morning made its presence known. She yawned and stretched just as Elliot pushed the door open with his back.

"Good morning!" he sang. "I'm so excited that we get to try Galactic Coffee. That's what this brew is called. Rex made it in this weird contraption."

Stella was not yet ready for Elliot's energy, and she hoped the coffee would perk her up.

"How many cups of coffee have you already had?"

Elliot handed her a mug. "This is my first one."

"Uh-huh. I wouldn't have any more if I were you. Thank you," Stella said.

He sat down across from her on the sofa and took a sip after he blew off some heat. "You're welcome. Now, let's see how this compares. Hmmm … nope. Coffee from home is still better, although I do love the aroma this one has. Caramel notes—"

"No, not for the coffee … for last night. For reading the book, for getting me through the shock."

Elliot grinned. "Hey, we're in this together, whatever this is."

After all the chaos she had just been through, she relished this moment feeling the sun on her back and a warm mug of coffee in her hand. Elliot eventually went back to his chamber for another "amazing bubble bath" while Stella ventured out to the main great room. The doors to the garden were open, sending a sweet breeze into the house. Gary and Iris were playing a digital board game at a small stone table as Rex looked on. They fell silent when Stella entered the garden.

"How does this day find you, my dear?" Rex asked.

"Better," Stella said. "I'm hoping to get more news about how we can get home."

"Yes, Rex. Let's please get these Terrans home," Iris said as she moved a piece on the board. "We have more important things to do than babysit."

Stella scowled. "Excuse me?"

"Uh, let's take a walk, shall we?" Rex said.

"Why did she say that?" Stella asked.

"Iris can be a bit icy toward newcomers."

"Oh, you mean she's rude to newcomers?"

"I do apologize."

"You shouldn't apologize; *she* should apologize."

"This is true. I simply offered that to soothe you somehow. But alas, it did not work, did it?"

Stella tried to hide her smile. "No."

The stone path in front of them opened up to a picturesque garden bursting with florals of all colors and sizes. Sunflowers standing six feet tall lined the edges. Bulbs of bright magentas sprang out of lime green shrubs. Stella closed her eyes, feeling like she had been transported to a tropical island. She inhaled, filling her lungs with the coconut- and vanilla-scented air.

"Enjoying the garden, are we?" Rex asked.

"Yes, it's beautiful here. I've never seen flowers like this. It's too bad I can't actually enjoy this."

"Well, we have crews working tirelessly repairing the portal, but I'm afraid you are stuck with us in the meantime. Maybe you can." Rex led her through a maze of thick boxwood shrubs and over a bridge to a clearing where a building sat in the middle of thick cherry blossom trees. "I was hoping we could chat about what happened in Aldemara now."

"Of course," Stella said.

They came to a gray building tucked into the trees. It didn't have any windows or markings of any kind and looked like something one would forget seeing the instant they passed it. Stella's mouth fell open once Rex opened the door. Computer screens lined the walls in the dim room. Stella squinted as her eyes adjusted to the dizzying mix of streaming data and flashing lights. Zimmer ended a call once Stella arrived.

"Good morning," Zimmer said.

"Good morning. What is this place?"

"Oh, a command center, so to speak, and a place where we can speak in private," Rex said.

"We are trying to put together the bits of what you said you saw in Aldemara, but I need more information if we are going to connect the dots," Zimmer said.

"My question is how did Ryder know who you were and where you were?" Rex asked. He pulled up the security feeds from when Stella was taken. "It is known that Ryder can cloak with his coat, which is why he remained undetected. But I can't, for the life of me, understand how he got to you so fast and knew your exact location. Your chip was not active when you were here."

"Did he say anything? Give you any understanding of how he found you?" Zimmer asked.

"No," Stella replied.

"But he was working with someone … the woman who you said assaulted you?" Zimmer pressed.

"Yes, someone named Kandice Shook."

Zimmer plugged the name into the computer. Images of Kandi, including her chip number, popped up. "We will get an operative to do some more digging on her, but yes, we are aware of her. She is Terran, a skilled inventor and engineer, actually. She makes deals and sells her products to whomever is willing to pay the best price, whether they are to be used for good or bad."

"She said she wanted me to go in a tank to 'suck out my healing juices,'" Stella added.

"What in the blazes does that mean?" Rex asked.

"I'm not sure, unless she has found a way to extract out what gives Stella the ability to heal. Hell, I don't know. It doesn't sound good. And it sounds like, if she needs a Healer, she is going to either keep coming for Stella or try to locate the only other Healer in existence," Zimmer said.

"Kate," Rex replied.

"My mother," Stella added. "But we don't know where my mother is."

"We don't now, but there is someone who can aid in our search," Rex said.

Zimmer laughed. "Maren. That's if she agrees to help. She's not as friendly as she used to be."

Stella recognized that name. "Maren? That's my mother's friend. I know her. She came to visit us with another friend named Willow."

Zimmer and Rex exchanged glances.

"Maren and Willow both came to Terra?" Rex asked.

Stella nodded.

"It seems that not all the Keepers were following their own decree of remaining hidden and separated," Rex said.

"We had no idea," Zimmer said. "Well, then Maren should be happy to see Stella at least."

"Why do you say she is not as friendly?" Stella asked.

Rex looked down. "Some of the Keepers changed when they went into hiding. Some have gone to great lengths to deny who they are, to deny what happened in the Great War. The last time I saw Maren, she was moving that way. Our attempts to contact her since have gone unanswered."

"But she can help us find my mother?"

"Yes, she is a Keeper of Mind; she can locate anyone who has ever been connected to you," Zimmer replied. "We need to find your mother before Kandice Shook does."

"We should leave for Vhalis straightaway."

"Vhalis?" Stella asked.

Zimmer cued up images of another planet. "Vhalis is where Maren moved to—Queen Maren, as the people of Vhalis call her."

Rex and Zimmer began to shut down parts of the command center so they could leave.

"Wait, what about the woman who I saw in the tank?" Stella asked.

"Oh yes. Did you get information about who she was?" Zimmer asked.

"I don't know her name, but the woman kept calling her sissy. Ryder's sister?"

Zimmer furrowed his brow. "I don't have any information on Ryder's sister, but I can put some people on it. For now, we need to find Kate. That takes priority. I'll get us ready to depart."

Zimmer rushed out of the building. Before they left, Rex turned to Stella, looking at her with a soft expression. "Did Driver come speak with you last night?"

"He did," Stella said. "It helped a little, but I need more proof."

"And you shall have it. We are about to embark on a journey of proof. Let's get moving, yes?"

"Wait," Stella said, remembering something that had bothered her from last night. "You knew I had lost a patient for the first time. How did you know that?"

Rex cringed. "I'm not sure you want to know this, but it's part of the data on your chip."

"But you seemed to think it was related to all of this—related to my so-called powers. I don't understand."

"I think Maren will be better suited to answer that for you."

# 27

# MARLON'S DEVICE

**AS STELLA AND REX WALKED BACK** to the main house, Zimmer radioed that Rex's ship was refueled and ready. Rex assembled everyone from his home and called for a Hovercar to take them back to the city. "It pleases me to take you to the destination of your choice," said the digital voice in the Hovercar once it pulled up in the driveway.

"To Starport, hangar 11," Rex said. He stepped into the front seat. Stella and Elliot followed, sitting in the second row. Iris jumped in the back with Gary, where he laid his head on her lap. She cooed at him and calmed him down to the point where she could switch him to sleep mode to quell his howls.

"What's in hangar 11?" Stella asked.

Rex leaned back in his seat. "My ship, of course. The vessel Zimmer and I brought to Stallworth's aid was just on loan from one of my colleagues. It was useful for our diplomatic mission, but The Pygmy Train is far too massive for my tastes. My ship is faster and can be run by our small crew here."

Elliot nudged Stella. "Did you hear that? We're part of the crew."

"That you are, Driver, so before we board, you and Stella will have to be fitted for uniforms."

"Why do we have to wear a uniform?" Elliot asked.

"So we know not to shoot you by accident," Rex said, winking.

The Hovercar zoomed above the city of Prehma. Stella closed her eyes. She did not enjoy the feeling of her stomach falling out of her with each shift and random drop of the car. She felt a hand wedge between hers. She normally would have pulled her hand away, but she held onto Elliot, and as she focused on his hand in hers, she was less aware of each subtle shift and drop of the Hovercar.

The Hovercar descended further until it landed in hangar 11. Stella pulled her hand away from Elliot, not wanting to keep holding on now that they were back on the ground. Zimmer and his ugly orange tie were waiting for them. Once they unloaded, Rex had an assistant measure Stella and Elliot for their uniforms.

"What is that?" Elliot asked, squinting to see the darkened object in the hangar's corner.

"This is my ship. Stella, Driver, may I present to you ... Marlon's Device." Rex pointed to the ship with his outstretched arms.

A scream sounded through the hangar as a maintenance worker ran to dodge a hefty metal chunk of the ship's right wing that broke free and hurtled to the floor.

"Looks good," Elliot said. "Uh, do you think we are going to need that piece?"

Rex scratched his head. "Possibly. We will look into that before we leave."

Stella frowned at the stained and tattered vessel that looked like a bulky, iron shark. It had a pointed snout and a fin on top. The glowing lights from the helm created the appearance of eyes. It looked more like a dead animal that washed up on shore than a ship that was ready to take them to the stars.

"While the outside is quite odd, the inside is surprisingly charming," Gary said.

"All right, friends, let's board. We will take off as soon as the uniforms come in and we, uh, repair that part of the wing. Zimmer, won't you uh … yeah," Rex said.

"Such odd names: The Pygmy Train, Marlon's Device," Stella said to Elliot.

He took a moment to answer because he was turning and looking up in all directions as they climbed up the ship's on-ramp. "Well, it's just the way we name boats back home, isn't it? My granddad had a boat in Florida named Gloria's Revenge. It was the one thing my grandma let him keep from the divorce. I bet all these ships have the best stories about how they got their names."

Stella snickered. "Gloria's Revenge, huh?"

"Yeah, she was a beauty."

For all its outward battle scars, the interior of Marlon's Device was cozy and quaint. Though it was not as brightly lit or luxurious as The Pygmy Train, it had character.

"See now—not so bad," Rex said. "Marlon's Device has everything we need."

Zimmer joined them later, announcing that they needed the piece that had fallen off, and asked Iris to join him to ready the ship for takeoff as they waited for the repair.

Stella noticed how relieved Iris was not to have to walk around with the rest of them. Iris always seemed to be in the background, not joining in unless she had a specific task to accomplish. Except for Gary, she didn't really talk to anyone unless they spoke to her first. Strange that someone so quiet surrounded herself with people like Gary and

Rex, who appeared to be warm and outgoing. As if she could feel Stella staring at her, Iris looked over her shoulder as she followed Zimmer to the helm. Iris's frosty glare lingered on Stella, and she wondered why Iris seemed to be especially cold to her.

Elliot caught the glare too but had a different interpretation. "I think she likes me. Do you think she likes me?"

"No. I think the only one she likes is Gary."

Rex was very proud of his ship. He beamed, sharing every detail of the ship while they made their way through it. The med bay contained only two beds, but it still looked as though it had the same technology Stella had noticed on the other ship. The living quarters were modest but decorated with inviting accents. The quarters Rex said Stella would stay in had a plush seating area set into the floor and a bed with a view out a hexagonal window. An emerald green plant with blooming vines curled across the ceiling.

Stella savored the aroma of old books and tobacco when they walked into the library. It reminded her of one her first mentors at the hospital. He had a library just like Rex's and smoked a pipe on his breaks.

"Wow, it's amazing that there are still leather-bound books here," Elliot said, pulling a book off the shelf.

Rex turned toward Elliot. "Why is that amazing?"

"Well, this is outer space. I would have thought printed books would be extinct. Everything digital, you know. A computer that talks to you in your brain, droids everywhere. Even this desk—it has pens and paper."

Rex laughed. "We do embrace some forms of technology— rather, we did—but there has been a movement to hold onto the old ways. We are trying to have more balance. We do employ droids to assist us, but we are sure to program them to have more human characteristics. You see, there was a technologically advanced civilization living on a planet in the system next to Verbatim. Technology did everything for them. It fed them, dressed them, carried them everywhere. We believe their technology even controlled their thinking. They depended so much on technology that they didn't know how to live any other way. They stopped speaking to each other, stopped going outside, stopped caring for their dead. Then, as was the plan all along, the machines rose up and killed them all."

Elliot looked up from the book he was skimming through with a look of terror on his face. "Whoa, I guess I don't feel bad about losing my iPhone."

"Right!" Rex clapped his hands together and then rubbed them eagerly. "Who's hungry? Let's see what we've got to eat around here."

Before anyone could answer, Rex walked out of the library just as Gary walked in. "Uniforms are here. Ship repairs are being completed. We will depart momentarily."

"Where are we going again?" Stella asked.

"Oh, to a haunting place. The planet of Vhalis. Strange and green and lush, filled with dense forests and winding waterways."

"Sounds incredible," Elliot said.

"It's not the scenery that will mystify you, but the inhabitants that may make your stomach turn. I believe there is a book on them." Gary scanned the shelves. "Right—"

"Here," Stella said, pulling out a thick book with *Vhalis and Its People* stamped in gold lettering on the spine.

She handed it to Gary, and he spread it open on the desk.

"They look like birds," Elliot said.

"The Minathi people are humanoid creatures with avian features," Gary added.

"This one looks like an owl," Stella said. The man in the picture was tall and muscular, with brown wings and brown feathers across his chest and eyes. He had tufts of feathers that stood up on his head just like a great horned owl.

"They are exquisite creatures, to be sure, but I must say that I never feel completely at ease on Vhalis. It's the way they look at you," Gary said. "It's like they are working out whether or not they want to dine on your flesh."

Stella cringed. "Can't wait."

"Please, make sure you don't stare at them," Gary continued. "They dislike it when you stare, and believe me, you will want to."

# 28

## SECRETS

**RYDER PAUSED BEFORE HE ENTERED** Kandi's chambers. She had summoned him from his apartment. "I need you," was the message that popped up on his smartwatch. He arrived in Kandi's high-rise moments later.

He cracked his neck and pushed on his knuckles, popping all his joints at once, then straightened his coat. He took a deep breath and buzzed at her door. Her voice told him to come in. Her desk, where she always sat when they met, was empty. Ryder frowned when he found her on the bed. She was wearing nothing but black, lace-embellished lingerie and a black silk robe draped around her.

Kandi leaned her chin on her hand. "Hey, handsome."

"What do you want?" Ryder balled his fists as she slinked out of bed and crept toward him.

"You," she breathed into his ear. Kandi walked around him dragging her hand across his shoulders. She grabbed his leather coat and yanked it down. He spread his arms to stop her.

"What are you doing?" he growled.

"Don't worry, baby. Just think you should take this off for a minute. Get comfortable."

"I'm not worried and I don't want to be comfortable. I want to know why you called me here."

Kandi ignored him and tugged at his jacket. She slid it off and threw it on the powder-pink chaise behind them.

"Unless you have a specific task or requirement ..."

Kandi rubbed his earlobe between her index finger and thumb. "Don't you ever get lonely, honey?"

"No."

"Well, I do. And I think it's time we add another layer to our relationship, don't you baby?"

"We don't have a relationship," Ryder insisted. He tried to remain calm, but the impulse to reach out and strangle her was growing in the pit of his stomach. There were no guards outside, no one to hear her scream.

"I'm sad to hear you say that after all we've been through," Kandi said. She wrapped her arms around his neck.

"I won't ask again. What do you want?" Ryder pushed her away from him, knowing he had to try to make a run for it before he killed her.

"You, silly." Kandi thrust herself onto Ryder, pushing him back onto the chaise. She plunged her mouth onto his, kissing him hard, her nails sinking into his cheeks. He grunted, shoved her away, and wiped his mouth with his forearm. She laughed as she toppled to the floor.

"What's the matter, baby?" She picked herself up and wiped the hair out of her face.

Ryder lunged for his jacket, but she cut him off, kneeling on it. "When are you gonna learn that you are here to do everything I ask of you? And that includes making me feel less lonely." Kandi slinked back to the bed and threw her hair over her shoulder. She tapped on the bed signaling that Ryder should join her.

"Keep the jacket," Ryder said. He rushed toward the door.

Kandi grabbed his coat and ran to the door, blocking his exit. "Relax hero, I'm just playin' with ya. You need to lighten up!"

Ryder snatched his leather coat and slipped back into it. He tried to push past Kandi, but she put up her hands and stopped him again.

"Oh, wait, we're not done here. I still need somethin' from you."

"Then tell me what it is," Ryder said.

Kandi stepped back and cinched her robe tight. "Calm down. I just need you to get something for me from the general's office." Kandi went to her desk and retrieved her phone.

"General Law? Her office is one of the most secure areas in Aldemara."

Kandi giggled. "Oh, that doesn't matter. You're the man for the job. You need to believe in yourself the way I do. Anyway, she's always reading this book, but when I come into her office, she puts it away like she doesn't want me to see it."

"So?"

"So, I don't like it. I want to know what it is." Kandi thumbed through images on her iPhone, finally seeing the one she wanted. She showed Ryder, but all he saw was a book with a leather cover hiding under papers.

"What's so special about this book?"

"That's what I want to know. It's her freaky secret, and I don't like it when peeps keep secrets from me. I don't trust her."

"You work for her. She has no requirement to tell you everything."

"I didn't ask for your opinion. She has a book. Every time I ask her about it, she changes the subject. I want to know what it is and why it's a secret, and I want you, lover, to get it for me."

"And how do you expect me to do that?"

"I'll keep her distracted; you figure it out."

Ryder looked Kandi up and down. "And what happens after this? I'm not going to last much longer being your errand boy."

"Oh, and why do you think you're not going to last?"

"Because every time I see you, I fantasize about wrapping my hands around your neck and squeezing it until it snaps."

The smile dimmed from Kandi's face and her color drained away. "The plan is the same. We need a Healer to close the deal with the Zuldari. You get me a Healer, and we can talk about you and sissy leaving. Until we can find one, you're going to have to keep doing these things."

Ryder knew Kandi was lying, but he also knew he had no other immediate options to rescue Pip.

**RYDER EXHALED AND TIPTOED** through the general's office, undetectable in his cloak. A signal sent from his smartwatch jammed the office's security and sent a false image back of what was happening in the room. He then could move about freely, though he was sure that whatever book Kandi was referring to, he was not going to find it. Lovella prided herself on being organized. Her desk was sparse and neat, with everything in its place even when she had to leave it suddenly. Not a speck of dust nor a rogue fiber existed on any surface. Her office was the perfect reflection of the order she preferred. It made Ryder admire her even more.

Short on time, Ryder skipped the usual places a book would be and focused on an area under her desk where he had caught Lovella placing something when he had entered to see her. There was a small drawer built into the side that, surprisingly, was not locked. Ryder pulled it open, and inside was a book with a tattered leather cover. *The Keepers of the Universe* was stamped into it. This had to be what Kandi was after. An urge to flip through its pages was quashed when he heard movement in the hallway.

He slipped the book into his coat pocket and moved to the wall so he could slip out the door again. A beep from the security pad on the door alerted him. Lovella was back sooner than he expected. The door opened, but Lovella did not walk in. She stopped in the doorway blocking any exit Ryder had.

"What are you doing here, Master Ryder?"

Ryder held his breath again.

"I am not granting you passage. You may as well reveal yourself," Lovella said.

Ryder uncloaked himself.

"I ask you again, why you are here?" Lovella asked.

"Waiting for you," was all he could come up with.

"You know, Master Ryder, you have many skills. Lying is not one of them." She adjusted her thick octagon-shaped glasses and brushed past him. He turned, but lingered in the doorway hoping he could still make his escape. Lovella drilled holes into him with her dark eyes, and he jumped as the door slammed behind him on its own. The lock beeped, signaling that it was activated.

"I will give you one more chance to tell me why you were lurking around my office before I have security come for you."

She sat down behind her desk and folded her hands across her lap.

Ryder sat down in a chair facing her. He knew he could not escape her, but he did not know how to reveal that he had taken the book. He thought of so many other things he could say to lie and get out of the room, but he knew she would see right through him. That's what made her such a good general: she could read people and find their weaknesses. His weakness in that moment was that he did not want to lie or deceive her even if it meant completing a task for Kandi.

Ryder reached into his pocket, pulled out the book, and set it on her desk.

She did not say anything at first. She just looked at the book and then back to Ryder. "Did she put you up to this?"

"She did."

"Then you better give it to her."

Ryder cocked his head, surprised that she would so willingly surrender something she had wanted to hide. "I don't understand."

"That book has only caused me pain. If she wants it, she won't stop until she gets it. It will be more beneficial for you if you complete your task."

"Why are you allowing me to do this?"

"You're a good man, Master Ryder. I want you to know that I disapprove of Kandi's abuse of you and your sister. You did not ask for this. And for this reason, I'm terminating your contract. I will see to it that your sister is revived, and you both are sent home."

Ryder raised his eyebrows. He was not sure he deserved her kindness, and he was speechless, though something told him there was more behind her desire to relieve him of his duties.

"General, I—"

"This is not your fight. While I can't guarantee the protection of your people once Aldemara is fully aligned with the Zuldari, the least I can do is give you the chance to return home and reunite with your family. You have done more than enough for us."

Ryder swallowed, the emotions welling up in his throat. "What about Shook? What of her role?"

Lovella paused. "My fear is that you will be forced to do even more to conspire against me to please Kandi. Her contract is also being terminated, though her fate differs from yours, which is a benefit to both of us. Give her that book. I know it will be returned to me once she is gone."

Ryder rose from his seat. "Thank you."

The corner of Lovella's mouth curled. "I must insist that you do not share this information. Just give her that book and wait for my instructions."

"Understood," Ryder said.

Ryder nodded again and left the room.

\*\*\*

Kandi was waiting for Ryder in her chambers. By the ferocity of her keystrokes, Ryder could tell Kandi was not happy.

"Took you long enough," she said. She looked up from her computer terminals. "Where is it?"

Ryder threw the book on Kandi's desk. Her eyes bulged when she saw it.

"I knew there was something different about her," she said, thumbing through it.

"Why? Why did you want that book?" Ryder asked.

"That's none of your business," Kandi said. She waved him away and Ryder knew that was his cue to exit, but Kandi called to him once more just before he left the room. "Hey hero, that Commander T'Adox is arriving tomorrow. Need you to be there."

Ryder nodded and left. His mouth curved into a smile as he got in the elevator. Soon the nightmare would be over, Pip would be free, and they could all go home. He had planned to storm the lab and rescue Pip on his own. He would be happy to take back control of his life even if he died trying. Having Lovella grant him and Pip their freedom was the best possible outcome. He only hoped Kandi would be sent someplace where she could never terrorize anyone else.

# 29
## CUTS

**AS MARLON'S DEVICE ROCKETED TOWARD** Vhalis, it passed through galaxies and stars and even a giant blue planet with four moons. Stella stood in front of a large window in the med bay as she waited for Rex. Brilliant wisps of magenta, purple, and blue lights moved past the window as the ship moved through space. She heard the door slide open behind her.

"Ahh, there she is," Rex said.

"Hello. What did you want to talk to me about?"

"Your healing abilities. And once we land, we will have you try a flight test."

"A flight test? You want me to fly a plane?"

Rex chuckled. "Oh my, no. Not yet. I want to see how you fly by yourself."

"Like the book says I can? Well, that's easy. I can't fly. That's nonsense."

"We shall see about it being nonsense. Now, back to your healing talents."

Stella glanced around. "Sure. I will need to know how some of this foreign technology works, but otherwise I can help with any medical emergency we encounter."

"No, not the abilities you used on Terra. I'm referring to your other abilities. Those of a Keeper of Healing."

Stella shook her head and she picked up a device that looked like a metal headband from a nearby counter. "Why don't you just show me what this does instead?"

"I need you to trust me and to try. It's time to begin. I want to assess your healing powers so we know what you can do."

Stella put down the device. "Assess away. I told you, I can't do what you think I can."

"You can and you will, and I'm going to show you how." Rex unzipped the jacket of his uniform.

"Whoa, what exactly are you showing me?"

He slung his jacket on the back of a lab chair. "Try to calm yourself."

"Trust me, I'm perfectly calm."

Rex rifled through a cabinet and came back to Stella with a scalpel. Stella watched in horror as he dragged the scalpel across the flesh of his forearm. Blood pooled and dripped from the wound, creating a rivulet that streamed behind the blade.

"What are you doing?!"

"It's as I told you. We are," Rex said between cringes, "going to work on your healing."

"Stop!"

"Clear your mind for a moment and focus on the wound."

Blood splattered on the steel floor.

"I can't do this with my mind. Do you have any gauze?" Stella turned to look through the cabinets. Rex stopped her by grabbing her hand.

"I don't need any cloth to stop the bleeding. I just need you. Bring your hand up. He guided her hand until it was hovering over the wound. "And then visualize the blood stopping, the skin healing, the wound reversing."

Stella tried to steady her hand.

Rex spoke in a soft tone. "See yourself repairing this wound the way you would normally … see the steps you would take … see it being cleaned … then see it closing."

Stella's hand jolted as she tried to follow Rex's instructions. A droplet of blood that had dripped off the skin reversed its course midway from Rex's arm and the floor. Moving in a circular motion, the droplet climbed back up to where it came from.

"Focus on the wound; focus on the healing," Rex said.

Her heart pounded in her ears, and her breath quickened. The droplet of blood stopped as it neared Rex and spun around. Stella's hand shook violently, and pain from what felt like lighting shot up her arm. The blood droplet stopped spinning and fell to the floor. A green spark flew out of Stella's hand, stinging Rex in the arm. She yelped when they both received a shock from it and Rex recoiled from the zap.

"I'm sorry."

"It's okay," Rex said. He grabbed a rag from a nearby tray and blotted the wound. "It's what I needed to see."

"I told you," Stella said.

Rex picked up a C-shaped electronic device that was no bigger than a pen. It had blinking red lights on each end. Rex placed it over his wound. Moments later the device's lights turned green, and when Rex peeled off the device the wound was gone.

"There now. All better."

"Why don't you show me how things like that work instead. That's how I can help you."

Rex smiled at Stella, and she could tell there was something else on

Rex's mind. She had a feeling that he was not going to give up on trying to make her believe, but she told herself that what just happened was proof that she was not who they thought she was.

Rex agreed to show Stella how the technology of medical equipment was not what she was used to. This was something Stella enjoyed, and she was even more pleased when Rex informed her that she would receive her own utility belt with some of the different medical tools included.

"I'm not wearing that uniform, though," Stella said. She remembered holding it up when Gary had brought it to her room and wondering how anyone could move around in something that felt so stiff.

"Oh?"

"They don't look very comfortable."

"Well for now, you can just wear your utility belt."

Elliot walked in, having tried his uniform on. He pulled and tugged at it. "Wow, this is not comfortable."

"You get used to it," Rex replied.

"I like how it automatically closes in the back when you put it on, but yeah, this is not going to be my weekend wear."

The suit fit him like a second skin and hugged every muscle Elliot had. He may not have been a real warrior as Rex and crew thought, but he looked the part, especially when Rex fitted him with his own utility belt.

"What's this do?" Stella asked, pointing to a sack of round objects that looked like marbles.

"Those are mini-hydrazone bombs. They are activated only when thrown at objects." Rex pointed to another gadget on both of their belts. "This will heal superficial wounds and ease pain with the press of a button. This object can stun someone for twelve hours, and this will burn through any substance.

"What do you usually take into combat, Driver? I really want to hear more about your past exploits." Rex patted Elliot on the back so hard Elliot coughed.

"Oh, you know…just…lots of bombs and guns and stuff," Elliot said, tugging at his collar again.

"Excellent. Do you prefer railguns or coilguns?" Rex asked.

Elliot wiped the sweat off his brow. "Yep."

Stella decided to interrupt. "Uh, I really was hoping Elliot could help me with something. He can help me with my gun—how to shoot it I mean." Stella grabbed Elliot's arm and took him out of the med bay.

"Thank you," Elliot said once they were out of earshot. He tried to pull the uniform sleeves down on his arms. "Oh my God, what is a railgun? I hope I never find out."

"You really need to tell them," Stella insisted.

"I'll tell them when you tell them your thing."

"Not going to happen because there is nothing to tell."

"Hey, how come you don't have on your uniform?"

"Rex said I didn't have to wear it."

Elliot scoffed. "Teacher's pet." He finally stopped fidgeting in his uniform when they reached the door of Stella's living quarters. "What are you going to do now? Do you want me to come in and show you how to use that gun?"

Stella chuckled when he winked at her. "Is there something in your eye, Mr. Driver?"

"Right, fine. I'll go see what Iris thinks of my uniform."

"I'm sure you will impress her. Just don't wink at her."

# 30
## DAMAGED

**STELLA STILL HAD TO SHUT HER EYES** as the ship flew low over the thick canopy of trees after breaking through Vhalis' atmosphere. The clearing they eventually found to land in was cramped and overgrown with mangled brush, and the ship creaked and rattled as it touched down on a patch of grass. She gulped. She was not sure how she was supposed to ever fly when her feet felt so much better on the ground.

"Oh, this thick air! My hair does not appreciate it," Gary said. "Though I do hope we get to stay in the same tree house as we did after the battle of Darna Thun. The feather bed in that one was divine."

"We are not on holiday, Gary," Iris said.

Two Minathi women stood on the edge of a riverbank just off the clearing and were waiting to take them to see Queen Maren. One woman had bright orange feathers that covered her chest and arms. Flaming red feathers went up from the base of her neck, stretched out over the sides of her cheeks and formed tufts on the top of her head. The other woman had dark feathers that framed her yellow eyes. Both were tall and thin with gangly arms and legs. Stella caught herself staring until Gary nudged her. They held spears that ran the length of their lithe bodies, and both bowed when Rex approached. Rex kicked a leg back and bowed as well.

"Everyone," Rex began motioning toward the two women. "This is Savu," he said to the bright red feathered woman, "and this is Teek." The owl-like woman bowed. "Thank you, dear ladies, for granting us safe haven on your wondrous world."

"The Queen expects you," Savu said in a raspy voice.

A boat was waiting to take them into the heart of what was called the Queen's Realm. It rocked, disturbing the water, as everyone piled in. Savu rowed with a long staff, pushing them down the river.

Stella had never been comfortable in nature. The city's noises and movement she understood. She knew how to navigate through the streets of New York City, but the woods and trees unsettled her because she did not know what to expect. The scenery above her was beautiful. Bugs that resembled fireflies danced in and out of the trees. Twinkling lights from tree houses added a golden glow to the twilight. Minathi men and woman came to their porches to peek at the visitors floating through the village. A network of bridges covered in vines connected each house. A child with bright pink feathers scampered out to a bridge that crossed over the river; she waved so excitedly at Stella that a single feather from her crown floated down and touched the water.

The boat made its way through the village and came to a dense patch of woods with a single dock that was overgrown with moss.

"We have arrived," Savu said.

One by one, the crew unloaded onto the dock.

Elliot whispered to Stella. "I don't see anything."

Teek appeared behind them and whispered, "Through here."

Elliot nodded nervously.

"Why was she looking at you like that?" Stella asked.

"Either she's flirting with me or she wants to eat me."

"Both those scenarios sound frightening," Stella replied.

Elliot cringed. "Yikes, she does look like a bird of prey."

The trees opened and revealed a larger, more ornate tree house. There were three levels that connected with twisting staircases. On the very top level, Minathi guards provided lookout over the Queen's expanse. Stella took a deep breath as she neared. She remembered Maren being more reserved than her mother or Willow, but Stella also remembered her being kind and gentle, a nice balance to Willow and her mother's outgoing nature.

*I wonder if she is even going to remember me. What do I say if she doesn't?*

Teek and Savu led the crew up a wide set of stairs. Symbols Stella did not recognize were carved into each step. They halted once they reached two heavy doors with more symbols carved into them. Two Minathi men stood on either side. A boom sounded when the men pulled the doors open.

"This way," Savu said.

"I'll wait here," Iris said. She took a seat on the porch in a chair made from chunky branches while the rest of the crew went in.

The interior of the tree house did not look fit for a queen; rather it looked like the modest home of an older woman. A fire crackled from a potbellied stove in the corner; a knitted afghan was slung over a woven wooden chair. Tattered stone tiles covered the floor, and oil lamps provided soft light in the house.

"Stella?" said a voice behind them.

Stella stifled a gasp. The woman standing in front of her was far from the woman she met so long ago. The woman who had visited her mother was young with wavy raven hair. Though she was short, she was shapely and had stunning olive skin that did not have one line or crease.

The woman standing before her looked as though she aged forty years in the last ten. Her hair was now ghost white, her skin pale and wrinkled. Deep scars went up and down from her left eye and she looked thin, almost frail. She was dressed in a black flowing dress with a high collar and long sleeves that almost covered her hands in their entirety.

"Maren," Stella said.

Maren crept toward her and then flung her slender arms around Stella. The second they embraced, a pop of green light connected between them and shot up through the middle of their bodies into the air. Stella and Maren stood apart for a moment, staring with mouths open.

"What was that?" Gary asked.

"It's two Keepers connecting," Zimmer said.

Maren smiled and hugged Stella again. "I almost didn't believe it when Rex sent his message that he was bringing you to see me." Her eyes began to tear up. She pushed hair out of Stella's face and cupped it with her hands. "It's so wonderful to see you, my dear."

"It's good to see you. I wasn't sure if you would remember me," Stella said. She felt a lump in the back of her throat. Maren was her mother's friend, and by seeing her, memories of those days with her mother came flooding back. Stella hugged Maren again and squeezed her tight.

"How could I ever forget you?" Maren asked. Slowly, the deep scar around Maren's eye began to diminish bit by bit until it was almost gone. Stella took a step back. Maren touched her face, feeling the smoother area around her eye, and gasped.

"Rex did not mention that your powers were so strong," Maren said.

"Because they aren't," Stella replied.

Maren narrowed her eyes and changed the subject. "Oh my, where are my manners? Rex, so happy to see you."

Maren welcomed the other crew members.

"And who is this?" Maren asked once she saw Elliot waiting patiently with his hands behind his back.

Elliot pulled at his uniform collar. "Oh, hi. I'm Elliot. Elliot Driver."

"A new Sentinel, I see," Maren said.

"Well, I'm more of a trainee. I'm actually her sidekick." Elliot pointed to Stella.

"She is lucky to have you," Maren smiled broadly. "Welcome, all of you, to Vhalis."

"Most appreciated, Queen Maren," Rex said.

"Please call me Maren. That's how you always knew me, Finnieous." Maren grasped Rex's hands.

"Of course. I was not sure how it was with you. We have tried to reach out many times, to no avail," Rex said.

Maren's gaze hit the floor. "A regret I have now, but I just couldn't ..." Her voice trailed off, and her gaze fixed on an empty corner of the room.

"We should leave you," Zimmer interjected. "Seems like you and Stella have some catching up to do."

"Maren, may Iris and I stay in that lovely bungalow I had before? The one right over the water?" Gary asked.

Maren smiled. "Of course, my dear."

Gary hugged Maren and left with the others. Rex remained with Stella.

"Stella, you certainly have grown into a beautiful young woman," Maren said.

Stella blushed and looked at the floor. "Thank you."

"As much as seeing you brings me joy, I must ask ... what are you doing here?"

Images of the events that led up to the moment when she walked into Maren's house ran through Stella's mind like a bad movie. "It's a long story," she said.

"I appreciate you seeing us, but I must say that this is not a casual visit. We need your help," Rex added.

Maren's soft expression disappeared. "Let's sit, shall we?"

They followed her to a seating area in front of the potbellied stove. "What help could I possibly be, Finnieous?"

"We need your help locating my mother," Stella interjected.

Maren raised her eyebrows. "Kate? I haven't seen her. The last time I saw her was on Terra all those years ago. I don't know where she is. Is she in danger somehow?"

"We are not sure, but we know something devastating may happen that can affect us all if she is not found," Rex said.

"We have all been in hiding for so long now. I thought the point of our isolation was not to be found."

"Yes, but there is another party searching for her. We believe they are working with the Zuldari and mean to use Kate's healing abilities for nefarious purposes."

Maren cleared her throat and swallowed. "The Zuldari?"

"Yes, they have recently resurfaced and—"

"As I said, I have not seen her in years. I'm afraid I don't know how to locate her," Maren said.

"It is our hope that you could work with Stella to try," Rex suggested.

Maren's face tightened. "I'm sorry both of you came so far, but I haven't used my abilities in years. We were supposed to repress them, which I have done."

"Maren please, I need to find her," Stella added.

Maren shot up from her chair. "I'm sorry. I can't do this. What I experienced in the Great War was nothing I care to experience again. I lost my husband and my son in that war. I came here to try to forget. I'm sorry. I can't help you."

Maren walked out of the room. She started to ascend the spiral staircase that was just off the seating area. "You all are welcome to remain on Vhalis for as long as you please. My apologies. I'm sure you can locate Kate another way. Good night."

Stella and Rex watched as she disappeared into the upstairs.

"So that's it?"

Rex rubbed his mustache. "It is as I feared. Let's let her be for tonight."

"Let her be? She has to help us."

Savu and Teek reemerged to show them to the door. Rex gently pulled on Stella's arm. Stella wanted to run up the stairs after Maren, but Savu and Teek made it clear that was not an option when they blocked her path.

"We can try again in the morning. Seeing you must have been quite a shock for her. I think giving her space tonight is the right thing."

The others were waiting for Stella and Rex outside.

"That was fast," Zimmer said.

"You found Kate already?" Gary asked.

Rex patted Stella on the back as she walked down the steps of the tree house. "Tonight was not the right time. Come, let's all retire and get some rest. I will try to speak with Maren in the morning." Rex followed Savu and Teek back to the boat. He and Zimmer whispered out of earshot. Stella and Elliot walked behind Gary and Iris.

"What did she say?" Elliot asked.

Stella stared at the ground. "She said she lost too much in the war and that she can't help us."

"That's terrible."

"She has to help. She and my mother were best friends. How could she not want to find her? I can't believe she just looked at me, said no, and then left."

"Well, isn't that what you did the other night?"

Stella stopped walking and grabbed Elliot's arm. "What did you say?"

Elliot gulped. "When we were at Rex's house and they told you about your mother and you said you couldn't help. Isn't that the same thing?"

"No, that is not the same thing, I ... that was different. Her friend is in danger."

"I think the person you need to talk to is yourself. You can't really ask her to help when you weren't exactly willing to do so."

Stella scowled, turned, and stormed away. She made it to the boat first and did not say a word as Savu rowed everyone to their accommodations for the night. Savu led Stella to her bungalow first. Stella had to steady herself when she followed Savu up a moss-covered bridge. The bridge squeaked under their footsteps, and Stella recoiled when she touched the railing. Dew from the thick forest air had made the twine slimy.

"You shall stay here," Savu said, opening the bungalow door. Stella thanked her and closed the door behind her.

She sat on a carved wooden stool in the room. A slip-like nightgown and matching robe were draped on the bed, and water with cut lemons and limes were laid out on a table made from woven grass threads. She slipped into the nightgown, which felt like luxurious silk next to her skin. She had a sip of water, but she couldn't stop pacing around the room. She was still fuming over what Elliot had said to her and not sure she could just settle down for the night. She heard him say goodnight to Gary and then the sound of a door closing. She paced the room, trying to think of the most appropriate way to respond to his comments. She had no choice. What she had to say couldn't wait. She stormed up another section of bridge and then pounded on Elliot's door.

# 31

## NEW BIC

**KANDI STRODE UP TO THE ELEVATOR,** waiting for it to hit the floor she was on. The door opened, revealing Lovella, whose calm expression dissolved into a scowl when Kandi joined her.

"Hello General Law. What's wrong? You look madder than a wet hen."

Lovella took a deep breath and shook her head. "What do you think you're doing?"

"Uh, I'm riding up to your office with you so we can plan for tomorrow's meeting with that T'Adox guy."

"You know I'm referring to that hideous piece of … I don't even know if there's a name for what you're wearing."

Kandi flipped her hair off her shoulder. "This is a pink, glossy, latex bodysuit."

Lovella looked up at the ceiling. "Elevator, stop."

"What? You told me I should be in uniform, and I was like, *you know, she is absolutely right.*"

"You will change out of that and be issued a standard office uniform after our meeting."

"The men of Aldemara really seem to enjoy this. Besides, pink can be professional. It's not what you're wearing; it's how you wear it, sweetie."

"I hope you understand; I put up with your constant impudence toward me because of what you contribute to this planet, but I will reach my limit," Lovella said, restarting the elevator.

"You've reached your limit, all right," Kandi mumbled.

"What did you say?"

"Nothing. Let's do this."

Lovella charged out of the elevator and entered the security protocols to open her office. She froze once she did so. Commander T'Adox was sitting in her chair. Four guards stood around him holding rifles, and Ryder stood in the center of the room with his revolver in his outstretched hand.

Commander T'Adox tapped his rubbery fingertips on her desk. He rotated his translator device, a small disc-shaped object attached to his neck, to English. "So good of you to join us," he said.

"Commander, I thought our meeting was not until tomorrow," Lovella said.

"We determined it would be more beneficial to meet at this moment."

"We? Excuse me? Who are you referring to as *we*?" Lovella asked.

Kandi slinked out from behind Lovella, bumping her shoulder as she walked past her.

"Me is we," Kandi said.

"What is this?" Lovella asked, her eyes bulging.

"Isn't it obvious? You are being relieved of your duties, General Law," T'Adox said.

Lovella's eyes narrowed. "That's impossible."

"Actually, it's not," Kandi said. "Looks like we don't need you anymore, baby."

"What did you do?" Lovella asked through clenched teeth.

"Made a new deal that does not include your sorry ass," Kandi replied.

T'Adox stood up from the chair. Kandi recoiled, seeing the shimmer of slime he left behind. She motioned to Ryder. "Search her."

Ryder hesitated, but then walked to Lovella.

He lifted three knives, a stun gun, and a blaster from inside the long vest she was wearing. He looked away from her but kept his gun steady.

T'Adox walked toward Lovella with his hands behind his back. "As part of my renegotiation with Aldemara, I have requested that you be replaced with Ms. Shook. She seems to have a better grasp on how we can obtain our goals. And you have now become more valuable to us as trade for the Sekke, which will allow us to free three of our military elders.

A wave of horror swept across Lovella's face.

Kandi grinned. "That's right. I'm the new bitch in charge. You're done."

"You cannot do this," Lovella growled.

"It is done," T'Adox said. "And we will see to it that you won't pose any interruptions to our collaboration."

"What are you saying?' Lovella asked.

"We know who you are," Kandi said. She threw Lovella's copy of *The Keepers of the Universe* onto the floor at Lovella's feet.

The color drained from Lovella's face. Kandi could hardly contain her excitement from seeing Lovella stripped of all her power and humiliated in her very own office.

"A brilliant but dangerous game you were playing, General Law, and one I'm afraid you have lost," T'Adox said. "I have to hand it to you.

You've done an admirable job of keeping your identity a secret."

"Neither of you will see this to its end," Lovella said.

"I wouldn't worry about us, honey. I'd start worrying about where you're going to find your end and, for now, that's gonna be in a pit on Kodon."

Kandi nodded to Ryder, who approached Lovella and fastened electronic cuffs around her wrists. Two of T'Adox's guards snatched her arms.

"T'Adox, you will regret putting your faith in this wretched woman. You know she is not of our world," Lovella insisted.

"That may be, but she has presented me with an aggressive new strategy that will allow us to significantly advance our efforts. Now if you don't mind, we have more business to attend to," T'Adox said.

The guards dragged Lovella from the room. Ryder closed his eyes and clenched his jaw. Kandi knew Ryder liked Lovella, which made it all the better that Kandi finally got rid of her. She was surprised that Lovella didn't fight back more. Kandi thought she was stronger than that.

"Do not be sullen, Master Ryder. You will be rewarded for your efforts here," T'Adox said.

Ryder turned and stood with his feet apart and his arms crossed in front of him. "I want only for my sister to be released. That is all," Ryder said.

"Ms. Shook has assured me that will occur when we finally acquire the Healer. Do we have an understanding, Master Ryder?" T'Adox asked.

Ryder hesitated and nodded before leaving the room.

# 32

# COMPLICATIONS

**RYDER BOLTED FROM LOVELLA'S OFFICE.** Even cracking his neck could not bring the release he needed from having to watch Lovella being dragged off. He only hoped that the small blaster he put back into her vest when he was searching her would help her in some way. Ryder pressed for the elevator, and when the door opened Taylor was waiting for him inside.

"Oh, hey."

Ryder stopped in the doorway of the elevator. "What do you want?"

"Nothing, but Kandi wanted me to give this to you. Are you getting in or what?"

Ryder entered and Taylor handed him a glass ball about the size of a marble. Ryder opened his palm and within seconds, the glass ball projected a message in the air. Ryder's heart sank as he read it. It contained the instructions for his next task, his final task.

"No," Ryder said. "I won't do this."

"Yeah, Kandi thought you might say that, so she wrote one more message into the orb. Keep watching."

Ryder looked down at his hand again. An image of his brother, Hunter, appeared. Hunter was walking into a building out of a blizzard of snow. "What is this?"

Taylor rolled his eyes. "What? You don't recognize your own brother? That's right, Hunter survived the blast and we caught up with him on Heelo, that yucky ice planet. Don't worry. Kandi's dogs are watching him. Finish this task, and she calls off the dogs. If you don't, well, you know what she's capable of."

The image of Hunter dissipated, and the glass ball evaporated into a mist that wafted out of his hand. Ryder would have punched Taylor in the face to purge some of the rage flowing through him, but the elevator door opened to the lobby and Taylor sauntered out waving goodbye as if he and Ryder had finished a friendly chat.

Taylor dropped the coffee he was holding. Ryder stepped out to see the two guards who had taken Lovella dead on the floor, with blood pooling around them. The metal cuffs lay broken in half. The blaster he slipped her lay on the ground next to one of the dead men. Ryder coughed to stop himself from smiling.

# 33

## VISITOR

**ELLIOT OPENED THE DOOR**, and before he could even open his mouth, Stella said "You were right."

His cheeks dimpled, and he leaned his head up against the door for a moment and then signaled that she should come in. The bungalow's roof was made of thatched reeds that formed a chevron pattern. In the center of the room was a circular bed with a twenty-foot-tall canopy that draped over it. A clay-domed fireplace stood off the to the right, and an S-shaped sofa separated the bed from the fireplace. The Minathi had lit candles that left a soft glow in the room. Elliot had already changed into pinstripe pajamas.

"Nice pajamas," Stella noted.

"Right? Not sure how every alien species out here knows what size I am, but I decided not to question it. So, what are you going to do?" Elliot took a seat at a thick, oblong wooden table and Stella followed.

"I didn't realize how it felt to be told no until it was said to me," Stella said. "I was so angry that Maren dismissed me like that, but you were right—I had done the same thing. I know now that I've got to find my mother even if I don't believe it all. I have to do something."

"That's awesome. I can't wait to see what you can do with those green sparks. Do you want to look through the tablet with me? Rex gave me another one he had on the ship," Elliot said.

"No, I want to go talk to Maren."

"Wait, tonight?"

Stella got up and pushed her stool in. "I need to convince her to help us. It can't wait."

"Fine, I'll go with you," Elliot said.

"That's okay."

"You want to walk to Maren's house, in a nightgown, on a strange planet full of creepy bird people, and you don't want me to go with you?"

Stella smiled. "I'll be fine. Maybe that one bird woman can escort me. Plus, I know I won't be able to sleep, and I need some fresh air."

"Uh, have you smelled the air? It's not fresh." He searched through the room for his shoes. "It's smells like my high school locker room out there."

"Elliot."

"Besides, we know those bird people live here; what about the things out there they didn't tell us about?"

"Elliot."

"Not that you are not capable. Obviously, you can take care of yourself. I'm just a worrier. I mean, people you can handle, but how about some prehistoric flying ant, which I'm sure lives in the trees."

"Elliot," Stella insisted. She grabbed his arm to stop him from pacing the room in search of his shoes. "Look, if I'm not back in twenty minutes, send help."

"Twenty minutes? How the hell am I supposed to tell time right now?"

"You'll figure it out," she said as she closed the door behind her.

The mossy wooden bridge moaned under her feet. She made her way down a series of steps to the forest floor. The breeze shifted, and she thought she saw a shadow dart across the path. A shiver bolted through her, but she kept walking straight down the road. She thought she remembered the way to the boat, and she walked where she thought they had come from when they returned from Maren's house.

Elliot was right; the air was not fresh but damp and stiff, and it sat on her like a thick cloud. Sounds of creatures chirping and humming as they called to each other through the trees signaled that nightly activities had begun.

The brush rustled to the right of her, and she could see only misty darkness as she peered in. A crack of twigs caught her ears, and she left the path and moved through the trees, hesitating for a moment before stepping into the bushes. Prickly bumps popped up on her forearm, but she continued to trek deeper into the woods. As she cleared vines from her view, a mass of dark birds rushed out of the trees, swarming her. She screamed and shielded her face, clinging to a heavy tree trunk as they blitzed past her, until one after another, they flew away screeching into the night.

She took a deep breath and pushed herself away from an enormous tree trunk, walking right into the end of a revolver with a glowing blue light cutting through the center. Ryder stood with his arm outstretched as he crept out of the brush. She backed up, her chest feeling like it was going to collapse.

"They thought you were dead," she said.

Ryder stood with his revolver extended. "I'm hard to kill."

"Well," Stella said, her heart pounding in her ears. "What are you waiting for?"

Ryder's eyes widened. "Quiet!"

"You want to hurt me. Go ahead. Just do it."

Ryder took a step back but kept his gun trained on her. Stella couldn't help but stare at his red eye. She wondered how the machine parts worked with the other parts of his skin, face, and internal systems. Around the red eye, small scars jutted out and cut like angry rivers into his cheek and forehead.

"I told you before, stop staring!" Ryder seethed. He threw her back against the tree and drove the revolver into her shoulder.

"What happened to you?" Stella asked.

"That's not your concern," Ryder said. Stella winced as Ryder jabbed her shoulder with more force. Her robe had slipped in their brief struggle, revealing the freckles on her fair skin and the rest of her scarred shoulder. Stella saw his eyes drop down to the remnants of where a bullet had torn through her flesh so long ago. Ryder's jaw tightened and then he swallowed. He stepped back, releasing her as he lowered his revolver. His eye bounced between her shoulder and her eyes.

*What's he doing? Why is he hesitating?*

An uneasy silence passed between them as they just stared at each other. Stella knew Ryder did not want to hurt her. Ryder was only trying to free his sister, and Stella was overwhelmed with the urge to try to help him. Just like the day the deranged man burst into the hospital with a gun. Stella tried to calm that man down; she tried to get through to him. Even though her life was in danger, she could not quell the urge to try to help, just as she felt now. The difference between the two moments was that Stella could see that Ryder's blue eye was still clear and full of color. The other man, who ended the lives of so many that day in the hospital, had eyes that had turned from green to black. It was like a switch had been flipped in him and there was no turning back. Stella did not see that in the man standing in front of her now.

The forest rustled behind them, but they ignored the sounds. Stella could see Ryder's blue eye dilate in the moonlight that sprinkled across their faces. Stella tilted her head; she moved closer.

"Who did this to you?" she asked.

Ryder didn't answer.

"I told the Sentinels about your sister. They are trying to find a way to help. If you just come with me to—"

"I said be quiet!" Ryder shook his head and brought his gun back up. "There's only one way you can help me."

"Come with me. Come talk to Captain Rex. He will help you."

"I doubt that."

"We all have choices," Stella said. "You can make a different one right now."

"I'm sorry," he whispered.

Ryder's finger touched the trigger, but Stella rushed him, shoving his arm up and away from her head. A blast of blue light exploded from the gun, narrowly missing her left ear. It hit the tree trunk behind her, spitting bark back at them.

The sound of something flying through the air cut through the leaves. Ryder cried out as a dart hit the back of his thigh. Another dart hit his neck, and another struck his hand. A second force flew in and flipped Ryder onto his back, then dragged him out of the bushes back to the path. Savu towered over him; Teek landed and pointed an electrified spear at his neck. Voices called out down the path. Elliot and the others sprinted toward her.

"Good God," Rex panted. "Ryder!"

Elliot reached out for Stella. "I don't know how long it was; it just didn't feel right."

Iris stared at Ryder's body with wild eyes. "I thought you said he was dead?"

"He was," Gary said, hunched over grabbing his knees and gasping for air. "I shot him myself."

"Gary, please, you are not out of breath," Iris said. She kicked the revolver out of Ryder's hand.

"How do you know?" Gary asked.

"Because you do not have lungs!" Iris spat.

"How did he find us again?" Rex asked. "Did your tracker light go off, Stella?"

"No."

"Of course it went off. That's how he found us," Iris said, scowling at Stella. "Captain, she is nothing more than a liability to us."

"I think I would know if a flashing blue light erupted under my skin," Stella said, glaring back at Iris.

"Would you?" Iris asked.

"That's enough!" Rex shouted. "Let's focus on Ryder for the moment." Rex kicked Ryder in the side. "How did you find us, Ryder? Did you come alone?"

"Forget it. He's not going to talk to you," Iris said.

"Are you all right?" Zimmer asked Stella.

She nodded and pulled bark out of her hair.

"Who is this man? He injured two shepherds of our watch," Teek asked. Ryder began to twitch and writhe from the Minathi poison eating its way through his veins.

Stella rubbed her neck. "We have to help him."

"Help him?" Rex asked.

"What is this? What's going on?" Everyone turned to see Maren running down the opposite path, followed by two Minathi men.

"Apologies, Maren. It seems this mercenary has been tracking Stella for some time. It's lucky for us we caught him," Rex said.

Stella turned to Maren. "What did they hit him with?"

"He has been poisoned from our darts. Most poisons take hold quickly, ours works slowly to cause the most pain," Maren said.

Sweat erupted over Ryder's pale face. Maren touched Stella's arm, and when she met Maren's eyes, Stella could tell she was questioning her even though Maren had not said a word.

"We can take him to the ship and put him in a HydrAtank to try to slow the poison. Then, maybe we can question him," Zimmer offered.

Ryder's body went limp on the ground, his head slacked to one side.

"Better do this with haste. Looks like that poison is working faster than it's supposed to. If we don't get him in the tank, he may not be of much help to us."

# 34

## TURN

GARY MORPHED INTO HIS SILVER mechanical form, threw Ryder's unconscious body over his shoulder, and started back to Marlon's Device with Iris and Zimmer.

"That man …" Maren started, "he is working with the Zuldari?"

"In a way, yes, although we have reason to believe he is not doing so by choice, but to free a captured family member," Rex said.

"Nevertheless, the Zuldari are mobilizing, aren't they?"

"That is what we fear," Rex replied.

Maren glanced up into the stars and then back down at Rex and Stella. "Which means that they won't stop until they have what they want."

Stella wanted to say something to urge Maren to help, but she waited, hoping Maren was coming to that conclusion on her own.

"Let's take a turn through my garden," Maren said.

Stella, Rex, and Elliot followed Maren back to her tree house. Rex and Elliot remained behind while Maren and Stella entered the garden. They walked on a narrower dirt path that was surrounded by giant forms of flowers Stella thought she had seen back home. Red poppies, iris, and sunflowers as tall as Stella lined the edge of the passage, and they all seemed to glow in moonlight.

"Stella, I want to apologize for my behavior earlier," Maren said. "It was such a shock to see you. And the moment I knew you were here, I realized that Kate must be in danger. I was … overwhelmed."

"I understand. I've felt the same way."

"Kate never told you? She never mentioned who we really are?"

"No, she didn't. She read me that book, but made it sound like it was simply a bedtime story. Once she was gone, I locked the book away in a safe. Never thought about it until the night I lost my patient."

"Patient? You did take on a medical profession then? When I saw you last, you were just starting school."

"I finished school and became a surgeon. I hadn't lost a patient in five years until the night they abducted me."

Maren sighed. "More proof to me that your mother is not well."

"Why do you say that?"

"In all my years, I had never seen a more powerful Healer than your mother. When she had you, I knew you had the potential to be the same. Your mother's strength was passed to you and remained with you all those years even after she was gone. If your powers of healing dimmed so that you lost a patient, it means she is losing power, like we all have because of our separation from one another. I fear her condition must be getting worse. If we lose Kate, we will lose all of us."

"Then help us … help us find her."

Maren turned to Stella and cupped her face with her hand. "I will do all I can."

Stella swallowed the lump in her throat. "Thank you, Maren."

Maren took her hand and led her to a stone bench that sat on the edge of a small pond. "Give me both of your hands."

Stella looked down at Maren's hands in hers and was shocked at the sight of them. They were spotted, wrinkled, and gray. The skin was so thin Stella could almost see the blood pumping through Maren's veins.

"What Keepers have is something we call the Connection ... our connection to each other. The Connection is the current that flows through all the Keepers, and it only grows stronger when we come together. Our powers are then amplified. When I connect with you, I can see anyone you know as long as you are picturing them. Once you think of Kate and keep her steady in your mind, I can then focus on her and I will be able to see where she is."

They both closed their eyes, although Stella kept opening hers a crack to see what Maren was doing. Maren became still and silent. She didn't move, not even a flutter. She just squeezed Stella's hands. Stella felt more alive than ever as what felt like electric current ran through her from Maren's grasp. Stella's heart raced, and a vision of her mother appeared in her mind as if out of a mist.

"I can see her ... she is unwell ... unsafe," Maren said.

"Where is she?" Stella insisted.

"Picture her ... focus, and I will find her."

Stella opened her eyes briefly and saw Maren's eyes flutter under their lids.

"Focus," Maren said. "I can see her, but not where she is."

Stella closed her eyes all the way this time and envisioned her mother reading the book to her. Stella was cuddled in bed facing her mother, watching her mother read the book. Her mother's face would get more animated when she read over parts of the story with more action, and Stella would laugh at the funny faces she made when she was reading.

"She is ... on Kodon ... office building A ... third level ... room 181," Maren said. Maren opened her eyes and exhaled. Maren's gaze shot to her hands, and Stella looked on with her mouth agape. Color flowed back into Maren's hands, and they turned from gray to a warm and fleshy pink. Veins that were once visible disappeared under the now plumped skin. Their fragility vanished, and Maren squeezed Stella with a renewed strength.

"How did they change like that?" Stella asked.

"From our connection," Maren said. She smiled and looked at her hands, flipping them open so she could see her restored palms as well. "You did this with your healing. And once we reunite you with your mother, you will grow even stronger. I see your healing is coming along, but how is your flying?"

Stella swallowed. "Why is everyone asking about that? I hate being in the air. Not sure I will ever fly."

A smile crept across Maren's face. "That may be for now, but that's definitely going to change, my dear."

Stella embraced Maren when she got up from the bench. Stella had never been one to show affection, mostly because she went so long without receiving any herself, but she felt the connection she had with Maren and knew it meant she was that much closer to her mother.

"Let's tell Rex so you all can be on your way. Although, I'm alarmed by the fact that we found Kate on the planet Kodon; that is truly a dreadful place."

"I'm prepared for anything at this point … well, except for flying."

Maren smirked. "Not easy to prepare when you don't know what is about to happen. What you really need to prepare yourself for is the possibility of having to trade a life for your mother's. You have been saving lives all this time, Stella. What you have to ask yourself is, are you prepared to end a life if you have to?"

This was a question Stella never thought she would have to answer. Her oath had been to do no harm. She never questioned whether a life should be saved. She did her job no matter who was on her operating table. There were times in her career when someone wounded would be wheeled in only to be followed by the person who wounded them. She didn't ask questions about their character; she just went to work.

"Hopefully, I won't have to make that choice," Stella said.

"This choice will be forced upon you at some point on this journey, and there will be consequences either way. You must prepare yourself for that."

Stella relayed her mother's location when they returned to Rex and Elliot. Rex's face twisted into a frown when Stella mentioned Kodon.

"Come with us," Stella said. "Mom would want you to be there when we find her."

Maren massaged her hands. "I'm afraid I'm too old to travel far beyond this world."

"No, you're not. You can help me, guide me. I still don't understand all this."

"You understand it; you just don't want to believe it. Deep down, you know what to do, Stella. You always have. You need to let go."

Stella sighed. "That is not easy for me to do. Please, come with us."

Maren's eyes watered. "When I started to age on Verbatim, people began to treat me differently. They thought that because my hair turned white and my skin had wrinkled that I was frail and weak. And when you are seen that way, you are treated that way more and more. I started to believe it was true. Maybe I was frail and weak. I never felt weak until others saw me that way. After years of isolation, I eventually felt invisible. I want to help, but the war cost us all so much. I can't bear to fight another one again. You're in capable hands. I helped how I could, but this is as much as I can do."

"I wish there was something I could do to change your mind," Stella said. Maren's shoulders slumped even more. Stella just nodded, and they embraced once more. It was difficult to let Maren go, but Stella turned her thoughts to her mother and to the fact that she would finally be reunited with her.

# 35

# ITEM FOR TRADE

**STELLA, ELLIOT, AND REX HUSTLED BACK** to Marlon's Device where Zimmer was waiting for them at the helm while Gary prepared the ship for takeoff.

"Is Ryder stable?" Rex asked.

Zimmer rolled down the sleeves of his white shirt, as he had just come from the med bay. "He is, for now. Iris is in with him, and she will administer more meds to help slow the poison."

"Good. When do you think we will be able to question him?" Rex asked.

"That may take some time. Minathi poison is no joke. It's going to take a while to reverse the effect," Zimmer said.

"Then he's not much use to us," Rex said.

"Actually, I think he has become very useful," Zimmer said.

"What do you mean?" Stella asked.

"It's great that we know Kate is on Kodon, but it's not as though we can land and tell the Sekke to bring her out to us," Zimmer said. "We need an item to trade for her."

"I don't understand," Stella said.

"Who are the Sekke?" Elliot asked.

Rex rubbed his chin. "How do I explain Kodon? How do I … explain Kodon?" Rex said. "Ahh, I believe you have something on Terra known as Wall Street, where people in suits trade stocks and currency. Am I correct in this?"

"Yes," Stella said.

"On Kodon, human men and women they call the Suits work for the Sekke, the native beings of Kodon. Instead of trading stocks and currency, the Suits brokers deal with trading people and other beings," Rex said. "Many of the Suits have defected from Terra and have found better business dealings on Kodon."

"Once deals are made, they are binding. Someone must have traded Kate in exchange for someone else. The only way to get her out is to have someone to trade for her," Zimmer added.

Stella shook her head. "So that's it? We don't have anything to trade, do we?"

Rex shot Zimmer a look. "I think we *do* have someone to trade for Kate. Someone who will be worth five people to the Sekke."

"No," Stella said. As the word floated out of her mouth, she immediately wished she could take it back. She wished she didn't have to trade Ryder for her mother. She wished they could save them both. "That man needs our help," Stella insisted.

"He kidnapped you and tried to kill you," Zimmer said with a furrowed brow.

"Ryder is wanted in twelve galaxies. It's probably safer for him if he spends the rest of his life on Kodon. He will be like a trophy for them and, therefore, no real harm will come to him unless he causes harm to someone."

"There must be a way to find my mother without trading. Can't we teleport in?" Stella asked.

"That's not how it works. Trust me, the Sekke are very powerful. No one just takes from them. This is the only way to rescue Kate," Zimmer said. "I'll start the call to Kodon."

Zimmer left the helm, and Rex turned to Stella. "You are truly remarkable for having sympathy for Ryder. and I feel for his predicament—I do—but this is the only way to reunite you with your mother."

Rex extended his arm out to round up Stella and Elliot so they could join Zimmer in the ship's conference room. Once they arrived, they took seats around a sizable square table. The top was an elaborate computer with a glowing blue screen. Zimmer had entered the communique link to Kodon, and they were waiting for a Kodon representative to pick up.

Rex rubbed his palms together. "All right, we're going to request the trade with the Sekke. If they accept, we will trade Ryder for Kate."

"And if they don't?" Stella asked.

"They will," Zimmer replied.

An image soon materialized out of the center of the table. A woman with a thin, turned-up nose wearing glasses greeted them cheerfully.

"Hello, and welcome to the Sekke trade line. Do you have an item you are requesting trade for?" she said.

"Yes," Rex said.

"Name of item or serial number?"

"Kate Walsh," Stella said, leaning forward.

"Yes, Kate Walsh. She's in our third-level holding. Quite valuable. I may suggest that you have two items to trade for this item."

"We have only one," Rex said. "We need only one."

The woman looked up over her glasses. "What is this one item you would like to trade?"

"John 'Ryder' Alexander," Rex said.

The woman's eyes widened. "One moment, please."

The screen went dark briefly until the woman returned, smiling. "We will accept this trade. Please arrive in exactly twenty-four hours with your item. Once condition of item is verified, the trade will be completed, and you may depart Kodon with your item. Instructions on landing site and point of contact to follow. Thank you, and have a pleasant day."

The screen went dark.

"So, that's it?" Stella asked.

"Wow, that was easy, "Elliot said.

"It seems easy now, but nothing related to the planet Kodon is easy. Many people who land on its dusty desert plains are never heard from again."

# 36

## CURIOSITY
## AND THE CAT

**"WHAT IS HIS STATUS?"** Rex asked as he, Elliot, and Stella walked into the med bay.

Stella cocked her head as she heard Iris whispering something.

"Who are you talking to, Iris?" Rex asked.

Iris cleared her throat. "No one." She kept her head down and entered information on a monitor next to the tank.

"I thought I heard you whispering something," Stella said. She walked to the side of the tank, but Iris would not look at her.

"Well, you heard wrong," Iris said.

"I see," Rex said with a furrowed brow. "So how is he doing?"

"He's stable. He will survive, but it will be a process," Iris said. "Not sure the Sekke will accept him in this condition."

Ryder was stripped to his boxers again and was lying faceup on a table on top of a large, rectangle tank of blue liquid. The word HydrAtank was printed in block letters on the side. The fluids kept Ryder's body stable and extracted the poison at the same time. Iris placed a silicone patch over Ryder's red eye so the fluids wouldn't permeate his skull. She tapped on a floating computer screen. After calibrating the tank to Ryder's body makeup and poison intake, the platform he lay on eased into the water.

"We'll get him there. Thank you, Iris. Will you return to the helm to assist Gary?"

Iris lingered at the edge of the tank.

"Iris?" Rex insisted.

"Yes sir." She threw a side glance at Stella.

"Why don't you take Driver to the helm with you. I'm sure Driver would love to learn more about how the ship works. Driver?"

Plastic beakers hit the floor as an object Elliot had taken off a shelf, slipped out of his hands. "Yes? Oops, uh, sorry."

Iris rolled her eyes, but Elliot was all too happy to follow her out of the lab.

"What's wrong with her?" Stella asked.

"Uh, Iris is a very complex being," Rex replied.

"You keep making excuses for her behavior, but something is not right with her, and she definitely doesn't want me to be here."

Rex paused. "I will speak with her after we finish here. Iris has always been a more reserved member of my crew, but she seems unusually hostile toward you, and for that I am sorry."

"Fine," Stella said. "As long as you trust her."

"I do."

Rex walked to the side of the tank. "John Alexander. This man has eluded every form of law enforcement and bounty hunter in the universe, and now he's here. I almost wish I could savor this moment more."

"So many tattoos," Stella said. A tattoo of what looked like barbed wire was wrapped around his right bicep; a large, black star on his chest; other symbols scattered over the rest of his body.

"What you Terrans refer to as tattoos are actually battle emblems to Kayguns. These are badges of battles hard-fought and won. Some also are a way to honor those who have died fighting at his side," Rex said.

"How did he become an assassin if he was such a decorated soldier? What happened to him?" Stella asked.

"From what Zimmer and I were able to figure out, he was betrayed," Rex said. "He was fighting in what was called the Miner's War. A few members of his own battalion made a deal with the other side. Ryder was ambushed in his bunker along with other members of his family. Ryder, most of his troops, and even his own siblings were found dead. Body dealers picked him up and sold him at auction."

Stella narrowed her eyes and stepped to the edge of the tank. "I'm almost afraid to ask ... what's a body dealer?" Stella asked.

"They are scavengers mostly. They skim battlefields for bodies, then sell them whole or for the parts," Rex said.

"That's despicable," Stella said.

"Sadly, it is a common practice in some areas. I believe that is how Kandice Shook acquired him. I'm starting to feel sorry for the poor son of a bitch now that I really think on it. It's a pity that he turned after working for Shook. He was a brilliant soldier and a good man. Now there is only death and destruction in his wake."

Stella shook her head. "We should be helping him."

Rex narrowed his eyes. "There is nothing that can be done now. Though he does have a sad story, make no mistake, Stella. This is a very dangerous man. Better for all of us when we hand him over. Come now, I want to show you how we deal with wound care."

Rex took her around and demonstrated some of the machines in the med bay. Stella soaked it all in. She had only started to see the advances in medical technology on earth. The advancements in the technologies scientific pioneers made in space exceeded even her wildest dreams.

Though there were so many machines that could diagnose, treat, and cure almost all wounds. Stella still felt comfortable only with the things she really trusted: her hands.

"Understand that I showed you how to utilize the lab just for the interim. Once your powers are fully realized, you won't ever need technology to heal again," Rex said. He powered down some of the lights in the med bay and left to join the others at the helm.

Stella's mouth curled into a smile. With everyone else occupied, she crept back to the med bay. The lights flickered back on when she waved her hand over a digital light switch. She moved to the tank and stared at Ryder floating in the water. A familiar feeling washed over her. It was a feeling she frequently felt examining patients at home. Something was wrong.

She needed to take a closer look.

The table lurched loudly as it brought Ryder out of the tank. The liquid beaded off him as he lay motionless. Stella inched toward him. His breathing was labored and his skin glistened a milky white. Something tugged at her as it always did back home whenever she saw a dying patient. The poison was eating away at him from the inside. The tank was not working.

She could see the poison in his veins clearly in her mind. She took a deep breath in and raised her hands over his body, moving from the top of his head slowly down to the open wound on his leg. The activity of the poison was clear in her mind. She closed her eyes. She could see and feel where it was pooling inside him. She guided her hands to the large wound in his shoulder. Though Ryder's tissue was fighting it, the poison was dissolving him from the inside out.

Stella focused on the poison, on seeking it out and visualizing it leaving Ryder's body. Her hands quivered, and her eyes jolted open when a spark singed her fingertips. She gasped and stared wide-eyed as the poison streamed out of Ryder's wounds to her fingertips as if they were vacuums sucking it out of his body. The streams glided under her fingertips and formed two balls of liquid under her palms.

Color eased back into Ryder's flesh. He twitched as the last bits of poison drained from his veins and the wounds made by the Minathi arrows sealed back to his skin's original state. Stella turned her palms upward. The poison had churned in a perfect orb like a ball of yarn that rewound itself after it had been unraveled. Stella hurried to a counter and turned her palms back down, releasing the balls into two empty glass beakers. "Oh my god," she said out loud.

She had been so preoccupied with the poison in the beakers, she almost forgot to check Ryder's vitals. She grabbed a device Rex had shown her how to use moments earlier and turned back to the tank.

A chill rocked her body.

The table was empty.

Wet footprints led away from the tank. She whipped around to see Ryder awake, seething, and blocking her exit.

"What did you do to me?" He said with a raspy voice.

"I ... I removed the poison."

He took a step closer to her. "Why are you helping me?"

"Because you need it."

Voices sounded in the hallway. Ryder pushed Stella back and snatched her blaster out of the utility belt she was wearing.

The door opened, and Rex pulled his blaster with one hand while Elliot fumbled with his.

"Put the blaster down, Ryder. You are outnumbered, and you have nowhere to go," Rex said, inching his way into the lab.

"I've had worse odds," Ryder said.

"Put it down," Rex insisted.

"I'm a dead man anyway," Ryder said. His finger pressed on the trigger, but before he could fire, Stella jabbed his stomach with the stunning device she pulled out of her belt.

Ryder lowered his weapon and fell back. He wobbled on his feet until he deflated to the floor.

# 37

# HALF-ROBOT

**"WHAT WERE YOU DOING, STELLA?"** Rex said, rushing into the med bay. "I told you …" He trailed off when he saw the beakers of poison sitting on the counter behind her. "What in the blazes?"

"The tank wasn't working, so I removed the poison … myself."

Rex's eyes bugged large. "By Thunder! It's happening already. That visit with Maren must have done more than I realized for your abilities." He pulled Stella to him, hugging her, though her arms remained stiff at her side. "Driver, help me get Ryder into a holding cell."

With a few grunts and growls, Rex and Elliot carried him to a holding room off the med bay. They laid him on a bed, and Rex covered him with a blanket, then closed the door.

"That dude was heavy. He's like a solid block of muscles," Elliot said.

Rex wiped the sweat from his brow. "That is the truth, my friend. We should've had Gary morph and move him. I'm afraid I will have a righteous kink in my neck in the morning. Okay you two, better get some rest. Enjoy your rooms. I've had them stocked with Terran goodies. I'll head to the helm to relieve the others."

Rex marched down the hallway and stopped, turning toward them while he was still walking backward. "Oh, and Driver, better practice with that new blaster. Can't have you fumbling if we see some action on Kodon."

Elliot laughed nervously. "Of course." He turned to Stella once Rex was out of sight. "So, still don't think you're a superhero?" Elliot asked.

"No."

"Well, only superheroes can suck poison out of someone with their fingers."

"It's not being a superhero. I could see the poison in his veins, and as soon as I focused on it, it started to come out."

"Sure, okay," Elliot said. "Do you want to chat about what else is going on here?"

"What are you talking about?" Stella asked.

"An observation I made while you were in the med bay."

"If you have something to say, say it. Otherwise, I'm going to bed. What observation?" Stella asked.

Elliot raised his brows. "You kind of have a thing for Mr. Roboto there, don't you?"

"Mr. Who?"

"Mr. Roboto. Ol' Red Eye. I saw how you were looking at him. You have a thing for him."

"A thing? I do not have a thing."

"I can't believe you like the bad guy, and a bad guy who is half Terminator no less. You really have interesting taste."

Stella's face flushed. "You are actually the worst."

"Ahh! But you do not deny it," Elliot said, pointing at Stella.

"I don't have to deny anything. I'm simply not acknowledging your ridiculous comments."

"Wow. I ... wow," Elliot said. "I never thought you'd be the kind of woman who would fall for the villain."

"He's not a villain." Stella stormed down the hall to her chamber, which was across the hall from Elliot's.

"And still not denying it," Elliot rubbed his chin and squinted at the ceiling. "Are you okay with them trading him for your mother?"

Stella's gaze hit the floor. "No, but we don't have another option."

"Remember, he *did* kidnap you."

"I realize that, but that wasn't his choice."

"You're making up excuses for him since you're kind of crushing on him. Am I right?"

"Goodnight," Stella said. She entered the code in the chamber's keypad.

Elliot stopped at his door. "Kind of makes sense to me, though. You like that half-robot because, you know, you're half-robot."

"What do you mean by that?"

"Goodnight," Elliot shut the door to his chamber, leaving Stella alone in the hallway.

She felt another wave of heat flush through her body as she raised her fist to knock on Elliot's door, but she stopped herself.

*Nope. Not going to deal with him.*

She paced around her chamber for a moment, came back out, and buzzed Elliot's door.

*Actually no. No. We are going to deal with this. We are going to deal with this right now.*

He opened the door grinning. "Oh hey, Stella."

"Did you say I was half-robot?"

"Yes."

"How dare you," Stella said.

"Honey, let's not fight now. Come in and have a drink."

"How many times do I have to tell you, I don't drink."

"Ahh, that was before. This is now. It will help you. Trust me."

Stella stepped inside his chamber. The room was big and cozy. A stainless-steel table sat in front of a small kitchenette. The bed was tucked into a separate room behind a seating area. The bright lights of the cosmos were visible through a circular window that ran floor to ceiling.

Elliot whistled cheerfully, took two glasses out of the cupboard, and began to pour from a bottle marked Terran Vodka. He sniffed it, his nose wrinkled, and then he threw the drink in the back of his throat. He poured a small sample in a glass and handed it to Stella.

"Drink this and sit, and tell me again how you are not half-robot," he said.

Stella sat down on a stool across from him. "No." She pushed the drink away from her.

"Listen, I get it. You like to be in control, but letting go a little doesn't mean you aren't still in control. You can have a drink and not go off the rails."

"Will you please stop talking to me like you have me all figured out?"

Elliot removed the glass and set it on the counter behind him. "Hey, I'm sorry. I don't want to pressure you. If you don't want to drink, don't drink. I will support that." He filled up fresh glasses with water.

"I used to drink … a lot. I stopped because … because of Brian Leemer."

Elliot cocked his head to the side. "You don't drink because of Brian Leemer?"

"That's right," Stella said.

"Wait, he didn't …" Elliot asked.

"No, no, not at all. In fact …" Stella paused. "… It was I who …"

Elliot sat down on the stool across from Stella, who squirmed on hers. She appreciated that Elliot was being patient and trying to listen.

*Maybe I am half-robot.*

She had not been forthcoming about herself with anyone in so long, she almost forgot how to open up. She glanced up at Elliot sitting there drinking water when she knew he preferred something else, and she thought it might be time to try.

"When I was in college, before I decided to go to med school, I wasn't very disciplined. I had no control. If there was a weekend party, I was there. My mom was gone, and I never knew my father. Didn't have many friends at first, so I blew off school because I didn't care. That's when I met Brian. Every time I was at a party with him, I couldn't help myself. He was so handsome, charming, and he made me laugh ..."

"Sort of describing me, but continue," Elliot said.

Stella smiled. "Anyway, I would start drinking and all I wanted to do was drink more and sleep with Brian Leemer. I was so drawn to him and the alcohol and anything that helped to derail me. I lost myself at those parties, and when I saw Brian I had no control whatsoever. I woke up one day and decided I needed to do more. I quit drinking, quit partying, and I quit Brian. I got control of my life and never looked back."

"That makes sense."

"It does, but that still doesn't make me half-robot," Stella said.

"Except that it does."

"Okay, so I can be a little rigid, but—"

"It's more than rigid. It's ..."

Stella narrowed her eyes.

"What I'm saying is not a bad thing. It's not a criticism. You have to be part robot to survive what you do back home. What you do is incredible. I can't imagine working in a hospital. All you have seen and done is amazing. But I'm sure it has gotten to you after a while."

Stella finished her water, trying to quench her dry throat. "I didn't realize it, but it did get to me. I gave up so much."

Elliot reached out and grasped her hand. "There is still control in letting go. That's the beauty of it. You still get to decide when, where, and how to let go."

Stella looked up and went to the counter, picking up the two glasses Elliot had set aside. He refilled his and splashed more vodka in hers, topping it off.

"It's okay. We don't have to drink at all. You opened up, and I'm proud of you for that. Water is fine with me," Elliot said.

"Except that it's not," Stella said. She pushed a glass to Elliot, and he took it.

Stella exhaled deeply and swirled the vodka around in the glass. She smelled it and jerked her head away.

"How can I drink this? It's lighter fluid," Stella said.

"Then don't drink it. Pour it down your throat." Elliot demonstrated by taking a shot. He grunted briefly, shook his head, and then waited for Stella to follow his lead. She did, and then her body erupted with coughs that shook her. Elliot got up and handed her some water.

"You okay?" He said, patting her back. "You all right?"

She nodded through her coughs. "Is there anything else in that cabinet that's less intense?"

"Shit, yes. There has to be. Sorry. You haven't had a drink in years, and I just took you from zero to vodka." Elliot took her glass and dug around. He found a bottle marked Terran Red Wine. "This will be better."

Elliot poured the wine in wine glasses. He handed one to Stella and then motioned toward the seating area in front of the window. Stella curled up in the cushions.

"So how are you feeling about tomorrow? About seeing your mom?"

Stella glanced out the window. "I don't know. It's been so long. I finally made peace with the fact that I was never going to see her again, and now she's alive. I have so many questions."

"Hopefully, everything goes smoothly. From what I've been reading about this planet, it's a bizarre place. Kind of wish I was a real warrior."

Stella chuckled. "You can do warrior things. I'm sure we'll be fine. What does the PKIS manual say about Kodon?"

Elliot retrieved the tablet from his nightstand table.

"It sounds crazy," he said. He sat down on the sofa and Stella joined him. "'Kodon is a desert planet with rocky mesas and red sandstone formations. This is home to the Sekke, humanoid beings that are part human and part lizard.' Look at this dude," Elliot said.

Stella gawked at the picture of a man, but with the head and markings of a lizard. He was bright yellow with black, jagged markings on his body. Elliot continued reading. "'Kodon is also home to many dinosaur species.' Oh my God, that sounds awesome! 'Dinosaurs were brought to live on Kodon to repopulate after it was determined they could not survive on Terra. Not all the species are represented on Kodon—only the desert species that can withstand the heat.' I'll believe that when I see it," Elliot said. He swiped right and revealed a picture of a city. Skyscrapers were packed together on a patch of land that had some lush oasis-like greenery in between them.

"'The capital of Kodon, and the only place humans dwell, is Duma City. This is where all the trade deals begin and end. This is also where the performance annex and sports stadium are located. The Sekke work with human business executives from all over the galaxy who handle the trading. The Lower Levels of the skyscrapers have holding cells and sparring pits where the Sekke place bets on the most skilled fighters. The sparring pits are also a way to allow prisoners to get some much-needed exercise.'"

Elliot set down the tablet.

"What's wrong?" Stella asked.

"Sounds like we better enjoy a little more wine tonight," Elliot said.

# 38

## KODON

**STELLA HATED THE HEAT.** She would much rather be wrapped up in a sweater sitting by a fire in the cold than feeling the swelter of Kodon's hot desert sands.

"Why did we have to park so far away?" Elliot asked once everyone disembarked.

"It makes it more difficult to escape," Iris replied. She and Gary were attached to each side of Ryder with electric bonds.

"Oh, this high temperature," Gary said, fanning himself. "My oil is boiling."

"Gary, is there an environment where you are truly content?" Rex asked.

"Yes. Verbatim," Gary replied.

A gust of wind pelted them with dusty bits of the planet. In the distance, a tall series of high-rises reflected the sun back into the atmosphere: Duma City.

"I thought you said someone was coming to meet us," Stella said.

There were no signs of any other living things, just wind and dust and rocks.

"The Sekke love to toy with us. We start walking toward Duma City," Rex said, pointing to the high-rises, "and they will come for us eventually. They know we are here, but they want us to suffer a bit. Keep your wits about you, my friends. Sekke are neither friend nor foe, which makes their behavior incredibly difficult to predict."

Stella and the others trudged through the blazing heat for what seemed like hours until the ship was a small speck on the horizon. Duma City did not seem to be getting any closer. They had started to wilt, each shedding various pieces of their uniforms to cool down. With only a light tank top on after she peeled off her long-sleeved shirt, Stella felt her shoulders getting crispy in the sun.

She stopped, shielding her eyes, when she noticed movement on the horizon. Multiple specks were moving toward them at a lightning pace, but in the sizzle that wafted up off the desert, she couldn't identify what they were.

Elliot squinted. "What is that?"

"Brace yourselves," Rex said. He stopped trudging through the sand and pulled a micro binocular lens over his right eye. "Criket."

"That's a pretty big cricket," Elliot said.

The crew paused, passing around a canteen of water as whatever was creating the dust storm neared.

Elliot nudged Stella with his elbow. "Punch me in the face."

"What?"

"Punch me in the face."

"I would love to, but why?"

"Because I can't believe what I'm seeing."

Stella looked back to the horizon. "What do you see?"

"Dinosaurs," Elliot said.

"Holy shit."

"Okay, so you see them too," Elliot said. "The tablet was right. They are real."

A pod of velociraptors sprinted toward them, shrieking as they ran. Some of the raptors carried Sekke on their backs, and some were running in tandem as they pulled passenger craft behind them. The raptors were smaller than what Stella had seen depicted in movies. They were brightly plumed with feathers from their heads to their muscular legs. The raptors screeched to a halt, and the dust settled down around them. A Sekke woman with lime green eyes hopped down to the sand. She had the body of a human woman, but she was completely covered with avocado-colored scales. She did not have hair, but three thick ridges that looked like humps on her head. She wore a tight, leather tank top and even tighter leather pants.

"Rex!" she said, throwing up her hands in the air.

"Criket. How have you been?" Rex asked. "Everyone, this is Criket, a Sekke elder."

"Ah, first, what do you call it? A hug? Yes?"

Rex opened his arms. "By all means."

"Oh, how long has it been?"

"Not long enough, I'm afraid. I don't relish seeing you in this unsettling place, my dear," Rex said.

"Reeelaaaxx! You are honored guest here."

"Aye, we appreciate your most gracious hospitality," Rex said.

"Zimmer, I did not know this that you would be in crew," Cricket said. She batted her eyes at Zimmer, who flushed under her gaze that was as hot as the sun. "We will be catching up on our chatter, yes?"

"Can't wait," Zimmer said with pursed lips.

"I will look forward to it," Criket said. She pulled him close; her lizard tongue whipped out and tickled his ear.

Stella recoiled from the sight.

"Where is your trade item?" Criket asked.

Iris and Gary brought Ryder up from the back of the pack. Criket took slow steps over to him.

She smiled from ear to ear, her forked tongue licking her lips. "Ryder."

"Criket," Ryder said.

Criket balled her fist and launched a swift punch into his stomach. He slumped over and grunted before rising back up.

"That's for my sister! For the stolen loot!" Criket shouted.

Ryder coughed. "It was a card game. She lost."

"She wouldn't have even been on Tasho-9 if it hadn't been for you! What do you have to say for that?" Criket shouted.

"Bad luck."

Criket hissed at Ryder. "I am to relish watching you grow old here." She shouted a command in her native tongue, and two orange men with long tails hopped over to her.

They hustled Ryder over to a raft-like craft that hovered over the sand. It was strapped to two of the raptors, and it bobbed in the air as Ryder was thrown into it. The two men slid onto the raptor's backs, and the fearfully great lizards screeched as they sprinted back to the high-rises.

"Now, where were we?" Criket asked.

"How about getting us out of this merciless heat?" Rex asked, wiping his forehead with a small towel he pulled out of his pocket.

"Yes. Ah, yes!"

She whistled, and another set of raptors whipped the Hovercart around so the crew could pile in. Stella was glad to be off her feet, which felt soggy and swollen in her uniform flats. Though it was being pulled by sprinting dinosaurs, the raft glided over the desert without jostling its

ANGELA HAAS

cargo. Criket rode along with them. Once introductions were exchanged with the others, Criket turned her attention toward Stella.

"So, you are the Healer's daughter, yes?" she asked.

Stella sat up in her seat. "Yes, how did you know?"

"You look like her. Your eyes are the same, but her hair keeps doing a turn to white."

"You've seen her?" Stella asked.

"I do this daily. She is friend. Is that how you say it?"

"How is she? Is she all right?"

"She is fair, though she has not the energy she used to," Criket said.

"When can I see her?"

"They are inspecting Ryder for trade. Once we clear him, the Suits will finish dealing. Then you get your item and gooooo." Criket whisked her hand up to the sky.

Stella caught her breath. She wondered if her mother had aged rapidly like Maren had. She only hoped she did not have to wait long for the trade deal to be solidified.

"What will happen to Ryder?" she asked. From the looks she received from everyone in the Hovercart, she wished she had not asked that question. She felt powerless knowing there was nothing she could do to help him, and she also knew it was the only way to get to her mother.

Criket's eyes widened. "Oh? Why ask? You are doing a concern for this man?"

"Not at all," Stella said, clearing her throat. "I was only wondering about the process. What happens when people get traded?"

"Depends," Criket said.

"Some meet horrid fates here," Gary said. He pulled a small fan from his fanny pack. He switched it on and enjoyed the breeze before sharing it with Iris. "I've heard that some are fed to the angry beasts that

207

live here. Some work in the skyscrapers making coffee for the Suits. I'm
not sure what sounds worse."

"How can I explain … oh you, you are from Terra?" Criket asked.
Stella nodded.

"Yes, you acting strange with your animals there," Criket said, leaning back and spreading out her arms on the back of the raft. "Some you
dress up and make pets, some animals you like to watch fight, some you
make do tricks and perform for you, and some animals you even eat."

"Well, now it just sounds weird when you say it like that," Elliot said.

"So?" Stella said.

"What gives you the right to decide?" Criket asked.

"Uh, I don't know. I never thought about it like that," Stella said.

Criket narrowed her eyes. "You should not have that right. Here
on Kodon, all animals, even the workers, are revered. Humans are the
animals here. So, you may get to dress up and play in the showtime, or
you may work, or you may fight, or you may get traded for someone
else. Ryder will spend the rest of his days doing one of those things, and
I will be there to watch."

# 39

# JACK AND JACK

**STELLA WAS RELIEVED TO BE SOMEWHERE** that felt familiar to her: an office building. The welcome relief of the air conditioning instantly cooled her once they stepped inside one of the main high-rises. After confiscating their weapons, including Gary's fanny pack, Criket waved them through an archway, and with a swift blast of air, all the dust that had collected on them was gone. Though it was on her home planet, Criket looked entirely out of place in the skyscraper. The lobby of the skyscraper was full of men and women in business casual attire. They darted in and out of elevators and shouted into smartphones. Stella never wanted to touch the railings in the elevators on earth, but the railing in the silver steel elevator they stepped into was so fingerprint-free, she felt fine wrapping her fingers around it.

"What is that?" Elliot asked, pointing to the speaker that cheerfully sprinkled instrumental music on them from above. "Journey?"

Stella listened in. "Any Way You Want It."

"This is so cool," Elliot said. "It's like we're home."

"Don't let down your guard," Rex said. "Easy to do, and a mistake you can pay dearly for here."

A breathy female voice announced their arrival. "Floor 18: Negotiations. Have a pleasant deal."

The elevator dinged, and the doors opened. Clear glass walls divided rows and rows of offices where men and women in suits sat behind desks, as beings from all over the universe sat opposite them, trying to finalize their deals. Across from these offices were other rooms that did not have windows but had doors with plaques that read "Private Deals."

Stella scanned the faces, wondering if her mother was in one of the rooms. Criket led them to a conference room with a long, oval table in the center. A watercooler gurgled with delight in one corner, and a happy little plant stood at attention in the other.

"You will wait in here for Jack and Jack. Once deal is done, they retrieve your item," Criket said. "After, I meet you down in the lobby and take you back to the ship, yes?" She then bowed and exited the room.

Stella sat down in a comfortable office chair between Rex and Elliot.

"Wait ... Jack and Jack?" Elliot asked, just as two men opened the door.

The men stopped and in unison looked at each other and then back to Elliot. "Driver? Elliot S. Driver?" they asked.

"Felton? Kline? Holy shit!" Elliot shot up to greet Jack and Jack. "Can you believe this? I went to college with these guys!"

The three men hooted and patted each other on the back.

"What ritual is this?' Gary asked.

"It's how males sometimes greet each other," Stella replied.

"What the heck are you doing here, Driver?" Felton asked.

"I don't know. Got picked up, I guess. Me and my lovely companion here were abducted." Elliot directed Jack and Jack toward Stella.

"Wow!" Felton said.

"What a beauty," Kline said.

"That red hair."

"Love red hair."

"Miss that about Earth," Felton said.

"Me too."

"You just don't see that many redheads out here," Felton said.

"It's a shame," Kline added.

"A real shame."

After Jack's and Jack's eyes lingered over Stella long enough to make her frown at them, they turned their attention back to Elliot. After a brief update from the friends, Jack and Jack bumped fists and sat down at the head of the conference table next to Stella, who could not believe Elliot could travel millions of light years from Earth and find two friends from college.

"So, let's talk business," Felton began.

"Yes, let's," Kline answered.

"We understand you brought Ryder in."

"Good job, by the way," Kline said.

"We hear he's quite a catch."

"And hard to catch."

"But you caught him, and that's good," Felton said.

"Very good," Kline said.

"Looks like we are doing a trade for a Dr. Kate Walsh," Felton said, flipping through images on a tablet.

"Yes, yes," Stella said. "That is the woman we came for."

Rex nodded his head and put his hand on Stella's arm. She sat back in her chair and crossed her arms. She grew impatient with all the formalities associated with the deal. Jack and Jack paused their chattering to answer a phone call which lasted only about ten seconds.

"Looks like we have good news," Felton said.

"Scratch that, we have *great* news."

"They have approved Ryder for trade. Now we can release your item," Felton said.

"She's not an item; she's a human woman," Stella said.

Jack and Jack both furrowed their brows and straightened their ties in unison.

"Steady," Rex whispered in Stella's ear.

"Wow, we've got a real firecracker here, Jack," Kline said.

"I see that, Jack," Felton replied.

Both Jacks simultaneously made a note on the legal pads they had in front of them. Stella watched them, noticing that she could not tell either of them apart. Each one could be differentiated only by minute details. Where one Jack's tie was a navy blue with gold checks, the other's tie was a lighter navy with stripes. One had slightly bushier eyebrows, while the other had a narrower nose. Both athletically built in stature, they almost seemed like two heads that shared the same body.

"All right, we will finish your paperwork and retrieve your item, and you all will be on your way," Kline said.

"Thank you for doing business on Kodon," Felton said.

"We'll be right back to get some signatures," Kline said.

"Driver, let's have a drink downstairs before you leave, all right broseph?" Felton hooted.

"Aw, I would love that," Elliot said. He got up from his seat again so they could all fist bump each other.

Jack and Jack sauntered out of the office. As they walked out, Stella stood up in anticipation of her mother coming into the room.

"I must say, this was seamless," Rex said. He got up to pour himself a cup of coffee and help himself to a Danish that was sitting out on a tray of pastries in the corner of the room.

"That's what makes me nervous," Zimmer added.

"How long does this usually take?" Stella asked. Her stomach was in knots. She exhaled to try to calm herself. She wouldn't feel better until she could embrace her mother and leave all this behind.

"Not long, usually. The Suits here are downright scoundrels for some of the deals they make, but they are also incredibly efficient," Rex said.

Moments later, Jack and Jack reemerged. A woman in a pencil skirt stopped them by blocking their path back to the conference room. She whispered something to them, and they both glanced back toward the conference room. Jack and Jack straightened their ties in unison and came back in the room.

"Uh, there's seems to be a slight issue," Felton said.

"What issue?" Stella asked, leaning forward in her seat.

The boardroom doors flew open and Kandice Shook stormed in, flanked by Suits on one side and Taylor on the other. "Hey, baby!"

# 40

# ANOTHER OFFER

**STELLA'S EYES BULGED**. "What the hell are you doing here?"

A grin snaked across Kandi's lips. "Making a new deal, honey."

"What is this?" Rex asked, turning to Jack and Jack.

Kandi and the others all took a seat across from Stella.

"We've already closed this deal," Felton said.

A Suit sitting to the right of Kandi pushed some papers toward the Jacks. "Miss Shook is offering quite a substantial counteroffer to your original deal. If we agree to hold this group here, and she is allowed to leave with Kate Walsh, she will make a payment of fourteen million credits. Quite substantial."

Stella shot up from her seat. "No, you are not taking my mother anywhere."

Rex touched her arm and gently pulled her back down to her seat. "This is completely irregular," he said.

"We are signing the original deal we made," Zimmer added.

"Y'all don't understand business very well," Kandi said. "Money speaks louder than anything I know, certainly louder than you little twerps. They aren't going to pass up that many credits. What I'm offering is worth thousands of their trades."

The Jacks straightened their ties in unison. "May we have a word outside please?" They stood up, as did the Suits sitting by Kandi.

"Wait! I want to see my mother. Where is she? I thought she was on her way here," Stella said.

"She was," Kline said.

"Is," Felton said. "She *is* on her way. Be patient, and we will see what we can do for Driver's friends here." Felton winked at Elliot.

"We ask that you please bear with us, while we both pitch our offers to the Sekke Elders," Kline said. "Sit tight, and please stay in this room."

"Any inappropriate actions may cause the deal to sour," Felton said.

"We hate it when that happens," Kline said.

"The worst," Felton added.

Stella tried to get up again, unwilling to sit across from Kandi who casually sipped her latte.

"Stay here. I'll go talk to them," Zimmer said.

"No, I want to talk to them, and I want my mother brought here now," Stella insisted.

"You can't do that," Iris added. "You're going to ruin this deal if you do something stupid."

Stella's face flushed as she glared at Iris.

Gary wailed from his seat, "This is wreaking havoc on my nerves!"

"Stella, I know this is frustrating, but you have to trust us. We need to be patient here," Rex said. "There may be another offer on the table, but we were here first. The Jacks have a bond with Driver, so that will help us."

"No." Stella left her seat and started for the door.

Rex and Zimmer rushed to the door, blocking her exit.

"Listen to me," Rex said. His voice left his body like a low rumble of thunder. "I need you to understand where you are right now. This is a dangerous place. We must not get trapped here, but that will be our fate if we don't follow their rules. We are so close to getting out of here with Kate, so please … sit down and let us handle this. Zimmer can help close our deal."

"But why does he get to go talk to them?" Stella asked.

"Because I'm a Suit. I can move a little more freely up here," Zimmer said, leaving the room to find the Jacks.

"Besides," Rex added, "Criket has an affection for Zimmer for reasons I cannot explain. Let him go. He wants to see you reunite with Kate as much as we do."

Stella nodded and went back to her seat.

Kandi giggled and clapped her hands together.

"Something amusing to you?" Stella asked.

"Oh yes, y'all really think they're going to take your deal. It's adorable."

"Shut up! You're lucky they took away our weapons," Stella said.

"Oh? And what would you do? You're a doctor, right? Didn't you swear an oath to do no harm?" Kandi asked.

"I can make an exception for you," Stella said.

"Oh honey, even though I am exceptional, I already told you, acting tough around me isn't a good idea, but I really appreciate your fire. You got spirit. I like that."

"Both of you stop it," Rex said. "The Jacks will honor our deal simply because we were here first. And we brought them Ryder. That will mean something."

"Hey, I'm willing to see what they say. I mean, I've offered them a ridiculous number of credits to hold all of you here while I leave with missy's mama. I get a Healer, and y'all get trapped here so you can't run and tattle on me. The Sekke make out like bandits because they get all of you and credits just for letting me leave with one Healer. Y'all are pretty valuable and will come in handy around here … even you, handsome."

Elliot blushed. "Oh well, I—"

Stella jabbed him in the ribs, and his boyish smile turned back to a frown.

"But hey, they may take your deal too. Either way, we all tried, right?" Kandi said.

"You aren't going anywhere with my mother," Stella said, gritting her teeth.

Kandi's mouth formed a crooked smile. "We'll see, sugar. We'll see."

Stella caught a movement in the hallway. She turned to see a stocky man who looked like someone had stuffed him in his suit and it was about to burst off his body. His arm was around a woman Stella almost didn't recognize. She had silver hair pulled back at her crown, and her face was weathered with lines and scars. It seemed like the man guiding her down the hallway was also holding her up.

The hair on the back of Stella's neck stood up, and goosebumps appeared on her arms. Stella rushed out of the room and froze in the hallway.

"Mom!" Stella cried.

# 41

## KATE

**"STELLA!"** Kate held out her hands, and Stella rushed into them. Once they embraced, a wave of green light blew them back as it rushed up through the center of their bodies. They held onto each other, and Stella watched as the deep lines on her mother's face faded instantly from Stella's touch. Stella's scarred shoulder stretched and eased as if it had never been injured. When they released, green light danced in the palm of Stella's hands before it evaporated into a mist. A wave of hushed whispers erupted in the offices as people stopped what they were doing to gawk at the commotion.

Stella tried to choke down her tears. The woman who disappeared from her life, who she only just stopped mourning was holding her again. Though Kate had aged rapidly from their separation, her arms held onto Stella tightly as they embraced again.

Kate whispered in her ear. "I can't believe you're here."

"Oh Mom," Stella said. She sniffed and tried to suppress them, but tears welled up in her eyes and she had to let them go. Kate released her again and wiped the tears from Stella's face and then wiped her own.

Stella had so much to say, but she knew they would not have time to linger. The hulking man who brought Kate down the hallway was behind them talking into his smartwatch.

"There is a situation up here," he said.

"We have to get you out of here," Stella said. She turned, pulling her mother's hand toward Rex and the others who had spilled out into the hall.

"Rex," Kate said. She threw her arms around him, and he hugged her tight.

"It's been so long, my friend," Rex said.

Zimmer marched down the hall followed by the Jacks and the other Suits negotiating for Kandi. "What's going on here?" Zimmer asked.

"I'm sorry, but the deal has not been finalized," Kline said.

"Then finalize it," Stella snapped.

Felton pursed his lips and shook his head. "This is not how we do things."

"Not at all," Kline said.

"Not like this at all," said Felton.

"Please understand these two women have not seen each other in years," Rex said. "They couldn't wait and for that I'm sorry, but—"

"That's a great story," Felton said.

"Really great," Kline replied.

"Heartwarming even."

"I've got chills."

"Same," Felton said. "But we have to do this right."

"Please get back in the room," Kline said. The Jacks went back to tapping on their tablets in unison. Stella sniffed and swallowed. She wanted nothing more than to get her mother back to the ship and catch up on the last ten years of the life she missed with her. She took her mother's hand, and Rex held the door open to their room, but

Kandi and her entourage blocked the entrance.

"Oops, that little outburst was not very becoming, Dr. Walsh," Kandi said, waving her index finger back and forth. "I would think a doctor, such as yourself, would have a tad more composure. Goodness, I wouldn't want to be on your operating table."

Stella dropped her mother's hand and charged Kandi, but hands from Rex, Elliot, and Gary held her back.

"Stella, don't," Rex said.

"Remain calm. She doesn't have anything signed," Gary said.

"You better say your goodbyes now," Kandi said. "They're gonna go with my deal."

Stella stepped in front of Kate. "I'm not letting you take her."

"Sorry, sweetie, but I don't think you're gonna have a choice," Kandi said.

Stella rushed toward Kandi. Elliot and Rex snatched her and pulled her back. Kandi threw her head back and laughed. Acid burned in the back of Stella's throat and she thrust her arm out trying to grab Kandi, but Rex and Elliot held on.

Kandi chuckled. "You really think you're hot stuff, but you have no idea who you're dealing with."

"Shut up!" Stella shouted.

"You've done it now," Kandi said. A Suit handed Kandi a tablet where she signed with her finger. "That bitch is mine."

"No!" Stella screamed. She turned to find her mother, but to her horror, her mother was being forced over to Kandi with a gun pushed into her neck.

"Iris!" Rex shouted.

"Iris, no!" Zimmer said.

"Iris, what are you doing?" Gary cried.

With her eyes wide, Iris shuffled Kate over to Kandi. "Stay back!"

she said as she shoved Kate into Taylor's arms. Stella saw how frail her mother looked. Kate was pale and tired, which must have been the only reason she was not fighting back. Iris stood in front of Kandi with a blaster extended. Taylor also pulled a blaster out of his belt and held it against Kate's temple.

"Iris, by God, don't do this," Rex said, moving slowly toward her with his hands in the air.

Iris's eyes glinted with sadness, but she kept her blaster trained on Rex.

"Too late friends; we're all leaving. Bye, bye bitches!" Kandi said. "Start transport now."

Behind Iris and Kandi, Kate and Taylor disappeared as the teleportation started. Stella screamed, and Rex lunged for Iris. Kandi then vaporized behind her. Iris shot off three shots from her blaster before vanishing, and they sped through the air even after she was gone. Rex covered his face, and Stella threw up her hands. Out of her hands a flash of green exploded, and the shots hit a shield that suddenly covered Rex, Stella, and everyone behind her. The blasts of light dissolved before they hit a single target.

The green light retreated into Stella's palms as if it were being sucked away. A phone ringing in someone's office was the only thing that made a sound. All movement ceased, and all beings on the floor were rendered speechless.

"Stella," Rex said, looking at her slack-jawed.

"Whoa," Elliot said.

"Her first shield," Zimmer said.

"Not her first," Elliot replied.

"Elliot," Stella said.

"What?" Zimmer asked.

"Rex, what are you be doin?" Criket hissed. She circled the crew and ushered them out of the hallway.

"Get in the elevator," Criket sneered. "You made too much trouble up here today!"

Several security guards shoved Stella and the others into the elevator. Not even the soothing smooth jazz could calm Stella down.

"We made a deal. Why didn't you honor it?" Stella asked.

"You are a foolish girl," Criket said. "We were doing your deal. Jack and Jack talked you all up because of their friend here." Criket pointed at Elliot.

"She's right, Stella. They were bringing Kate down to go with us, but when you ran to her before we signed, you forfeited our deal. They honored the deal; you did not," Zimmer said. Not only did Zimmer's acidic tone rattle her, but she was devastated by the realization that she was the reason her mother was not riding down in the elevator with them.

"How could I not run to her? She's my mother. How could something like that cause the deal to fall through?"

"Because there is a way to do business here. You may not understand it, you may not agree with it, but it's the way things are," Zimmer replied.

"Now the new deal stands," Criket said.

"It's not fair to penalize everyone else," Stella said. "Can't you let everyone else go?"

"You are not getting this, girl," Criket said. "That's not how it be."

"Oh no, what will be done with us?" Gary asked. His face was streaked with saltwater from him wailing over the loss of Iris.

"I do not be knowin' this," Cricket said. "You all can remain up here with the Jacks and me, and we can see what we doin' about all this. As for you ... lady. It's the pits for you."

"Criket, is that really necessary?" Rex asked.

"I'll go with her," Elliot said. "I'm her sidekick."

Criket cocked her head to one side. "What is sidekick?"

"It means they can't be separated, my dear," Rex said.

"Doesn't matter. I've been ordered to send her down. I will need this sidekick man to return to negotiations since he friend for the Jacks."

They spilled out into the lobby, and two security guards grabbed Stella from behind.

"Criket, please," Rex protested. "I'm begging you, do not do this."

Stella tried to push them off as they dragged her back into the elevator.

"Nothing I can do. She has been remanded to the Lower Level for now. Little lady needs to cool off," Criket said.

Elliot ran to the elevator, but a guard pushed him back as the door closed.

"Get off of me!" Stella shouted. The elevator rocked back and forth from her trying to pull her arms from the guards' grasp. As the elevator dinged, signaling that it had reached the cellblock of Lower Level, a guard hit Stella with a stun gun. Tingly numbness shot through her, and it was enough to immobilize her so one of the guards could pick her up and sling her over his shoulder.

The cellblock they carried her through consisted of a long stretch of cells that were set on one side of a narrow hallway.

"Where we takin' this one?" one of the guards asked.

The other one answered as he walked ahead. "Cells are more full than usual, but there is only one in 12 B at the end."

The blood rushed to Stella's head, and when it felt like it was going to pop, she was set on the floor of the last cell on the block. The chilled pavement under her felt like ice on her back. Though she was awake, she couldn't move. The guards slammed the door shut.

The dim glow from the flickering oil lamps out in the corridor didn't provide much light, and it was only when she heard someone's shoes scraping over dirt on the floor as they walked over to her that she realized she was not alone. She lifted her neck up and tried to move, but even her toes were numb. She closed her eyes and tried to will her body to move, and that's when a familiar voice said, "Welcome to cell 12 B, Stella Jayne."

# 42

# THE PITS

**STELLA HEARD A POPPING SOUND** that made her stomach turn. Ryder emerged from the shadows and crouched down beside her. She cringed as he brought his hand down on the pavement just missing the right side of her head. She opened her eyes to see him wiping a squished, blue insect from his hand. Without a word, he took her limp arm, placed it around his neck, and scooped her up into his arms. Her eyes locked with his for a moment, and her face flushed. She wondered what changed in him that he was being so gentle with her.

Ryder cleared his throat, set her down on the bench, and leaned her up against the brick wall. "Give it minute. Stunning agent should be wearing off now."

"Why wait? Aren't you just going to kill me now?"

"Not at the moment," he said casually. He took a seat across from her, leaned back, and folded his hands across his chest.

"That's reassuring I guess." Stella extended her arms as the tingling numbness subsided. "How do you know my middle name?" Stella asked.

"It's my job to know."

"And what else is in your job description?"

Ryder looked at the floor and scratched under his chin. "Depends. I'm hired to get information, to find things."

"And to kill things?"

"Sometimes."

"Don't you get tired of killing things?

Ryder paused. "Sometimes."

"I see they took your jacket."

Ryder looked slightly less threatening wearing a white T-shirt and leather pants.

"They did. I'll get it back," Ryder said. He shifted on the bench. "So what happened?"

"What do you mean?"

"They only send the troublemakers down here."

Stella glanced at him sitting in the corner as if he were riding on the A Train and was trying to make conversation to pass the time. She figured time was what she had now in the cell, so she shrugged and decided to answer.

"I lost my deal," she said. "I didn't listen, and I reacted. Now I'm down here, and I lost my mother again."

Ryder slid forward on the bench. "Your mother, the woman you wanted to trade me for?"

Stella gulped. "Yes. They told me to wait, and I couldn't. When I saw her, I couldn't help it. For the last ten years I thought she was dead. When I saw her, I lost it."

"I see."

Stella shook her head. "It's my fault. I should have followed the rules. Now she's gone with that woman you work for."

Ryder nodded. "Your mother must be the Healer she was looking for."

"Yes. What's going to happen to her?"

"She won't be harmed. Shook means to use her in one of the tanks. Not sure how it works exactly. Your mother is more valuable alive and healthy, if that's any consolation."

Stella felt tears of frustration welling up in her eyes. *If only I had listened to the others. If only I had sat back down in the conference room* … Those thoughts repeated over and over in her mind. It stung her to be that close to her mother and to now be so far again.

"There was nothing you could have done," Ryder said. "Whether or not you waited, Shook doesn't stop until she gets what she wants."

Stella glanced at Ryder silently, wondering what had changed in him. His expression was softer; almost concerned. Before she could ask him, footsteps echoed in the corridor. The sound of clanging keys against cell doors and doors opening followed.

"What's happening?" Stella asked.

"They're taking us down to the sparring pits," Ryder replied.

"The what?"

"The pits." Ryder stood up and made his way to the door. "Down here, they pick some of us to fight for them while Sekke Elders place bets on who will win. Only way in or out is the way we came. They let us out in there for a while, and then you either get to walk back to your cell or they drag you back. My advice … keep your head down and do what they say."

Two guards entered their cell. Ryder stuck out his hands, and a guard fitted him with electronic cuffs. Stella reluctantly stuck out her hands, and though it was not her instinct to fall in line, she learned a lesson by not following the rules earlier. Another guard bent down and attached a thin single cuff around one of Ryder's and Stella's ankles.

"What's that?" Stella asked.

The guard smirked. "Keeps you from runnin'. If you run past the pit barrier with this on trying to escape, you'll be dust before you know it."

Stella gulped as her ankle monitor beeped from being activated. The guards then grabbed Stella and Ryder and shoved them in line with prisoners they were releasing from the other cells on the cell block. One by one, the prisoners made their way down a long, stone staircase that descended into the sparring arena. The shrieks from the Sekke sitting in viewing balconies high above sent a chill down Stella's spine as her eyes adjusted to the dim lights of the arena. It resembled a prison yard except for pits dug in the dirt floor where some prisoners were fighting. A wooden half-wall with one gate separated each pit where other prisoners cheered on whomever was sparring.

"Stay back; blend into the crowd. Don't get too close to the pits or they might toss you in," Ryder said.

Stella nodded and tried to swallow the lump in her throat. Aromas of sweat, blood, and dirt hung like a cloud in the arena. Some prisoners sat at stone tables talking to one another; some looked like they were recovering from a fight they just lost.

The arena appeared medieval compared to what Stella had seen in the rest of the city except for digital screens attached to the walls overhead that appeared to be keeping tallies of which fighters were winning, which were losing, and which had, as the screen said, "Expired." Guards with guns patrolled from scaffolding that ran below the viewing balconies.

A scream sounded, and one of the guards from above yelled. "We've got a runner!"

The line of prisoners stepped out of the way just as a man yelled something in a foreign language and made a run for the exit. An alarm sounded, and a red laser grid appeared in front of the staircase. The man ran into it and evaporated into gray dust that fell to the floor. The ankle monitor hit the ground with a thud. A man smoking a cigarette came over with a long vacuum hose that was attached to a backpack. He causally sucked up the ashes of the runner, and the commotion in the pits resumed as if nothing happened. Stella was frozen, staring at the last few ashes that still sprinkled the ground, but soon she felt a poke in her side from a guard grunting at her to keep moving.

One guard turned to Ryder. "You're up, mate. They couldn't wait to get you down here. Got a lot of credits riding on you." He pushed Ryder through the crowd of prisoners, and a hush fell over them as Ryder walked to the first sparring pit. Two men were throwing jabs at each other in the circle, but they stopped once Ryder entered the ring. The two men scooted out, and for a moment Ryder stood in the pit by himself. The normally loud and boisterous crowd of onlookers now whispered to each other. The guards on the ground signaled to those guarding from above to train their blasters on Ryder. One guard entered the pit so he could release Ryder's hands in preparation to fight.

It was no problem for Stella to fade into the mass of people that swarmed Ryder's pit. They pushed against each other and stood on their toes, eager to see who would enter to take up the challenge. A scruffy man finally approached the pit. His tank top was splattered with blood and grime. He sauntered in, chest puffed out, and stood in front of Ryder with clenched fists. He was taller, but leaner. From the reactions of the spectators, it appeared Ryder was not their favorite to win.

Ryder twisted his neck to each side and pressed down on his knuckles, popping them all together. He took off his shirt and threw it to the side. Murmurs from the crowd broke the silence, and Stella heard one of the human men looking on say, "Whoa, so many emblems."

"Remember gents, fair fight," said the guard. "Loser is the first one to cry truce."

Ryder and his opponent eyed each other, and then the other man decided to make the first move. He crouched into a fighting stance with his fists up and began to circle Ryder, who remained still. The man threw a punch, and Ryder ducked and hit the man in the ribs. The man fell back but rushed at Ryder again. Ryder snatched the man's hand and whipped it around his back. Ryder pulled the man's fingers back and, with an unsettling crack, broke two of them. Ryder blocked another punch with his forearms and then landed a punch to the man's jaw. The man cried out, and the crowd cheered. Ryder released him, and the man stumbled. The man's face was flushed, and he charged at Ryder, this time forcing him to the ground.

The group watching the action grew as others rushed in. Stella was pushed to the side, and though she could no longer see what was happening she could hear grunts and moans mostly coming from Ryder's opponent as they struggled on the ground. Stella pushed her way up to the platform and saw that Ryder had the man on the ground in a headlock. Ryder's legs were wrapped around his torso. The man must have landed a couple of punches because Ryder had a gash above his eye and blood streaming down the side of his face.

The man spit and struggled. He couldn't move with Ryder wrapped around him. He cried out, "Truce! Truce!" and Ryder immediately released him. An explosion of cheers and jeers followed. Stella overheard someone asking the person next to him what was coming next. "He has to stay in until someone puts him down," the man said.

Next, a stubby and thick-set man entered the ring. The crowd on the platform jostled so much that Stella stepped down, not wanting to get pushed around with the screaming spectators. Three other pits had fighters in them, but only one toward the corner had as many people watching and cheering as Ryder's did. It sounded like a woman laughing in between punches, which piqued Stella's curiosity. She caught two Sekke men leering at her from a table, and she thought it might be better to blend in as Ryder suggested. She climbed up onto the platform surrounding the pit. She forced her way through the railing surrounding it and gasped.

One of those sparring was a muscular man partially covered in fur and the other a curvaceous, dark-skinned woman who sent him to the ground with a kick to the chest. Everyone cheered, but Stella remained frozen, clamping down on the railing, eyes wide. Fighting in the pit and laughing with every blow she landed was the last person Stella expected to see.

# 43

# WILLOW

**"WILLOW!"** Stella shouted.

Willow looked up into the crowd and her eyes locked with Stella's. "Stella?"

Stella calling to Willow distracted her long enough that the man she was sparring with could whip out an illegal knife from the waistband of his pants. He threw the knife, and as it sailed through the air, Stella caught a glint of light off the blade. She shouted for Willow and raised her hands. Green light burst out of her palms. An auroral shield surrounded Willow just in time, and the knife bounced off it, clattering to the ground. Willow stood motionless for a moment and then glanced down at her own hands, which appeared to change although Stella could not make out what was happening from where she was.

The light eventually retreated, and those watching the fight fell silent. Those on the platform inched away from Stella as the crowd began to disperse. Willow called two guards over to bring attention to the fact that the man she was fighting with had an illegal weapon. The crowd dispersed, and the guards hauled the hairy man away. Stella jumped down and ran to the entrance of the pit, but Willow had already left and hustled to an area behind a section of stone tables. She ducked behind a wall and Stella followed, calling after her.

"Willow?" Stella entered a room with a marble fountain in the center. A man was drinking from it and splashing water on his face. He slipped out and that's when Stella heard someone whisper from the corner.

Willow waved her over and extended her arms. Stella ran to her, and when they embraced, a sonic boom of green light shot up between Stella and Willow. They stepped back for a moment and embraced again. Unlike Maren and her mother, Willow did not look as though she had aged except for her hair. Her once lovely, dark braids were now snow-white dreadlocks, which were a shocking contrast to her ebony skin.

"Stella, what are you doing here? How? How did you get here?" Willow asked.

"I can't even begin to tell you," Stella said. "I was abducted by a man, and then Captain Rex found me, he told me everything—about who I am, about the Keepers—we went to see Maren, and we came here. Willow, my mother was here—"

"Slow down, slow down," Willow said. Willow's eyes lit up and her mouth formed into a smile. She kissed Stella on the cheek and hugged her again. Stella squeezed back. After losing her mother again, it was good to be in the company of one of her dearest friends.

"Let's sit down," Willow said. "I need to rest. That last guy gave me a run for my money. Thanks to you, I will fight again."

They sat down on a stone slab across from the fountain. The lights in the water were reflected in blue, glowing ripples on the walls.

"I can't believe you are fighting in these pits," Stella said. "I thought the separation was supposed to make you weaker?"

Willow clasped Stella's hand in hers. "The separation impacts all of us differently. My powers are gone, I can't see into minds, I can't control energy, I'm more forgetful than I ever was, but I can still fight. And, you know, being stuck down here, fighting makes me feel like I'm still alive."

"You're a Keeper of the Mind, so that's how it affects you—your mind isn't what it used to be?" Stella asked.

"That's right. I have good days, but the days that go by without stimulation … my mind gets fuzzy."

"How long have you been down here?"

Willow looked up and took a deep breath. "You know, I don't remember." Willow shook her head. "What is stuck in my mind is the fact that I had a dream about you the other night. You were floating toward me out of the sky, and when you touched my hand, I was lifted out of my cell and flying with you. And now, here you are. I'm beside myself."

"Well, that was definitely a dream because I hate to fly."

Willow laughed and then put her arm around Stella, hugging her again. "That's going to change, believe me. I'm beyond filled with joy seeing you. I just wish it was under different circumstances. Now, tell me, how did you get down here? You said you saw your mother and Maren?"

Stella brought Willow up to speed, telling her of the abduction, waking up next to Elliot, their encounter with Stallworth, and Captain Rex and Zimmer telling her about who she really is. Stella talked about Ryder and Kandi's plan, seeing Maren, and the events that unfolded upstairs.

Willow rubbed her neck. "My, oh my, you have been through it. And now, if what you say is true, the Zuldari are moving out of the shadows with that woman's help. What was her name? Shook?"

Stella nodded.

Willow continued. "She doesn't know what she's getting into by helping heal the Zuldari. The Zuldari always find someone they can use and then lose. If they have your mother, she will no doubt be used to lure you. Oh goodness."

"And now we are probably stuck down here because of me," Stella said.

"Possibly," Willow said. "You should have waited and listened to Rex."

"Thanks, that makes me feel better," Stella said.

Willow laughed. "Feel better, my dear. You made an error in judgement—one that led you down here to me. We just need to get out of here and get to Kate as soon as we can. Talk to the Elder, Criket. She seems to be one of the more reasonable Sekke. You and Rex have to convince her to let us go."

"Don't we have to make a deal?" Stella asked.

"Tell her the deal is our freedom for the future of all Criket holds dear in the universe. She makes deals. Try to reason with her by suggesting this will impact her and the Sekke way of life because if the Zuldari come back to power, they will not stop until every planet is under their control."

The deep reverberation of a gong rattled through the alcove, and guards began to shout that the fighting for the day was done.

"They're rounding us up," Willow said as she stood up.

"Wait! How will I know how to find you? What if we can't get Criket to help?" Stella asked.

Willow wiped a stray piece of hair out of Stella's face. "When you saw me in the pit and you saw the blade flying, what were you thinking?"

"I … I don't know. The word *shield* popped in my mind, and it happened. I didn't think; I just did it."

"And that's how you do it. It's all about turning your questioning thoughts around. Instead of how will you find me, say you *will* find me. Instead of wondering if Criket will help, think Criket *will* help. Just start to think it, and it will come. It may not seem like it at first, but if you set your mind to what you want, it will happen."

"Seems easier said than done," Stella said, kicking at some dirt on the floor.

"Trust me, it works. Get back to your cell. Hopefully, you won't have to stay down here much longer."

Stella left Willow at the entrance of the alcove and guards forced her back into a line. Ryder remained, trying to win one last brawl in the pit. He was bloodied and beaten but still standing. The last bit of onlookers booed as his opponent landed a punch to his face. Ryder spit out a glob of blood and charged, blocking another punch and landing one of his own to the man's ribs and then the man's throat. Everyone watching shouted and hollered, and the man went stiff and fell to the ground in a heap.

Ryder picked up his shirt and limped out of the pit. The guards allowed him to splash his face with water and rinse out his mouth before they put the cuffs back on him. He then fell back in line behind Stella as everyone made their way up the staircase. The guard shoved Stella back into cell 12 B, but kept the door open so Ryder could hobble in. Stella gaped at him when he stumbled in and collapsed on the floor.

He wiped blood from his nose and his cheek. The gashes were healing on their own, but a large cut on his forehead wasn't as quick to repair. Stella tried to help him sit up.

He moaned and touched his side. "I'm fine," he winced.

Stella moved his hand away, and her eyes zeroed in on where his hand had been. It was if she could see right through his flesh. A picture as clear as a photograph appeared in her mind, and she could see the broken rib in his body.

She put her hand on his side and he squirmed.

"Please stop," he said. He looked at her, his eye wide.

She scooted closer to him on the floor. "Your rib is broken."

"Pretty standard for me. It will fix itself after a while."

"I can fix it right now," Stella said.

"Don't …" Ryder protested. Stella placed her hand on his side and one thought appeared in her mind. The word "repair" was all she could see. She then saw bones moving, creeping back together. Ryder cried out, but she maintained focus and the bones eventually grew back together, healing as if they had never been broken. She then gently touched his forehead, and before her eyes, the blood stopped dripping and the wound vanished.

Ryder's chest heaved as Stella pulled her hand away. "Thank you," he said.

Stella remained close to him and his eyes met hers. "Why didn't you do it?" she asked.

"Do what?"

"When you had the chance to hurt me, to kill me, even with your sister's life on the line, why didn't you?"

A flush of red filled Ryder's cheeks. "I don't know."

Stella inched closer to him. "Yes, you do," she said.

He didn't say anything for what seemed like the longest time; he just sat looking into her eyes.

Ryder then cleared his throat. "Lots of reasons, I guess. My sister, Pip—she would not want me to do all this for her. I'm a Kaygun soldier, and we swear an oath to protect those who need it. The man I was … I would have fought for you, Pip would have fought for you, and we would have done anything to safeguard the Keepers."

"You're still that man," Stella said.

"Not after what I've done. I don't know what I am anymore. What I do know is in the past few months, I've felt sad and lonely. I've missed my family and the life I knew, and lately, I've felt so much anger that I've wanted to rip out my own guts just to find a release, but … I feel better … when I'm around you."

He tried to look away, but Stella reached out and turned his face back to hers. His eye dilated and his lips parted. Stella leaned in and could feel his breath on her lips, but the jingle of keys on the cell door interrupted them.

"You, Red. You're going back upstairs," the guard said, opening the door.

Stella took one last look at Ryder as the guard pulled her out. She cringed hearing the door slam, knowing she had to leave Ryder behind. She ascended with the guards on an elevator, and Elliot was waiting as a door opened at the top.

"Hey," Elliot said. Stella rushed into his open arms. "Are you okay?"

"I'll live," Stella said.

"I talked the Jacks into letting you come back upstairs."

"Thank you. But it was good I was down there."

"Eww, why?" Elliot led Stella back to the conference room.

"I saw Willow."

"Your Mom's friend? She's a Keeper of Mind, right?"

"She is, and we need to find a way to get her out," Stella said.

"I may have found a way. I talked to the Jacks and they have a new deal for us."

"Who do we have to trade?"

"It's not a who, but something we can do to get out of here."

# 44

# OBSTACLES

**ZIMMER, GARY, AND REX STOOD UP** when Elliot and Stella made it back to the room. Rex reached out his hand for Stella.

"I want to apologize," Stella said, taking Rex's hand.

"Not at all," Rex said. "Stella, you have been through so much, seeing your mother must have put you over the edge. We'll find a way to get out of here, and you shall be reunited with Kate soon. You didn't come all this way for it not to happen."

Stella smiled at Rex, appreciating his kindness even as part of her did not feel she deserved it. "I don't know how. I messed up everything by not listening." Stella took a seat at the conference table, and the others followed.

"Stella, when you worked at your hospital, did you work alone?"

Stella looked at Rex, wondering where that question came from. "No, I had a team, an amazing team that supported everything I did. I miss them every day."

"I'm sure you do, and while I know we can never replace them, I want you to think of us as your new team. We are here only to support you. The only thing we ask in return is that you trust us."

She didn't say anything but nodded and mouthed the word, "Okay."

"What happened down there?" Elliot asked.

"I spoke to Willow," Stella said.

Everyone perked up.

"Where did you speak to her?" Zimmer asked.

"Down in the pits," Stella replied.

"You were actually in the sparring pits? Were you fighting?" Gary asked.

"No, but she was," Stella said.

"Incredible," Rex said. He sat forward in his seat and began to rub his chin.

"She said we should talk to Criket and find a way to convince her to help us," Stella said.

Slowly everyone in the room all turned their gazes toward Zimmer. He furrowed his brow and tried to change the subject. "How was Willow's health?"

"She said her mind felt fuzzy. Her hair has turned white, but other than that, she looked the same as I remember her. She was actually fighting well in the pits."

"Sounds right," Rex added. "We'll talk to Criket as soon as we are done with these blasted Suits."

It was then that Jack and Jack walked in and sat down at the head of the table. In perfect unison, they pulled out tablets and pieces of paper and then rested their chins on their hands.

"All right, well it appears that ... how do I say this?" Felton asked.

"I'll say it," Kline offered.

"Will you?

"Of course."

"Thank you, because it was really going to be difficult for me to say."

"That's why I'm here," Kline said.

"And for that I'm grateful," Felton said.

Fist bump.

"You two are exhausting," Stella said.

"I'll pretend we didn't hear that," Felton said. "We had a deal with you; that is true."

"Very true," Kline said.

"But at the last minute, a Kandice Shook pitched a better offer."

"Way better."

"However, since Driver here is our bro, we pushed to get you all a new deal since the other one fell through," Felton said.

"You are going to love this new deal," Kline said.

"Love it!"

"It's the best deal possible," Kline said.

"Just spit it out man!" Rex shouted.

Felton continued. "We had to really fight for this."

"But we did because Driver is our bud, am I right?" Kline said, winking at Elliot.

Elliot laughed nervously, and the Jacks continued. "We have secured your release once Driver here successfully completes our obstacle course," Felton said.

Fist bump.

Elliot glanced at the Jacks. "Wait, what? What obstacle course?"

"One we have had specially built," Kline said.

Felton said, "Show course site A," and the TV on the wall turned on. An aerial image revealed a set of obstacles.

"Once he finishes, you are all free to go. That's the new deal," Felton added.

"I have never heard of a deal being changed like this," Zimmer said.

"To be fair, she changed the course of the deal, not us," Kline said. Both Jacks threw a look of shade toward Stella. Stella already felt guilty;

she did not need these two talking heads to make her feel worse. She
opened her mouth, ready with an insult, but she caught Rex and Zimmer
glaring at her. She closed her mouth and decided to follow the rules.

Elliot asked, straightening in his chair. "You mean …"

"You got it, buddy," Felton said.

"The same course you've run on. Just like the one at home."

"This is your moment, Driver."

"Excuse me? What moment?" Rex said.

"Don't you know who this guy is?" Felton asked.

"He's famous."

Elliot blushed. "Uh, almost … almost famous."

"No, you are. We told the Sekke Elders about you, and they want
to see you do their course."

"This is it, buddy!" Felton said.

"Driver?" Rex asked. "What are they talking about?"

"Driver here is an American Ninja Warrior," Felton said.

"Take a look," Kline said.

Felton pressed a button on the table. The wall separated and
revealed a screen. Kline got up and entered in a code, then said, "Elliot
Driver, Earth, USA, Denver, American Ninja Warrior semifinals," out
loud.

A video appeared of Elliot on the starting platform waving to the
crowd as the announcers introduced him. Elliot made it through all the
obstacles, and then a sea of cheers erupted from the crowd watching.
Stella eyed Elliot as his eyes remained glued to the screen. She could
see that he was proud, seeing himself finish each obstacle. He waved
to the audience after each one. That is, until he got to the last one—
something called The Warped Wall. It consisted of a massive, curved
wall that warriors had to clear by running at it and then trying to push
themselves to the top where they could press the buzzer signaling they

made it through the course. Jack said, "Pause," and froze the video.

"How? How did you get this?" Elliot asked.

Felton winked at Elliot. "We have our ways, my friend."

"What am I looking at?" Rex asked. "Is this some strange prewar … warrior rite of passage?"

"Uh, yes, in a way," Elliot said.

"All right!" Kline said.

"This is exciting," Felton said.

"It is, isn't it?"

"Anyway, if Driver finishes our course, you get to go," Felton said.

"If he does not, you stay," Kline said.

"And we negotiated it down so that if you all find yourselves permanent residents of Kodon, you will be free from danger and perform in our entertainment division," Felton said.

"No fighting or working—just performing in a set of lovely costumes," Kline said.

"They are lovely, aren't they?" Felton asked.

"The best," Kline replied.

"Driver, can you complete this course?" Rex asked.

Elliot's eyes were glued to the screen as he saw himself frozen in time falling down the wall.

"Yes … um … I mean, I'd have to check it out. How long do I have to train for this?"

"You will compete in exactly twenty-four hours," Felton said.

"We can't wait," Kline added.

"Um, I won't be ready by then," Elliot protested. Elliot stood up, but the Jacks were not phased.

"You got this, bro!" Felton said.

"Yeah, you're the beast!" Kline said.

"We will draw up the papers for this new deal, and you can sign before you go out tomorrow," Felton said. He got up and patted Elliot on the back.

"Criket will be right up to take you to your accommodations for the night," Kline said. He offered to fist bump Elliot's hand. Elliot reluctantly accepted.

Jack and Jack chuckled with each other as they left through the glass doors.

"Goodness, did you just fall down?" Gary asked as he pointed to the screen.

"No, it's the way the camera is ... uh ... the angle is off," Elliot stammered.

Gary laid his head in his arms on the table. "Oh, we are going to die here! And Iris is gone. I'm not sure how to cope with this information."

Rex tried to comfort Gary. "Come on now. Driver does look like a beast. I'm sure this will be easy for him, right?"

Elliot scratched his head. "Sure, of course."

Stella was relieved to see Criket come through the door. She couldn't bear to see Elliot squirm any longer.

"Where are you taking us?" Stella asked once Criket waved her hands for them to follow her.

"A place where we can talk, do rest, and do thinking things," Criket said with a smile. "My abode."

# 45
## LIZARDS IN THE NIGHT

**THE VELOCIRAPTORS SHRIEKED** as Stella and the crew piled into the Hovercart. Criket rode ahead on her own raptor. The night air felt cool and a welcome relief from the hot dampness Stella experienced in the Lower Levels. At first, they all rode in silence until Zimmer broke it.

"Why didn't you tell us you threw your first shield?" Zimmer asked, crossing his arms. His expression was tight, and he glared at Stella, waiting for an answer.

By the looks she got from the others, Rex and Gary also had the same question, although Rex tried to diffuse the tension. "We can speak about this later, my friend. Stella has had a pretty rough go of it."

Stella appreciated what Rex was trying to do, but she thought it best to answer. "Because I didn't know what it was. I thought I was hallucinating."

"When did it first happen?" Zimmer asked.

Stella paused, and then reluctantly answered. "On Stallworth's ship."

"You should have told us," Zimmer said, and then he turned his attention to a pod of dinosaurs running over the hills next to the Hovercar.

"I didn't tell you because I didn't want to believe it. You know, I had a life in New York ... on Earth. Whether it was real or not, or who I was meant to be, it was my life and it was all I had ever known. I was ripped out of that life and told things no normal person would just believe willingly. I'm not going to say I'm sorry for not telling you something I didn't even believe could be true."

Zimmer glanced back to Stella and nodded as if he understood, though he did not say another word the rest of the way. Lights in the distance popped up as they neared. As they got closer, Stella could see a grand house nestled in an oasis of lush palms and ferns. A fountain stood, rising out of a reflecting pond to the side of the house. Stone pathways led from the front drive through a garden.

"Hey, hoooo! Welcome to the house!" Criket cheered from the doorway.

Stella and Elliot exited the Hovercart, slack-jawed and speechless.

"I thought she was going to be living in some cave," Elliot said.

"It makes houses in the Hamptons look tiny," Stella added.

"Ha! You shall have a grand rest tonight before your big day tomorrow," Criket said, ushering them inside. A purple-and-black-striped Sekke man greeted them, wearing a white sheathe and a tiny hat. He bowed as everyone walked in, and then he tended to the raptors who screeched as he took them to the back of the house. Inside, there were thirty-foot-tall ceilings and a winding marble staircase that connected to a long hallway upstairs. Tiles were arranged in intricate patterns under their feet. The foyer resembled a five-star hotel lobby.

Criket wrapped her scaly arm around Zimmer and pulled him close. "Come now, my sweet, loosen that tie. No Suits allowed in this house." She took off his jacket and threw it to another Sekke man waiting in the foyer. Zimmer loosened his ugly orange tie. "You shall have food and drink and sleep. Yes, there is plenty of space in my room."

Zimmer chuckled and yanked at his collar.

Stella bit her lip. *Ha! I love how uncomfortable Criket makes him. He's so tightly wound he could use a little romance, even if it's from a woman with green skin.*

Zimmer and Criket plopped down on a maroon sofa while a servant handed them glasses of champagne.

The servant then offered Stella a glass as she stood with Elliot, Gary, and Rex; they watched Criket cuddling with Zimmer.

Rex's mouth fell open when Stella took a glass. "You are drinking now?" Rex also took a glass. "My, you never fail to surprise me."

Stella shrugged and took a sip. The bubbles danced off her tongue, and the aroma of apples and pears filled her with instant comfort.

The Sekke man offered a glass to Elliot. "Sure, why not? Lizard people riding dinosaurs, living in mansions, and drinking champagne. I'll say cheers to that."

Stella laughed.

"This is my favorite planet so far. It's like, anything goes," Elliot said.

"I suppose we are here only because Criket has a big crush on Zimmer, is that it?" Stella asked.

"You are correct in that, though it boggles the mind, doesn't it?" Rex said.

They all glanced over to see Criket kiss the side of Zimmer's cheek.

"A welcome distraction, I say, after the day we have had. The loss of Iris ... well, I don't think I can recover," Gary said, taking a seat in a leather chair.

Stella saw Rex's mouth turn down as he took a seat across from him.

"What do you think happened?" Stella asked.

"I don't know. Once we get off this godforsaken place, Zimmer will try to gather some intel on her. But I surmise that her working on the inside for Kandi was how Ryder was able to find us and stay a step ahead for the most part. We will track her down, and I will interview her myself. I loved her and trusted her as one of my own. Her betrayal has left a deep wound." Rex sipped his drink and his eyes focused on the floor. "I knew Iris was always different—quiet and reserved—but I never saw this coming."

Gary sobbed in his hands.

"For all that is holy, I wish his engineers would not have fashioned him with tear ducts," Rex said quietly to Stella and Elliot.

"She was perfect in every way!" Gary said.

"Cheers to that, Gary," Rex said, lifting his glass.

"I'm sorry about Iris, but I think we have a bigger problem," Stella said. "How are we going to get out of here with Willow?"

"Well, that depends on how confident we are that Driver can clear that course," Rex replied.

Stella and the others turned to Elliot, who trembled under the weight of their stares.

"Driver?" Rex said.

"Um, yes, I'm pretty confident ... well mostly ... some. I have mostly some confidence, although I haven't been training, but hey, all I can do is try, am I right?" Elliot guzzled his champagne.

Rex narrowed his eyes. "Right."

"For what it's worth, I believe in you," Gary offered.

"Thank you," Elliot said.

"And I do as well. You can do this," Rex added.

Stella was not sure she was as confident as the others were saying they were. Then she remembered what Willow had said to her.

"Yep, he's going to do it," Stella said. "You're a beast, right Elliot?"

Elliot grinned at her. "That's right. I ... I can do it."

"What is this chatter about?" Criket asked, calling from the separate seating area. "Come here and sit by us."

Stella got up, but Rex pulled her aside before they made their way to the separate sofa.

"Let's not stress how valuable Willow is. Best not to mention that she is a Keeper. Criket may not want to let her go," Rex said in a hushed voice.

Stella nodded.

She sat down on the sofa across from Zimmer and Criket.

"What are you speaking over there in hushed voices?" Criket asked.

Stella didn't want to wait for the others. "We need your help."

Criket stopped playing with Zimmer's ear and leaned forward. "What is this? My help?"

"There is a woman in your Lower Level. She is one of our dear friends and our crew member. We need to secure her release when Driver passes your course," Stella said.

"You trade for her?" Criket asked.

"No, we have nothing to trade, but—" Stella started.

"If you have nothing to trade, then we cannot speak of this."

*Criket will help us. She will help us.* She repeated those phrases over and over in her mind.

Rex stood up and paced around the back of the room. "Criket, there is a threat growing that will affect all of us."

"So? The Zuldari do not bother us," Criket said.

"They will. This time they will, if we don't stop them," Rex said.

"You know that Sekke do not war. We do trade; we make deals. We do not choose sides."

"A war is coming, whether the Sekke want to choose a side or not," Rex said.

"It's true," Zimmer said. "If you help us, we can offer Kodon protection."

Criket's eyes bounced around everyone in the room, and her brow furrowed. "Kodon has never needed this protection from anyone."

"Trust me, this new threat from the Zuldari will affect us all," Rex said. Rex shot Zimmer a look and cocked his head quickly.

"Er, we know that Kodon is a strong and powerful nation. You are brave fighters and wise with your business," Zimmer said. He reached for Criket's hand. "But we fear if the Zuldari are not stopped now, we will all lose. We need your help."

Criket's eyes softened, and she squeezed Zimmer's hand. "And what is this help you need?"

"The woman I saw in the sparring pits. She is a friend, a member of our crew. She can help us in the fight," Stella added.

"Who is this?" Criket asked.

"Her name is Willow," Stella replied.

Criket thought for a moment. "Ah yes, Willow. She is good. She wins much credits in the pits. Not thinking it is good for business to release her."

"Please, Criket, she is a long-lost member of our crew. It would mean so much to be reunited with her," Zimmer said, wrapping his arm around her.

Stella pulled her lips inward so that they would not give way to a smile. Zimmer had always seemed so grumpy to her. From what she could gather from her interactions with him, he did not suffer fools and was not a patient or warm person. And yet, he was cuddling up to Criket as if he knew it was wearing her down. Criket stared into Zimmer's eyes and then touched her nose to his.

"Okay, I will do this for you, my sweet," Criket said. "Once your man wins the course, I will take you to the Lower Level to get that Willow.

Though, I cannot be seen as helping you without a deal. Best to make it look like I did not assist."

"How will we get her out without making it look like you helped us?" Stella asked.

Criket rubbed her chin. "I will sneak you out in a hush, then give you a head start. You will run, I will make a chase after you. If you can make it back to your ship, the escape is yours."

"Thank you. We will not forget this," Stella said.

"Better not, and better not forget the trouble you caused. You have been doing me much hurt to my head," Criket said. "Now, enough business. Let's eat and drink and ..." Criket turned to Zimmer and ran her finger along his chin, "... make much love."

"Oh, my word," Gary said. He fanned himself with his hand.

Rex spit out his champagne and choked on what was left in his throat.

Stella got up and patted Rex on the back. "Well, we should, uh, leave you two to catch up," Stella said.

Zimmer shot her a warning look.

"Yes! There is much refreshment in the kitchen, and you can take any rooms upstairs," Criket said.

Stella and the others left the room just as Criket was trying to unbutton Zimmer's shirt. A Sekke servant led them to an open kitchen with a spread of food that caused Stella to salivate, not only from what was laid out but also from the salty, sweet, and savory smells that tickled her nostrils.

"Please, you may enjoy," the servant said. "Much Terran food has been gathered for you." He promptly left the room.

"I want to shovel everything in my mouth right now," Elliot said as he hovered over a meat tray.

"Wait," Stella said. "How do we know what all this is?"

Rex tossed a carrot. "Gary, can you scan this?"

Gary stepped up and examined the spread, his eyes darting back and forth across the counter. He fell silent as his head shook, and then he looked up as if he just came out of a trance.

"I can verify that this is a mix of favorite Verbatain and Terran foods. All derived from plant sources though some are made to look like Terran meat products. Definitely safe to …"

Everyone looked at Elliot, who already had his mouth full.

Stella set her plate down. *How can I eat when the people I care about are out there … suffering?*

"What's wrong? Is it possible that you are not hungry?" Rex asked.

"That seems impossible," Gary added.

"How can I eat and enjoy this food and this place when my mother and Willow and …" Stella paused, "… others … are hurting and in danger."

Rex wiped his hands on a napkin. "I hear you, and I don't have a sterling answer to what you're feeling. Maybe think of it as not really enjoying, but resting, refueling, and getting ready for the next battle. We do enjoy these moments in between at times, but it's nothing to feel guilty about. It doesn't take away from how worried we are about the ones we love. Besides, Kate and Willow are no wallflowers. They have seen battlefields your mind cannot even fathom. They are so strong, and it will do you no good to make yourself sick with worry."

"I agruffered," Elliot said, trying quickly to swallow his food.

Rex's comments reassured her, but she couldn't help but feel anxious about how the next day would unfold.

After they had their fill, they made their way upstairs. Rex and Gary bid Stella and Elliot goodnight and retreated into two rooms. Stella heard a sound below and peered over the railing to see Criket dragging Zimmer, by his ugly orange tie, into a room off the sitting room. She waved to Elliot, and he glanced down as well. They watched until they heard a door close and then the click of a lock.

"That guy is about to earn his stripes tonight," Elliot said. "Can't believe he's going to debase himself for the cause. Glad all I have to do is finish the course."

"You wouldn't shack up with the lizard lady for a night to save us?"

Elliot looked up at the ceiling. "Actually, I would."

"Oh, please," Stella laughed.

"Hey, I do not discriminate when it comes to saving the universe," Elliot said. "Just set phasers to 'love me'... am I right?"

# 46

# THE WALL

**STELLA PACED IN THE VIEWING AREA** that ran parallel to the obstacle course in the main outdoor arena of Duma City. The seats in the stadium were full of cheering Sekke while some of the Suits watched from enclosed balconies in a separate section. The course was a mix of obstacles that Stella recognized from TV, but the pools of water were larger underneath. The viewing area she was in was shielded from the blazing heat, even though it was open so the breeze could come in. With the help of fans overhead, it was surprisingly cool inside.

She waited with Gary and Rex for Elliot to join. He was being kept in a separate staging area and fitted with the clothing he was to compete in. Moments later, Elliot entered the room, but without his usual swagger and confidence.

"Oh my God," Stella said.

Rex walked over to Elliot with his mouth open. "What the …?"

"The final insult," Elliot said, looking down at the rainbow-striped, silken leotard he was dressed in.

Stella turned away. *Don't laugh. Do not laugh.*

Elliot looked as if he were headed on stage for a clown ballet performance rather than trying to compete for their freedom in an outdoor obstacle course. The suit had a tank top but was one solid piece like a jumper. It hugged him like a second skin, and when Stella turned back, she could not help but stare.

"Eyes up here, Stella," Elliot said, pointing to his chest.

Stella cleared her throat. "Uh, is it comfortable at all?"

Elliot jumped up and down extending his arms and rolling them around. He twisted, turned, and touched his toes. "I guess, but not sure if it's moisture wicking."

"I think that's the least of your worries," Stella said. "How are you feeling?"

Elliot exhaled loudly. "Not great, but I guess if I pass this, it will count as me helping you out of a jam, right?"

"That's right, and you are going to be great. You *will* get up that wall," Stella said.

Just then, Criket strolled in, arm in arm with Zimmer. He sat down in a chair as she walked out of the viewing room and onto a platform where she waved to the spectators and spoke in her native tongue. The crowd erupted and then started to chant and beat on their railings.

Stella grasped Elliot's hand as he walked to the door waiting for Criket to call him out. "You got this," Stella said. She almost did not get those words out as she could feel her heart in her throat.

"Do I? Is it too late to just start running?" His hand felt cold and clammy. "This is the exact course. I don't know how they did it, but this is the exact course."

"What exact course?" Stella asked.

"The one I can never finish."

Criket motioned that it was time for Elliot to come out.

Stella grabbed his face in her hands. "You will finish this. You will." She saw how scared he was and, in the moment, she threw her arms around him and kissed him. He kissed her back, and a jolt of lightning rocketed through her.

Elliot's face flushed when he pulled away. "I will." He tugged at his costume and jogged out into the arena. He panted on the entrance platform, squinted in the brutal sun, and then bent down to running stance as he waited for the starting horn.

Criket returned to the viewing area, excited and laughing.

"Why did you put him in such a costume?" Stella asked.

"Ah, so he is better seen from under the water," Criket replied.

Stella gulped. "What?"

"Nothing, my dear one. Now sit, watch, and enjoy the show." The door to the room opened, and a guard entered. "This is Gio," Criket said. "He will take you down to the Lower Level after the event to find your Willow if your man wins."

Rex and Stella nodded in agreement.

"I will be meeting you at the entrance of Duma City after your friend is free. Bye for now." Criket kissed Zimmer on the way out. Gio waited outside the door.

Zimmer took a glass of water that had been sitting on a nearby table. He drank some and then splashed the rest on his face.

"How you holding up, old boy?" Rex asked. "Rough night?"

Zimmer scowled and wiped his mouth. "I will not be discussing it. Let's just hope Driver can finish this, and if he can't, I'm stealing some weapons and I'll shoot my way out before I have to endure another night with that woman."

The horn sounded in the arena, and Elliot pounced off the platform and across steps that were slanted so he had to jump carefully, one at a time. Stella and the others came to the railing.

"Oh, I am not sure I can watch this," Gary said.

The crowd cheered. He made it through the first obstacle. He launched himself at a giant punching bag and wrapped his arms and legs around it as it slid rapidly down over one of the bodies of water. He launched off it and landed on the platform of obstacle three. Next, he had to swing from a rope into a wall made of thick, braided twine cables. He flew across on the rope and landed into the cable wall. He climbed up the wall and was about to make it over when a beast that looked like an alligator with the head of a porcupine living in its mouth screeched and burst out of the water. It squealed, and a tentacle that shot out of its mouth just missed Elliot's leg. Laughter from the Sekke echoed in the arena as Elliot kicked and hustled up the rope wall.

"What the hell was that? That's not a part of the courses back home," Stella said.

"I don't know," Rex replied. "Damn Sekke bastards always have a trick up their sleeves."

Another monster roared out of the water as Elliot dangled over it, hanging from a bar with two wheels at the end. He cried out and kicked it away, but his right hand slipped off the bar as the monster flew out of the water again.

Stella gasped and covered her mouth with her hands. At that moment, everything else she was fighting for melted away. She just wanted Elliot to survive. The monster's jaw snapped, grazing his calf. He threw up his hand, grabbing the bar, and he cringed as momentum slammed him into the mat of the next obstacle. Cheers erupted from the Sekke.

"This is amazing," Rex said, rubbing his mustache. "Look at that son of a bitch. He *is* a warrior."

Gary threw his arms around Stella who squeezed the railing in front of her. Her knuckles turned white, and sweat beaded across her forehead.

Elliot ran and pounced onto an unstable inflated bridge that wobbled under his feet. More cheering sounded as he flung himself off the bridge to the landing platform. He grabbed his knees and caught his breath. The two toughest obstacles remained: The Salmon Ladder and the Warped Wall.

The Salmon Ladder was a bar resting on two parallel walls. The walls had seven sets of rungs for the bar to rest on, with gaps in between each rung. Elliot shook out his arms, and he would have taken more time to rest if two Sekke warriors hadn't jumped onto the platform with spears. They shouted and jabbed their spears at him. He yelped and jumped up to the first rung of the ladder.

He thrust the Salmon Ladder bar up and through, missing one wrung and almost falling into a dusty pit under the obstacle. Elliot held on, adjusted his grip and re-centered his hands. He grunted each time he pushed the bar onto the next rung. He pulled up his legs and moved the bar twenty times to make it through the ladder. Elliot grunted as he finished. He let go of the ladder and rolled onto the mat of the next landing.

He lay motionless on the mat, and a hush settled over the arena. Stella leaned forward to see if Elliot was getting up, and her throat tightened as she saw his body roasting in the heat of the sun.

"Get up. You can do this. Just get up," Stella whispered.

"Oh, he's dead. I knew it!"

"Shut up, Gary!" Rex said.

Stella gasped as Elliot twitched and pushed himself up to all fours. Slowly, he stood up, and the crowd screamed and applauded. Elliot stretched his neck and turned to see the wall in front of him. A low rumble of chanting came from the crowd. He sprinted onto the lower wall and scrambled up the curve of it, only to fall to the bottom, just missing the top with his hand.

"No," Stella gasped, touching her neck. "C'mon Elliot." Stella knew the last obstacle was all that mattered, and the one Elliot could never complete.

Elliot sprinted again and felt himself glide up the curve. He got two fingers on top of the ledge, but it wasn't enough, and he fell again, rolling to the bottom of the wall. He slammed his fist into the mat and remained on the ground.

"Well deary, looks like we need to find a place for you here on Kodon. Precious man out there isn't going to make it. I think I will keep him in my house," Criket said.

"He's going to finish," Stella said, keeping her focus on the arena.

"So sure? That is interesting since he is crumpled up on the ground. You such a pretty, fiery ting. Better get used to doing a dance in our show." Criket tickled Stella's neck with her forked tongue and then sat down next to Zimmer.

Stella shook off the creepy feeling of Criket's tongue, and her heart jumped as the cheering started again.

Elliot made it to his feet, but he hesitated as he stared at the wall. He lifted off his toes and ran as fast as he could into the curve. He threw his hand to the ledge, and this time his fingers stuck. One hand, then the other, he pulled himself up and slammed his hands down on a giant buzzer. A great horn sounded, and the stadium erupted into a level of sound that could have shattered glass.

Stella felt a lump swell in her throat. Elliot waved to the crowd as they hollered and jumped up and down in the stands. Stella grasped her chest, relieved. Gary hugged her, crying. Rex and Zimmer both cheered. Elliot climbed down the ladder on the other side and made his way back to the viewing room.

Stella pulled his limp arms around her. "You did it!"

"I did it, I did it," Elliot gasped. He hugged her.

"Never doubted you for a moment," Rex said.

"That was the most inspiring thing I have ever seen! Such a warrior to behold," Gary said, clapping his hands together.

"Water. Must…have…water," Elliot breathed.

Stella held him up as Gary brought two glasses of water from the table. Elliot drank one and poured the other one on his head. "I think I'm dying," he said. "So … hot out there and did you see? There were monsters in the water. Actual monsters … what the hell, man?"

"Let's get you back to the ship," Stella said. "Go with Rex. I'll go get Willow."

Rex held Elliot up. "I hope you have enough gas in your tank to run for your life across the desert."

# 47

## CELL 12 B

**STELLA FOLLOWED GIO DOWN** to the Lower Levels. Once the elevator touched down in the cell block, she ran out into the corridor. She called for Willow in a hushed voice, but no one answered. She searched and searched, but Willow was not waiting in her cell as she said she would be.

"Where is she?" Stella asked out loud.

"Where is who?" Gio asked.

"Willow, the woman we are supposed to bring back up?"

"Stella!" Willow called from behind her. She was just coming up the stairs from the pits. "I knew it! Let's get out of here." Willow ran past her, but Stella froze. She looked down to the end of the hall. She knew she could not leave him behind.

"You," Stella said to Gio, "I need to get the prisoner out of cell 12 B."

Gio furrowed his brow. "This was not the agreement."

"Stella, we need to go," Willow said, trying to pull her into the elevator.

"No, not until he opens cell 12 B."

"Get in the elevator," Gio commanded.

Stella glanced quickly at the blaster hanging from his belt. She stepped back in the elevator, but when she was next to Gio, she snatched his blaster out of its holster. "Open 12 B," she said.

"What are you doing?" Willow asked.

"I don't have time to explain this," Stella said.

Willow grabbed Stella's arm. "The hell you don't. Why would we take a prisoner with us?"

Stella swallowed and looked down at the floor. "Because he doesn't deserve to be here."

"And why are you making this judgement?" Willow asked.

"It's a long story. I will explain it later, but you have to trust me right now."

Willow pursed her lips and let go of Stella's arm. "Fine. Quick, quick though. We need to get to the others."

Stella nodded and motioned for Gio to move down the corridor.

"Criket will hear about this," Gio said.

"I'm sure she will," Stella replied.

Willow waited in the elevator to hold it open as Stella kept the blaster trained on Gio. He turned his key in the lock and pushed open the cell door. For a moment, the cell was quiet, and then the sound of Ryder's boots scratching the cement broke the silence.

"C'mon," Stella said.

Ryder glanced at Stella and then at Gio.

"Let's go. You're coming with us," Stella insisted, and Ryder finally followed them back into the elevator.

Willow stared at Ryder, who was still covered in blood and dirt. The door closed.

"Madame," Ryder said. He saluted her, and without warning, pounced on Gio. Ryder wrapped one arm around Gio's neck while the other arm held his head still.

"Goodness!" Willow shouted.

Gio tried to claw at Ryder's head and face, but Ryder didn't budge. Gio's face turned tomato red, and after another attempt to free himself, he closed his eyes. Ryder guided him to the floor of the elevator.

"Is he dead?" Stella asked.

"No, but it should give us some time," Ryder said.

The elevator opened to the main floor of the lobby. Willow and Stella rushed out while Ryder pressed the button for the highest floor in the building and kicked Gio's feet to the side. He jumped out just as the door closed.

With most citizens still celebrating in the arena, Duma City was all but empty. Once they made it out of the high-rise undetected, Stella handed Ryder Gio's blaster. "Go get your jacket."

Ryder's eye widened and he managed to smile. He took the blaster and shoved it in his waistband.

"Stella, please," Willow urged.

Ryder nodded and then ran off in the opposite direction.

# 48

# RAPTORS

**ZIMMER, REX, GARY, AND ELLIOT**, still in his rainbow leotard, waited on the edge of the city where the pavement stopped and the desert sand began. Criket sat on her raptor with a spear in her hand. "And there they are," she said as Stella and Willow ran up. Criket slid off her raptor, who squawked from the motion.

"Captain Rex," Willow said, embracing him.

"My heavens! Thrilled to see you, Willow," Rex said.

Zimmer and Gary both greeted Willow, but Criket cut their reunion short.

"You must go. I will give you a head start, but Sekke will start to head back from the arena, and I need to give chase, yes?"

Rex grabbed Criket's hand and kissed it. "We are in your debt."

"Of course you are! This was a fun. I will be doing you all a great miss!" Criket said. "You most of all." She kissed Zimmer on the lips and then climbed up on her raptor. "Now... run."

"What? We really have to run back to the ship?" Elliot asked.

"We'll never make it," Gary said.

"Run, fools! In a time, I shall sound the alarm," Criket said.

Rex guided everyone out into the sand. "Let's away."

They started running, their feet sinking in the dirt. Stella kept glancing over her shoulder and saw that Criket was still on the edge of the city waiting.

"We'll never make it," Gary said again.

"Wait, Rex." Willow stopped them. "What ship did you fly?"

"Marlon's Device, of course," Rex replied.

"That bucket of bolts can still get off the ground?" Willow asked.

"Absolutely! You remember it?"

Willow nodded. "I think so. I have an idea."

"We need to keep moving," Stella said.

They ran through the heat and the dust, but Stella knew she could not keep up the pace on foot. Suddenly, she heard the sound they all dreaded.

Criket blew the horn. It reverberated behind them, as did the screeching of the raptors.

Willow ran beside Stella. "We need to fly to the ship, Stella."

Stella glanced over at Willow and then over her shoulder. The horn sounded again, and she could see other raptors gathering near Criket. "I can't fly," she shouted.

"Yes you can!" Willow replied. "Give me your hand."

Stella sprinted beside her and shook her head. She would rather run for miles than be in the air.

"Give me your hand!" Willow extended her hand again. This time, Stella took it. "Now repeat this word in your head ... fly. Fly!"

Stella tried to clear her mind and she heard the word. She said it over and over, *fly, fly, fly.*

She gasped as her feet skipped off the sand and, for a moment, she was in the air, but she immediately touched back down. Willow squeezed her hand and Stella's eyes met hers.

*Fly.*

Willow's feet left the ground. Stella felt her hand lifting.

*Fly.*

Stella popped off the ground and bolted into the air. Her stomach dropped into her feet and she wobbled but then began to pick up speed. The g-forces flapped her cheeks, and Willow's hand slid out of Stella's grip until they were only touching fingertips. Stella picked up speed and tucked her arms against her body.

*I'm flying. Oh God, I'm flying. Don't look down, don't look down.*

She sputtered in the air and then stabilized as she sped above a pod of dinosaurs that scattered as the two Keepers passed over them. *How is this happening? How can I do this?*

Stella looked down, and her eyes bulged. She screamed as she dropped suddenly.

*Fly.*

Stella shot back up, even again with Willow. On the horizon, the familiar shape of the ship came into view. They were coming up on it at a rapid pace, and a horrific thought entered Stella's mind. She had no idea how to land. Willow stuck her arms out wide, slowing herself down and aiming her legs back to the ground. She landed ahead of Stella, and the ground shook when she touched down. Stella tried to extend her arms, but instead of landing as Willow did, she fell out of the air, hit the ground, and rolled. She coughed and spit dirt out of her mouth.

Willow ran to her. "Are you okay?"

"I think so," Stella said. She stood up with Willow's help and wiped the dirt off her face. "How did you do that?"

"I didn't do that. You did that. Now, come on."

Willow hustled back to the side of the ship. She pulled down a panel and entered the code. The ship's ramp creaked open, dust blowing out of the sides, and it landed in the sand with a thud. Willow stood motionless in front of the panel.

"What's wrong?" Stella asked.

Willow looked at her. "I remembered the code."

Stella grinned. "Let's hope you remember how to fly this thing."

Willow ran to the helm, flipping switches and sending life back into the sleeping vessel. It rumbled and groaned as it woke up.

"How are we going to get the others?" Stella asked.

"We will port them in," Willow replied. She tapped on the computer terminal, and it scanned her hand. She passed the security protocols, and she got up from the captain's chair and went back to a terminal to the right of it. The screen in front of them came alive with the image of Elliot, Rex, Zimmer, and Gary running as fast as they could through the desert, an army of Sekke riding raptors chasing them. Rex and Zimmer were starting to slip behind Gary and Elliot.

"Please hurry," Stella said.

Willow stared at the panel. Stella's heart raced as she looked at the screen of her friends running for their lives and back to Willow who was frozen at the control panel. Willow touched her lip and then went to touch a part of the panel. She pressed a button, and a sensor alarm went off.

"Can't you remember?" Stella asked. She glanced back up at the screen to see three raptors breaking from the line and gaining ground on Rex and Zimmer.

"I can, I just …" Willow pressed another button, but nothing happened.

Stella's breath quickened and she wanted to scream, but she calmed her mind and focused on the one thing Willow needed. Stella reached out and touched Willow's forehead. "You remember," Stella said.

*Help her remember.*

Energy flowed out of Stella's hand, and Willow closed her eyes. Seconds later, her eyes shot open and she looked back down at the panel. She punched in a new code and guided her hands on the terminal. The screen now showed brackets that looked like targets zooming in on each of the others.

Rex cried out and tried to dodge one of the raptors closing in on him. Criket chased down Zimmer and had almost caught him, but he vaporized just in time. One by one, they all disappeared. Rex vanished just as the raptor reached out with its jaws and clamped down onto thin air.

"Go check on them. I will get us in the air," Willow said, rushing back to the captain's chair. Stella raced off the bridge and back to the teleportation room. Everyone was there, covered in dust and lying in a pile on top of each other. They rolled off one another and all, even Gary, were gasping for air.

Rex popped up and squeezed Stella's arm. "You were flying. By all that is sacred, you flew!"

"We can celebrate that later," Zimmer said, pushing himself to his feet and grabbing Rex by the arm. They darted out of the room to man the helm.

Gary rolled onto his back. "I think I shorted out something."

Elliot stepped over him to get to Stella. He pulled her to him, and she squeezed him tight. He pulled away from her, still holding onto her waist. "You were, uh, you were flying in the air."

Gary called out from the floor. "Hello, I'm still here."

"I know," Stella said. She let go of Elliot and they both helped Gary to his feet.

"I'm so proud of you!" Gary said.

"Thank you," Stella said. They hustled back to the bridge and tried not to get knocked off their feet as the ship throttled out of Kodon's atmosphere.

"How did it feel?" Elliot asked.

"Terrifying, exhilarating, terrifying."

"You're amazing and hey …" Elliot said. He turned to her in the corridor as Gary ran ahead. "You kissed me."

Stella gulped. "I was caught up in the moment."

"Well, if that's you letting go, I'm all for it."

"It was amazing, watching you on the course. You really did get me out of a jam," Stella said.

He swallowed. "I did. It was easy, actually. I mean, the giant four-headed tentacle monster was a surprise, but he probably just wanted to be friends."

Marlon's Device had gotten a little windblown from sitting in the desert, but it took to the stars as if it was happy to be reunited with its crew.

Rex sat in his captain's chair alongside Willow, who helped him with the controls. Zimmer manned communications behind them.

"Where are we headed?" Stella asked once she and Elliot reached the helm.

"Omnibus," Rex replied. "It's a space station not too far from here." He swirled in his chair and reached out for Stella's hands. "And fear not, Zimmer is bombarding our comm channels to find Kate's exact location. We will find her. We *will* find her."

# 49

## SISTER

RYDER'S LEATHER JACKET MELTED into his skin, but he needed to leave the cloak on as he sprinted away from Duma City. Waves of heat pulsed over the land, distorting his view. He stopped and switched the settings on his eye to read the land. He could see for a mile in the distance. As he approached, he saw his transport was there as promised. He threw a glance over his shoulder to make sure he was not followed as he dashed up the ship's ramp, thankful to be out of the swelter.

He threw down his jacket on a rear seat and climbed into the chair at the helm. He fired up the controls for takeoff when he heard a click behind his right ear. He turned slowly in his chair to see Iris on the other end of a gun.

"I talked Kandi into letting me come get you, so it's a good thing Stella let you out. I was about to leave you behind," Iris said.

"Glad you didn't," Ryder smiled. "Where have you been?"

Iris balled her fist and punched him square in the face. He choked and shook the ringing from his ears as little drops of blood from his split lip stained his tongue.

"I have been stuck on this rock waiting for you! I should have gone with Kandi. You completely lost your head in this!"

"I'm sorry."

"I can't believe you let yourself get captured! What the hell happened, Ryder? All you had to do was kill her! We would have been free and with Pip and far away from all of this!"

Ryder shot up from his chair. "It wasn't that simple."

"It was, it was that simple, until you cocked it all up!"

"Have you forgotten your oath? Have you forgotten everything we used to stand for?"

"We have an oath to fight for our family," Iris said.

"Wrong, we swore an oath to protect those who need it. Stella and her mother are Keepers. The Kaygun way is to give our life for people like Stella. Pip would have done the same."

Iris stared at him. "You can't speak for her."

"We were not made to be mercenaries, Iris. That's not who we are," Ryder said. "And yes, I can speak for Pip. I know what she would say and so do you."

Iris blinked away tears. "Why couldn't you just stick to the plan?"

"Because ... the things Shook asked of me ..."

"So what? Do you think I enjoyed pretending to be a Sentinel, all the while funneling intel and spoiling their plans? Having to smile in their faces knowing I was deceiving them? No, but I did it for Pip."

"At least you were surrounded by people who kept you safe ... who cared about you. You have no idea what I've been enduring having to be at that woman's beck and call. I have been suffocating under the weight of her disgusting advances." Ryder gritted teeth; his eye stung from angry tears. "You were being asked to lie; I was being asked to murder people. And if I deviated at all, I had to sit there and watch our sister being tortured. I did what I could, but my soul has its limits!"

Iris crept toward Ryder and took his hand. "I wish we would've all died in the Miner's War. That would've been a better fate than this."

"We did die. Shook just brought us back to this unnatural life."

"So, what do we do now?"

Ryder cracked his knuckles. He had been thinking of ways to rescue Pip for weeks, but he knew he couldn't do it alone. Now, with Iris by his side, they had a chance.

"We go get Pip," he said.

"How? Shook isn't going to let us walk out with her."

"Who are we?" Ryder asked.

"What do you mean?"

"We are Kaygun soldiers."

Iris sat down in one of the chairs at the helm. "Wrong, we *were* soldiers."

"The betrayal of a few doesn't change the fact that we are still Kaygun. Together, we can save Pip. Once we have her, we can then find Hunter."

Iris perked up. "Hunter?"

"He's alive."

Iris's eyes bulged. "How do you know?"

"Shook showed me. They found him on Heelo." Ryder rummaged through the ship, searching for any weapons that might be on board. What Stella had said to him was true; he was still that man. He started to believe he wasn't Kaygun any longer only because of Kandi's poisonous words. He was the man he used to be, and it was time to get his life back.

Iris sat back in her chair. "What's the plan?"

"We walk in," Ryder said, powering on a large blaster. "And take the lab. We get Pip out of the tank and head to Heelo. See if you can use some of the ship's comm links to try to get word to Hunter."

"Shook is the only one with a code to the tank," Iris said.

"That woman has lied so many times, that may not be true. If it is, we find her and force her to open it."

"This is a suicide mission."

"Maybe," Ryder said. He hopped back into the seat at the helm and entered the coordinates for Aldemara into the system. "But nothing that happens to us now will be worse than the nightmare we have been living. Are you in or not?"

Iris climbed into the seat next to him, put on a headset, and belted herself in. "I'm in."

# 50

## ASHES

**RYDER'S LANDING CODE** had not been revoked, which allowed them to touch down on the outskirts of Aldemara. With their cloaks on and armed to the teeth, they made their way to the laboratory. The usual two guards paced outside. One guard asked the other for a cigarette, but before he could ask for a light, Ryder and Iris snapped their necks. They fell to the ground and Iris pulled one of the guards closer to the door. She guided his right hand to the security screen, and the first door unlocked when it verified his palm.

Two more of Kandi's security guards hustled through the door. Iris struck one of the guards from the side, kicking him into the other. Ryder slipped behind another. He thrust a revolver in the man's back and blew him to the floor. One by one, security ran down the staircase, and one by one, Ryder and Iris picked them off like they were flies being swatted out of the way.

They took the stairs up to Inventions and Experiments and removed the last two guards who were waiting outside. Neither of the guard's fingers unlocked the doors, so Ryder fitted a small explosive device to the outside. It blew the door lock without so much as a tremor. This time, Ryder and Iris did not tiptoe up to the door. They undid their cloaks and burst in with guns drawn, ready for a shoot-out with those guarding Pip. Mr. Owen screamed and threw up his hands.

"Ryder, Iris … um … what are you doing here?"

Ryder scanned the room. Three large, empty tanks of green liquid fizzed and gurgled. Three flat med bay beds sat empty. Little hums and beeps escaped other machines, but other than that, the lab was quiet and there was no sign of Pip anywhere.

"What is this?" Iris asked, eyes wide as she walked through the lab with her arms and energy revolvers extended.

"I don't—"

Ryder charged Mr. Owen and grabbed him by the collar. "Where is she?"

"Who?" Mr. Owen asked with a shaky voice. "Ms. Shook is gone for the night."

"Where is Pip?" Iris asked. She stormed over and pushed one of her revolvers into Mr. Owen's temple. "What did you do with her?"

Mr. Owen coughed and cleared his throat. "We didn't, … um … do anything with her."

"Stop it! Just tell us where she is," Iris said, pressing harder with the revolver.

"She was never here," Mr. Owen said.

Ryder clenched his jaw. "What did you say?"

"Um … she was never here. Please don't hurt me. I was threatened. I had to do what Ms. Shook told me to do."

"I don't give a shit about that. Tell us where Pip is!" Iris roared.

Ryder shook Mr. Owen, and Iris pulled the trigger on a warning shot that flew past Mr. Owen's head, singeing one of his eyebrows.

"Please! Okay! Okay! I can show you." Mr. Owen pulled at his collar, and Ryder released him. He pushed his glasses back up his nose and hobbled to a computer terminal.

"It was Shook … she, she, she created a digital version of your sister to trick you. But Pip was never here. You and Iris were the only ones who came in with the body dealer."

"But I saw her!" Ryder said. "I was standing right here when I saw her."

"You saw this." Mr. Owen tapped the keyboard. Ryder and Iris stood in disbelief staring at the tank they thought Pip had been in. An image of Pip appeared just as he had seen her floating in the liquid, looking as if she were asleep. Mr. Owen pressed the buttons again and Pip faded away. "It was merely a digital representation. Ms. Shook is a digital engineer. She researched your sister and found her information from your home world's military database. It was all her creation."

The color drained from Iris's face, and she leaned over onto a table with her hands out to steady herself. "Pip never made it out of the bunker."

A wave of nausea welled up from Ryder's stomach. He could hear Mr. Owen continue to explain, but it was if everything started to move in slow motion. Ryder's vision blurred, and for a moment he felt as though he might pass out as he came to grips with the fact that he thought he was close to rescuing his sister only to find out she was just ashes blowing off the battlefield on a distant planet. All the blood on his hands, all the nights he was called away from his safe house to answer to Kandi; it was all for nothing. There was never a chance to save Pip. All the anger and rage he had been suppressing for months boiled over, and he fired into the lab. Shots ricocheted off counters, sliced through glass, and shattered equipment. He fired at the tanks, but the reinforced glass didn't budge.

Mr. Owen screamed and ducked under a desk as sparks flew from the terminals, short-circuiting. Iris slammed her fists down on a computer terminal and then took a beaker of liquid and threw it to the ground. She took a chair and threw it into one of the other tanks. The glass of the tank cracked, but the tank held. Bits of glass popped into the air along with liquid from beakers torn apart by laser blasts.

"Please stop! Stop!" Mr. Owen pleaded.

Ryder did not want to stop until the lab was reduced to rubble, but he heard Mr. Owen's cries and knew they had burned too much time. He wiped his mouth and holstered his revolvers. He put up his hand to stop Iris. She threw one more beaker on the ground and wiped tears from her face.

"You need to go. Ms. Shook is watching. She will be sending more security here," Mr. Owen said.

"Where is she?" Iris asked. "I'm not leaving here until she's dead."

"You won't be able to get to her; she's too strong. She's too protected here." Mr. Owen said.

"She's not protected from something she can't see," Ryder said.

"Your cloaks are useless around her. She … um … invented your cloaking devices, you see, which means she also invented a device that helps her see them. Trust me, Miss Iris, she is unbeatable here. If I were you, I would run from Aldemara and never look back."

"I don't care. I want her head for what she's done to us!" Iris screamed. "I want to sell her to a body dealer and see how she likes it!"

"You two have your lives, but you won't if you try anything with Ms. Shook."

Ryder didn't move. He faded in and out. He was back in the bunker, back with Pip. He could hear her, see her. His ears were ringing. He felt lightheaded. He heard someone calling to him, and when he looked up, he saw Pip reaching for him, but her voice was low and hushed.

"Ryder," Pip said. He shut his eyes and shook his head, but he heard it again. "Ryder."

He held his head.

"John Alexander!" Iris shouted.

Ryder snapped back to the present.

"We're done."

Ryder glanced back up at the tanks and noticed they were all empty. He couldn't rescue Pip, but there was still someone he could try to save. Stella's mother wasn't in the tank, which meant there was still a chance to get to her.

"They're coming," Mr. Owen said when he noticed a beep on a screen that tracked movement outside the lab.

"Where's the Healer Shook brought back here?" Ryder asked.

"I … uh … I don't know," Mr. Owen replied.

"Tell me now or you will be leaving here in a bag," Ryder said, pulling out his revolver again.

"Ryder, let's go!" Iris shouted. "Pip is gone. There's nothing else for us to do here."

"I won't ask again. Where is the Healer?" Ryder asked.

"I told you, I don't know. I just know that I heard whispers of a plan for Ms. Shook to lure the Healer's daughter here so she can use both of them. That's why she … um … is bringing in more Zuldari troops. If the Healer's daughter returns for her mother, there will be an ambush. Now please, I'm begging you … um … you can't help anyone else if you're dead, and you will be if you stay here any longer. Ms. Shook will most likely have a kill order out on you now."

Ryder pulled Iris aside. "We need to warn Stella. We need to help the Keepers any way we can."

"They didn't need Kaygun help in the Great War, and they definitely don't need us now. Ryder, please, if you won't let me go for Shook's head, please let me go home."

"Kayguns don't retreat. We fight."

"Pip was our fight, and now she's gone," Iris said. "I'm done."

"We can still fight for her. We can still make Kandi pay for what she's done, and we can help the Healers at the same time."

Two guards breached the lab door. Ryder and Iris activated their cloaks, raised their guns, and shot, putting the guards down. They slipped out of the lab.

"I can't go back there," Iris said. They ducked behind the lab, out of sight of the other guards rushing in. "How can I face the Sentinels after what I have done? I'm the reason Stella's mother is here."

"You know them, Iris. Do you think after we tell them what we have been through they will punish us?"

"I would."

Ryder smiled. "You definitely would. Let's hope they are more forgiving. Listen, let's get them information that will help them. That's all we have to do. Then, we can get back to Hunter knowing we did the right thing."

Iris looked down.

"Hey, we're almost done. And at least we're together now, and if we do this right, we will be with Hunter again too. If we help the Keepers and the Sentinels, they will help us."

Iris met his eye, and Ryder could see she was trying to hold back her tears.

"I hate it when you make insane ideas sound reasonable," Iris said.

Iris turned to head back to the ship, but Ryder realized they couldn't leave yet. He knew Iris was not going to like it, but there was someone Ryder had to see.

# 51

# TIME'S UP

KANDI SWITCHED OFF HER MONITOR and leaned back in her chair. Watching Iris and Ryder destroy the lab didn't even make her twitch. She just let it play out and let them go, knowing they would bring the mouse back to the mousetrap. She admired her fingernails and hit replay on the security footage.

"Why are you just sitting there?" Taylor asked.

Kandi didn't answer.

Taylor set Kandi's coffee on her desk with such force it bubbled up through the lid. "Hello? They're ravaging the lab." Taylor snapped his fingers rapidly in front of her eyes.

"Doesn't matter. I can repair it and they didn't see the fourth tank, which is the only one I need. I allowed them to blow shit up so they felt like they were doin' well."

"So you just let them go?"

"Yeah. Now they'll bring me back all the Keepers when they come looking for the Healer."

"You're losing your head in this," Taylor said. "They may bring back a freaking army and destroy us all."

"I don't remember asking for your opinion," Kandi said.

"That's right," Taylor said. "You don't ask for my opinions because you stopped listening to them."

Commander T'Adox buzzed Kandi's intercom, requesting a meeting with her.

"That wretch is so vile, I don't know why you would ever want him here," Taylor said.

"Because he and the Zuldari can help broker even more deals for me. They're starting a war and by the time it's over, I'll be Queen Bee here and we can do whatever we want, baby. We won't ever have to worry about the Keepers spoiling our party."

Taylor set down his own coffee and rummaged through his tote bag. "Well, you can be Queen Bee around here alone because I'm out." Taylor slid a lab key and ID badge across the desk. "I'm not waiting around for Iris and Ryder to come back with more firepower."

"What did you say to me? Who do you think you are?"

"Oh girl, the shade of pink your face is right now does not flatter you. I'm out. This used to be fun, you used to be fun, but you don't know what the hell you're doing now. You should've listened to Lovella. All she ever tried to do was help you."

Kandi shot out of her seat and pounded on her desk. "Shut your damn mouth you wormy little bug!"

"All your lying and scheming, and for what? To get in good with the Zuldari? I can't believe you trust them. I certainly don't."

Kandi's eyes were wild, but she slowly sat back down in her seat. "I'm sorry you feel that way, baby."

Taylor put his hand on his hip. "That's it? Is that all you have to say to me after all we've been through?"

Kandi shrugged.

"You really are something, you know that?"

"I know. I *am* something."

Taylor shook his head, turned on his heel, and stormed off. He made it halfway through the door when Kandi called to him. "Oh honey, don't forget your coffee."

Taylor charged back to the desk and took a sip. "You know, you're going to wake up one day and realize you're all alone and the only person at fault for that is—" Taylor grabbed his throat. He looked at his coffee with eyes wide. It fell from his hand and splashed on the floor. White foam billowed out of the sides of Taylor's mouth as he stumbled back. His throat constricted and he coughed and choked on the foam, which was turning pink from the blood mixing with it. He fell over the ottoman, and Kandi slinked out from behind her desk.

He reached out to her, but she only laughed and waved a small syringe in the air. The poison eating through his body kept him alive long enough for him to see Kandi standing over him with a wide grin on her face.

"You should know by now, honey, that if you're not with me, you're against me. And that's a bad place to be."

**T'ADOX HAD TAKEN OVER** Lovella's office once it was confirmed she was no longer in Aldemara. Kandi sauntered in and froze once she saw the changes T'Adox had made. The stench from T'Adox hit Kandi before she even walked through the door. Lovella's office always smelled of rose oil, and the space was always spotless with everything in its place. Soft music played, and there were fresh bottled beverages Kandi enjoyed pilfering.

Now, T'Adox's slimy body left a residue wherever it lingered. The office was dark and dank, and Lovella's things were thrown in a pile in the corner. T'Adox sat in a large, wooden chair and was happily snacking on giant live insects that had been flown in from his home world.

Kandi decided to stand close to the door, especially since her favorite leather chair had been removed. Kandi hated Lovella, but T'Adox was proving to be a horrible replacement. He was just a means to an end, however, which meant Kandi would have more power—something she would never gain with Lovella sitting behind that desk.

"Well, you have certainly redecorated," Kandi said.

"I'm not sure what that comment indicates so I will not acknowledge it."

"I don't expect you even understand it," Kandi laughed. "What do you want?"

T'Adox took a bite out of a three-headed rat-looking bug and then licked his rubbery fingers. "I would like you to understand that the time I have given you to complete your task is near to expiring."

"The hell does that mean?"

"It means that you have failed to deliver time and time again, and while Lovella was willing to cater to your opulent demands, I am not. This latest plan of yours better result in the acquisition of the Healer's daughter or you will lose more than your accommodations here."

Kandi scoffed. "I got you the mother, didn't I?"

"And due to your lax security in the lab, the individuals who broke in caused a great deal of damage to the tanks."

"We will repair the lab."

"Another delay," T'Adox said.

"Don't worry. That daughter of hers will be coming for her, so you'll have your little family reunion."

T'Adox slithered away from his desk and approached Kandi, who stood with balled fists in front of him. "You speak so casually, which means you do not understand how dangerous the Keepers are to our civilization."

Kandi let out a high-pitched cackle. "What? Those old ladies? What are they going to do? Hit you with their canes? I read that book. They all scattered like roaches when the light comes on. There's nothing to worry about."

Kandi stepped away from T'Adox, seeing his eyes turn black.

"Foolish, insolent girl," he said.

Kandi wiped his spit from her face. "Oh my Lord, you're disgusting."

T'Adox grabbed her arm and yanked her toward him. "Do not underestimate those women based on their aged appearance. They are as powerful as all our armies combined. If they are allowed to reconnect and reunify, their first strike will be most deadly. Your henchman has failed, General Law evaded our capture, and we still don't have a Healer for our tank so we can begin the healing process."

It had been a long time since she felt a lump form in her throat. She had gotten so used to always controlling the room. She turned her nose up at T'Adox to show a brave face, but her legs felt like jelly.

"Get off me!" She wrenched her arm out of T'Adox's grasp. "You'll have your Keepers. They will come runnin' for the mother. Then, we will kill them all. Now, leave me alone so I can get the job done."

# 52

# MORE HUMAN

**RYDER BLASTED THROUGH THE DOORS** of Tana's repair shop. She yelped and dropped the soldering iron she had in her hand. The droid she was repairing looked up, swiveled its head around, and beeped.

Tana pushed her glasses up to her forehead. "It's okay, P42. Ryder? And Iris? What the—"

"We don't have time," Iris said, as she slammed the door behind her and locked it.

P42 beeped again; Tana switched off the droid so it could not overhear the conversation.

"What are you doing here? I thought you both defected?" Tana asked.

"Working on it. I need that eye." Ryder pushed P42 off Tana's table. It rattled and crashed onto the floor.

"Hey! Have you lost your damn mind? I was in the middle of that."

"Not anymore. Do you still have that prosthetic eye you made for Ryder or not?" Ryder situated himself on the operating table.

Tana folded her arms across her chest. "I do, but I'm not doing anything until you tell me what's going on."

"We need that eye to help make him less noticeable," Iris said.

"Less noticeable for what?" Tana asked.

Ryder sat up. "Shook never had our sister. We never had a chance to save her. Every image I saw of Pip in the lab was a digital manipulation. She was never here. We've been doing all of this ... for nothing."

"We need to get to the Sentinels for help," Iris added.

Tana's face softened. "That's nasty business. Shook is a monster." She paused, putting her hand on Ryder's shoulder. "But you may need more than the Sentinels to help you. More and more Zuldari arrive here every day. That's a much bigger problem than Shook."

"That's why we need backup, but I can't get through Sentinel security looking like this," Ryder said.

Tana thought for a minute. "Lie down." She pulled her glasses back down over her eyes and retrieved the prosthetic eye from a lucite display case on her workstation.

Ryder twitched after Tana injected something into his wrist. "What was that for?" He asked.

"For the pain. Try to keep your face relaxed."

Ryder groaned as Tana removed the machine eye from its socket and tossed it into a steel tray beside her. With steady hands, she fitted a blue eye into Ryder's empty socket. She next laid a flap of synthetic skin over the hole on the right side of this face. She punched commands onto a computer screen. The skin of the eye immediately reached out and bonded with Ryder's surrounding flesh. He clenched his fists and fought the urge to scratch the itch on his face where the synthetic skin was bonding to his own.

Tana worked to fuse the new eye with its socket and restimulate the nerves surrounding it. Ryder squirmed as a current from the prosthetic zapped the dead nerves in his eye.

Tana tried to comfort him. "It stings, I know, but we're almost done."

The warmth from blood flowing into the dead cold side of his face sent a shiver through him. He saw only darkness out of his right eye, and then a sensation to blink came over him. At first, he felt as though he was wearing an eye patch, but as he blinked, the sight began to come back into that eye. He did not have to strain from seeing heat signatures and digital information; he saw the room as he used to before he woke up in Kandi's bed. It was the first time he felt human in a long time.

"It looks so real," Iris said, peering at him.

"It will look and feel real," Tana replied. "You can even cry with this eye again."

Tana helped him sit up and gave him a mirror so he could see her work. He swallowed the lump in his throat as the man he used to be looked back at him from the mirror. He turned his head side to side, amazed that there was only minimal scarring on his face.

"Thanks Tana," Ryder said.

"Now, I need to tell you—"

Ryder shot off the bed. His vision blurred, and because his eyes were not used to working together, he wobbled on his feet. He grabbed onto the side table full of tools to break his fall, but it did not save him, and he tumbled to the floor.

Iris exhaled loudly. "I'm not dealing with this."

"What I was about to say is that it may take some time for your eyes to adjust." Tana grunted as she helped Ryder off the floor.

"I thought you were tougher than this," Iris said.

Ryder used Tana's arm to steady himself. He could tell his sister thought it was amusing to see him fall to the ground like a drunken idiot. It was the first time he heard her laugh in so long that he didn't mind. Iris took Ryder's hand as he tried to walk toward her.

"This is incredible," Ryder said.

Iris chuckled. "You look … better."

Movement outside the window caught their attention.

"We need to go," Iris said.

Ryder turned to Tana. "You need to leave here too. It's no longer safe."

"Safe? Ha!" Tana said. "It's never been safe here." She threw some of her tools back to the table.

Ryder looked at Tana—his confidant, his friend, one of the only people who really understood him. "I can get you out of here."

"Fool, you can't even stop yourself from falling down."

"There's a transport leaving for Heelo tonight."

"Heelo? Why would I go to that dismal planet?" Tana asked.

"My brother, Hunter, is there," Ryder replied. "Iris and I will meet you there as well."

"No good. I don't like the cold. I'll be fine. You worry about yourself and Iris."

Ryder blinked and pinched his nose. He knew Tana was stubborn, but he couldn't bear to leave her behind. "Get your stuff. We aren't leaving without you."

"Can we discuss this as we move?" Iris asked. She ducked as ten Zuldari guards rushed past the window.

"I really appreciate you looking out for me, but you needn't fuss," Tana said. She opened a cabinet filled with all types of weapons and pulled out an energy rifle. "I can handle myself."

"Where the hell did you get all of that?" Ryder asked.

"If she wants to stay, leave her be, Ryder. We need to go. No offense Tana."

"None taken, Iris." Tana set her rifle down and embraced Ryder. "I'm going to miss you. I hope our paths cross again. Please don't worry. P42 and I will be departing shortly."

When they pulled apart, Ryder stared at her. She was oddly unbothered by the Zuldari invasion outside her window. There was something she was keeping from him, but he didn't have time to press her about it. "Thank you, Tana...for everything," he said.

"You bet." She winked at him and turned her attention back to P42 as Ryder followed Iris out of the building.

# 53

# OMNIBUS

**STELLA STOOD AT THE HELM** of Marlon's Device marveling at Omnibus as the ship rocketed toward the bustling space port. Omnibus was established as a Sentinel safe zone after the Great War. In the years since, it had become a haven for weary travelers and Sentinel allies. Other space craft zoomed in around them, flicking off and onto landing pads that sat on top of massive circular rings. In the center of these rings was a cylinder that acted as the power generator. The cylinder was fitted with unprecedented defense systems that had enough power to vaporize a small moon. There were very few safe havens in the universe like Omnibus.

The top level consisted of the landing docks. Ships glided onto hundreds of landing pads on the top deck. Once they passed the security clearance, they were lowered into the docking bays for further inspection. The middle deck served as a military base and galaxy checkpoint for the Sentinels and other armies. The lower deck consisted of lodging and dining options. Travelers could relax and rejuvenate after long journeys.

Marlon's Device creaked to a landing, eager to rest inside one of the Omnibus hangars. A hangar cleaning crew descended on it, spraying off grime and filling up its fuel tanks before Rex and crew had even unbuckled their safety harnesses.

"How long are we staying here?" Stella asked.

"Not long," Rex replied. He pushed his way through the sea of uniforms and alien beings of Bay 47. Willow hustled along beside him. Gary and Elliot followed, Gary chatting on and on, delivering every facet of Omnibus history into Elliot's curious mind.

Stella tried to be patient as Rex and Willow were greeted by other colleagues, but she found it difficult to stand still while others were chatting. "And how long will that take?"

Rex turned to her. "It takes as long as it takes, but I promise you, we will leave straightaway."

"I'm going to touch base with my intel team. See what information they have for me. I'll meet you in one of the roundtable rooms," Zimmer said. He scooted off in the opposite direction and disappeared into the busy crowd.

An Omni employee pulled Rex aside and informed him someone was waiting for them in one of the lounges of the lower deck.

"Who is waiting?" Rex asked.

The Omni employee shrugged. "Dunno. I was just told to give you the message when I saw you. Lounge 21."

As they rode a moving walkway and then down on an elevator to the lower deck, the voices of the team laughing and taking in the sights of the space station faded, and Stella could think only of Kate.

*Where is she? What is she feeling?*

Stella closed her eyes, trying to focus positive thoughts on her mother.

*We will find her in time.*

She felt a nudge in her side. Elliot cocked his head, waiting for her to leave the elevator and follow the others.

"You okay?" Elliot asked.

Stella sighed. "I'm fine."

The corridor leading to Lounge 21 was lined with square windows. Rex walked into the lounge first, and Stella pushed past him, eager to see what mystery person was waiting for them.

"Maren!" Stella said. "You're here?" She hugged Maren, and Willow ran in, wrapping her arms around both of them.

Gary wailed in delight from the moment. Elliot worked to calm Gary down by hugging him.

"It's been too long, sweet friend," Willow said.

Maren blinked rapidly. "Willow, what are you doing here?"

"Stella found me in the pits of Kodon, of all places," Willow replied.

Maren's eyes widened. "The pits? How horrid."

"I've been in worse places."

Maren nodded. "True. And where is Kate?"

Stella cast her eyes downward. Before she could open her mouth to speak, Rex stepped in. "We lost her. Could not get to her in time."

"Which is why we're glad you're here," Stella continued. "We need your help to find her."

"Precisely why I left Vhalis. I want to help. You were right, Stella. I cannot remain in my solitude any longer," Maren said. "You had come all this way. I know I need to be at your side."

"You're damn right," Willow said. "We need you, Maren."

"I'm rusty, but I will do what I can."

"I'll take rusty right now," Stella said. "I'm just happy to have you both here." Stella reached out for their hands.

"We're happy to be here with you. Just wish it was under more pleasant circumstances," Willow said.

Zimmer radioed to Rex that he had some information. Stella and crew made their way to a meeting room toward the end of the corridor where Zimmer was waiting. Judging from the way his tie was ruffled, Stella knew he did not have good news.

"What's wrong?" Stella asked.

Zimmer cued an image on a monitor on the wall. "Before we left Verbatim, we sent a scout team to Aldemara to see if we could gather information. They have since disappeared, and their comm channels are dead."

Rex sighed heavily. "Which means that we are no closer to learning more about what we are up against."

"So, we take this crew and break into that lab. We don't need another team; I was there. I saw the lab and what she wants to use my mother for," Stella said.

"It's not that simple," Zimmer said. "The prospect of taking your mother will serve as way to lure you there, Stella. We can't risk it. We need to get more information."

"I'm willing to risk it," Stella said.

"I appreciate that, but we can't fly in there blind," Zimmer said.

"What are we supposed to do? Sit here and twiddle our thumbs?"

Zimmer rubbed the back of his neck, and his face tightened. "We are not twiddling our thumbs. We can't just land in Aldemara without knowing what is waiting for us. We have teams trying to gather more information. Until then, we wait."

Stella folded her arms across her chest. "This is just ... I've never in my career waited if I had to save a life."

"I get that, I get it," Rex said in a soothing tone. "But if we don't wait until we have the information we need, more lives will be lost."

Everyone stood up from their chairs and began to file out of the room. Stella remained in her seat, wondering why the meeting was adjourned before they had come up with a plan. "What are we doing now?"

"Taking a break. I'm taking Gary to get his circuits cleaned," Rex said. "Stella, Driver, there are other lounge rooms at the end of the hall where you can rest. We have the run of this corridor while we are here."

"I'm looking for a shower to get the smell of Kodon's pits off me," Willow said. "Then, Rex, you need to go over how to fly the Device with me again."

One by one, they all went in separate directions except for Elliot. "What do we do now, boss?"

"I don't know, but I have to do something. I can't just sit here," Stella said.

"Okay, do you know how to fight off the army they were talking about?" Elliot asked.

"No, of course not."

"Do you know how to find that planet you were on?"

"No."

"Can you fly a spaceship?"

Stella paused and kicked at the floor. "No. I know what you are going to say. Trust my team, right?"

Elliot nodded. "Which is not easy in this case, but I think it's what we have to do."

"We?"

"Yes, we're in this together, so yeah … we."

Stella smiled. "Okay, but still, I need something to do. I can't just sit in a room."

"I have an idea," Elliot said. "But we need to find a room with a couch."

"Elliot, just because I kissed you does not mean—"

"No, not for that, dummy. I have more stuff to show you in the tablet. I've been doing my own research, and I want to show you. Did you know Shook is from Earth too?"

Stella followed Elliot to the end of the hallway. "I did hear that."

Elliot found a room with a wide sofa with fluffy cushions. They sat down in unison, and Stella nestled her shoulder into Elliot as he pulled up images from the tablet. He smiled with accomplishment as images of Kandi projected into the air.

"I just learned how to do that," he said.

"I'm really proud of you."

"I know, right? Anyhow, she's supposed to be an inventor," Elliot said. "She probably will have lots of booby traps in her secret fortress."

"Oh?"

"Most evil genius inventors have lots of booby traps."

"You just like saying booby traps, don't you?"

"Pretty much."

# 54

# THE BLUE LIGHT

**ADRENALINE HAD BEEN SURGING** through her veins for so long, Stella didn't realize how exhausted she was when she stretched out on a large sofa in her room. She tried to close her eyes, and though she was grateful to lie down, she still couldn't sleep. Getting up to pace the room also did not calm her nerves. She looked down at herself, not remembering when she put on a silky nightgown. She shook off her bewilderment and floated toward the door, where she turned off the light. She whipped around, sensing a presence behind her.

There on the bed, outstretched and hovering, lay Ryder, once again stripped to his underwear. His arms and fists were clenched at his sides. Stella looked around, wondering how he got there. She opened her mouth to call to him, but no words came out. Her heart pounded in her rib cage like a prisoner trying to get out of its cell.

She crept toward him. His eyes were open, his face whole as he stared at the ceiling. She looked him over, noticing all the machine parts of him were gone. He looked like a normal man. He didn't move even as she peered over him. He just hovered and stared. Her hand trembled as she reached out to touch his arm. Maybe if she shook him, it would wake him from his trance. She barely grazed his skin with her hand when in one jerk he reached up, grabbed her, and pulled her down onto the bed. He flipped over on top of her, now fully awake and now just inches from her face.

She shot up and out of her dream. She had dozed off on the sofa next to Elliot who was slumped over and snoring. She exhaled deeply, trying to clear the images of the dream from her mind. She touched her forehead and that's when she saw it.

The blue light.

She slowly rose from the sofa so as not to wake Elliot. There was no one else in the room so she crept to the door, opened it and waited. The hallway was eerily still.

She held out her wrist and walked down the corridor. The light started to blink faster as she turned through the corridors of the building. Each time she rounded a bend, the path lay empty in front of her. She swore she heard movement behind her, but there was nothing there. She kept walking, holding her wrist in front of her, only stopping when the light stopped blinking. She shook her wrist as if she were shaking a dimming flashlight to get it going again. She stopped and turned around.

*What am I doing?*

That's when two arms reached out from a hidden corner, pulled her behind a wall, and pushed her up against it. He stepped back, released his grip on her, and removed his cloak.

"It's okay, it's okay," Ryder said as he put up his hands.

"The hell it is. What are you doing here?" Stella said in a hushed voice.

Ryder took a deep breath. "I needed to see you."

Stella cocked her head. That was not what she was expecting to come out of his mouth, but she let that statement drift out of her mind for a moment as she noticed his face. Instead of seeing a deep cavern of red light carved into his face, she saw two eyes looking at her. Two blue eyes.

"Your eye…it's …"

"… a prosthetic," Ryder said. "This is what I used to look like."

"It looks good," she said. "Wait, what do you mean you needed to see me?"

Ryder turned pink. "I mean, I needed to get information to you, from Aldemara."

"If you're found here …"

"It's worth the risk."

Stella tried to keep her wits about her, which was difficult to do with him staring at her and standing so close. She cleared her throat. "Let's find Captain Rex. You can tell him what you know."

Ryder took a step toward her. "Why did you help me?"

Stella's lips trembled. "What?"

"Why?" Ryder leaned in toward her. "Why did you get me out of that cell?"

Stella looked away for a second and then back into his large, intense eyes drilling into her. "I don't know."

"Yes, you do."

Her eyes lit up at that moment because she did know. She did. She couldn't suppress what was happening inside her any longer. Her lips parted then, as her eyes dilated and she leaned in looking at his mouth, feeling his breath. She slipped her hands around his neck and pressed her lips against his. The explosion inside both of them almost rocked the building because it was as if two hearts, long dead, started to beat in unison. The machines inside of them fell silent as they surrendered to something they had long desired, although neither could really understand why it was happening. Ryder broke from her, his eyes rolling into the back of his head as he tried to catch his breath.

"I'm sorry. I ..." she whispered.

"Why? I've been ... wanting to do that for a long time."

"You have? Since when?"

Ryder smiled. "I'd say from the moment you leveled me with a throat punch."

She kissed him again. This time, she could feel his powerful arms wrap more tightly around her. They lingered in the kiss and then released each other again. Stella exhaled and they touched their foreheads together for a moment. Ryder clasped Stella's hand and wrapped his other arm around her waist. Her stomach did several flip-flops before it finally calmed down.

"I'm the one who needs to apologize," Ryder said, taking a big gulp.

"What do you mean?"

"I didn't ever want to hurt you. Please understand, I was only trying to free my sister. All of it. It was nothing I ever wanted."

Stella's heart thumped in her throat. She couldn't quite say it was okay, but she could see the pain is his eyes. She pulled him to her once again and hugged him. She released him and cupped his face in her hands. "I'm sorry for what Kandi did to you."

"The more I think about it, I'm not."

"You're not?"

"No. Everything that happens to us, good or bad, we just have to try to make sense of it. If I had not been picked up by the body dealer, I would be dead and gone on some distant planet. Instead, I'm alive, Iris is alive, and I'm standing here with you."

"I'm glad you are standing here with me and glad you got your jacket back," Stella said.

The sound of multiple weapons being cocked and pointed at Ryder's head cut the conversation short.

"Step away from her," a voice said.

Three Omni security officers surrounded them. Ryder immediately did what he was told, and the officers dragged him out from behind the wall. One of the officers spoke into his smartwatch. "Yeah, we found him. He was assaulting a woman. We will bring him in."

"Ma'am are you hurt?" another officer asked.

"Did he harm you?" asked another.

"I'm fine. He's with me," Stella replied.

The officers exchanged glances.

"It's okay; you are safe now," the taller officer said. "No need to pretend. We can see clearly by your watery eyes and flushed skin that you are in distress."

Stella cringed. "I ... no, you don't understand."

"We are taking him to Captain Rex. We have his sister in custody as well."

Stella took a deep breath, and seeing that Ryder was not resisting, she said "Fine, let's go see Rex."

# 55

# BOOTS ON THE GROUND

**AS RYDER TAPPED HIS FINGERS** on the cold, steel table, waiting for his latest inquisition to begin, he hoped it would not end as the last one did. Ryder had been through a handful of interrogations in his career as a hired hitman. The last one began with him being electrocuted through his fingertips with long needles. It ended with the needles sticking out of the dead interrogator's neck. When Rex entered the room with two glasses and a bottle of whiskey tucked under his arm, Ryder realized this one would be different.

Rex filled the glasses a quarter of the way and slid one glass across the table to Ryder, who caught it in his palm. Rex then reached forward and released Ryder from the magnetized power cuffs. Rex eased into the chair across from him and laid the cigar he had been smoking across the top of his glass.

Ryder swirled the liquid in the glass, smelled it, and set it back down on the table. "Is this poisoned?"

"I hope not," Rex said, taking a big gulp from his glass.

"Where's Iris?"

"She's in the other room."

"Let's just get this over with. Whatever cage you're going to drag me off to, whatever torture you've got lined up for me, whatever hole you want to dump me in, just do it. Release Iris though. She doesn't deserve any of that."

Rex sipped his whiskey. "Hmmm, sounds tempting. I did have a hole picked out to dump you in, but we've already talked to Iris. She has informed us about what you have been through and what you endured with Shook."

Ryder sat back in his chair and finally took a sip of his drink. "This isn't an interrogation?"

"Not unless you would like to ask me anything," Rex replied.

Ryder nodded and his heart, beating like a drum in his chest, started to slow down. He had been running through one nightmare to the next; he forgot what it was like to feel like he had an ally.

"I've actually come to ask you for your help."

Ryder raised his brows. "Help?"

Rex stood up and began to pace. "What you and Iris have been through—well, there is no horror that I can equate to it. What I appreciate is your willingness to risk your safety to return to us and bring us the valuable intelligence we have been seeking."

"It was the right thing to do."

Rex rubbed his chin. "It was, and now our interests have aligned."

"Have they?"

"Yes, we need to infiltrate Aldemara, retrieve Stella's mother, and help stop T'Adox."

Ryder took another sip of his drink and clenched his jaw. Just the thought of potentially seeing Kandi again caused acid to boil up from his stomach. "And this is where you ask me for my help."

Rex nodded. "You know Aldemara and Shook's movements better than anyone on my team. Help us get through Aldemara. Help us retrieve Stella's mother."

Ryder sighed. "I'm tired of being the hired man. Tired of taking orders. Iris and I have been through enough."

Rex slid forward in his seat. "I understand that. John, we know who you are. You are a soldier, a warrior for your people ..."

Ryder gulped at hearing his birth name, a name he kept forgetting he had. "*Was.* Was a soldier. Now you can add mercenary to my resume—a job I never thought I would have. So many people I had to kill didn't deserve to die. It was all to try to save my sister, and the entire time, I had no idea she couldn't be saved."

"How is it with you now?" Rex poured more whiskey in Ryder's glass. "I am sorry that you could not recover your sister."

Ryder focused his gaze in his glass. "At first, the thought of murdering Shook was all I could think about, but the more I thought on it, the more I realized, Pip died the way she would have wanted to, on the battlefield. She did not die because I couldn't do the things I was ordered to do to save her. The truth is, I'm relieved to know that I never had a chance to save her after all."

"The rosier side of things, I suppose. Even more reason to show us the way inside Aldemara," Rex said.

"I can give you any information you require ... I just don't know if I can go back to Aldemara."

"You're not the sort of man who backs down from a challenge."

"It's not me; it's Iris. We've gotten word that our brother, Hunter, survived the attack. I'm not sure I can persuade Iris to stay and help when all she wants is to be home with the rest of our family."

"If you have his location, we can send Sentinels his way to offer protection."

"I appreciate that, but Iris and I need to go ourselves."

Rex let out a long sigh. "Listen, we know this is difficult for you and Iris, but we need you. Stella needs you."

Ryder laughed. "Stella does not need me. She can handle herself."

"Well, I for one could use your tactical support, and to be frank, Iris is the only one who can manage Gary, our droid."

Ryder smiled, remembering how Iris spoke of Gary. Iris never shut up about him. He knew deep down that Rex was a man of merit, but he was not sure he wanted to put his life or Iris's in Rex's hands. "And if I can't convince my sister? What happens then?"

Rex sat back and finished his drink. "Nothing. You are free to go. I've arranged for your full pardon, whether you help us or not. You were prisoners being manipulated into doing the things you did. You shall be prisoners no more."

Ryder cocked his head. "Wasn't expecting that. I would do anything for Stella. I'll do what I can to convince Iris to stay, but she is stubborn as hell."

"You're a good man," Rex said. He got up and pushed in his chair. "I could use you on my team. If the Zuldari get more strongholds in the universe, you and I won't be the only ones to suffer."

"I don't know. The last time I was on a team, they betrayed us and I woke up in that woman's bedroom missing an eye."

Rex's mouth formed a thin curve. "I can assure you that will not happen on my team. You help us with this one mission, and you may return home. You and Iris would be free. You can return right now and be free, but at least you know you earned your freedom by doing something just and right for the universe. Talk to Iris, and take some time to think about it."

# 56

# TWO TEAMS

**STELLA SAT BEHIND** a two-way mirror watching the interrogation along with Gary, who had been gnawing at his fingernails. Rex stood up and shook Ryder's hand as the door opened, and Iris entered, her eyes looking at the floor. Rex hugged her and reassured her that all was forgiven. Rex left the two of them, and Iris ran to Ryder and embraced him. He rocked her back and forth in his arms.

"Do you think they are going to help us?" Stella asked. When no one answered, she glanced around and saw she was alone. Gary had burst into the interrogation room and scooped up Iris and Ryder. Ryder didn't seem shocked, but he did slide out of the group hug and let Iris calm Gary down.

Rex and Elliot joined Stella behind the mirror.

Stella asked again. "Will they help us?"

Rex stroked his mustache. "I'm fairly certain they will."

"Fairly?" Stella asked.

"Mostly."

"That doesn't give me much confidence," Stella said. "I know he can give us information, but having those two lead the way would give us a much better chance."

"Yeah, those two are total badasses," Elliot added.

"Badasses? I'm not familiar with this term, Driver," Rex said.

"Oh, uh, it means they are tough," Elliot replied.

"Right," Rex said. "They are tough, as you say, but they have both been through so much. Iris is not on board, and Ryder is committed to honoring her wishes. We will let them talk it over. Staring bullets into them will not bend them to our will. Let's get the rest of the team. We need to create two plans of attack—one that includes Iris and Ryder, and one that does not."

**STELLA SAT NEXT TO GARY AND ELLIOT** with her cheek resting on her fist. *This waiting is unbearable. How hard is it to fly a ship? If only I could just go myself.*

Willow, Maren, and Rex whispered to each other in the corner of the conference room. Zimmer entered moments later. Stella perked up, hoping to see Ryder and Iris enter as well, but no one followed. Willow and Maren took their seats at the table just as Zimmer began his presentation.

"Well?" Rex asked. "What's the word?"

"Haven't seen Iris or Ryder, and there was a Jumper ship departing Hangar 47, but I didn't see who was on it."

Everyone in the room let out a collective exasperated sigh.

Zimmer continued. "Hey, it would've been great if they were coming with us, but it looks like they've departed. We will press on without them. At least I was able to get some information from Iris." Zimmer took out a remote and cued an image on a monitor. "It appears that this Shook woman has made a deal with a Zuldari commander."

"No, not—" Rex started.

"Afraid so." Zimmer paused an image on the screen. "Commander T'Adox, First Leader of the Midway Zuldari Alliance."

"Shook has made a deal with him to sell a liquid form of Kate's healing essence, which is intended to heal great numbers of the Zuldari people who are sick from living on their toxic home world. The Zuldari are a threat to the success of our mission, but Shook is an even greater one. The security measures she will have in place could be our undoing."

"The booby traps," Elliot whispered to Stella.

She tried not to smile.

"Can't we call Sentinel units in for support?" Maren asked.

"No, you can't."

Everyone turned to the door.

"Hi, Iris," Elliot blurted out. He turned pink when everyone in the room stared at him.

Rex stuck out his hand to Ryder. "Glad to see you, man. We need your eyes on this. Iris, it just isn't the same without you."

Iris nodded and smiled.

Willow leaned across Gary. "I see now why you wanted to free him," she whispered as she winked at Stella.

Ryder shook Rex's hand. His eyes briefly connected to Stella's, and then he cleared his throat and continued. "You need to see this as two critical missions. The first team will have to handle the extraction of an asset. That team will get in, locate Stella's mother, and get out. The second team will have to keep the Zuldari distracted, giving the first team time to complete its mission."

"And Shook and T'Adox?" Rex asked.

Ryder punched keys on his smartwatch. Images of a high-rise in Aldemara and the laboratory appeared on the monitor. "Shook likes to frequent her chambers, located in this office building, as well as a place called the Inventions and Experiments room in this laboratory. The lab is most likely where she'll be keeping Stella's mother. T'Adox could be on the twenty-fourth floor of this high-rise or the coward may have gone back to his home world, leaving his soldiers to do the dirty work for him."

"What's the best way to extract Kate?" Zimmer asked.

"We could use Maren to locate her and just teleport her onto the ship," Stella said.

"Shook is too smart for that. She'd block the teleportation signal and then shoot us out of the sky before we could lock onto her," Ryder replied. "We're going to have to land."

"We can land on the outskirts of the city," Iris said. "Our allies in Aldemara will make sure we get to a safehouse undetected."

"I still don't understand why we can't call for backup," Maren said.

"Because there isn't time. We've already lost time on this floating bus. Shook has Kate, and if we don't get to her soon, there won't be much left of her to salvage," Rex said.

"That's right. Verbatim is too far away from Aldemara. We're closer," Ryder added.

"What about the people of Aldemara? You said you had allies there?" Stella asked.

Iris shook her head. "Aldemarans don't fight. Even if they wanted to, Shook hoards most of the weapons. Our allies will be able to lend us some ammunition they've smuggled in, but it won't be much."

Stella tapped her finger on the table. "Two teams."

"I think I know which team we will be on," Maren said.

"That's right," Willow said. "Maren can zero in on where, exactly, Kate is in that lab, and then we'll go get our girl."

"It's not that easy," Iris said. "We're going to have to get you into the lab, and once you're in, who knows what to expect. Don't underestimate Shook. She's incredibly intelligent and resourceful."

"She probably won't even let us land," Zimmer said.

"Landing will be easy," Ryder said. "She'll let us land. But she won't let us leave. She knows we're coming, and that's exactly what she wants. She wants to lure the Keepers to the lab. She will attempt to eliminate Willow and Maren and keep Stella and Kate in the lab to syphon their healing essences. She'll be ready for us."

Rex paced at the back of the room. "So if we charge into the lab, Shook will have the Keepers there … together … on her turf. It's the perfect trap."

"She could take all of them out in one shot," Zimmer said. "Willow, Maren, and Stella should stay here while we go for Kate."

"The hell we will!" Willow said.

"You don't get to decide this for us," Maren added.

"This is my mother we're talking about here. You actually think I'm going to stay behind? Have you learned nothing?"

"Hello," Elliot said quietly. "Have you met her?"

"We may be rusty, but no one is taking us out in one shot," Willow said. "You need to remember who we are."

"I know who you are. You all are too valuable. Why give Shook exactly what she wants?" Zimmer asked.

Gary massaged his temples. "My head is pounding."

"Gary …" Iris said.

"Iris, I know you will insist that I can't possibly have a headache, but trust me when I say this back-and-forth is causing my gears to grind in a horrific fashion."

Iris smiled. "Apologies, my friend."

Rex sat back down at the head of the conference table and stretched out his hands in front of him. "Listen, all of you. This mission is unlike any that we've been saddled with before. We are used to fighting wars together with massive armies and artillery at our disposal. We are used to facing foes with more predictable movements. Instead, we have no army, not much artillery, and we are facing an unpredictable foe who means to lure us into her trap."

"Precisely why the Keepers should remain here," Zimmer said.

"Well, while this mission could be doomed to fail, Maren is right. It is not our decision whether these Keepers assist or not. As Sentinels, we live to serve the Keepers any way we can. So ... Keepers? What say you?"

"We already know what they're going to say," Zimmer said, shutting off the computer and tossing his remote on the table.

"You need to watch it, little man, and let us speak for ourselves," Willow said.

Rex chuckled. "Stella, what do you want to do?"

"We've been hiding for too long. Yes, we'd be taking a risk, but there are risks either way. We're coming with you."

"Maren? Willow?"

Maren nodded.

"Like you even have to ask me again. Have you not heard me hollering?" Willow said.

Rex laughed. "Oh, I hear you Willow. I always do."

"Let's get going then," Zimmer said. "I'll ready the ship."

Everyone began to filter out of the room. Stella caught Ryder on the way out the door. Before she could speak, Elliot stepped in between them.

"Well, well, Mr. Roboto," Elliot said, folding his arms across his chest.

"What?" Ryder said, taking a step toward Elliot.

"I haven't forgotten that you abducted Stella and hurt her in the process."

Ryder stiffened. "And you are?"

"Elliot Driver, warrior and Stella's sidekick."

"Doesn't seem Stella's the kind of woman who needs a sidekick."

Elliot cleared his throat. "She doesn't need a new robot, that's for sure."

"You're suggesting I'm a robot?"

"That's right."

Ryder took one more step toward Elliot. "You need to get your facts straight."

"Excuse me," Stella said, throwing up her hands in the air. "Excuse me. That's enough. Elliot … a word, please." Stella pulled him away and shoved him into a nearby elevator.

"What was that?" Stella asked, stopping the elevator. "You were literally puffing out your chest back there."

"I'm, like, a foot taller than him. That's got to count for something."

Stella narrowed her eyes. "What are you talking about?"

Elliot shook his head. "I don't know. I don't know what came over me. Maybe I have space madness. Is that a thing?"

"No, space madness is not a thing."

"I'm sorry. I think I reacted because … I don't like that he hurt you."

Stella raised her eyebrows. *This man never ceases to surprise me.*

Elliot ran his fingers through his hair. "And, yes, I know you're a genius surgeon, you can shoot green fire out of your hands, and you're this unstoppable, beautiful, she-Godzilla, but still … I hated hearing you scream for help on the other side of that door back on Verbatim."

Stella gulped. It was if someone had knocked the wind out of her. She had spent the last ten years on her own; she had forgotten how it felt to have someone looking out for her. "I appreciate that, and I get it. I do. It wasn't right, but at the time he didn't have a choice. If it makes you feel any better, I kind of hurt him too."

"Oh?"

"I split his lip when I headbutted him. And ... um ... I punched him in the throat."

"Yeah, that does make me feel better. Maybe he's right, though."

"Right about what?"

"You don't need a sidekick."

"Well, I may not *need* a sidekick, but it has been nice to have a warrior like you to fight all these battles with."

"I'm not really a warrior. I've kind of just been telling people that to fit in."

"Elliot you *are* a warrior. Look at everything you've done since we've been here. And as far as everything I've done ... I couldn't have done it without you. You saved us on Kodon, and you've been that one familiar constant I've had in a place where nothing is familiar or constant."

Elliot's cheeks dimpled.

"And if we ever make it back to New York, I will definitely hang out with you."

"All right! It's a date. But first ... let's go get your mom."

Stella hugged Elliot, cupped his head in her hands, and gave him a quick kiss. He hugged her tight and then started the elevator.

# 57

# FIST BUMP

**MARLON'S DEVICE WOULD REMAIN HAPPY** and resting at Omnibus while the crew took a small Jumper ship to Aldemara, since Marlon's Device didn't have stealth capabilities to land undetected with Kandi's technology scanning the skies. Stella paused as she strapped herself into the seat. Her stomach wasn't burning and churning. Hands were steady, no jitters, no nausea. Even when the small ship bounced around as it pushed through Aldemara's atmosphere, Stella wasn't shaken. She smiled and snapped the buckle of her seat belt in place.

"Almost there now," Rex said as he flipped switches from the pilot's chair.

Zimmer sat to the right of Stella. "Seems like you've adjusted to being off the ground."

"I ... I have. It's not the flight that's bothering me, but what we're flying into that makes me anxious. I hate that everyone is risking so much for me."

"No one is doing this for you," Zimmer said with a flat tone.

Stella raised her eyebrows.

"You're so used to saving one person at a time. This is so much bigger than you. Saving Kate, stopping the Zuldari from restoring themselves to their full power, reuniting the Keepers ... that's the mission now. It's not just our lives; it's the lives of untold millions in this galaxy."

Stella nodded. "Somehow, that doesn't make me feel better."

"It's not supposed to," Zimmer said. "It just gives you a different perspective."

"You mean the perspective that we're flying into a trap totally outnumbered with a crew half-assembled from the island of misfit toys?" Elliot said from her left.

Stella scanned the room and saw Iris in her black catsuit, Ryder in his leather coat, Maren and Willow in flowing, silk gowns, Gary wearing his traditional tourist garb, Zimmer in his suit and ugly orange tie, and Elliot packed into a Sentinel uniform. *Yep, the misfit toys.*

She leaned into Zimmer when she caught him also glancing at the crew. "Do you ..."

"I see it and am now making a mental note about equipping us with a more cohesive set of uniforms."

"Does that include you?" Stella asked.

Zimmer ran his tie through his fingers. "No."

The smile broadened on Stella's face. *This guy is growing on me. I'm even starting to like the tie.*

The Jumper kicked up dirt as it touched down behind the safe-house on the outskirts of the city. The modest tin house was empty except for some furniture, dust, and a meager stockpile of weapons and ammunition.

"Hot damn! Haven't seen one of these in a while," Willow said, grabbing a blaster no bigger than her hand. She held it up in the dim light of the house and then shoved it in her pocket.

"You've never needed one of those before, Willow," Maren said.

"Don't you trust your hands?"

"I do, and while I feel more alive than I have in years, I'm not sure I'm up to full speed just yet. This little cutie will be my fail-safe."

"These are some sweet finds, to be sure. You've got some bold Aldemaran friends, Iris. Especially considering they had to smuggle all this in," Rex said.

"Aldemarans are good people," Iris said. "We're fighting for them too."

"Agreed. Willow, won't you take us through the battle plan as you used to do back in the day?" Rex asked.

"I would love to, if it's okay with the Suit here." Willow winked at Zimmer, who scowled and folded his arms across his chest.

"It is very important that we hold a formation until we are fully inside," Willow said. She signaled to Rex, who projected digital images from his smartwatch showing a rendering of how they were to line up. "Mr. Gary in front, Iris and Ryder on each side. Stella in the middle, with Maren and I flanking her. Stella, how's that shield of yours?"

"Uh, good," she said. She briefly looked at her hands and then back to Willow.

"Okay. Elliot, Zimmer, and Rex will bring up the rear. Who has the map of the building we're headed to?"

Ryder stepped forward and projected images of the interior of the lab.

"Once I give the signal, we break. You six stay back to provide some cover so Stella, Maren, and I can search for Kate."

"I've got her," Maren said with her eyes closed. "She's on the second floor."

"The Inventions and Experiments room," Iris said. "Makes sense that's where Shook is holding her. I'm going with you up there so I can kill Shook myself."

"No," Stella said, her gaze fixed on the floor. "No. Stay with the others. I've got Shook." Stella's usually lilting and sweet voice left her body with a low growl. No one said a word in protest. Only the sound of Ryder cracking his knuckles broke the silence.

"Right. We know the enemy is waiting for us; let's give them one hell of a fight," Rex said. "All that matters is retrieving Kate and then getting the Keepers safely out of the building. Take one extra moment to compose yourselves, pray to a deity, stretch, or whatever you need to get ready for this battle. Though we be small, we are mighty. This is for Stella, Kate, and for the fate of all that is good in our universe."

Zimmer cleared his throat. "Right, and everyone take an earpiece so we can talk to each other."

Ryder checked the battery pack on his revolver and shoved it in its holster. "You ready for this, warrior?" he asked, turning to Elliot.

Elliot winked. "Yep, bringing up the rear is my specialty."

Ryder chuckled.

"Good. Then you better take this." Iris shoved a long steel club with a spiked ball on the end into Elliot's hand.

"Whoa, what is this?" Elliot asked, almost dropping it.

"It's a stunning mace. It stuns larger targets so you can finish them off with a few more blows," Iris said.

"Neat. How about … uh … do you have anything for smaller … smaller targets are the ones I like … yeah."

"Or maybe you'd like a plasma canon?"

"Uh …" Beads of sweat broke out on Elliot's forehead when Iris handed him a weapon almost as large as he was.

Ryder rolled his eyes. "C'mon, Iris." He gave the canon back to her and grabbed a pulse rifle. "Take this. Just point it and shoot. It fires a big blast not even a blast repulsion vest can stop. It's set to hit the chest of a target so you don't even have to aim."

"I can handle that. And hey," Elliot pulled Ryder off to the side. "Uh, about what I said on that Omnibus thing, I apologize—"

Ryder held up his hand. "No need. You care for Stella. You're looking out for her, and that's a good thing. The only apologies owed were from me to her."

"Okay, cool. Yeah, that's awesome, man."

"Good. Now, are you ready?" Ryder asked.

Elliot stuck out his fist. "You better believe it, bro."

Ryder stared blankly at him.

"Now you make a fist too."

Ryder stuck out his fist. Elliot pounded his fist first on top of Ryder's, then from below, and then right in the middle.

Elliot walked away. Ryder looked at his fist and shrugged.

Stella laughed as she set her comm link in her ear.

"I don't have to ask you if you're ready, do I?" Ryder said.

"No, you don't."

"You didn't select a weapon, though. You can't go in there unarmed."

Stella turned to the table behind her with different sizes of blasters, pulse rifles, knives, railguns, and other weapons on it. She ran her fingers over a small blaster and briefly grasped it before setting it back down on the table.

"Why don't you want a weapon?" Ryder asked.

Stella rubbed the back of her neck. "Because I'm afraid I'll use it."

"And that's a bad thing?"

"For me, it is."

"You're going to need something for protection."

She paused again, looking over the table. The others had already started to shuffle out of the safehouse. "I've got stuff on my belt, I've got my shield, and I've got all of you. I'll be fine."

# 58

# SITTING DUCK

**THE NIGHT SKIES OF ALDEMARA** were clear, although the streets in the distant heart of the city still looked barren. A metallic-scented breeze danced around them as they crept single file to the lab. A commotion ahead of them caught their attention, and Ryder threw up his fist, signaling them to stop. A Hovercar rode up, stopping in front of the lab. Ryder motioned for them to duck behind the back of the building.

"Commander, are you really meaning to leave them?" asked a voice.

"My troops are willing to die for the cause. There is nothing more I need to do here. Shook is of no use to us now."

"T'Adox," Iris said. She lunged out of line, but Ryder reached out and grabbed her. "We can't let him leave," she said.

Ryder shook his head. T'Adox and another Zuldari man crawled into the Hovercar. It blew a blast of air back on Stella and crew as it whipped away into the night.

"Look at that dastard," Rex said. "Doesn't even have the guts to stand with his own army."

"He will get his sooner or later," Ryder said. "Let's go."

The doors that normally required the guard's handprints and retinal scans were propped open. Wind whipped through the doorways and created an eerie echo that sent the hair on the back of Stella's neck straight up. The crew filed through the passageway, silently and in formation. Stella held her hands up in the middle of the formation, ready to throw the shield. Her hands trembled, but she clenched her fists and focused. She kept her gaze fixed in front of her while Iris and Ryder shifted theirs, sweeping their weapons back and forth as they scanned for Zuldari soldiers in the lab.

The lobby's floors were gleaming and polished. A potted plant near a column by the entrance swayed in the breeze that wafted behind them. Nothing was out of place, and not a soul could be found except for Mr. Owen standing in the middle of the lobby shaking and dripping with sweat.

"Don't come in here," he said, his voice quivering.

"Mr. Owen, what are you doing?" Iris asked.

"Please ... don't come in here. You don't want to be here, please."

The crew stepped forward until they were fully in the lobby. Stella let out a yelp when the doors slammed behind them. The sound echoed through the lobby and created a distraction, so no one saw who fired the shot that hit Mr. Owen. Blood burst from his shoulder, and he fell to his knees. Another blast ripped through his side. He rolled on his back, writhing in pain.

Stella gasped and tried to push her way to him, but Maren and Willow held her back. "Do not break formation," Willow whispered. "Not yet."

Knowing she couldn't help Mr. Owen, Stella's skin felt like it was being pricked by a thousand needles when she heard the gurgling sounds he made as he writhed around on the floor.

"Hang in there Mr. O. You hang in there," Ryder shouted.

"We have to help him," Stella said.

"We will," Iris said. "We will."

"We can't just leave him here," Stella said.

They stopped in the middle of the lobby. Mr. Owen was almost within Stella's reach.

*I can help him. If I can just reach him.*

"Stella don't do it," Maren said. "There's no time."

"This man doesn't deserve to die like this."

"Everyone get ready," Ryder said.

Mr. Owen turned on his stomach and began to crawl toward them with an outstretched hand.

"Cover me," Stella said.

"What?" Iris shouted.

"No. Stay in the middle," Willow said.

Stella jumped out and grabbed Mr. Owen's outstretched hand. Laser light from invisible sources bounced off the floor around her. Ryder and Iris returned fire over the railing of the balcony, though they didn't connect with anything but the walls above.

Stella pulled Mr. Owen in between Willow and Maren and ducked down. "You're going to be okay."

Mr. Owen nodded in between panting breaths. The wall Gary created with his giant silver battle form blocked blasts. Other shots whizzed over their heads.

"Stella! Leave him!" Zimmer said, shooting at something behind him.

She ignored them all and pressed her hands gently on Mr. Owen's wounds.

"We need your shield!" Rex said.

Stella focused on Mr. Owen: the blood clotting, his seared flesh repairing, the holes in his body closing. "When I tell you to, you run. Crawl out in between us and then get out of here, okay?"

Mr. Owen's eyes were wide, but the color was slowly returning to his face. "Okay, thank you. Okay, I'm okay."

"On one, two …" Stella popped up, and with one arm extended, she threw a shield around Gary and the others in the front. "… three!"

The shooting increased as Mr. Owen scrambled to his feet. With her other arm extended toward him, Stella fired green sparks out of that hand, forming a bubble around Mr. Owen as he ran to the door. He flashed his hand across a control panel and the doors swung open. Blasts ricocheted off her shield as Mr. Owen sprinted through the doors closing behind him.

"Okay, Shook got us in the building. Now what?" Rex asked.

One by one, armed Zuldari soldiers appeared out of their cloaks. Hundreds of snarling, shrieking soldiers emerged wearing helmets and blast repulsion vests. The sound of the small army creeping toward them sent a shiver up Stella's spine. They were slinking in from all sides, and Stella wished now she had grabbed a blaster.

"Okay, uh, yeah, should've gone with the stunning mace," Elliot said.

"Stick to the plan," Ryder said.

"Counting down," Willow said.

Stella extended her palms, creating a ball of green light around them.

"Three … two…"

A shot went off behind them. All eyes focused on a Zuldari soldier crying out. Blue slime cascaded out of his chest as he dropped to his knees and slammed to the floor.

"Oops, my bad." Elliot said.

Stella gritted her teeth, feeling the weight of every Zuldari blaster unloading on her small circle of friends. The crew returned fire from within the shield, bringing down soldiers on all sides. But when one soldier fell, it seemed like twelve more appeared in his place.

"We're going to have to fly to the second floor," Willow said.

"Okay," Stella said out of breath.

"Go!" Rex yelled. "We got you!"

Some of the shooting paused as the stunned Zuldari watched Willow, Maren, and Stella pop off the floor. Stella turned and aimed her shield at the ground to protect the rest of the team. She glanced over her shoulder to find a spot to land. Willow landed on the second floor, opened her palms, and sent a chain of lightning through ten Zuldari. Maren landed on her feet but stumbled. Stella extended one of her arms and shielded her from a shot. Stella held one arm down to the lobby, blocking shots until the crew broke away, ducking behind various objects. Ryder and Iris cloaked themselves and ran off in opposite directions. Stella was so preoccupied with what was going on below her she didn't see the Zuldari soldier she slammed into when she tried to land.

She coughed from the wind being knocked out of her and rolled off him. She sent a shield up to protect herself as he jumped to his feet and fired. He immediately dropped when Willow fired into his back. Willow helped Stella up, and they ran into the Inventions and Experiments room, followed by Maren. Stella looked over her shoulder, surprised the Zuldari didn't follow, and ran right into Willow's extended arm.

"Who is that?" Willow asked.

Stella tiptoed toward the body sprawled out on the floor. Kandi's blond hair reached out from her head like pale tentacles swimming in the ocean of blood around her.

"Shook."

# 59

# FIRST STRIKE

"WELL, THAT'S DISAPPOINTING," Willow said. "I was looking forward to ending her life."

"Who did this?" Maren asked.

Before anyone could answer, Kandi's body rattled with coughs. "Please … help …" she said between gasps. Her hand shook violently as she raised it, reaching out toward Stella. Her other arm was bent awkwardly underneath her.

Stella took a step forward, but Willow pulled her back. "Stop. Something isn't right here."

"I know that, but …"

"But nothing," Willow said. "We need to get rid of this thing, find Kate, and get out."

"Please, I can take you to the Healer … it was all T'Adox. He just shot me. He forced me to do all these things … I was his prisoner. Please … help me and I will help you," Kandi said.

"Let's waste her, Maren," Willow said.

Kandi erupted in violent sobs. "I'm begging y'all. I didn't want any of this. Give me some healing ... let me make this right."

Stella wrenched her arm out of Willow's grasp. "Where is my mother? Tell me where she is and I'll help you." She inched toward Kandi and knelt beside her.

"I'm so cold. Please, if I pass out, I ... I can't help you."

Stella hesitated but seeing Kandi drowning in blood, she knew she had to try to help. "Stay awake, stay with me," she said, reaching for Kandi.

"Stella, leave her!" Willow shouted. "We can find Kate without her."

"I doubt that," Kandi said.

Stella cocked her head. "What?"

Kandi whipped her hand out from under her, revealing a large blaster in her hand. "Back up, bitch!" she yelled, hopping to her feet.

"What ... the ...?" Willow gasped.

"Honestly, y'all made this way too easy."

"Where is my mother?" Stella asked through gritted teeth.

Kandi pressed a button on her smartwatch, and the heavy steel doors closed behind her with a resounding thud. She tapped on her watch again, and out of a dark corner emerged a smaller fourth tank locked into a mobile transport with three wheels. "Told you! Mommy's here, babe."

Kate looked like a doll suspended in the teal liquid of the tank. Her crimson hair floating around her made her look almost peaceful. Stella clenched her fists and felt as if she were staring into a fire from the heat pulsing through her body. She opened her mouth to scream, but before she could, Kandi fired.

Willow and Maren wailed as they fell to the floor. Willow's blaster slid out of her hand, stopping near Stella's foot. Stella froze, staring at them wide-eyed. She lunged for the blaster, but was stopped by a white-hot laser slashing through her hand. The burning numbness shot all the way up her arm.

Kandi threw her head back and cackled so loudly that it almost shook the room. "I can't believe it. Is that all you got? Look at you! You're supposed to be this superhero, and you brought these two spoons to a knife fight. Y'all actually thought two grandmas wearing muumuus would be a match for me?"

Stella ducked just in time to miss another incoming blast and then threw up her hands. "Stop! Stop! Let me help them, let my mother go, and you can have me."

"Hmmm … tempting … but I think I'll just take y'all."

"Not going to happen," Stella said, taking a small step closer to Willow's blaster.

"You just don't know when to quit. Oh my gah! Listen, I don't need you and a bunch of grannies ruling again. The only woman who should have any power anywhere is me. The universe just isn't big enough for all of us."

Kandi raised her arm again and laser light erupted from her blaster. Stella deflected two shots, but the pain from her hand clouded her mind, and the shield fizzled like fireworks dying in the sky. Stella collapsed to her knees, clutching her chest. Blood filled her hands and flowed to the floor.

"Ha! Y'all think you're heroes. I've read that book of yours—you fight in some war and then just run and hide like ants from a squirt gun? What's up with that? If I had the superpowers y'all have, I'd be blowin' shit up left and right." Kandi snatched a book off the computer terminal next to her and tossed it at Stella's feet. "This was General Law's book. She just gave it up and ran away like the freak she was. I'm going to hunt her down too when I'm finished with all your sorry asses."

Kandi slipped her blaster back into its holster that was hidden on her back and began to tinker with the tank Kate was in.

Stella touched the wounds on her chest.

*Heal ... you can heal.*

She fought to keep her eyes open, but they felt heavy and weighted. She pressed on the deep laser gash on her chest and tried to concentrate, but she couldn't shake off the painful sleep that was overtaking her. An icy sensation crawled through her limbs, and her head slowly lowered to the marble floor.

# 60

# OVER THE EDGE

**RYDER WIPED THE SWEAT** from his brow as he hid behind a column. While cloaked, he had mowed down dozens of Zuldari, but he turned it off so his team wouldn't shoot him by accident—something he felt was entirely possible since Elliot had a rifle. He called to Stella through their comm channel and felt his stomach churn when she didn't respond.

"We need to head up to the second floor … give those ladies some backup," Ryder said.

Rex yelled over the gunfire. "Agreed. Gary and I will try to finish off the last of them down here. The rest of you get up those stairs."

Elliot bolted up the stairs behind Iris, who cleared a path with her plasma canon. Zuldari screeched as they flipped over the sides of the staircase. Ryder and Zimmer darted up behind them. They picked off multiple Zuldari once they reached the second floor, but it didn't seem like they made a dent in their numbers. Elliot, Zimmer, and Iris shot through a line of Zuldari that charged them while Ryder ran to the Inventions and Experiments door. It was locked from the inside, and even multiple laser blasts at the lock couldn't get the door to budge. He pounded on the door, calling for Stella but heard nothing in return.

Out of the corner of his eye, Ryder saw a Zuldari soldier aim his weapon, but he blew a hole in his torso before he could get a shot off. Another fired from behind, and Ryder ducked, narrowly missing a plasma shot. Gary pushed himself in front of Elliot, Iris, and Zimmer once he and Rex finished in the lobby. He acted as their shield while Rex and Ryder provided cover from behind.

Rex's blaster jammed, and a shot tore through his leg. "I hope those ladies are faring better than we are," he said. Rex hopped on one leg, and Ryder stepped in front of him, turning on his cloak once more so he could run through a pack of Zuldari.

"Something's wrong," Zimmer shouted. "None of them are answering our calls."

"We have to get into that room!" Ryder said.

Gary gritted his silver teeth and rushed through a mob of Zuldari. He picked up two by their necks with his massive, steel arms and slammed their heads together. They died with a loud crack, and he threw them to the ground. He punched another in the face, snapped the neck of another, and then suddenly came to a screeching halt. Three Zuldari were setting up a plasma rocket launcher.

"Get back, Gary!" Zimmer yelled.

Gary turned and ran. Iris charged her canon and stepped in front of him, while Elliot opened fire from behind her. "Let them get through this!" she exclaimed.

"Iris, get down!" Ryder screamed.

An ear-numbing boom sounded. A rocket burst out of the cylinder. Iris fired. The plasma ball of light and the rocket connected, creating a stunning fireball. The force blew Iris back into Elliot, sending them both over the railing.

"No!" Ryder fired into the crowd of Zuldari near the rocket launcher. Their bodies shook from the energy tearing through them, and they all slumped over the launcher. Gary and Zimmer kept firing as Ryder sprinted to the railing. He closed his eyes for a moment, not wanting to see Iris's lifeless body at the bottom of the lobby. When he opened them, he saw Elliot with clenched teeth holding onto a rung of the railing with one hand. His other hand clutched Iris's leg as she swung upside down. Ryder grabbed Elliot's wrist and reached his other through the rungs. "Iris!"

Elliot grunted and groaned as he tried to pull Iris up to grab Ryder's hand, but a blast ripped through his arm. He cried out, lowering her again. Ryder hopped up and pumped six shots into two Zuldari firing from the left. Rex snatched Iris's canon and blew away a massive group of them, and Ryder slid his hands back through the railing. This time Elliot raised Iris just enough that she could pull herself up and grab Ryder's hand.

Fewer and fewer Zuldari appeared to challenge them, and Gary rushed over to help pull Iris and Elliot back up to the solid ground of the second floor. Smoke from all the crossfire hung in the air like a drifting ghost, and the lab was quiet once more. Ryder pulled out a healing cloth from his jacket, tore off a piece, and wrapped it around Elliot's arm. He propped him up against one of the banisters and then tended to Iris who was nursing a shot in the leg.

"Good job everyone. Teamwork makes the dream work, am I right?" Elliot said, gasping for air.

"Incredible action you took there, Driver," Rex said.

"Thank you for not dropping my precious girl," Gary said, morphing back to his human form.

Elliot helped Iris up when he got to his feet. Her hand lingered in his and she leaned into him.

"That's some grip you've got there," she said.

Elliot coughed. "Uh, oh, I mean … thank you … for noticing."

Shots erupted on the other side of the Inventions and Experiments door followed by a woman crying out.

"Stella," Elliot and Ryder cried in unison.

# 61

# TIDAL WAVES

**A WARM HAND CLASPED** Stella's lying limp at her side.

"Stella don't pass out," Willow whispered. "Stay with me."

Willow rolled over and laid her other hand on Stella's chest. Stella's eyes burst open from the charge that surged through her. She touched the burning wound on her chest, closing her eyes to visualize it healing. She touched her arm and sealed another oozing lesion. Blood flooded back to her head, and the heaviness that had been crushing her was gone.

Kandi kicked the tank, which was not moving on her command. She didn't see Stella reach for Maren, who was stirring to the side of her. Maren squeezed Stella's hand and slowly sat up. Kandi shouted into her phone, calling for assistance. Stella, cringing, sat up and helped Willow, who silently motioned to Maren. Willow whispered, "Focus your energy on the tank. The tank—we need to hit the tank."

"I don't care how y'all do it; you need to get someone up here to help me move this tank because it just shorted out ... Of course I can fix it, but there's no time. We need to get it to the landing pad on the roof and move it ASAP."

Kandi turned. Her phone slid from her hand, shattering on the ground. "Oh, I'm not having this!"

The Keepers were standing facing her. Maren and Willow each had a hand on one of Stella's shoulders. "Sorry to disappoint, 'babe,'" Stella hissed. "You need to learn that acting tough around us is a bad idea."

Willow and Maren reached back and then thrust their arms forward. Green lightning exploded out of their palms and hit the tank.

"No!" Kandi screamed, unsheathing her blaster. Her shot bounced off Stella's shield, and gallons of liquid flooded the room, sweeping Kandi off her feet. Kate's lifeless body was flushed out of the tank and ejected onto the floor.

"Help her!" Stella said as she ran through the liquid toward Kandi, who was scrambling to retrieve her blaster. Maren and Willow pulled Kate out of the deluge, trying to resuscitate her. Kandi had one finger on her blaster when Stella pounced, smashing her hand to the ground. The blaster slipped out and flew across the wet floor. Stella yelped when Kandi punched her in the side of the head, knocking her down. Stella crawled on her stomach, still in reach of Willow's blaster. She reached for it, but Kandi tugged on her leg, pulling her away from it. Stella whipped around and kicked Kandi in the face. Kandi covered her mouth and writhed on the ground.

Stella flipped back around and scurried to the blaster. She finally grabbed it and rolled onto her back, but Kandi had reached her blaster and was standing with her arm extended. She seethed and gritted her teeth.

Stella aimed, but her blaster jammed. She gasped as Kandi pulled the trigger. A surge of light sped toward Stella but fell when it hit the shield that suddenly enveloped her. Stella's eyes widened when a burst of green electricity struck Kandi. The electric charge zapped every molecule of Kandi's body. The light surging through her was so great that Stella saw Kandi's skull as if she were looking at an X-ray image.

Kandi crashed to the floor. Steam wafted up from her body, and blood cascaded out of her eyes and mouth. Stella hopped to her feet. Her mother stood behind her, soaked to the bone and holding her palms forward. Willow and Maren stood on either side of her.

"Mom!" Stella said, running to her. "Are you okay?"

"I'm okay," Kate answered.

"I'm all for family reunions, but we need to go," Willow said.

"Do you think that thing is finally dead?" Maren asked.

"Not sure who could survive being electrocuted like that," Kate said.

Just as Stella thought she should check Kandi one more time, an alarm sounded overhead. Lights flashed around them, and Kandi's voice spoke from above.

"I guess I must be dead because that's the only time this protocol initiates. Don't think you can kill me and run. I'm going to burn down this lab and take y'all with me. See you on the other side, bitches!"

The computer terminals sparked and exploded into little fires. Monitors burst into flames, and the other tanks started to drain.

"The door won't budge," Willow said, testing it.

"What do we do now?" Maren asked. Stella didn't answer. Her eyes darted around the room. Bars slid down over the windows, and there were no other exits she could see until she looked up at the twenty-foot-high ceiling.

"Mom, are you strong enough to fly?" Stella asked.

"Do I have a choice?" Kate asked.

"Ladies, can you blow a hole through the roof?" Stella asked.

Another explosion behind them caused Maren to yelp. "I think so," she said.

Willow and Maren stood shoulder to shoulder.

"Put your hand on Willow's shoulder," Kate said to Stella.

Stella did as her mother instructed. The smoke stung her eyes, and she coughed from the chemicals released into the air by the fires. Kate put her hand on Maren's shoulder, and Maren's posture improved. She looked at Willow and extended her hand. Willow took it and raised her other hand. Maren raised her hand at the same time, and a giant green fireball burst from their palms. The ceiling quaked, and they shielded their heads. When Stella opened her eyes, the roof was still intact and the fires inside were growing.

# 62

# NO EXIT

**RYDER CONTINUED TO POUND** on the door while Elliot called to Stella from his comm link.

Kandi's cloying voice echoed through the building.

"She's dead," Ryder said.

"That's excellent," Rex replied.

Iris shook her head. "No, we need to go now!"

"I'm not leaving without Stella," Elliot said.

Stella's voice came through his earpiece just then. Zimmer connected her to his smartwatch speaker so everyone could hear.

"We're okay. You need to leave before the building blows. We'll find another way..." Then her voice cut out.

Everyone jumped when steel bars slammed shut, locking them out of the other passages and corridors. Muffled explosions on the other side of the exam rooms caused smoke to billow out from the doors.

"Let's go," Ryder said. "C'mon! Let's go!"

Elliot didn't budge. "I'm not leaving."

"Listen, they are more powerful beings than all of us combined, especially now since they are in there together," Rex said, grabbing both of Elliot's arms. "They must have Kate, which makes them unstoppable. We have to trust Stella. She wouldn't want you to get yourself killed because you got stuck waiting by this door. Now, let's go."

Elliot nodded and followed Rex down the staircase. They hopped over the dead Zuldari bodies, whose rotting flesh had already started to smell. More bars cut them off in the lobby, leaving the way they came in as the only way out.

"That's it," Iris said. "The only way those doors are going to open is by a retinal and palm scan."

Zimmer fired at the door, but the blasts sparked off the glass, not even leaving a scratch. "Stella, can you hear us? Stella? If you make it out, you need to try to blow the lobby doors from the other side."

Only a garbled voice responded.

Gary sobbed as Iris picked up a blaster and fired into Zuldari carcasses out of frustration.

"Iris, please. Give it a minute. Stella and the others may have made it out by now. Let's not fall apart just yet," Zimmer said.

A conference room to their right erupted into a fireball, and Ryder wrapped his coat around Iris to shield her from the spray of glass. The once cheerful potted plant was now in flames. Burning smoke invaded Ryder's lungs, and he ran to the glass doors, pounding on them in a sheer act of desperation. Another explosion from their left sprayed them with concrete from a beam that was blown to bits. Iris and Elliot fell to their knees, choking on the thick smoke.

Ryder kicked at the door, his eyes stinging from ash. "No! No! We are not going to die today!" He balled his fist and punched the glass. He stepped back, eyes wide, as the first door to the lab opened. Through the haze, the silhouette of Mr. Owen appeared as he leaned in to let the computer scan his retina. He called to them, waving them through, and though he was still covered in blood, he managed a smile as he pushed his glasses back up his nose.

"Sweet mercy, that little man did it!" Rex said.

Ryder helped Iris up and shuffled her out, the others not far behind. Dust blew through the passage after them as another explosion brought down a chandelier.

Ryder picked up Mr. Owen and swung him around when they were a safe distance from the building. "You did it. You came back for us."

"Well, I … um … heard the alarm and I knew Shook had expired," Mr. Owen said. "I was forced to help her build in that protocol, so I knew what was going to follow. You all saved me, and I felt I needed to return the favor."

They all took turns thanking Mr. Owen, but Ryder knew they couldn't celebrate just yet.

"Mr. Owen, is there any way Stella and our other friends can get out of the Inventions and Experiments room after the protocol has been initiated?

Mr. Owen brought his hands to his mouth. "Oh no! She's still in there?"

"Yes, she's in there. Is there a way she can escape?" Elliot asked.

"Well, no … uh … not unless she can fly."

Ryder and Elliot exchanged glances, and all eyes turned back to the lab.

"C'mon Stella," Elliot said under his breath.

The windows in the lobby blew out into the street as explosion after explosion tore apart the building. Ryder swallowed the knot in his throat. He was trying to tell himself that it was going to be okay, but with every bomb exploding in the lab, his heart sank further into his stomach as he realized time was running out for Stella.

*If only I could get back in there and get Mr. Owen to open the doors.*

"I wish there was more I could do to help," Mr. Owen said. "But the entire place is rigged to blow and trap any remaining lives inside. I'm sorry for your loss, Master Ryder."

Ryder furrowed his brow. "No, she's going to make it."

Another detonation sent more pieces of the lab out into the night, but this time it came from a green fireball bursting through the roof.

Maren, Willow, Kate, and finally Stella popped out of the hole in the roof. As Ryder sprinted towards them, he saw the three Keepers touch down. Stella overshot them and rolled to a stop when she hit the pavement. She coughed and sputtered, out of breath as Ryder swept her into his arms.

"I thought we were going to die in there," Stella said, clutching onto him.

Ryder pulled her face into his chest as they held each other on the ground. "Nah, you're a Keeper, Stella. Nothing is going to stop you now."

# 63

# RECONNECTION

**STELLA PAUSED THE VIDEO** she had been watching as Rex jolted from his sleep. He had been showing her how to operate Marlon's Device when he dozed off in the chair next to her. They made a quick turnaround on Omnibus, and Marlon's Device, washed and refueled, was only happy to take off into the stars.

"How long was I asleep?" Rex asked.

"Long enough that you started to snore," Stella replied.

"Oh my, an abysmal sound to be sure. Apologies, my dear." He straightened his uniform. "Who has been flying the ship?" Rex glanced around the otherwise empty bridge.

"Me."

"You?"

"Yes, me. You showed me some things, and I figured out the rest so far."

Rex's fingers touched his parted lips. "By thunder, you never cease to amaze me. When you first arrived you almost vomited when you got off the ship, and now you're flying it."

Stella grinned. "Thanks in part to you. And ... I kinda like being at the helm."

"It definitely suits you." Rex flipped some switches and pushed up a lever, increasing the ship's speed. He then turned in his chair and reached for Stella's hands. "We can't begin to thank you, Stella. I know this was not an easy journey, but I'm proud of how far you have come in such a short time."

"Thank you for not giving up on me," Stella said.

"I never will," Rex said.

Stella reached out and squeezed him tight. She had never known her father, but she had come to see Rex as the father she had always missed having in her life. "I'm going to go find the others."

"I believe your mother is resting in the med bay and the other Keepers are in your chamber. Mr. Owen has settled into a guest chamber and we've sent a scout team to Aldemara to pick up his family."

"That's great. Are you sure you don't want me to keep you company?"

"Thank you, my dear, but I am perfectly at peace alone up here. I absolutely revel in these moments of solitude. I can sort through my thoughts as I listen to the delightful whir and hum of the ship."

As Stella passed by the main crew lounge, she leaned against the doorway, beaming as she took in the picture in front of her. Elliot was spread out and sleeping on his stomach on the floor. He had finally made it up his wall, gotten Stella out of a jam, and fought off Zuldari soldiers with a blaster. He, too, had come a long way from the day he woke up on the Inspirion. Gary had been switched to sleep mode, and his head was resting on Elliot's back. Ryder had dozed off sitting upright on the sofa, his arm around Iris, whose head rested on his chest. Even Zimmer and his ugly orange tie looked peaceful, sleeping with his feet slung over the arms of a chair in the corner of the room.

*This is my team. This is my team now.*

Ryder's eyes peeled open for a moment as Stella's mouth turned upward. The corner of Ryder's mouth curved as well. He winked at her before his eyes closed again.

Stella tiptoed into the med bay, where her mother had been sleeping in a bed. She had a headband device attached to her head.

"Hey, Peanut."

Stella reached out for her mother's hand. "How are you feeling? Are you hot or cold?"

"I'm just fine. I'm near you." Kate pushed herself up and hugged her. "So many years, so many things I missed with you, and now I hold you and you are the most beautiful thing I've ever seen."

Stella pulled away and could see that, just from that brief embrace, the color had returned to her mother's face. Her eyes were brighter, and she stopped the coughing she had been plagued with since they got to the ship. Kate removed the headband once it beeped.

"What is that thing?" Stella asked.

"It helps with headaches, and my head was throbbing. All better now, though. I realize all these devices must be so foreign to you. Very different from our medical technology on Earth."

"That's for sure."

Kate's eyes welled up with tears, and she took Stella's face in her hands. "I'm sorry, Peanut. I'm so sorry I had to leave you. I thought we had outrun those who were looking for us, and when they found us on earth, I fled to get them away from you. I only wanted you to be safe, but I wish I had not left you behind. I'm going to spend the rest of my life trying to make it up to you."

"I know. I understand that now. Just rest, Mom. It's okay."

"I don't want to rest." Kate pushed herself up.

Stella tried to stop her. "Mom, please."

"I want to see the others. Come on. I can't sleep anyway." Kate slid down off the bed and took Stella's hand. Maren and Willow were in Stella's quarters, and their eyes lit up when she and Kate entered the room.

Willow brewed some Verbatim tea and passed each of the ladies a steaming hot cup. They took seats on the same sofa where Elliot had told Stella about Kodon. Stella had always kept her veins charged with coffee, so she had never become a tea drinker. But the aroma and taste of this tea was very soothing—a wonderful brew after what they had just been through. For a few moments, they sat in silence, reflecting on the events that occurred in the lab as they watched the wisps of steam rise out of the steel mugs. Willow broke the silence.

"You know, that girl was right," she said.

Stella raised her eyebrows. "What girl? Kandi?"

"Yes, such a lost soul and so full of hatred, but she was right about one thing. We've been hiding for too long. We fought in the Great War, after all."

"And we lost that war," Maren said. "That's why the Zuldari are growing in numbers. We failed to completely eliminate them."

"And that's why we should have stayed together," Willow said.

"It was too dangerous not to separate at the time," Kate said. She held her mug with both hands while blowing to cool it down.

"I think it was too dangerous to separate and scatter; our strength faded with each passing day. Now here we are, older, tired, and rusty as hell," Willow said.

"What are you saying, Willow?" Maren asked.

"I'm saying we need to fight. I'm saying we are done hiding and watching our skin sag and our hands shake. We need to reconnect and find the others."

"I am too old, and too much time has passed. I am not the same person I was in the Great War," Maren said.

"Oh come on," Willow said. "Seriously, just because we've aged, just because we've let time march all over us, we aren't who we once were?"

"Willow, have you looked at me?" Maren said. "My hair practically glows in the dark."

"And you still look beautiful. Whatever has been lost over time, we can recover, especially when we are all together," Willow suggested.

"While I have to agree with Willow, I'm torn," Kate said. "Where would we possibly look for the others?"

"We just start," Stella said. "I wasn't even looking for anyone, but Rex led me to Maren, we found Willow, and then you, Mom."

"That's right, that's right." Willow set down her cup. "Listen ladies, I get it. My bones are creaking, and half the time I can't remember one day from the next, but now that I'm with you all, I feel better. If we reconnect, we will all be better. We were always stronger together."

Willow extended her hand. Kate smiled and grabbed her friend's hand. Willow stretched her other hand to the side and Stella took it. Stella then reached out for Maren, who hesitated but slowly let a smile spread across her face and took Stella's hand.

A warm current flowed into Stella's hands and tingled all the way up her arms. A scar on Willow's right eye vanished, and the skin around it looked as if it had never been damaged. The age spots on Maren's hands faded away.

Stella never felt more alive and supercharged than she did from the connection of that moment. She saw her mother's color had been restored and she did not look worn or tired any longer. When they all finally released, they all collectively let out joyous sighs.

Willow spoke first. "Now, don't we all feel better?"

Another collective sigh of gratitude and relief.

"So? What say you? Do we want to go back to our home worlds and shrink away, or do we stick together and fight?"

"We fight," Kate said.

"Maren?"

Maren exhaled and rubbed her temples. "I'm with you."

"Who do we seek out first? The other Keepers, I mean?" Stella asked.

Willow paused and glanced at *The Keepers of the Universe*. She had grabbed it from the lab, just before they escaped. "Maybe we should start with Lovella. I'd love to ask her what she was doing in Aldemara, and I would *love* to give her book back to her."

# 64

# GOODBYES

**A FRENZY OF VERBATIM CITIZENS**, military personal, friends, and family greeted Stella and crew once they landed at the Starport. Word had spread at the speed of light through the galaxies that the Zuldari were defeated in Aldemara, and some of the Keepers were reemerging from hiding. Stella was not used to the fanfare. Usually when she saved a life in the hospital, she would wipe the sweat from her brow and move on to the next patient. Occasionally, one of her coworkers would give her a pat on the back, but she just continued to do her job.

It was something different entirely to walk into the main terminal with her mother and be smothered by people marveling at her and the other Keepers. Willow beamed and soaked up every smile that greeted her. Maren blushed and stayed behind, but the crowd still stared at her in awe of finally seeing the elusive queen.

Elliot walked in front of them talking to Iris who stopped, grinned, and kissed him on the lips. Stella chuckled at seeing Elliot's skin turn pink. Gary hopped up and down with glee and threw confetti that he stored in his fanny pack. Stella smiled as her mother was greeted by old friends and colleagues who were happy to see her alive and still looking radiant, though gentle streaks of gray ran through her red locks.

Zimmer tried to hustle by Stella, but she reached out for his arm, stopping him. "Really proud of you, Stella. You've come a long way."

"Thank you."

"What is it?" Zimmer asked.

Stella narrowed her eyes. "I want to ask you something."

Zimmer glanced around and shoved his hands in his pockets. "Sure, but make it quick. I've got a lot of paperwork to complete after all this."

"I've been trying to get to the bottom of who you really are."

"I really need to take this—" Zimmer fumbled for his phone that hadn't been ringing.

Stella shook her head. "No. No more fake phone calls."

Zimmer relaxed. "What's your question, Stella?"

"You knew I was a Keeper from the very beginning, didn't you? You acted surprised when you realized I had the book, but it didn't surprise you at all. You knew."

Zimmer wiped his forehead and pulled Stella away from the crowds. "Yes ... I knew..."

"Then why the act?"

"There's a lot I'm not at liberty to discuss. All I can say is ..."

Stella leaned in. "Yes?"

Zimmer patted her on the shoulder. "It was time for you to come home."

He looked relieved when his phone really did start ringing. He waved and walked off toward the heart of the city.

Stella wandered over to them as her mother was swallowed by a swarm of old friends. Ryder thanked Rex, who joined up with Willow, Kate, and Maren.

Stella and Ryder smiled at each other briefly before Stella broke their silence.

"Where are you headed? Rex said he offered you a position in the Sentinel army."

Ryder nodded. "He did, he did."

"Are you going to take it?"

"No."

Stella kicked at the ground.

Ryder continued. "At least not yet. We are headed to Heelo to reunite with Hunter, and we have gotten word on where Pip is. We are going to bring her home and give her a proper burial. What about you?"

"We may have a lead on another member of the Keepers. Either way, I'm looking forward to spending time with my mother."

"I'm happy for you," Ryder said.

"Are you leaving right away?" Stella asked.

"Yes. Rex secured a ship for us."

Stella's heart sank and she stared at the ground. "So that's it? After all this, that's it and we go separate ways?"

Ryder lifted her chin with his finger. "Only for now. When we get Pip and figure out what's going to happen when we get home, I'll find you again."

"How?" Stella asked.

Ryder turned her wrist over and rubbed his thumb over where her chip was. He kissed her wrist, pulled her to him, and kissed her again. When he pulled away, he smiled at something behind her.

"Oh, uh, didn't mean to interrupt," Elliot said.

"Not at all. Happy you approached. I wanted to thank you again for your efforts in Aldemara and for saving Iris." Ryder extended a balled fist to Elliot.

Elliot's grin almost overtook his entire face. He happily bumped Ryder's fist. "Just doing my job as a sidekick."

"You're not a sidekick. You're a warrior, my friend."

Elliot nodded. "That's right. I'm a warrior."

Ryder saluted him, then turned and disappeared into the crowd.

"What's up with Mr. Roboto?" Elliot asked. "Where's he going?"

"Away. To find his brother and sister," Stella said.

Elliot raised his eyebrows. "You going with him?"

"No. I'm going to stay here with Mom." Stella watched until Ryder was out of view.

"That's too bad he's leaving."

Stella rolled her eyes. "Yeah, right."

"No seriously. I think I have a crush on him now. He's looks pretty good without that weird red eye."

Stella laughed. "And what are you going to do? Are you going home?"

"Dunno. I think I may stick around here. Rex just told me the Jacks called him. They actually want me to keep competing on those obstacle courses, and they even promised to remove the tentacle monsters from the water."

"Really? But that place was awful."

"It wasn't that bad. I like the dry heat, plus they promised me my own mansion and a pet raptor. Dreams really do come true."

"Your dream has been to live with lizard people and complete obstacle courses in the desert?"

"Well, it was one dream of many. I'd love to tell you about it. I know this little coffee shop around the corner. They have excellent bottled water." He winked at her and held out his bent arm.

Stella exhaled, remembering the coffee Elliot raved about the first time they touched down on Verbatim. She smiled and took his arm as they walked back to the Starbucks.

# 65

## FOUND

**STELLA WIPED THE SWEAT** from her brow. She watched intently as her mother floated through the crowd. Kate was making the rounds through the sick and dying who were scattered all over the floor of the last remaining shelter on the planet. Months before, they had been called as Healers to the planet of Ketnar 1, a small desert world the Zuldari had ravaged before pulling up stakes and heading to Aldemara. Before the Zuldari occupation, Ketnar 1 was a happy trading village, home to a mix of civilizations like Tamerlan and Spreeti, but the Zuldari drained all the planet's resources and then moved on, leaving those left behind starving and on the brink of death. The Sentinels had sent a small team with the Healers to help, and they had been stranded for days as a sandstorm raged outside.

Stella left the primary area of the building where the sick were scattered. She massaged her aching hands and sat down in a rusted chair that groaned from even her modest weight. She tried to wash the sand from her throat with a glass of water—some of the last water they brought from the ship just before the storm hit. Her mother joined her.

"You know, Mom, when you said we should catch up on lost time together, this is not what I had in mind."

The corner of Kate's mouth curved upward. Stella passed her mother the water glass.

"What are the supply levels?" Kate asked after taking a small sip from the glass.

"About a day left. How long do these storms typically last?"

"Much longer than that." Kate pushed the glass back to Stella and got up. She peered out the window at the makeshift hospital she and Stella had created. "At least we are making progress here."

Stella joined her mother at the window. "Healing these people is not going to do them much good if we can't get more supplies. The storm has wiped out all our communications."

"We have to keep trying. Every time there is a break in the storm, we will send out another signal," Kate said. "We did not come all this way to perish here. I know this is not the end of our story. Somehow, the signal will break through and we will be found. In the meantime, we work on healing these people."

This is what Stella had missed about her mother. Whenever Stella wanted to give up or quit as a child, Kate knew how to motivate her. While she appreciated her mother's optimism, Stella's logical mind couldn't help but have doubts. There were hundreds of people occupying this small apartment-like building. Their ship was miles away, grounded by the storm, and food and water were dwindling along with oxygen. Stella knew the odds weren't good.

She tried not to think about that as she straightened her shoulders and went back out into the sea of sickened inhabitants. She stopped near an older Tamerlan woman who extended her hand toward her. Stella smiled and grabbed the woman's hand. She placed her palms on the woman's head and could instantly feel the woman's head throbbing. For a moment, Stella's head throbbed in unison, but Stella could see what was causing the ache in the woman's brain and focused all her energy on it.

The woman exhaled, feeling instant relief as her pain subsided. Stella held her for another moment until the woman closed her eyes and slipped into deep sleep. Stella stretched to her knees when she caught something out of the corner of her eye.

The blue light.

The chip in her wrist blinked slow and steady under her skin. A prickle of excitement shot through her. She glanced around the room, but the scene was the same. She raced toward the door and began to wrap herself in cloth to protect herself from the sand. She reached for the door handle when a hand stopped her.

"What are you doing? You can't go out there," Kate froze, seeing the blue light blinking.

Stella could hear her mother calling to her as she threw herself out into the sandstorm. The wind whipped sharp pieces of dirt into the cloth around her face. She scanned the landscape, trying to make out any movement in the dunes ahead. She ran further out into the storm and nearly got blown off her feet. The sun briefly cut through the dusty haze, bringing more light to the terrain. She steadied herself as one last whirl of grit blew over her. Through the murk, she saw a shadow moving toward her. The light in her wrist flashed excitedly, and she burst into a sprint. She could see someone flying on an enclosed Hoverbike. The bike touched down in the sand, and the figure, face covered in a protective shroud, took off running for her. Stella ran so fast her feet didn't have time to sink. The dust calmed around them as Stella ran right into Ryder's arms. He scooped her up and squeezed her.

"You found me," she said, catching her breath.

"Told you I would, although Ketnar 1? You could have made it a little easier."

"You shouldn't have come here," Stella said, taking a step back. "We are out of supplies; our ship is dead ..."

Ryder smiled. "That's why I brought some reinforcements."

There was more movement behind them. An entire fleet of vehicles, sandswipers, a rolling med unit, and dozens of Kaygun soldiers wearing Sentinel uniforms pulled in behind Ryder. Iris rode up on a Hoverbike and stopped, along with a man with a beard riding a sandswiper.

Ryder shrugged. "Just a few of my friends."

Stella's mouth fell open.

Iris rolled by them. "Hunter and I will head in," she said before taking off.

The man with the beard rolled by on his sandswiper. "Ma'am ... brother." He saluted and rode on.

The wind swirled around them again, and they knew they needed to get inside. Ryder and Stella ran back to his Hoverbike. She hopped on behind and wrapped her arms around his waist as the bike's shield closed in around them. They raced back to the building to see Kate open the door to greet the welcome site of aid. The Kaygun army helped gather the sick and the well in the decaying building. The last of the planet's population was loaded into a large Star Cruiser bound for Verbatim, where everyone would be healed and given opportunities to remain or be relocated. Stella was exhausted, and her ears reverberated from the weeks of hearing the wind whip around them in the storm. The quiet hum of the Star Cruiser was a welcome relief. The ship's captain was briefing Stella and Kate in one of the crew lounges when Ryder walked in.

"Master Ryder," Kate said, reaching out her hands for him.

"Ma'am," Ryder said, taking her hands. "I've made contact with Captain Rex. He is preparing for our return. There will be aid and shelter for the refugees."

"Thank you."

Ryder bowed his head. "My pleasure."

An awkward silence passed through the room as Stella's and Ryder's eyes lingered on each other. Kate winked at her daughter and then left to sit at the helm.

Stella grinned and stepped closer to Ryder, now that they were alone in the room. "You look good in a Sentinel uniform."

Ryder looked down at the pristine white and rose gold suit he was wearing and shrugged. "I miss my jacket, but this will do."

"I really ... I can't thank you enough," Stella said. Her stomach flip-flopped from being near the only man to have that effect on her.

"Didn't do much. You and your mother are the ones who kept those people alive."

"We would not have made it much longer. I'm glad to be on this ship and out of that dying building."

"And I'm glad to be here with you."

"Oh?" Stella said. She leaned in and kissed him softly. "Well, we've got a long trip to Verbatim. What should we do?"

Ryder ran his hands down her arms. "I know I said you didn't need one, but is there room for a sidekick like me in your story?"

Stella smiled. "Hmmm. I already have a sidekick, but I do have an opening for a love interest."

Ryder pulled her to him. "I can start right away."

They shared another deep kiss as a pink and green galaxy passed by the window. The same glittery stars flickered outside, just as they did when Stella first woke up in space.

# ACKNOWLEDGMENTS

**I HAVE SO MANY STORIES ON PAPER**, in my head, and scattered in fragments throughout my computer and various notebooks, but actually sharing those stories with others is as terrifying for me as jumping off a cliff. This novel exists only because of the following people. They encouraged me, believed in me, and—in one case—did *not* believe in me.

First, my best friend, my compass, my everything—my husband, Tim Haas. You seem to have an unwavering faith in my abilities, and this has kept me going even when I thought *I'm not cut out for this*. You have supported and backed my writing career, and I owe so much to you.

This book wouldn't exist if it weren't for you, Catherine Spader. You are an incredible writer and writing coach. You displayed endless grace and patience while helping me transform this fledgling story into an actual novel.

Thank you to Bobby Haas for your wisdom and perspective as editor. You brought this story to such an elevated place, and the extra time you put into it means so much to me.

A million high fives to Kirsten (K.B.) Jensen, Polly Letofsky, and everyone at My Word Publishing for all your support and cheers from the sidelines as you helped me cross the finish line. An extra thank-you goes to K.B., who helped keep me on track even when I did my best to veer off course.

Mom and Dad, you always gave me pens and paper and anything else I needed to fuel my creative side. Thank you.

Thank you to University of Colorado Colorado Springs for giving me a job I love through good times and bad. Thanks to everyone in the Communications Department for believing in me and supporting me even during low points in my personal life.

To J. Thorn and all the friends I have made at The Author Success Mastermind, you inspire me every day to be better and to not lose myself in the imposter syndrome that creeps up on me when I'm in the glow of your greatness.

I also want to thank the agent from the writing competition I paid to enter, who told me my story was garbage and that I should quit writing. As the words in that agent's email settled on me, I sat at my kitchen table thinking I should quit. Instead, I posted my experience in a writer's group on Facebook, and that's when I found Cathy Spader, My Word Publishing, J. Thorn, and everyone else who changed my life as a writer. If you are reading this and you've been rejected or told by someone that you should quit, don't. Use that setback, learn and grow from it. Every villain in your life also can be a teacher.

Finally, I want to thank *you*. You chose to read this book, and that's amazing. I thank you for picking it up and reading it through to the end.

# ABOUT THE
# AUTHOR

**ANGELA HAAS** was born in Colorado
Springs, Colorado. A professor of communication, she writes novels about superheroes and spaceships. She loves not camp-
ing, salty snacks, and soft blankets. She has
been writing since she was a kid and still
has all the spiral-bound notebooks she filled with her early stories. Her
series Keepers of the Universe features older women as the superheroes
because she was tired of the standard entertainment tropes of older
women being the evil queen, jilted first wife, or wise grandmother. She
and her husband live with an English bulldog, French bulldog, pit bull
mix, Rhodesian ridgeback, and Maine Coon cat that thinks he's a dog.
Visit firststrikenovel.com for details. To contact Angela about attending
your event, email her at ahaaswrites@gmail.com